Lily Monadjemi

THE SCENT
OF LOVE

Hero, an imprint of Legend times group Ltd
51 Gower Street
London WC1E 6HJ
United Kingdom
www.hero-press.com

Paperback ISBN: 9781835632079

Lily Monadjemi was born in Iran, educated in England and the United States. She holds an Honour degree in Social Welfare and a Masters in Educational Psychology.

She was a lecturer at the National University of Iran up to the Iranian Revolution when, with her family, she emigrated to Sydney, Australia. Now she lives between Paris and London. Her previous books, successfully published in Australia and the UK are entitled:

Blood and Carnations

A Matter of Survival

The Mulberry Tree

Angels Can Hate Too

Golestan: The Garden of Memories

This is for Betsabeh and Parissa, Julien and Joerg.

Acknowledgments

My sincere thanks goes to my very dear friend Sousan Majidi who spent so many hours on reading the manuscript, discussing it and giving me valuable suggestions, and my wonderful husband who has put up with a boring wife for so many long years.

Last but not least I would like to thank Haley Knight, Rose Northwood and Vinh Tran at Austin Macauley for their invaluable assistance.

Those of you who feel no love
sleep on.
Those of you who do not feel the sorrow of love
in whose heart passion has never risen
sleep on.
Those who do not long for union
who are not constantly asking, 'Where is He?'
sleep on.
Love's path is outside of all religious sects
if trickery and hypocrisy is your way
sleep on.
If you don't melt like copper in your quest
for the alchemical gold
sleep on.
If like a drunkard you fall left and right
unaware the night has passed and it's time for prayer
sleep on.
Fate has taken my sleep but since
it has not taken yours, young man
sleep on.
We have fallen into love's hands
since you are in your own
sleep on.
I am the one who is drunk on Love
since you are drunk on food
sleep on.
I have given up my head and have nothing more to say
but you can wrap yourself in the robe of words and
sleep on.

Jalaledin Rumi 13th Century.

Chapter 1

June 30th of the year 2009

Fifth Street is a dull cul-de-sac running off an avenue christened in the honour of the liberator of India: Ghandi. Like his build, the avenue is narrow and long. It languidly inclines uphill, towards the north and then suddenly is aborted by a busy highway that cuts its head off. This quarter used to be a prestigious residential area, but no more. Teheran, with a population of twenty million, has spread its periphery in all directions, particularly, up the wide breast of mount Alborz, where the air is cool and fresh and the price of land astronomically high. However, the commercial section of this avenue has been modernized and is celebrated for its fashionable restaurants catering to the rich who, on their way, pass an endless strip of jewellery boutiques with display windows lit by the glutinous glitter of eighteen carat gold pieces and diamond-studded jewels tastefully exhibited to lure them in. Lunching at a restaurant along Ghandi Avenue is a double joy for most females as it often coincides with the purchase of a luxury good. Women in Iran, particularly the nouveaux riche wear jewellery to exhibit their husbands' love, loyalty, and success in business. In turn, their spouses indulge their whims without a whinge. This, most of them do to hide their infidelity under the guise of attentive generosity, which in reality is a commercial prudence. In a country with an annual inflation of almost thirty percent, investment in gold and precious stones is safer than holding cash.

Fifth Street tilts downhill. On its right side, just before the road ends, a set of steps descends to the noisy Africa Street. Close to the ridge of the cliff stands a moderately tall apartment block that has seen better days. The entrance hall of this monument to bad taste is as cold as its stained white-marble façade. It has a lift that hardly ever works and inhabitants who hardly ever use it – so old and disillusioned are they. These folks find peace and security only within the confines of their four tired walls. Outside is no longer a familiar and affordable place to shop or take an afternoon stroll to purchase an ice cream or some pistachio nuts from a favourite confectionary shop that has changed hands and decor several times; thus losing its intimacy. These disillusioned souls belong to the social segment that was strangled by the indiscriminating tentacles of revolutionary zealots. Through persistent struggle and some luck, they had managed to break loose and scrape a meagre sustenance out of the limited resources they had salvaged out of the grip of a Foundation or two – in a city recognized as one of the most expensive in the world.

Now, almost thirty years after the dawn of the Islamic Republic, their only affordable social activity is to meddle in each other's affairs or take an afternoon tea with the neighbour they are on speaking terms. Mostly out of touch with the outside world, gossip is the flavour they savour most.

Regardless of the cheerless ambiance of their community, these folks are all thankful that none of the apartments has changed hands. To have a fundamentalist neighbour would have been a kiss of death – even in spite of their, by now conforming life style.

They are aware that within the stronghold of an autocratic rule, whether monarchy, religious or military, treacherous faults in foes are found quicker than a wink of an eye. The strangers, could not only disturb their peace, but offend their sights and olfactory senses by the smelly shoes they discard in front of their flat's entrance before stepping inside. They are pedantic about the cleanliness of the floor upon which they spread their prayer mat and pray to a God they fear more than they love. Many of these pseudo-believers, live comfortably in confiscated properties which in a true religious term were 'usurped'. In Islam, property ownership is sacred and unjust confiscation sacrilegious. Nevertheless, anything, even crime can be justified, if an appropriate cause, however fraudulent, is improvised, or like a miracle descends from heaven.

Fortunately now that the revolutionary fervour has thawed, many people have been able to repossess their properties.

Turan and Shamsi are the sole owners of the fifth floor flats. These two widows went through the anxieties of the Revolution and fears and shortages of an eight-year war together. Time, the struggle to survive, and loneliness were instrumental in binding them in a sincere friendship which now-a-days is a rarity in Iran.

Turan lives with her rather simple-minded son Homayon, and Shamsi is taken care of by Tirdad, her unemployed, perpetually drunk younger son; the only one of her three children in Iran.

When Shamsi was well, her joy was to bake, and her pastries were celebrated as the tastiest, even by those who had tried Lenotre's pastries in Paris. The two neighbours used to pass pleasant afternoons on one of their balconies that face the city's crisscrossing highways and avenues that were beleaguered by ancient vehicles entangled in traffic jams, with carbon monoxide puffing out of their exhaust pipes further polluting the air engulfing Teheran. With all sorts of sanctions hanging over the country, in those days, few new cars traversed the roads.

Flirting with their afternoon tea and enjoying Shamsi's treat, the two ladies used to gab about the bygone days, when they could laugh from the heart and Shamsi could earn money from her highly valued skill. She used to be an envied cook; had taught cooking at a high school and published a cook book. But now, almost incapacitated, God knew what Tirdad was feeding her. To the chagrin of Turan, she had become skin and bones. From her pretty face remained a long Roman nose spidered with veins and a pair of large, lifeless eyes that stared into nothing but a dark void.

Turan, old and frail, irrespective of her own problems, was a conscientious neighbour. She had lost a son in the Iran-Iraq war, and thus was the recipient of several government benefits. Yet, every time her heart warmed up to God she asked him to put some compassion, mercy and forgiveness in the hearts of those in power, so that they would stop, twisting his commandments to suit their selfish purposes – as though there would be no Day of Judgement. All the mayhems that had affected people's lives seemed to her utterly senseless. After her husband had seen the remnants of his bomb-blasted soldier son brought back in a wooden box for burial, and amongst all the razzmatazz and cries of Allah Akbar due to a martyr, carried through the street leading to the local mosque for a requiem; he had grieved himself to death. Now in the wide world she was left with an intellectually handicapped son and an almost senile neighbour for whom she was grateful. Such was her nature – always content – never complaining. So she lived and enjoyed the brilliant rays of the morning sun pouring in through her bedroom window, fluttering over her creaking old wooden bed, waking her up by their brilliance and pleasant warmth, to face the challenges of a new day – with an open heart and a clear mind.

Although the tea sessions had become a sweet memory, yet out of concern, she made sure to be aware of what was going on in her friend's flat in case her assistance was required. She often heard Tirdad's joggle of keys when opening and slamming the door shut, and then yelling and swearing at his mother. Unfortunately, she could say nothing and do nothing. What does one say to a drunkard? Besides, he was so mean that he had not even opened the door to her knocks on the few occasions she had lost patience with his blasphemous language that had been loud enough to reach her ears and offend her sense of propriety. She had not seen Shamsi for almost a month now. Nevertheless, she knew Tirdad spent the nights with her rather than at his own home with his family. It was common knowledge that his was not a happy marriage and his wife and mother never saw eye to eye. But to spend the nights away from home was strange for a middle-aged man. Didn't he need the company of a woman? She wondered often with a wistful sigh. She never understood why Tirdad did not commission a domestic for his mother and find an occupation for himself. She knew that Datam, Shamsi's oldest son, had offered to contribute to the cost – so it was not a question of affordability. Even once, when in Iran, Datam had actually employed a mature lady who seemed pleasant and capable. But alas, as soon as he had left for London, the woman had been dismissed.

Once, desperate to be of help to Shamsi, she had sought the advice of Amir Khan, their neighbour upstairs and Tirdad's Arak (homemade vodka) mate. Amir Khan had shaken his bald head in sympathy for Shamsi's situation and divulged that Tirdad took care of Shamsi so that he could pocket her monthly pension to support his own family and keep a respectable roof over their heads. Unemployable because of his prison record, the man had no other choice. An aid's fee would devour a good portion of the pension and leave him with little to fulfil his primary obligations. The information had broken her heart and kept her quiet for a while. Yet, vigilant she had remained. Often, when she heard footsteps on the stone floor of their landing, she opened her door a slit to see if Shamsi had a visitor.

This morning, a week had passed without hearing a single sound of activity floating out of Shamsi's apartment, nor any light flickering through its entrance door gap. That was strange indeed. At first she had thought perhaps Shamsi was bedridden – as often as she was. But not hearing Tirdad's noises was bizarre – in fact worrisome. Her curiosity reaching its ebb, she gave vent to a heavy groan, dropped on her sofa, picked up the phone from the side table and dialled

Shamsi's number. When no one responded, she banged the receiver on its cradle, pulled up the shawl hanging over her shoulders, spread it over her head and hastily moved to rise. A sharp pain shot through her arthritic limb and paralyzed her for a second or two. Then, she gripped the arm of the sofa and forced herself up. Once on her feet she stood still to catch her breath. Now-a-days the slightest hasty movement exhausted her. She waited a bit longer and then limped towards the door, opened it and stepped out. Just at that moment, she heard Homayon's deep-voiced call.

"Mother, where are you going?"

"Not far son."

Hating the thought of being left alone, he sat up in bed and began contemplating whether to get out and follow her, or remain in, and carry on teasing his erect genital. Getting up also meant following her orders which he detested. He just wanted to be left alone so that he could remain in bed, dream of his girlfriend and masturbate. He made no demands from his mother and expected her to do the same. But, alas! He had to set the table, help with the dishes and do the shopping. The last was the most difficult chore. Often, while carrying all those heavy grocery bags, he had got lost in the streets that kept changing names. Disoriented, he had to wander around for hours before he could navigate his way back home and face her reprimands for being late.

Homayon had led a normal, healthy life until the age of thirteen, when a dreadful disease, no one could put a name to, had sent him into coma for six weeks, and then, when he had opened his eyes, most things had seemed foggy, unrecognizable and meaningless. He was kept in hospital until the fog in his head had cleared and he could recognize a few people, utter a few simple words and move his limbs. That is when his father made a pilgrimage to Mecca to thank the Almighty for the miracle.

Now, he was thirty five, with almost the mind of an adolescent in the body of a pleasant-looking, tall and well-built man. Agitated, he brushed his sticky hand over his bottom sheet, threw away his blanket and was about to rise when he heard his mother say: "I am just going to see what has happened to Shamsi." Shaking his head, he wondered why on earth she wanted to know what had happened to the neighbour.

In the empty corridor, Turan reached Shamsi's door. She rested a palm on the wall for support, took couple of breaths, and then slowly bent and put her good ear to the key-hole and listened. The stillness accelerated her heart beats, rushed blood into her head and tensed her facial muscles. Her eyes wide with worry, she slowly unbent her back, leaned her gross bulk against the wall and stared at the doorbell she knew had stopped functioning months ago. Suddenly the cold empty corridor seemed like a deserted sepulchre. Horrible thoughts assailed her and she began to shiver. To calm her nerves she started to murmur the Fear Prayer she knew by heart. It soothed her a bit. She looked at the door again, a barrier between her and dear Shamsi. She clenched her fingers and with her crocked knuckles began knocking at the door. The loud tapping sound echoed in the corridor and died down.

What on earth could have happened to them? She kept asking herself while waiting for the door to open. And when it didn't, a terrible feeling of helplessness beset her. Her eyes began to sweep the corridor in search of help. No one was around and besides, no one cared about their neighbour's welfare anymore. In fact they had become weary of each other's problems.

Desolate, she became aware of the awful pain in her knuckles. She grabbed her aching fingers with her good hand and tried to squeeze the pain out without success. Lost in dark thoughts, like a retreating soldier, she hobbled back into her domain; banged the door shut, dropped on her withered red velvet sofa and shook off her shawl. It slipped down over her stooped shoulders. Aggravated by its weight, she pulled it off, threw it on the sofa's arm and picked up her address book that lay next to the telephone. Impatiently she flipped through its pages until she found Golnar's number. She laid the book on her lap; picked up the phone and, staring at the digits, dialled.

Golnar, the unmarried daughter of Shamsi's eldest uncle, the late Mohammad Hassan Khan, is the family's lawyer. She attends to the affairs of their various estates, which due to the change of regime have become notoriously difficult to manage. In spite of all the hassles involved, the task not only gives her a feeling of importance but also is favourable to her branch of the family's interest. Her father, having been the eldest son of a landed aristocrat, had inherited the right to supervise the affairs of the farmland and needless to say none of the siblings, out of respect for his seniority, dared to question his annual account. They all thanked him for the pittance they received and then whispered their complaints behind closed doors. Now, Golnar was doing the same as her father had done, albeit under such complicated circumstances that one wouldn't wish for an enemy. The first and some of the second generation having passed away had left their shares to their numerous descendants who were now scattered all over the world. In such a situation and with all the rivalry that exists amongst the various cousins, nothing tangible can be achieved within a reasonable time, if at all. Many believe this suits Golnar but not Shamsi who, when still in command of her mental faculties, had given her a total power of attorney to deal with all her affairs. Turan knew that Golnar was the only reliable relative Shamsi has. The rest had either left for safer shores or were as old and as ill as she – or in their graves. So she was her only hope for help.

Out of bed, hair unkempt, face black with stubbles, eyes drowsy, Homayon aimlessly wandered in his untidy room wondering why his forever calm mother had banged the door. Something must have angered her? He surmised shaking his head side to side. Then, he heard her desperate voice: "No one opens the door, nor picks up the phone."

"Who doesn't open the door?" he yelled in concern.

Turan put her palm on the mouth of the receiver, turned her face towards the narrow corridor that led to his room and replied: "I am on the phone, talking to Golnar Khanum."

She turned back and removed her hand. "Sorry Khanum joon (lady dear), Homayon thought I was talking to him; and no, I do not have the phone number of Tirdad's flat. Can you hold on please, I have to get something to write with?"

Homayon heard sounds of shuffling which made him imagine his mother searching for something.

"Son, hurry, give me something to write with."

"Yah, I was right! The old bitch is summoning her servant again!" He whispered tying the waist strings of his blue-striped pyjama pants. He delved his feet into his frayed cotton sleepers with such ferocity that one toe tore the fabric and popped out. He sent a curse and dragging his feet on the hardwood flooring, skulked into his mother's bedroom where he knew he would find her eyebrow pencil next to her looking glass on the window-sill. He picked the pencil up and holding it like a gun aimed to kill, carried it to her. He knew this would annoy her. It made him feel good to see her lined face crinkle and her thin lips twitch. Perhaps one day she would understand his resentments and stop treating him like a servant. He was an Agha (gentleman), like everyone else.

"Here you are, Mother," he said, a sardonic smile tilting on his face. Unshaved he looked more like an ape than a man.

Turan looked at the pencil pointing at her heart and then at him with a frown on her narrow forehead. She swallowed the obscenity that was about to fly out of her mouth; shook her head in disappointment and grabbed the pencil. She bit her lower lip hard, dropped the receiver on her lap; pushed the phone's loud speaker button down; leaned towards the telephone table on which sat an old newspaper waiting to be discarded and said: "Ok what is his number Golnar Khanum?"

Golnar's soft voice flowed through the loudspeaker.

Homayon towered over Turan and focused on her scribbling. He noticed the trembling of her hand and felt a pang of guilt which quickly turned into a frustrated irk.

Turan finished writing and straightened her stiff back. "Thank you Golnar joon. I shall call you as soon as I know what is going on there."

"I wait for your call Turan Khanum and I hope nothing is wrong. And also thanks for your concern."

"Nothing at all. Shamsi is like my own sister," Turan replied before returning the receiver on its cradle.

"Can you read your squiggles?" Homayon ridiculed.

Holding the pencil up, she whispered: "Son, please return this to its place." The sound of her voice was as rueful as the feeling in her heart. When she looked at him, she only saw the brilliant child that he had been before that dreadful evil eye settled on him. But his callous words always took the joy out of her fantasy. Why was he so nasty to her? Why? She couldn't figure that out. She shook her head in despair and heard him snap back: "Do it yourself."

Wordless, she just watched him turn and walk to the kitchen. Then she murmured an 'Allah Akbar' (God is great), placed the pencil over the address book, leaned her head against the back of the couch, closed her eyes and prayed to be forgiven for the resentment she had felt towards her son. Had he died from that awful disease, she could not have been able to live this long. Suddenly she remembered Shamsi. Her eyes opened wide. Hurriedly she sat up. A sharp pain shot through her back and came out as a moan. She picked up the phone again, consulted her squabbling on the paper and dialled.

"Hallo?" A seductive voice whispered.

"Salam Nary Khanum. I hope you are in good health."

"Thank you Turan Khanum and I hope you and Homayon Khan are well too."

"Not really my dear. I am afraid something is amiss at Shamsi's. No one picks up the phone, or opens the door and I haven't seen Agha Tirdad for some time now. Have you seen or heard from either of them lately, my dear?"

"No. We are not on speaking terms."

"Sorry to hear that. Dear, I am terribly worried about Shamsi. Could you please come here and help me to find out what is going on behind that locked door?"

Nary paused and then replied: "I am terribly busy these days. What can I do that you cannot?"

"I do not know. You are a kin and know better than I. Please come?"

"OK. But I cannot stay long."

"Just come please. You are family and I am just a neighbour my dear."

"I am not much of a family either. But to rest your mind at ease, I will drop in."

"Thank you Khanum." Turan said before disconnecting.

"What a wife to have. No wonder he lives with his mother!" Turan whispered before dialling Golnar's number. Anxiously waiting by the phone Golnar took the call, heard Turan's report and promised to join her immediately.

Relieved that the burden was off loaded from her conscience, Turan stretched on the sofa and closed her eyes to relax.

An hour elapsed in serenity. Then the ding-dong of the bell disrupted her nap. Disoriented, she opened her eyes and looked around. Consciousness crept in. The bell rang again. Carefully she swung her legs and rested them on the floor. Then she put her hands on the arm of the sofa and very slowly stood up. She heard the ding dong again and swore. She lumbered to the door and asked: "Who is it?"

"Salam Turan Khanum. It is me, Golnar."

Turan unlocked and opened the door to a sweating, panting Golnar, whose flushed cheeks were pulsating with exhaustion.

"The damned lift doesn't work again!" She mumbled while loosening the knot of her black scarf.

"Come in my dear, come in," Turan invited, spreading her arms around her round shoulders and kissing her on both cheeks.

"Thank you for coming. Thank you," she whispered into Golnar's ears before unfolding her arms.

"Imagine climbing all those steps clad in these heavy layers! Summer is an awful season for us wretched women," Golnar complained, unbuttoning her black coat.

"I never wear a coat – just my chador (long veil). It is ugly but cooler and more convenient."

Golnar who would rather die than appear in a chador gave her a timid smile.

Turan closed the door without locking it and then pointed to the sofa. "Sit here dear; I'll be only a minute." Golnar dropped her black handbag by the side of the sofa, sat down and fixed her concerned eyes on the kitchen's open door. Soon Turan emerged carrying a silver tray on which was a cup of tea and a tarnished silver sugar dish filled to the brim with sugar cubes. Careful not to spill the tea, she placed the tray on the coffee table.

"It's a bit on the strong side. It has been brewing since breakfast time."

"Thank you Turan Khanum. I like strong tea," Golnar replied, picking up the cup and looking at her hostess, who warily lowered herself onto the sofa and when lodged comfortably, released a sigh of relief.

"What do you think has happened Turan Khanum?" Golnar asked before taking a sip of her tea.

Turan shook her head in wonder. "I really do not know. Shamsi never goes out, but I usually hear Tirdad's noises, at least twice a day – but now, it is a good while, I have heard nothing at all, nor seen any light flutter through the door gap. Tirdad usually leaves the light in the hallway on."

"This is strange indeed. Shamsi calls me once a week and I have not heard from her for almost three weeks now. I have not called her myself because sometimes Tirdad picks up the phone, and I really do not want to talk to him. He is always so rude and aggressive, as though we are to blame for his misfortunes!"

"Do not talk about his rudeness! He is just awful to everybody, especially poor Shamsi. When he starts shouting at the dear woman, he uses words that make my hair stand out. He is so unlike his father!"

Golnar nodded her agreement and placed her empty cup on its saucer.

"And of course his better half is no better," Turan added, shaking her head in repugnance.

"She is another wrong choice. They are not birds of the same feather. We do not even know who her real father is – such distinguished family!" exclaimed Golnar, wrinkling her round nose.

Turan exhaled, pursed her lips, and shook her head in consent.

"And all the airs and graces she gives herself – utterly repulsive! The worst is that he always backs her, even when he knows she is wrong. Poor Shamsi, from among three children, she is left with the black sheep."

"Well, that is her fault. I know for a fact that Datam, before leaving Iran, asked them to go and live with him in London. But no, cousin Shamsi had to remain with Tirdad – the rotten apple of her eyes."

Turan sighed wistfully, changed the position of her legs, and began to massage her left thigh.

Homayon, sitting on his bed with a French text on his lap, could, to his annoyance, hear every word exchanged between the ladies. Their voices were disrupting his concentration and he couldn't make head or tale of the sentence he aimed to memorize. Frustrated, he threw the book aside, dived for the door, kicked it shut and swearing under his breath returned to the task at hand. He was rather proud of his elementary French skill. Through persistent endeavours he had managed to learn a few sentences by heart. This achievement he had kept from his mother whom he knew, didn't believe him capable of learning anything at all and had angrily scolded him for wasting his pocket money on the purchase of the book, even though second-hand. It hurt him to think she considered him an imbecile. Deep down he knew he was, but not all the time. He picked up the text and looked at the sentence he was trying to memorise. Now he couldn't even read it, let alone commit it to memory. He focused harder to no avail. Nothing entered his head except the aggravating noise from the sitting room. Exasperated, he threw the book on the table, dropped on his bed, folded his hands behind his head and leaning on them murmured: "Well, today is one of those bad, imbecile days!"

In the sitting room they heard the sound of footsteps echoing in the corridor.

"I hope it is Nary," Turan said patting Golnar's knee. It jerked up.

"Dear, you must be very nervy."

"Who isn't Turan Khanum? Life has turned into a repertoire of problems for all of us. Just look at your elevator. With all the maintenance charges you pay to the management, they should, bloody well have changed it by now."

"Management – my foot! No one really knows what they do with the money, and no one has the sense or the audacity to question."

"Why Turan joon?"

"Because we have to save face and also we do not know with whom we are dealing. No one wants to jeopardise his or her safety. At our age we like to die in our own homes my dear! Our own homes! And a wrong word to the wrong person, your home can be confiscated and you thrown out into the street." Turan stopped and began massaging her bad leg.

"Surely it isn't as bad as that?"

"It is worse than that my dear."

"But, you know all your neighbours. Shamsi told me that none of the apartments have changed hands."

"No – they have not, but people have changed. The new social system, with its new values, has affected most of the people, at least all those I know. They are not the same anymore. Some have turned pseudo-fundamentalist, some anarchist and some, like me, weary, waiting to die in peace."

The bell rang.

"It must be her," Turan murmured, rising to open the door. When she reached it, she looked through the security eyelet.

"It is them." She whispered, pushing the handle down and opening the door to a puffing Nary behind whom stood her son Ahmad.

"Salam Nary Khanum."

"This is awful – having to climb up so many steps," Nary blurted out, shaking her loosely wrapped foulard off.

"I know and I am sorry about it."

"Salam Turan Khanum," Ahmad greeted in a warm tone to compensate for his mother's rudeness.

As Nary's eyes fell on Golnar her frown tightened.

"Salam Nary Khanum."

"Salam Golnar Khanum," Nary replied, her tone as cold as clay.

"Nary Khanum please sit down. I will get you some tea."

"As I told you, I do not have much time and really do not know why I am here. My so called husband hasn't called me for a long time now, and I have not seen him since Kobra left for Paris."

"This is not strange is it – given your relationship with him?" Turan replied, her frank eyes on her long face.

"No Khanum, it is not strange, but all the same a fact. And now, I see our marital problems have been publicised by my very dear mother-in-law!"

Golnar, tensed, straightened her shoulders and looked at Nary with distaste, "my cousin cannot ask for a glass of water, let alone gossip behind you. Please do not be insolent about my family members or else I will leave."

Nary, shook her plump shoulders, fixed her audacious eyes on Golnar's stern face and replied: "Do as you wish. I did not expect to find you here. Had I known you would be present, I would not have bothered to come – you are the one who has power of attorney from Shamsi Khanum – so it is your responsibility to see if she is dead, alive or whatever else."

Turan, ever so discretely, hit her thighs, bit her lips and shook her head at the sharpness of the woman's tongue.

Clearly embarrassed by his mother's unnecessary insolence, Ahmad pinched her arm and whispered: "Enough is enough."

"You are right Nary Khanum. I am here to see what has happened to my client and you, my dear, should be here to see what has happened to your husband, by grace of whom, you have socially climbed high and lead a comfortable life. You were just a widowed secretary when Doctor Tirdad Amiri married you my dear. Be grateful for your luck and act according to the demands of your acquired status – like a lady."

Not expecting such an assault from a usually reserved Golnar, Nary paused to collect her thoughts. Then throwing Golnar a venomous glance she replied: "I am not going to grace your stupid remark with a response. You are all the same – heartless and arrogant."

Shocked, Turan watched her turn and walk out.

Golnar, swallowed the insult with a pinch of salt, picked up her bag, stood up, took Turan's arm and together they followed her out. Neither uttered a word.

By the door, Nary, covered her hair with her foulard and then pushed the bell button.

"It doesn't work Khanum. Had you been visiting your husband and your sick mother-in-law, you would have known." Commented Turan, a sarcastic smile on her thin lips

Nary shrugged off the remark and whispered: "Trust him not to have had it fixed."

"Bang at the door, Mother." Ahmad suggested impatiently.

She did – with all the frustration inside her. The echo in the corridor compounded their irritation.

"Stop it Khanum. It is useless. No one is there." Said Turan, snatching Nary's hand.

Nary pulled her hand out of her grip and threw the old woman a nasty glance.

"I think we better break the lock," Ahmad suggested, his bushy eyebrows creased in genuine concern. He loved his step-father. The man had been exceptionally kind to him. He was only four when a bomb- blast had turned his biological father into a martyr. The only father he had known was Tirdad: kind, caring and genuine until lately.

They were all contemplating what to do, when Homayon who had quietly joined the crowd, ran inside and returned with a hammer which he proudly offered to Ahmad with both hands.

"We need other tools as well, not just a hammer Homayon Joon!" Ahmad said in a kind tone. Embarrassed, Homayon hid the hammer behind his back, dropped his eyes to the floor, then mumbling incoherently ran indoors, threw the hammer on the floor, rushed to his room, sat on his bed and began to cry like a despondent child. Blushing, Turan turned her gloomy eyes to Ahmad and whispered: "Son, run to the kitchen where you will find the tool box in the bottom drawer, on the right of the sink."

A few minutes later, Ahmad returned with the same hammer and various screw drivers.

He knelt by the door and began to work. The noise of repetitive pounding exploded in the corridor, alerting the neighbours to an unexpected calamity. Eventually the lock gave in. Satisfied, Ahmad set aside the tools and stood up. As the door slit open a loathsome wave of odour gushed out churning their stomachs. 'Oh my God.' They cried, stepping back and colliding with each other.

None uttered a word. None dared to think of what to expect, and none dared to take the first step in.

A few long, frightful minutes passed before Golnar summoned her courage and ventured into the darkness in which the interior was drowned. The stink was too pungent to bear. Hearing the thumping of her own heart, she swallowed the bile in her mouth, withdrew a handkerchief from her coat pocket, exclaimed a noiseless "Ya Allah", covered her nose and took another step in. The others took courage and followed suit.

Only thin wisps of light whizzed in through the slits of the drawn curtains.

As their eyes became accustomed to darkness, Nary turned left and switched the light on. The surrealism of the illuminated scene forged out yelps of horror from each of their throats. The noise frightened the cockroaches parading in the kitchen. Their peace disturbed, the insects rushed towards safety. A few hastened out, into the living area, a gruesome mess in which even a derelict could not have survived. Stained dining chairs were strewn around and on the dining table remained two moulded, malodorous plates, some cutlery and a large takeaway container filled with dead flies which must have feasted themselves to death. Dead ants lay on the tablecloth that once must have been white muslin, embroidered in pistachio green. A thought, uglier than the scene in view occurred to Nary and made her whisper: "Oh, please God prove me wrong."

At the far end of the sitting room, next to a wall, Tirdad, in his creased, blue-striped pyjamas sat on a spread of dried blood. His head was skewed to the left and his deeply cut forehead was coated in blood. Fear was frozen on his open eyes and an expression of pain sculpted his grey, swollen face on which streaks of blood had scabbed over his skin and unshaved barb. There was a disorderly trail of blood between him and the glass coffee-table, the edge of which was also blood stained. On an aged, pink sofa lay Shamsi, her grey hair long and rumpled, her skin a pallid, crinkled sheet of parchment paper punctured by a set of closed eyes sunken in a deep inky cavity. Her toothless mouth was half open, her pale lips chapped; a peppery beard on her narrow chin; her skinny right arm dangling down the side of the sofa and her chipped nails longer than those of a card's joker. By the sofa lay a pair of soiled dentures on which couple of ants had fossilized.

In the open space, patches of loose excrement were buried under mounds of dead ants and cockroaches.

Turan let out a loud scream and began hitting her head with both hands. Golnar rushed to the toilet to vomit and Nary, steadily walked to where her husband sat and stood staring at him with awestricken eyes. Images floated in her head and words rang in her ears making her heart gloat inside her chest. No tears moistened her eyes.

Tears streaming down his pinched face, bent under a heavy load of guilt, Ahmad slumbered to the phone and dialled 110 for police and ambulance.

Golnar, as grey as ash, returned from the toilet, knelt by the sofa, took Shamsi's cold hand, kissed it several times and then instinctively searched for her pulse. After a few seconds of intense concentration, she detected a faint beat. She focused further. Yes it really was a heartbeat. Gently she placed the hand on Shamsi's thigh; stretched up; put her cheek against her nose. A tinge of warmth brushed her skin. To make sure that the sensation was not illusory she remained still. Then sure of the breath of life, she shouted: "Shamsi is alive – quick – call an ambulance."

"I have already done that Golnar Khanum." Ahmad responded from under his breath. He was kneeling by his father and stroking his head with love, wooing him in his heart and letting his tears drop on his lap. He stole a kiss from his cold face, placed his head on his swollen stomach and kept cursing himself.

Nary walked to the window, drew the curtains, opened the window and then glided away to inspect the bedrooms. On the right-hand side of the narrow corridor was Tirdad's. Its door was open and an awful smell drifted out of it. She entered and switched the light on. Shocked, she took a step back and with her palm muffled the cry of horror that was about to escape her tight lips. Patches of dried faeces on which lay dead insects were all over the grey carpet. At the right corner, facing south, Tirdad's wooden bed was broken, feathers of its torn quilt everywhere and its crumpled sheet terribly soiled. A dusty, torn, blue curtain hid the window and creased clothes were scattered all over the single chair that sat by the bed acting as a table.

He must have had bad diarrhoea or perhaps was food poisoned? And why did not the stupid man call me? She wondered with a touch of guilt. The broken bed did not surprise her at all for he was prone to violent behaviour especially when drunk. She stepped in and began searching for his wallet which she found under his dirty skewed pillow. She took it and shoved it in her pocket. She swept the area with her eyes. Nothing of value lay there, so she left for Shamsi's bedroom. There, nothing of interest attracted her attention, except couple of suitcases lodged on the top of the wardrobe. She would inspect them later.

In the kitchen, behind the fridge, she found several empty bottles of white alcohol. It didn't surprise her. She knew he used to mix it with lemonade as a substitute for vodka which he could not afford to buy. Alcohol poisoning – an inevitable end for an alcoholic on white alcohol. She mused, her voluptuous lips parting in a smile that appeared and disappeared swiftly. In her mind, the earlier suspicions vanished and she exhaled with ease.

Nary was in her mid fifties, still sexy and appealing to men who have a preference for blonds. She had inherited her ivory skin, blond hair and power of deception from her Georgian mother. A mask of grief on her face, she returned to the living room, knelt by her son, threw him a strange glance, took Tirdad's cold clenched hand and tried to pull his wedding band off. The finger was too bent and swollen for the band to move. To save face, she kissed the hand, gently placed it on the dead man's thigh, turned her eyes to Golnar who had been watching her, and whispered: "There are several empty bottles of white alcohol in the kitchen – white alcohol is what he mixed with lemon juice or lemonade to drink – that must have poisoned him."

Disgusted by her ignoble act, Golnar gave her a cold, demeaning look and ignored her remark.

The news had already travelled through the building and the landing was raucously crowded by inquisitive neighbours. Turan, unable to remain in the apartment was spread on the corridor's floor, her head cupped in her palms, crying ceaselessly. By her stood Homayon, busy describing his perception of the events for those snooping for information. Suddenly sounds of purposeful footsteps announced the arrival of the police. The buzz turned into a hush. Eyes turned to the stair-case. A tall youngish officer, followed by a pair of petulant policemen reached the landing. The officer, his posture erect, his pleasant shaved face serious, swept his large, curious black eyes over the crowd and politely, yet firmly, ordered the non-relatives to disperse. He had prominent cheekbones, probably growing sharper with age, and a look of calm but determined authority, as if he was used to taking charge of situations. He turned to Ahmad who appeared at the door and asked: "I assume this is the Amiri residence?" "Yes sir. Please come in." Ahmad replied stepping aside, to let him go through. As the officer entered, the stench hit him hard. He paused for a minute, decided against covering his nose with a handkerchief, (a sign of weakness for a man of his rank) and introduced himself to the audience, as Sarvan (officer) Amir-Hussaini. Everybody rose and whispered their greetings. Amir Hussaini, endeavouring to disguise his horror at the state of the interior, roamed his eyes around, forming a first impression of those present. Then he focused his attention on the two victims, assuming both dead. No one spoke. The silence was as thick as the film of dust covering the furniture. He turned his eyes back to the crowd. Golnar's dignity and composure captured his attention. He took a step towards her and politely asked: "Khanum what is your relation to these victims?"

"I am the cousin of Khanum Amiri who, God be praised is still alive."

"Alive?" Amir- Hussaini exclaimed, astounded. The woman seemed as lifeless as a statue.

"Yes, God be praised. She breathes, Sarvan."

Regretting his reckless assumption, he went to Shamsi, bent down, took her pulse, and concentrated. Then he turned his eyes to Golnar and said: "You are right Khanum. What great luck! "

Golnar gave him a serene smile and then turned her sad eyes to Tirdad. "Doctor Tirdad Amiri is her son. This morning Turan Khanum, the next door neighbour and a close friend of the family, having been unable to get in touch with anyone in the flat, called me. And since I too, had not heard anything from either of them, I hurried here to see if anything was amiss – and this is what we found after breaking the lock." Golnar paused and then with her head gestured towards Nary, without looking at her face. "That lady there is doctor Amiri's wife, and the young youth standing by her, his step-son."

Amir Hussaini threw Nary a compassionate glance and then turned and knelt by Tirdad. He swept his eyes all over him and then released a heavy sigh. There was no need to check his pulse. The man was as dead as stone. He stood up thinking how he could have met his end. The signs were contradictory. The door had been locked from the inside and they had to break its lock to enter. So there had been no intruder unless he had had a Key. The pool of blood indicated obvious injury and the excrements disease. It was lucky that the old woman was still alive – a miracle indeed – but what had really happened? If the son had been sick, the mother could have asked for help from her friendly neighbour. If or when he had fallen and hit his head on something, most probably the glass table, again she could have sought help. Why had she not done so? Something must have happened to incapacitate her, or both of them, before the death occurred. Could she regain consciousness and remember? She must have seen what had happened. And the room's shocking state! Even a pig couldn't live in it – let alone respectable folks. The pictures on the walls indicated class and wealth and yet the outfits on the mother and the son were shabby, craggy and dirty. What tragedy had caused this drama – what? He felt his left eye twitch – as it always did when distressed. He had an old, sick mother, as frail as Shamsi. For a second he visualized it was her on the sofa and felt a whisper of Allah Akbar fly out of his mouth. He shook his head to get rid of the bad thought.

No one spoke. Staring at the Sarvan, they waited for his opinion, assumption or questions. As he moved his head, they straightened their necks and sharpened their ears.

He turned to Nary and asked: "Khanum, when did your husband become ill?"

"I do not know Agha Sarvan. He was living here taking care of Shamsi Khanum. He hardly ever came home."

"Hmph!" Exclaimed Amir-Hussaini and turned his attention to Golnar.

"Who saw the victims last Khanum?"

"Agha Sarvan, you should talk to Turan Khanum. She lives here and knows more about what goes on in this flat than the rest of us." Golnar replied turning her eyes to the door.

"Shall I fetch her for you Agha Sarvan?" Ahmad volunteered and then without waiting for any response headed for the corridor.

A few minutes later Turan leaning on Homayon's arm entered the room, her eyes closed, howling in a grating voice: "God make me blind so that I won't be able to see my Shamsi in this state. My poor, poor Shamsi!" Golnar went to her, took her free hand and together with Homayon led her to the nearest chair to the standing officer. She sat down, released a deep sigh and opened her tormented eyes, focusing them on the interrogator.

"Khanum, I understand you called Golnar Khanum for help. Can you please explain why?"

"Homayon give me your handkerchief."

"I do not have one, Mother."

Ahmad, now standing by the dining table, saw a box of Kleenex there. He withdrew a tissue and respectfully handed it to Turan.

"Thank, you son." Turan whispered before blowing her nose and wiping her tears.

Ahmad stepped behind her chair and gently began rubbing her shoulders. She threw the tissue over her lap, turned to the officer and said: "Agha Sarvan, Shamsi Khanum is like a sister to me. I love her very much." She paused, sniffed and then began shaking her head and hitting her chest with her fist. "Oh my God! Why has this happened to my poor dear friend? Why? No one can imagine the hell we went through – together. The poor, poor lady! Against all my counsel, she took life far too serious – so serious that she made herself ill and dependent on him." She swung her head towards Tirdad, threw him a quick cold glance and began shaking her head in pity. Amir-Hussaini did not miss the derogative tone in her voice when referring to the dead man. It surprised him. Turan, hysterical now, began beating at her laps.

"Please calm down Turan Khanum. You will make yourself sick." Golnar implored, taking hold of her hands. She composed herself, picked up the wet tissue from her lap; wiped the beads of sweat from her forehead, fixed her eyes on the Sarvan and continued:

"As her health deteriorated, our visits became less and less frequent. The last time I saw her was when Kobra was here. After she left I heard nothing from her and then didn't even hear the noises Tirdad made in the corridor and inside the flat. That is when I became concerned; came to the door and knocked. No one responded. I returned home and phoned. When no one answered, I called Golnar Khanum."

'Khanum who is Kobra?" The officer asked.

"She is Shamsi Khanum's daughter who lives in Paris and works for a pharmaceutical company. She often comes here to visit us all." Homayon, so far reticent, volunteered in a voice laced with pride.

The arrival of the ambulance paramedics stopped the interrogation. Faced with two victims, the senior paramedic politely addressed the Sarvan: "Your Excellency we can only take one corpse."

"Call for another ambulance. You take the lady who is alive to hospital and we wait here for the second ambulance to take the dead to the morgue."

The man pulled out his mobile from his pocket and called his centre.

As the two paramedics were heading out to go and bring up their stretcher, the Sarvan, with his hand gestured them to stop. "Don't waste any time. She might finish at any moment. The two of you carry her down right now and do what is necessary in the ambulance. Also never come to a scene such as this without your stretcher."

Murmurs of "sorry Sir," reached Sarvan's ears. To compensate for their negligence, the men hastily set to work. They gently lifted Shamsi up, one holding her shoulders and the other her legs. At that moment Golnar ran to Shamsi's bedroom, picked up her Islamic coat that was hung behind the bedroom door, brought it in and spread it over her. Then she thanked the Sarvan, adjusted her foulard, buttoned her coat, picked up her bag and ran after the paramedics down the stairs. Fortunately they were taking Shamsi to Mehr Hospital which was nearby.

In the flat, Amir-Hussaini thanked Turan for her help and then ordered all present to leave so that the police could start their search. Ahmad and Homayon, each took an arm and helped Turan out to her home, ignoring the questions that were thrown at them by a prying bunch still lingering in the corridor.

Once the flat was under his control, Amir-Hussaini asked one of the policemen to draw a line around the corpse and the other to follow him looking for clues. They went from one room to the next, pulling out drawers, opening cabinet doors, making the mess messier without finding anything that pointed to violence except the broken bed which was ancient and the torn quilt. So at some stage there must have been a struggle. Between whom only God knew! Amir-Hussaini extracted his note pad from his coat pocket and noted his observation.

The search proved futile. The team gathered around the corpse, eyeing it with pity while disputing over the cause of death. Dysentery, food poisoning, giddiness, heart attack – all of which could have caused a loss of balance and a subsequent head hit on the sharp edge of the glass table which was evident from the cut on the victim's forehead and the blood stains, extending from the table to where he sat. Amir-Hussaini listened with care and smiled at the way their minds worked. None of their theories seemed plausible to his rational thinking. If death was caused by a fall, how could the corpse be sitting upright, leaning against a wall? Why so many dead insects accustomed to feasting on filth? And why was the mother in that state? He smelt a rat, but in the absence of solid evidence he couldn't surmise murder without an autopsy now that the bloody lazy forensic pathologist had refused to accompany him because he had to go to a funeral. Restless, he took out a cigarette and was about to light it when the second ambulance paramedics arrived to take the corpse to the morgue. Once they had placed the body on the stretcher, he bent over it, fixed his eyes on the dead man's face and tried to see if he could decode a message from the midst of its folds. All he could detect, especially from the open eyes was emission of deep suffering. He sent a silent 'Allah Akbar' and with his head pointed to the door. Then he turned to his team and ordered them to go down and wait for him in the car. He wanted to go through the flat once more. Perhaps he had missed something. A disturbing feeling was haunting him. A voice in his ears was telling him that the key to the riddle was within his reach and he could find it if he used his sixth sense. For the second time he went through the flat, like a dog sniffing for drugs at an airport. His instinct led him to the kitchen and the garbage bin where a very small glass container with a foreign label caught his eyes. He picked it up, smelled it and threw it back, assuming it to be a medicine container probably brought or sent by the chemist daughter for her mother or brother. Had it been containing a poison, the murderer wouldn't have left it in the garbage bin, unless he was an imbecile.

At a secluded corner, almost hidden behind the fridge, he noticed a row of empty bottles some with labels and many without. He picked one up, took it to his nose and sniffed through its mouth. A slight smell of alcohol tickled his nostrils. He smiled. Nowadays everyone including, him, kept a couple of arak bottles at home. That wasn't a crime as far as a policeman was concerned. He put the bottle back and stepped out of the kitchen terribly annoyed – annoyed at his own inability to resolve the enigma that was challenging his capabilities as a professional. The rational man that he was, he decided to report the death as 'accidental', hoping the autopsy might prove him wrong. There was something disturbing in the ambiance of the flat. And, he definitely did not like the wife. Her eyes were cold and her behaviour void of any grief. There was something about her air that repulsed him. But the death happened behind locked doors without her knowledge! Shaking his head in bewilderment, he walked out of the kitchen, closed the windows, switched off the lights and opened the door to leave when he came face to face with Nary and her son. Surprised, he heard himself say: "Folks please accept my condolences. I believe the deceased died hitting his head on the table."

Nary shook her head and in a wistful tone commented: "He must have been drunk."

"Did he drink heavily?"

Looking at the Sarvan with sad eyes Ahmad replied: "He had become an alcoholic Agha Sarvan."

The information lifted a heavy load off the Sarvan's conscience. He shook his head left and right, cut the air with his index finger and in a definitive tone exclaimed:

"That is it then. Now everything makes sense."

"What makes sense Agha Sarvan?" Both Nary and Ahmad asked simultaneously.

"Assumption of an 'accidental' death: inebriated he lost his balance, fell and hit his forehead on the sharp edge of the glass table. Injured, he crawled to the wall where he sat and bled to death. His mother saw his fall and the shock sent her to coma." He paused, smiled at his logical conclusion and then looking at the two, added: "Alcoholics often meet with unpredictable deaths." He paused again. Thought for a second or two and then asked: "Did the chemist daughter ever send her mother or your husband any medicines?"

"Yes Sarvan. She sent all the medication her mother needed because she could get them without paying. She is a French citizen and apparently they can get all their medicine free."

Amir-Hussaini shook his head in envy and exclaimed: "Lucky them!"

Then he pointed to the door with his head and suggested:

"Khanum joon you should bring a locksmith to repair the lock and forbid anyone entering the apartment until you receive the morgue's report. It will, roughly, take a month."

"Thank you Agha. I shall follow your advice as soon as I can."

"Enshallah God will grant you patience to bear your loss." Amir-Hussaini consoled, bade them farewell, turned and ran down the stairs. Outside suddenly he stopped, looked back at the building and whispered: "But what about the bloody excrements and the dead insects?" He hit his temple with the heel of his hand regretting not taking any samples for the lab.

"What is wrong Sarvan?" asked one of the policemen in the car.

"We didn't collect any samples of the filth on the floor and the dining table."

"Don't worry Sir, the doctor at the morgue won't need our samples and if he does, he will send someone himself."

Amir-Hussaini climbed into the jeep, "let's go," he commanded, utterly confused.

The traffic to the hospital was light and the ambulance reached it within twenty minutes. There, in that overwhelmingly crowded place, Golnar, running behind Shamsi's stretcher, came face to face with Dr Mehran, Shamsi's physician and the Managing Director of the hospital.

"God be thanked that you are here, doctor!" Golnar cried, before grabbing the man's arm.

Conscious of his rank in front of the crowd, the doctor gently shook her hand off his arm, whispered a low Salam, and looked at the patient's face. Instantly recognising her, he turned to Golnar and asked: "What happened to her?"

"I do not know doctor. We found her like this."

Mehran turned to the senior paramedic and ordered:

"Take her to the operating room this instant."

"God bless you doctor." Golnar whispered.

"Wait for me in the waiting room Khanum." The doctor said hurrying after his patient.

During the long hour that dragged on and on, Golnar paced up and down the corridor, trying to figure out what had caused this inconceivable tragedy. The more she thought, the more her head ached. Then she saw the doctor coming towards her, his eyes smiling. "She will live, won't she doctor?" She asked him in hope.

"Yes Khanum." He replied, with a nod acknowledging a passer-by's greeting. "Shamsi must have a very strong constitution – probably it is all the fruit and vegetables she kept eating. Nothing but a strong constitution could have kept her alive under such acute dehydration. Nevertheless, she will have to stay at the Intensive Care Unit, until she gains consciousness. Go now, and rest assured that her chance of waking up is great."

Golnar controlled the impulse to kiss the doctor, something not done in public. Instead, she heard herself say: "Thank you dear doctor and God bless you and your family." The doctor smiled and walked away.

Golnar flew out of the hospital, hailed a taxi, negotiated a fair fare and climbed in, accidently banging the door. "Khanum be careful another bang and the door will fall apart." "Sorry Agha, I did not mean to bang the door. It just happened."

"Then be careful it won't happen again when you leave."

"OK Agha, and again I am very sorry." The driver looked at her through his rear view mirror and when he saw her tears, he became guilt ridden.

"Khanum please do not cry. I did not mean to upset you. You know how expensive everything has become, particularly now that they have increased the petrol price, introduced coupons and rationed petrol purchase. I have several mouths to feed and any additional expense takes the food out of a mouth."

"I understand Agha." Golnar whispered, wiping her tears with the edge of her scarf.

Soon he reached her home, and when Golnar handed him twice as much as the sum negotiated, he forgot about the mouths he had to feed and refused to accept the money. Frustrated, Golnar dropped the notes on the front seat, opened the door, got out and closed it as gently as possible. She waved him a good bye, walked to her gate, took out her key and let herself in.

Inside the courtyard she took no joy in seeing her pistachio tree inundated by fresh nuts in their green skins, nor the roses perfuming the dusty air. Her servant, who had seen her enter from the kitchen window, opened the door to the building with a "Salam Khanum." She didn't even hear her. Her mind was elsewhere; in that awful room where she had witnessed drama in its most odious form. Suddenly a fit of nausea hit her. She ran to the bathroom and let the bile of distress gush out into the toilet bowl, brutally hurting her throat and inducing tears of pain in her sore eyes. Relieved, she took couple of deep breaths, rinsed her mouth; undressed and took a long cold shower. The chill of the water relaxed her a bit. Then she dressed in a loose comfortable gown; went to her neat kitchen where she knew tea was being brewed. The maid asked if she wanted a large glass. "Yes," was her answer. The maid poured the tea and handed it to her. Golnar walked to her sitting-room, placed the glass on the low mahogany table, sank deep into the couch, closed her eyes and began exercising yoga breathing. For five minutes her mind stopped wandering. Then feeling in control again, she opened her eyes and in peace enjoyed the taste of her tea. She let a further, few tranquil minutes pass while savouring the feeling of safety she always enjoyed within her own space.

"Khanum would you like more tea?" Asked her servant concerned about her mistress who seemed in distress. She stood by the door looking at her with inquisitive eyes.

"No thank you Zahra." She replied, picking up the telephone from the side table.

In Paris, Kobra was concentrating on the report she was writing. As the phone started shrieking, a deep frown formed on her wide forehead. "Merde," she exclaimed picking up the receiver and into it murmuring a curt, "Allo."

"Kobra joon, Salam."

"Salam Golnar."

"I am sorry for disturbing you at your office."

"It must be something urgent? Has anything happened to my mother?"

"Yes. She is in hospital and Tirdad dead."

"Oh, my God!"

Golnar swallowed the lump in her throat and then recounted the story as gently as possible.

"This is just devastating." Kobra exclaimed, sounding shocked.

"It really is. I cannot close my eyes without seeing Tirdad in that tragic state. Yet we must be thankful that Shamsi is alive. You know that I love her very much, don't you?"

"Yes, yes. We all know that, Golnar joon."

"You know that you have to come to Teheran as soon as possible."

"Yes. Unfortunately I am inundated by work at the moment, but I will come."

"When would that be?"

"I cannot give you a date right now. I have to talk to my boss."

"Ok, my dear."

"Thank you Golnar joon and God be with you."

The phone went dead, leaving Golnar stunned beyond conception. She was expecting some sort of emotional outburst from a sister who had been so close to her brother. Her coolness was indeed odd. She put the receiver down, closed her eyes and recommenced her yoga breathing – for one day, she had had enough of tragic surprises.

Kobra had no intention to cancel her long weekend at Mount St. Mitchell with her new boyfriend! Her mother was in good hands and the burial had to wait. Still holding the phone, she consulted her watch. It was 9.30 a.m. which meant 8.30 in London. She dialled her older brother's number.

Rose, lingering in bed, picked up the phone and whispered a cloudy, "Hallo."

"Good morning Rose."

"Good morning Kobra joon and how are you my dear?"

"As well as I can be, under the present circumstances. Tirdad is dead and my mother in hospital."

"Oh my God!" Rose exclaimed, tears welling up in her large black eyes. Her voice trembling with grief, she asked, "What happened?"

"I do not exactly know and I do not know why Golnar delivered the news first to me instead of Datam, the eldest of the family."

"Wait, I will pass you to him. Please break the news gently. He is not well today."

"He seems to be ill all the time. What's wrong with him now?"

"Just a bad cold," Rose lied, throwing off her bed-cover. She slipped her feet into her silk slippers and hurried to the TV room where Datam, his breakfast tray on his lap, was watching the news. From behind the sofa, she stole a kiss from his bald patch and handed him the receiver.

"Darling it is for you."

"Who is it?" He asked, looking up at her, his amber eyes glowing with love.

"It is Kobra."

"What does she want at this time of the morning?

Rose did not answer. Silent, she removed the tray from his lap; put it on the table and sat by him.

"Salam Kobra joon." Datam said into the phone, his voice kind and warm.

Rose fixed her eyes on him. As he listened, she saw the remnants of colour vanish from his face and the veins in his temple throb hard. Her heart bled for him, for she knew how much he loved and missed his family.

Then, in a husky voice she heard him say: "Do not worry Kobra joon- I will leave for Teheran as soon as possible. See you there my dear."

He disengaged the phone, threw it on the table and fell into a deep silence.

"Darling, I am so sorry for your loss – such a tragic end for poor Tirdad. Nevertheless we must be thankful for your mother."

Without looking at her and in silence, he leaned back, rested his head on the back of the sofa and closed his wet eyes. She stretched across and hugged him tight.

They had been married for forty years and she had been not only his wife but friend and mother – totally in charge of their life – totally. She had no other choice. He was suffering from three different cancers, unrelated and progressive. She wanted him to live in peace for as long as possible. She believed by removing all responsibilities from his shoulders and allowing him to do what he wished during his borrowed time, he could live longer. Without him life would become meaningless for her. She had no one – no one at all in the world – except him and God.

After a little while, she unfolded her arms and let him deal with his grief in his own peaceful way.

Looking at the TV screen without seeing anything, she heard herself whispering, "The poor man."

"Yes. The poor, unlucky man!"

He, too, whispered shaking his head in grief.

Rose picked up the TV monitor, pressed the off button, threw the gadget on the table, picked up the phone and dialled their travel agent's number.

The booking was made for the day after Datam's medical check-up.

Kobra was the first to arrive in Teheran. She lodged at Golnar's and then went to her mother's flat. Surprised, she found its door without a lock. She gently pushed it open, stepped in and then out. She stood still, her heart pounding savagely, her mind frozen by an emotion hitherto foreign to her – guilt. 'What had gone wrong?' She asked shaking her head left to right and right to left. Finding the smell too overpowering she withdrew a lavender infused tissue from her bag, covered her nose, entered and opened the nearest window. Then, she walked to the chalk- drawn human shape, stood by it and stared at the void in between the lines. Memories paraded in her mind – good and bad. Suddenly, in spite of the suffocating heat surrounding her, she felt terribly cold and began to shiver. She closed her eyes and took several deep breaths of the foul air that upset her stomach and made her sick. She ran to the toilet and spewed. Feeling better, she washed her face with cold water, and looked for a towel. There was none. Then her eyes fell on the heaps of clothes in the bath tab. Instinctively she began throwing them out, as though searching for something. Yes she had to look everywhere and make sure that the flat was indeed clean of clues to a murder. The police had found nothing! Perhaps she could? So she started with Tirdad's room. There, the mess and his broken bed surprised her. By habit he had been a tidy man, then what had happened to induce this carelessness – what? Probably another row with his bitchy wife, she assumed, leaving the room with a groan of disgust. In her mother's bedroom, on the floor, she found the suitcases that were usually lodged on the top of the aged wardrobe, opened and almost empty. That bitch Nary and her bastard son must have done it. She murmured kicking the edge of one, as though it was Nary's shin. In fact nothing of value had been in the suitcases except couple of table cloths, some towels and a few blankets which were now in Nary's linen cupboard. She, herself had taken most of her mother's valuables before becoming accessible to Tirdad. Yet the thought of Nary, this once, having had the upper hand, flared up her forever hatred of the woman. From the bedroom's window she saw plumes of dust spiralling up like a whirlwind and making visibility difficult for the drivers. The heavy traffic had come to almost a halt. The wind was strong, lashing at everything in its path. She heard the window latches clack and the entrance door bang.

In her sitting room, Turan was knitting a jumper for Homayon and swearing at the wind that was whiffing through the window sills, bringing in all the pollution and dust in the air when the loud banging of a door made her jump out of her skin. Her zigzagging hands stopped and she murmured: "It must be Shamsi's – still without a lock!" Shaking her head in disgust, she put her knitting on the sofa, slowly rose, walked to her door, opened it and popped her head out. She was correct. It was Shamsi's. Again someone must have been there and when leaving hadn't closed it properly. She growled in annoyance, lumbered back to her sofa, took her foulard from over its arm, threw it on her head, took a few steps and with the tip of her shoe pushed the door stopper in place so that the wind could not lock her out. She ambled to the neighbouring flat and as she stretched to grab its door knob her eyes fell on Kobra's back. Surprised, she let out a cry. Frightened, Kobra turned with a jerk, saw Turan, and ran to embrace her. At that precise moment, they both heard Homayon's yell of: "Mother, where are you?"

"Kobra Khanum is here. Come and express your condolences to her."

"Heaven above!" Exclaimed Homayon from behind his desk where he was doing his French exercises. He threw his pencil on the desk, jumped up, pulled off his dirty shirt, threw it on the floor; sprayed some deodorant under his arms, took out a new T-shirt from his drawer and wore it with utmost care. He combed his hair, checked his appearance on the wall mirror; satisfied, dashed to meet Kobra; savouring the delicious feeling rising in his loins.

Inside the flat, smiling salubriously, he leered at her with eyes that sparkled with desire. 'Salam Kobra joon, it's so great to have you back so soon.' The words flew out of his mouth and settled like thorns on his mother's mind. She threw a measuring glance at Kobra and detected a flutter of unease pass over her countenance. A wave of presentiment hit her heart. She sent a silent 'astakh-far' (God forbid), bit her lower lip, and giving her son a chiding glance said:

'Dear, you address this lady as Khanum and not joon.'

Homayon was about to say something when Kobra intervened with a sweet smile: "Do not worry Turan Khanum. We all know Homayon joon well." Then, she threw Homayon a warm glance which sealed his lips. His eyes fixed on Kobra, his hand, discretely, pointed to his erected organ. Kobra threw it a quick glance, paled and immediately diverted her eyes to Turan who had been watching them.

As wise as ever, the old lady controlled her shock, faked a smile and asked: "Dear would you like to come and have tea with me?"

Ready to run away Kobra replied: "Thank you Turan Khanum, I cannot right now. I arrived late last night and must go to the hospital and see my mother – perhaps tomorrow." Then remembering the door needed a lock, she asked: "Turan Khanum do you know of a nearby locksmith?"

"Yes Khanum, I do, and I am surprised Nary has not taken care of the lock as yet."

"She doesn't care what happens to this flat anymore – after all, it is not hers."

"But she is family."

"She never was Turan Khanum, never!"

"Do you want me to call him for you?"

"Yes please, but I cannot wait until he comes"

"Never mind, I will deal with him, keep the keys and when you return come and get them from me and not Homayon. You want two sets, won't you?"

"Yes please: one for me and probably one for Golnar."

"Come as soon as you can Kobra joon – Khanum." Homayon demanded, his lascivious eyes gleaming with lust. Kobra pretended not to have heard him.

Turan caught the glow in his eyes and a whisper of 'God forbid' followed by a curse escaped her mouth and melted in the stinking air. The pain in her joints intensified. She bit her lip and grabbed her son's arm as though protecting him from harm. Kobra assumed an air of innocence, took Turan's free hand and leading them towards the door said: "Turan joon, I really do not know how to thank you for being such a decent human being. Had it not been for your caring, my mother would have died." The duplicity hidden in her soft voice was not lost on Turan. Avoiding her conniving eyes she stepped out, and replied: "Your mother is my single friend in this wide world. Enshallah, she will recover soon."

"Enshallah Khanum joon." Kobra replied closing the door behind them.

Once inside their own apartment, Turan grabbed Homayon's arm, stared into his eyes so that he couldn't lie and asked:

"Is there anything between you and Kobra that I should know, son?"

"Yes, a close and pleasurable liaison."

Feeling faint she let his arm drop and leaned against the closed door.

Frightened by her pallor he asked: "What is wrong mother?"

The door knob was pushing against the hollow of her waist. She twisted her torso to avoid the protrusion. Then she put her palm over her aching forehead and massaging it whispered: "Whatever is between you and her must stop."

"Why mother?"

"Because she is not for you."

"I do not understand what you mean?"

"Just trust me, son. She is no good for you."

"Do you mean I am not good for her, because I am not as clever as others?"

"No. No son! No. Please don't get me wrong."

Agonized and humiliated, Homayon frowned, turned his back to her and ran to his room. There he fell on his bed, closed his eyes and began to cry – like a child robbed of his treat.

In the kitchen Kobra found the bottles. They did not surprise her. On the dining table she saw the sickening mess and moved to clear it. Then she stopped. She shouldn't touch anything until they receive the morgue's report. The police might want to inspect the flat again. She returned to Tirdad's bedroom, to check if there had been any important documents that had missed her perusal. Again, she went through the drawers one by one. In the depth of the last drawer she found an unsealed envelope addressed to Nary. She took the envelope to the sitting room, sat on a chair; took out the letter and began to read it.

10th Khordad 1388. (May 2009)

My darling Nary,

I hope you are well and happy. It seems when with you, a curse seals my lips preventing me to tell you how much I love and miss you azizam.

Once upon a time, Rumi made these verses for his beloved Shams. His words express what I feel for you:

You are my life, my senses, you are everything!
Be the rising Moon in my dark nights
I am thirsty for your light.
Use my hands, look through my eyes,
Listen with my ears.
You are the soul of every living thing.
Come, come back dancing like the rays of the Sun
And chase away the shadows.
Come back my love
My broken heart cannot bear more passion,
No more promises.
I've had enough of sleepless nights,
of my unspoken grief, of my tired wisdom.
Come my treasure, my breath of life
Come and dress my wounds and be my cure.
Or else I will die my Nary.

Azizam I have made many wrong decisions in my life for which I only blame myself. I loved my country: I ended up on the side of its greatest enemy. I loved my family and managed to harm them all: I sent my father to his grave; I betrayed my brother and Rose's trust, and I ruined your life.

I am taking care of my senile mother, within the best of my ability, so that she can forgive me. I am stealing from her to provide a comfortable life for you, so that you can love me back and I drink because I cannot live with myself. I know one of these days your absence and alcohols will kill me. That is why I implore you, for the sake of the good times we have shared – by the goodness that I know dwells in your heart, forgive me and believe that only for you I have struggled to continue with my wretched life.

Please forgive me for not being the husband you wanted me to be. Only in your forgiveness can I continue to breathe. Come back to me, my darling, and let us try to find some semblance of what we used to have, during the short time that is left to me. I am very ill and will die soon. Be generous and let me die a happy man. The sun of my life, please, let your rays illuminate the abyss I am drowning in. Come my love – come back to me and let me die with my lips on yours.

Forever Yours,
Tirdad

"The sentimental bastard was pathetic to the end!" Kobra whispered, tearing the paper into pieces and throwing the scraps into the overflowing wastebasket that surprisingly still stood erect.

Two days later, Datam and Rose arrived early in the morning and lodged at Esteghlal hotel. Datam took a quick shower, changed and left for the hospital. Rose did not accompany him. She wanted him to have some private moments with his mother.

He found the hospital as jam-packed as ever with a long, creeping queue by the reception desk. Nurses, doctors and all sorts of staff in uniform were rushing around or talking to people. In that hectic environment he stopped three personnel, asking each for direction. All in a hurry referred him to the Reception. He was too tired to join that unruly queue. Lost in thought, he stood in the middle of the corridor, his eyes aimlessly roaming around. No one paid him any attention. Suddenly it occurred to him to ask for doctor Mehran. He spotted a matronly nurse coming out of a room. He dashed to her and politely asked: "Khanum Salam. Could you please be kind enough to help me? I have just arrived from overseas and am searching for my mother, Shamsi Amiri who is doctor Mehran's patient."

"Salam Agha and welcome to Iran. Of course I will help you. I work with doctor Mehran and have been taking care of your mother myself. Thank God she is responding well to treatment. Please follow me. She is still in the Intensive Care Unit."

Datam smiled his gratitude and followed her with long strides, hastening towards the end of the corridor where the Intensive Care Unit was. She pushed the double door open and hung to one until he was inside. Then she let the door swing back and led him to Shamsi's bed where, he found her, tied to various tubes and monitors. The sight stabbed his heart with million shards of grief. A bombshell of guilt blasted in his head, causing an excruciating pain in his eyebrows and eye sockets. He stared at her shrivelled, sunken face, tears streaking down his quivering cheeks. Toothless and pale, she resembled a breathing skeleton. Fortunately the beard had been removed, and the nails trimmed, but the expression of horror and suffering that had remained frozen on her face shocked him beyond measures. 'What did she see that was so horrific?' Datam asked himself bending to kiss her forehead. Suddenly he remembered the other time, when he had kissed her forehead. It had been as cold as now. But she had been awake and alive – though pregnant. Pregnant! He pushed the ugly memory out of his mind and replaced it with forgiveness and compassion. He gently stroked her grey hair spread over the white pillow; kissed her hollow cheek and then turned to the nurse and asked: "Will she return to us again?"

"Her condition is steady. That is all I can say to you Agha. She will live but in what state I do not know. It is all in the hands of the Almighty."

He nodded his understanding and whispered:

"Thank you for your frankness Khanum."

Then with shoulders hunched, he turned and walked out of the Unit.

Outside it was getting hot. Yet he decided to walk to Nary's. She lived nearby. A walk could clear his mind. He hoped in vain.

He knew the neighbourhood well. It only took him ten minutes to reach his destination which was an impressive apartment block. He smiled his satisfaction. After all, Tirdad had been able to maintain a respectable roof over his family's head. Knowing how he had been financing his lifestyle, he felt no resentment.

He pushed button three. "Who is it?"

He recognized Nary's voice echoing through the intercom.

"It is me, Datam, Nary joon."

"Come in."

The door clicked. Datam pushed it open and entered a well-lit hall. He took the elevator to the third floor. Stepping out of the lift, he saw her waiting for him. They shook hands and he expressed his condolences before stepping inside her apartment. He had never been in his brother's home. The open space in which he found himself was furnished well, and adorned with his mother's antiques and valuables. Then at a corner, he noticed a display cabinet exhibiting several of Rose's antique objects that had been left in the custody of her in-laws. Suddenly he remembered his father's remark in the park and sighed. Nary's eyes following his, noticed them rest on the porcelain plates with Nasser Al-Din Shah's portraits painted on them in blue and gold. "Your mother bought those for us when she was selling Rose's household belongings, stored at our previous apartment."

"They go well with your furniture Khanum." Datam remarked sitting on an armchair.

He is very different from his brother, she thought before asking him if he wanted any tea. "No thank you Nary Khanum. I have come to talk to you about the funeral and see if you have received any news from the morgue's doctor." Without responding, Nary turned her back, walked away and into a room that was just off the sitting room. She returned with an envelope she handed to Datam before sitting down.

"This arrived three days ago. According to the morgue doctor's report, the cause of death was an accident – a fall."

Datam read the report and then threw it on the table. He had never seen such a brief, legal document. He raised his eyes to her, "this report is so short and vague that cannot possibly be taken as a genuine legal document. Cause of death a fall. What fall?" He asked staring at her in awe.

"I do not know. I am neither a doctor nor a pathologist. Somehow, he must have fallen and hit his head on the edge of the glass-table. His forehead was slit open and the edge of the coffee table smudged with blood. We all saw that. I am sure you know that your brother was an alcoholic?" Datam found her tone strangely cold and bitter, and he was too tired and shaken for any kind of dispute. He moved in his chair, intertwined his long fingers together and looking into her cold eyes asked:

"Nary Khanum, how can I help with the funeral arrangements?"

Lifting an eyebrow she replied: "Well, you can pay for it. Your brother was perpetually broke. I had to borrow money to buy his grave. He was buried the day his body was released from the morgue. He rests at Behesht-Zahra cemetery."

Astonished, Datam found himself raising his voice. "Khanum you had no right to bury my brother without us. Golnar told you when we would be arriving in Teheran. Out of respect, you should have waited for us."

Narrowing her eyes, she gave him a long, taxing glare; then leaned forward, and shaking her index finger under his nose said. "Do not ever raise your voice at me again." To avoid her hand touching him, Datam moved backward. "Did you ever think about the welfare of your brother?" As Datam opened his mouth to reply she answered: "No. None of you did. You let him become the slave of your demanding, selfish mother who destroyed our marriage and eventually caused his death. Now, Agha, you come here and dare to raise your voice at me – me who has received nothing from any of you except blames, humiliation and insults." She removed her blazing eyes from Datam's flushed face, turned them to the door and with her hand pointing to it urged. "Please leave my home and forget that your brother ever had a wife." Stunned by her unexpected hostility and rudeness, Datam withdrew his pen and cheque book from the inside pocket of his jacket and put them on the table. With an unsteady hand, he wrote down the sum of a hundred thousand rials. He tore off the cheque, slid it on the glass table towards Nary, returned his pen and cheque book to his pocket, rose, and wordless, left the house, feeling like dirt. He had gone with all the good intentions in the world and parted bearing the weight of universal guilt on his thin shoulders. Almost delirious, he kept asking himself why the woman had behaved so begrudgingly; why she had buried him in a hurry and why the letter from the Morgue's doctor was so brief and hastily delivered. A bureaucratic correspondence usually takes at least a month to reach the recipient. This had taken less than a week.

As Datam waited to catch a cab, Nary picked up the cheque and called out: "Hashem, come out and let's take this unexpected gift to the bank.

Chapter 2

Summer of 1936

As the Air France plane finished bumping on the airport' s tarmac and came to a complete halt, a whisper of 'thanks to the lord' filled the air turning the passengers' anxiety into a sense of relief. A hasty commotion broke the hushed silence and even though the 'fasten seat belt' sign flashed red they moved to unbuckle their seat belts, stand up, open the luggage compartments and pull out their bags and boxes. No one paid any attention to the air-hostess's stern warnings. They just wanted to get their feet on the ground as soon as possible. Those days, people were still in awe of flying, being considered a daring venture, attempted out of necessity.

One of the first to exit the plane was a tall, smart, young man, his name Mohammad Amiri. A beige rain coat over his arm and a brown leather brief case in hand, he descended the landing steps with the air of a man in command of his destiny. On the ground, he stopped to inhale the dusty air he had longed for during the past five years. How much he had missed his country, its air, its noise, its intimacy, even the donkey driven carts and doroshkehs (hooded carriage) that worked the streets, side by side the handful of newly arrived motor cars and buses that were frightening the beasts of burden and their owners!

Contented, he turned his glittering, amber eyes towards the milky sky, and whispered his thanks to providence and not God. He was an atheist believing, like Carl Marx, that religion opiates the mind. Suddenly a hurrying passenger bumped into him. The man gave him a dirty look for barring his path and passed him without a word of apology. Mindless of the insult, he straightened his thin shoulders and joined the wave, but with a steady pace. Unlike the rushing crowd, he was not expecting any family members waiting to welcome him. That knowledge did not disturb him at all. He was one of those lucky individuals with an understanding and forgiving nature. All he thought about was his best friend, whom he knew, would come for him. The two had shared several wonderful years of bachelorhood – a prince and almost a pauper – an odd couple, yet true friends. Amongst his peers, the Prince was the only one, genuinely enchanted to see him receive a doctorat d'état degree in nuclear physics, the thesis of which he had written under the supervision of doctors Marie and Pierre Curie. Marie had been so fond of him that she had given him, as a souvenir of their teamwork, a gold biro with her name etched on it. That pen was guarded with outmost care, secured on a hook in his brief case.

In Isfahan of those days, hardly anyone, including Mohammad's relatives, knew what nuclear physics was, let alone knowing the Curies and their contribution to science. Therefore Mohammad's relatives, ignorant of their kin's privilege of studying under such luminaries, remained envious of his luck for having been sent to France. From the tone of the few letters he had received from them, Mohammad had sensed their resentment, but without a single pang of bitterness. He had just smiled at their naiveté and shrugged off their envy.

A superior student, he had been among the Dar-al-Fonoon (the Centre for all Sciences) graduates whom Reza Shah had sent to France, to study at the University of Paris. These students, financed by government grants, were under obligation to return and work at a government institution, preferably to lecture at the Faculty of Science, in the recently inaugurated University of Teheran, which had replaced the ancient Dar-al-Fonoon established in early nineteen century by the order of Nasser Al-Din Shah Qajar.

Mohammed was born into a respectable family, none of whom had ever cared for higher education, in its modern sense, except him. During those days, wealth and power were held in the tight grips of the landed aristocracy, the successful merchants of bazaars and the clergy. He belonged to none of these groups. He was orphaned at an early age and his elder brother had robbed him out of their father's inheritance. Not interested in the accumulation of wealth, even in adulthood, he had not fought him for his due. He wanted to become a scientist like his ancestor who had been astrologer to Shah Abbass the Great, (1571-1629) of the Safavid dynasty. He loved the world of academia – non-existent at the time, in his home town. Now, with a secure position at the University and an acquired taste for French lifestyle, he planned to forget about life in Isfahan, marry a damsel from an established family and settle in the Capital city where he was a total stranger. He was prepared to face facts for what they were. He knew where he came from and where he wanted to go. Yet, he was unaware of the social strictures that prohibited his entrance to the class he aspired to enter. Nevertheless, luck was on his side. His best friend, Mohsen Mirza was a prince of the expired Qajar dynasty. An extraordinary individual for his era, the Prince, to his chagrin, was aware that no one of inferior blood could socially climb high. Even Reza Khan, the first Pahlavi Shah, in order to acquire a semblance of national grace, had married two Qajar aristocrats. However to Mohsen Mirza's delight, the value of education was becoming nationally recognized and that played on his friend's favour.

Mohammad passed through the visa check point, ignored a porter's offer of assistance, picked up his shabby suitcase, and hearing his own heart beats carried it through the custom area without a glimpse at the custom officer busy pulling out the contents of an unfortunate traveller's suitcase. Before exiting the zone, Mohammad put his loads down, took a deep breath to relax his mind. His eyes glittering with mischief, and as jubilant as a naughty teenager, he congratulated himself for successfully smuggling in, an extra bottle of Armagnac to share with his friend. He lifted up his luggage and with steady steps entered the bustling arrival hall where his expecting eyes began to sweep the area for his friend. Suddenly he became conscious of the admiring eyes of young girls on him. Self-conscious, he felt blood rush into his cheek. He dropped his head for a second, then, lifted it up, corrected his posture, elongated his neck and recommenced his visual search, this time with an air of indifference. After ten minutes', anxiety settled in his mind and he wondered what had happened to his reliable friend. Mohammad did not have a rial in his pocket, nor did he know where to go. Fear made him resent the crowd. The area was packed. It seemed as though half of the city's population had come to the airport – an outing to boast of. Iran was on the modernization path, a progress happily welcomed by the population in general. The only segment of society that begrudged change was the clergy. Reza Shah, in his earnest endeavours to modernize Iran, had recently, prohibited Islamic Hejab, and subsequently curtailed the power of the clergy – albeit ruthlessly.

Apprehensive that his friend may not have received his telegram, he lifted up his case aiming to go to the telephone booth when from behind a boisterous group Mohsen Mirza emerged, his waving hand cutting the air. As their eyes met, the Prince exclaimed a loud "Bienvenue mon ami."

Mohammad, beaming with delight, let go of the case's handle and spread his arms wide. They embraced, kissed each other's cheeks, separated and stared at one another with brotherly affection. Then they burst into a joyous laughter.

"Let me help you mon ami?" Mohsen Mirza offered, patting his friend's back.

Mohammad handed him his brief case and together they marched towards one of the few cars parked under the shade of an acacia.

"Where are you taking me Mohsen joon?"

"To my cousin, Farhad Mirza's house. He was posted to London last month and I asked him if you could stay in his house until you find something for yourself. And he agreed. He is a rather accommodating fellow."

"That is kind of him. What does he do in London?"

"He is our Ambassador there."

Mohsen Mirza opened the boot, put the brief case in a corner and allowed Mohammad to fit in his suitcase. Then he shut the boot's top and unlocked the two front doors. They climbed into the white Cadillac. Mohsen Mirza ignited the engine and headed north, towards Zafaranieh, one of Teheran's most fashionable suburbs. In their view lay the majestic Alborz range with its peak, crowned by a thick layer of snow. Damavand is so high, that from a distance it seems it kisses the sky.

Their conversation was light and moist with juicy gossip about the girls they had left behind and those Mohammad had to meet.

The Prince was aware of his friend's desire to marry well. The task was indeed difficult but he liked a good challenge. It added spice to his boring life. Mindful of Mohammad's pride he had to be extra cautious. Teheran was not Paris where men could allure the girls by their charm and good looks. Here blood and land were the determining factors in the choice of a spouse.

Their drive was pleasant and fast. Mohsen Mirza stopped the car in front of an impressive building half of which was hidden behind a high red- brick wall. He blew his horn couple of times before the gate opened wide and the caretaker in his white shirt hanging over a pair of black pantaloons stepped out bowing to the Prince. Mohsen Mirza waved his acknowledgement and drove in. The domestic shut the gate, rushed to the huge oak entrance door by which he stood to catch his breath. Then, he pulled out from his pantaloons' large pocket, a bundle of keys hanging from a narrow chain. He found the one he wanted and with it unlocked and opened the door. Quickly he rushed back to carry the luggage. He faced the Prince and with both hands offered him the keys. "Welcome shahzadeh (Prince). I am at your service." he said politely.

The prince took the keys, handed them to Mohammad and then smiling said: "Thank you Hamid. We can manage the luggage ourselves. Just prepare a light dinner for us; look after doctor Amiri while here and feed him well."

Mohammad stretched his hand to shake Hamid's. The rare gesture of respect embarrassed the old man. He bowed first before taking Mohammad's hand.

"Sir, please let me know what you like to eat."

"Anything you make will do Agha Hamid."

Surprised and impressed by the guest's affability Hamid bowed again, turned and returned to his quarters with a light heart. Others who had stayed in the house had been so arrogant and demanding. This one seemed different – a genuine Agha. Folks thought rank and money brought nobility. They did not know that even a pauper could be an Agha. A noble soul was far more respectable and loveable than a soulless noble – which most of those he knew were. Thus he decided to serve the gentleman well and cook him good, nourishing food. He seemed as though he had been fasting all his life. The thought gave him a reason to become active again.

Mohammad watched Hamid until he disappeared inside his room by the gate. Then he turned to Mohsen and asked:

"Is Farhad Mirza a millionaire?"

"No. Just well off. He inherited this from his father. He believes it to be a burden; but nonetheless, he keeps it because of his childhood memories."

"Lucky guy!"

"It all depends what you call luck Mohammad?"

"I assume so."

They stepped inside a wide and bright hallway from the high ceiling of which hung a large crystal chandelier. Mohsen Mirza led the way to an elaborately decorated bedroom, with a large window framing the garden view.

"This is your room." Pointing to a half-opened door he added: "And that is your bathroom."

Awestricken by the breathtaking luxury Mohammad paused to admire its movie style decor. Then, he turned his smiling eyes to his friend and exclaimed: "A bath? That is just what I need right now. Would the bathtub be porcelain and the taps pure gold?"

Mohsen Mirza smiled and teased: "Almost!"

Half an hour later, refreshed from his shower, attired in cream cotton trousers and a white shirt, both slightly creased, Mohammad joined his friend in the large but neglected garden, where he was sitting on a bench reading an old magazine. The sky had remained cloudless, the sun rays warm and the birds happily chirping away. It was such a pity that the lawn had overgrown and there was nothing in the swimming pool except dead, shrivelled leaves, and some garden refuse lodged there by the wind.

The two men, delighting in true friendship and parading in paradise, went through the bright morning speculating about the position that would be offered to Mohammad and the brilliant future that lay ahead of them both – all positive stuff of sweet dreams.

As the sun's rays became warmer and their stomachs craved food, they rose and walked to the nearby kebab restaurant where they enjoyed tender pieces of lamb and chicken marinated in saffron and lemon juice, followed by a large portion of Persian Ice cream tasting of cardamom and smelling of saffron . Mohsen Mirza paid for the feast and knowing that Mohammad had no Iranian money, took him to the nearby Currency Exchange shop belonging to a Jewish friend, so that he could change his francs to rials without being cheated. Then, they walked home for a short siesta.

The sun had set, leaving behind an inky blue sky and a horizon edged by a thin thread of gold. The Muezzin had already called the pious to prayer and the stars had begun their dazzling parade when the door bell sounded. The two smartly dressed gentlemen, whisky glasses in hand, winked at each other, and raised their glasses in honour of the pleasures the evening promised. Mohsen Mirza, swallowed his drink, put the crystal vessel on the nearby mahogany table, hurried out of the sitting room to open the door. Hamid having served dinner had been given the rest of the evening off. A waft of delicious French perfume preceded the reappearance of Mohsen Mirza, holding the bare arms of two smiling French beauties. Mohammad immediately recognized one of the ladies – his Air France hostess. They smiled their recognition and automatically gravitated towards each other.

Wine, music and pleasurable intimacy, under the moonlight, lasted till dawn when the early morning breeze made it too cold to remain outdoors. Mohsen Mirza and the girls parted in the Cadillac and Mohammad went to enjoy the luxury of sleeping in a gigantic bed, covered by a colourfully embroidered silk spread.

Mohsen Mirza always went to bed after midnight and rose past nine in the morning. He did not have to work. He supervised the foremen who managed his father's several agriculturally prosperous villages and collected the income to pay for his mother's upkeep in Iran and his father's lavish lifestyle in Monte Carlo. In fact, not many aristocrats worked for a living. They just went through their inherited wealth turning it into ash that later covered heaps and heaps of regret. Some sought solace in opium others in alcohol and those with self-respect committed suicide. However, the world was changing and so was Iran.

It was Friday and Mohsen Mirza was at his Aunt's house gossiping with his cousin Shamsi, when suddenly he had a brain wave: why not her for Mohammad? She was nineteen, pleasant looking, only a bit short and reserved. She had finished high school and was impatiently waiting for her prince charming – none other than her handsome cousin – she prayed and he knew. Conscious of her infatuation, Mohsen Mirza felt rather uncomfortable when in her company. This idea of introducing her to Mohammad relieved his guilt. Why he should feel guilty at all was a mystery in itself, which at times bothered him. Perhaps it was because he did not want to hurt anyone – the way he had been hurt.

Shamsi, her large, black eyes on him was chatting away without being heard. He never participated in her female gossips; it bored him particularly now that he was preoccupied with his grand plan. His silence didn't bother her at all.

She just wanted to have his attention, be near him and inhale the deliciously scented breath that exuded out of his shapely nostrils.

His teasing eyes on her, he was thinking about her elder sisters who were married, one to an aristocrat, and one to an engineer from Isfahan. This indicated that his Aunt was prudent enough to value education. Therefore, she may not reject Mohammad. The thought produced a bright smile on his handsome face. Shamsi presuming it was for her blushed and stopped talking. Suddenly the air became perfumed by the aroma of spicy food being carried in large trays. At the same time, a commotion commenced towards the large rectangular dining table, dressed in white embroidered cotton cloth, about to be brimmed with mouth-watering dishes of rice, stews and kebabs. Determined to have a chat with his Aunt, Mohsen's eyes meandered around till they fell on her standing by the pool. Frowning she was disputing something with one of her unfortunate domestics. She was known for being an unfair mistress, especially towards those who were not endowed with pleasant features. Which servant ever was, particularly in the Middle East? The poor souls, almost all, bore the marks of poverty on their faces, or figures. Trachoma, small pox and polio were the prevalent diseases of the underprivileged. Often Mohsen Mirza pondered upon justice in this world and often he was convinced that it did not exist.

At the age of fourteen Aunty Afsar had been given away to a respectable lawyer who was short, plump and crossed-eye, with a bulbous nose smothered with red veins. She had hated the union in which she had had no say. Soon, to everyone's delight except his wife's, the gentleman proved to be a tolerant, kind and considerate husband. Now that he was dead and buried, Afsar was displacing her life's grudges on those whose appearances offended her discerning eyes. Anyone, not endowed with beauty, had no claim to respect. They were just beings to be abused, as though they had to pay for reminding her of her husband.

Mohsen, feeling sorry for the poor skinny, pockmarked fellow, who most certainly was being reprimanded over nothing of importance, gently padded Shamsi's round shoulder, "My dear, I must go and say hello to your illustrious mother before part-taking of her salt." Then, without waiting for her response, he turned his back and ran down the steps, fully aware of her burning eyes chasing him.

Humming an Edith Piaf tune, he loitered out of his Aunt's vision until her discourse with the wretched, one-eyed, young fellow ended. Then, like a jinnee he appeared in her sight with a loud: "Salam Aunty Afsar."

"Salam Mohsen joon. It is always such a pleasure to set eyes on your handsome face."

"Thank you Aunty. From what I see on the table you have surpassed your usual hospitality. Are you feeding an army?" He asked raising an eyebrow.

"No, I am shutting up gossipmongers."

"You must never worry about them. Even if you offer them the world, they will find something amiss. Aunty, your hospitality is renowned and I wonder how any of us could ever match it."

He paused, produced a playful facial expression, scratched his head full of black hair, and fixed his teasing eyes on her plain complexion, wondering why her nose seemed larger than ever. Even though she was chubby and short, yet she was not as ugly as his other aunts. Besides she knew how to dress and that he liked. He believed elegance gave grace and grace was more appealing to him than beauty for it lasted while beauty faded. Aunt Afsar certainly did have grace. She was a nice person and, in spite of her abominable treatment of her servants, he liked her very much. He knew her only worry was to find a decent husband for Shamsi who was getting on in age – as the saying was, soon to be "pickled". This fact was a trump in his matchmaking scheme.

Flattered, Afsar smiled and lifted a thin, arched brow, (Greta Garbo style brow was a la mode). She took a deep breath, fixed her eyes on him and shaking her head, replied: "I do not need anyone to match my hospitality. You my dear, to please me, can find Shamsi a husband, as eligible as yourself." Smile still tilting on his tanned face, he replied: "Aunty that will be very difficult. But, if you lower your expectation to just as educated as me, I have the right man for her. He is handsome, elegant, tall, complexion light and a lecturer of physics at the University of Teheran."

"Do not joke with me boy." Afsar exclaimed, furrowing her eyebrows in jest.

"I am not joking at all. His name is Mohammad Amiri; he comes from Isfahan, his blood is not blue, but his background outshines that of your existing Isfahani (from Isfahan) son-in-law. His family is well established and respected in Isfahan."

Afsar suddenly noticed her servant lingering within hearing reach. Her countenance blazing with anger she demanded: "Why are you still standing here, you lazy imbecile?" The humiliated man, crimson with shame, dropped his good eye to the ground and replied: "Your ladyship, I was waiting to be dismissed."

"Do not lie, you ass. You were eavesdropping. Now run; Jafar Khan needs your help with the dishing out of the desserts."

Mohsen, dumfounded, marvelled at her unreasonable insolence. How could a woman who is so kind to her family members be so cruel to her servants? He wondered in vain.

Cursing his luck and the unreasonableness of his employer, the servant rushed away. Afsar relaxed again, grabbed Mohsen's arm and pulled him away from the crowd, towards a private notch, under a weeping willow, a short distance from the pool in the midst of which a fountain danced joyously, its tear drops bouncing on the water like tiny translucent marble balls. There, in the shade, she stopped, looked into his serious eyes and asked: "Are you sure he is worthy of my daughter?"

"Aunty, would I dare to propose a man unworthy of your daughter – my own cousin – would I now?"

"I wouldn't know. You always have a trick or two up your sleeves."

"Not when such serious matter as marriage is concerned. Mohammad is a good man. His only fault is that he is a bit thrifty – but one cannot blame him because he lived on government grants in Paris and did not enjoy the privilege of having a rich father like mine. He will make a good husband for Shamsi."

Afsar, turned her gaze on the rose petals floating on the pool surface, contemplated for a short while and then returned her concerned eyes to him and suggested: "Why don't you invite him to dinner with us at your home, without mentioning anything about the matchmaking to any one – in case I do not approve of your choice?"

Mohsen bent and stole a quick kiss from the powdered cheek of the contented lady, raised an eyebrow, and shaking his index finger at her conditioned: "I will do so only if you promise to be less unreasonable to your servants."

"Don't be naive son. They need to be reprimanded at all times. If you compliment them, they will feel indispensable, demand privileges and a wage increase. Learn Agha: never be nice to the class below. They are a non-deserving lot. Always remember the saying: God knew the ass and that is why he didn't give it horns!"

"I do not agree with you Aunty, but I am not going to argue with you either. The feast on the table is getting cold and I do not like cold food. Voila!"

"When are you going to arrange a meeting with this professor friend of yours my dear Agha Voila?"

"Do you know what VOILA means?"

"No and I do not want to know. I want to know when I am going to meet your professor friend."

"He is not a professor yet – but soon will be."

Afsar, who did not know the academic meaning of 'professor', frowned, pondered and then asked: "Well if he is not a professor, what is he?"

"Aunty, it takes years of lecturing and publishing before an academic earns the title of professor. At the moment he is only a lecturer."

"Is that respectable enough?"

"Yes Aunty dear. Nevertheless since in Iran all who teach at the university are addressed as 'ostad' (professor), no one would know the difference. So if he becomes your son-in-law, you can address him as 'professor', and boast about his position in front of your friends who, I am sure, will be impressed, since none of their husbands would have even passed through Dar-Al Fonoon."

"Don't be impertinent young man."

Mohsen smiled, patted his Aunt's shoulders and asked: "What about this coming Thursday evening?"

"That will do well – we often come to you on Thursday evenings, so no one will suspect anything unusual, would they?"

"No dear Aunty. No. And do not fret so much over what people might think or not think. Their opinion should not bother you and besides, life is too short to worry about unimportant things such as gossipers' vicious tongues!" Mohsen replied taking her sagging arm and gently leading her to the dining table which had become less tantalizing. The dishes were half empty and the elegant tablecloth stained by stew drippings and saffron infused rice grains. But the kebab aroma was still lingering on. He inhaled it deep, savoured it with delight, walked to the square table on which china crockery and silver cutlery were neatly laid. He picked up a plate, knife and fork, returned to the dining table and attacked the kebab dishes, being particularly selective with the pieces. He only liked chicken breast and filet kebab, very few pieces of which were left. The hostess headed towards her other guests who were still by the table either eating, or chatting while waiting for desert which they knew would be ice cream, topped with shredded pistachio, pomegranate jelly with fresh cream and Noon-Khamei, (Persian cream puffs). Mousse, cream caramel and other European deserts had not as yet conquered the Iranian desert menus.

Thursday morning arrived sooner than Afsar had expected. Her widowhood days flew away so fast that she sometimes lost count. Without a husband or a son, she had to deal with the boring male chores of accounting, running a large household, minding the incessant family disputes over their inherited villages, dealing with demanding tenants and pickling of Shamsi.

Those days, in the absence of hair-dressing saloons and beauty parlours, beauticians performed their various tasks at clients' homes. Thursday afternoons were dedicated to preparing the wealthy socialites to outdo each other, during revelries. Afsar Khanum's expert was punctual. She always arrived at four, when her client had had her siesta and bath. Usually she was taken to the bathroom to curl Afsar's hair, trim her eyebrows and remove her facial hair; and, once in a blue moon, cut Shamsi's long, wavy hair. But today, she was ushered into the dining room where her arrogant and fastidious client was waiting to have tea with her. Perhaps, the sun rose from the West today! Thought Fatimeh, while kicking off her shoes. "Salam Khanum," she said stepping in. Afsar, smiling at her for the first time in five years of service, acknowledged her greeting with a nod of her towel-wrapped hair and gestured her in. "Come my dear and have tea with me." In a way intimidated by her familiarity, Fatimeh took couple of quick steps, dropped her heavy work bag by the chair facing Afsar, took off her foulard, neatly hung it around the back of the chair and timidly sat down, not knowing what to do with her hands. Afsar turned to Mariam, her new maid and ordered tea.

Fatimeh Khanum used to be a Dalak. Dalaks or better say masseuses worked in public baths, where they scrubbed and battered their clients with olive soup and removed their unwanted hair with strings or honey wax. As people began getting accustomed to bathing at home, in their modern bath tubs, their visits to public baths became less frequent. This reduced the income of the Dalaks. The enterprising ones left the occupation, called themselves 'beauticians', and visited their bath-clients at home. There, they cut, washed, hennaed and curled their hair by heated metal rollers; removed body hair with home concocted honey wax or threads and plucked and shaped eyebrows.

A few minutes passed before Mariam arrived and placed her tea tray on the table.

Afsar looked down at the tray, and then up at her. "Why there are no tea spoons?"

Mariam handed them each their cups and then looked at her Mistress and replied:

"Your Ladyship, neither you nor Fatimeh Khanum put cubed sugars in your tea. You always suck them. That is why I did not bring any tea-spoons. Any extra washing will use water and soap, both costing you money."

The girl's rational response silenced Afsar for an instant and then forming a tight frown she chided: "That is not for you to decide. Etiquette requires tea spoons on the saucers."

"Khanum joon, I am just a village girl. I do not even know the meaning of this word 'etiquette'. I just know one has to save when one can."

"She is right Khanum." Fatimeh volunteered, smiling at the girl's courage and prudence.

More important things on her mind than wasting time on a servant girl, Afsar threw her a dark glance and in a harsh voice ordered: "first go tell Shamsi Khanum to come down, here, and then wait on Fatimeh Khanum."

Afsar picked up a piece of cubed sugar, put it in her mouth and took a long sip of her tea. The sweet taste relaxed her a bit. She put the cup down and began scratching her itching head from over the damp towel. Then nervously she untied the towel and threw it over the dining table. Somehow a horrible feeling was nagging at her. She was terribly anxious about tonight. Arranging a marriage was something she did not like. What if her daughter became a victim of social necessity as she had been? But, on the other hand, she couldn't bear people assuming her pickled. Scratching her head again she turned to Fatimeh and ordered: "Do my hair first. Then, spend the rest of the afternoon on Shamsi. We are going to the Marble Palace for dinner and she must outshine all the other damsels there. If she does, than all the mothers present will be asking me for the name of her beautician, won't they?" Afsar asked, raising, an eyebrow. Fatimeh, a bright smile parting her thin lips, moved her head up and down.

"Do you know what that will mean for your business, my dear?"

"Yes Khanum joon I do, and, I promise you will not be disappointed with the outcome of my endeavours today."

"Enshallah! Now, drink your tea quickly. You have a lot to do this afternoon."

Fatimeh Khanum pushed away her cup and in an ingratiating voice said: "I will have tea later on Khanum joon."

Thus, dreaming of stacks of money, Fatimeh set to excel herself. Afsar's hair did not take long to do. It was almost dry. On Shamsi, she had to work hard. The girl was as hairy as an ape. First she asked her to sit and rest her head on the back of the chair. Then she turned to Mariam and asked her to bring a bowl of boiling water. From her bag she extracted a plastic container in which was her home-made honey wax. Mariam returned with a steaming bowl on a tray which she put on the table. Familiar with the process, she took Fatimeh's container, unscrewed its cap before gently dipping it into the bowl. The only sound that could be heard while waiting for the wax to melt was of Shamsi's nervous breathing. Like a dummy, her head was fixed on the chair's back, her frightened eyes on Fatimeh and her hairy legs crossed stiff. After a few minutes Fatimeh took out a wooden spatula from her bag, delved it into the container, twisted it around and pulled it out with a thin layer shining on its width. She blew over the wax to cool it a bit and then set to work. The inflicted pain rushed tears to the girl's eyes. Once finished, Fatimeh pulled out from her bag a little mirror and handed it to Shamsi to look at herself. The girl, unaware of the reason for such suffering, refused. "Look at yourself my dear. You are very beautiful." Fatimeh insisted. Reluctantly Shamsi took the mirror and gazed at her crimson but pure and glowing reflexion. Her joy evaporated the pain. She touched her face. It felt as soft as a skinned peach. She turned her happy eyes to Fatimeh and said: "I cannot believe how different I look."

"You look like an angel my dear."

"Thank you Fatimeh Khanum. Thank you." The girl's genuine rapture touched Fatimah and made her more diligent. Once beautification was accomplished she dressed her; tidied the back of her hair that had slightly moved out of shape; took her hand and led her to the Khanum's chamber. There, they found her sitting behind her dressing table, applying rouge to her cheeks. As she saw Shamsi's reflection on the mirror she swung around and exclaimed: "How beautiful!" Then, smiling her satisfaction she looked up at the Dalak and remarked: "You have done well my dear." The complement surprised and delighted Fatimeh. She expressed her thanks, turned to Shamsi, "dear turn around so that Khanum can check everything."

Shamsi swung around and then sat on the edge of her mother's bed. "Madar you should thank Fatimeh Khanum. I never knew I could look so nice."

"You were born nice. Fatimeh Khanum only did her job for which I am paying her ample money."

Uncomfortable with her mother's comment, Shamsi turned to Fatimeh and with her lips mimed another "thank you".

"Mariam bring my handbag. It is in my closet."

The maid obeyed. Fatimeh was paid without the expected gratuity. However, in view of what she thought awaited her, she forgave the frugality. She had her tea at the servant's quarters where she felt more comfortable than in the sitting room, and left dreaming of becoming the Court's beautician.

Sharp at seven thirty, Hussain Agha, the senior domestic, brought a doroshkeh by the gate and up climbed Afsar Khanum and Shamsi, leaving behind a trail of delicious aroma where one could only inhale the scent of dust. At the time, the popular perfume was Balmain's Jolie Madame and if you did not stank of it, you were not considered fashionable enough to deserve a glance. This Afsar knew and hence had Mohsen Mirza bring two bottles for her from Switzerland, where he had gone to ski.

Reza Shah had prohibited Hejab and everyone had to appear in western clothing and hats or a foulard. Most women of taste did have a matching hat for each suit that made them look like the movie stars in movies just arrived in Teheran. And there were also those who did have a few, without knowing how to wear them. Fortunately Afsar had enough sense to seek the advice of the French couturier commissioned by Reza Shah to train the royal family in the art of Western elegance. Thus, both she and her daughter, looked perfect in their (uniform like) black suits, white shirts and black silk hats, decorated with a large white bow that sat at the right corner of the hat's delicate brim.

Once Hussain Agha saw his charges comfortably seated side by side, their backs erect and their arms resting on their side of the carriage, like two princesses on an official parade; he gave the coachman the address and made him promise to drive cautiously.

The carriage commenced its wobbly ride, through Avenue Shademan to Old Shemiran Road, towards the north, and Mohsen Mirza's palatial villa, on Avenue Ehteshamieh. After a shaky ride, almost giddy, they reached the gate of their destination, in front of which was parked two American cars, one white and the other black. Their chauffeurs were standing face to face, by their vehicles, boasting to each other of the wealth and importance of their respective employers. The presence of these two Cadillacs signified the presence of Prince Ehtesham, a cousin of Afsar Khanum and Prince Salari another relative. At the time, there were only twenty cars in the whole of Iran and those who owned a Roll Royce, hid it from the covetous eyes of Reza Shah, apprehensive of his demand for a Royal gift that no one dared to refuse – such was the fear of the Pahlavi Shah.

The coachman brought his horses to a smooth halt, jumped down, and opened the carriage door. The mother first and then the daughter, holding his hand for support stepped down, mindful of not laddering their expensive French silk stockings. Afsar Khanum paid him his tariff without a rial more. Then she turned her attention to her daughter, who, like a meek poppy, was watching her. "Come close girl." She commanded, while adjusting her own hat that felt skewed.

Shamsi took a step and faced her with a timid smile. Afsar hastily smoothed the crease on her collar. "Do not forget to walk straight, keep your head up and do not smile at strangers."

Shamsi tucking her black clutch under her arm shook her head in obedience. Afsar extracted her perfume bottle from her handbag, sprayed a little on her own wrists and behind Shamsi's ear-loops. She paused, sniffed the fragrance and finding it redolent enough, returned the bottle to her bag, straightened her hunched shoulders, elongated her neck, took Shamsi's arm and led her through the open gate. The illuminated garden was breathtakingly beautiful with its masterfully designed luminous waterway that rushed down its smooth path, dividing the terrain into two zones joined at intervals by arched wooden bridges – a design Mohsen Mirza had borrowed from Monet's garden at Giverny. The artificial rivulet seemed endless – so long was its bed.

The two-story white-washed house, its oak entrance door impressively wide and high, nestled on an elevation. The edifice was engulfed by a wide veranda allowing for placement of beds that in the evenings were enclosed within mosquito nets. Sleeping outside was a pleasure most Iranians indulged in during hot summer months.

Like all buildings in Iran, this mansion faced south, towards Mecca. Wooden beds covered by Persian rugs were arranged in an ad hoc fashion, under the shade of tall ancient trees that aimed to reach the star- packed sky. There were also plenty of cushioned garden chairs set around colourfully clothed tables. The south-facing veranda belonged to the musicians tonight and the famous Ghamar Vasiri was singing to Maestro Mahjoobi's violin; her voice so enchanting, that even the frogs had come out of their aqua-habitat to listen. A mild jasmine scented breeze was fluttering the leaves of various fruit trees and caressing the petals of flowers in full bloom. One uniformed waiter carried around a tray of alcoholic beverages, another Caviar on Sangak bread and the third, tea, for the teetotallers, mainly the ladies. It had not become fashionable for females to drink alcohol in public yet.

Afsar Khanum smiled at the copiousness of the glittering assemblage. It promised a great evening during which enshallah (putting all hopes in the hands of God) a match would be made. Relying on Providence, she found her way towards the host who looked his princely self. He was in a black suit, crisp white shirt and bow tie. His jet black hair was parted in the middle, slightly brushing against the edge of his shirt collar and his moustache, thin and meticulously shaped upwards, quivered as he spoke. Posture majestically erect and slightly tilted to the left, he was standing within the right distance from the gate to greet his guests. His eyes twinkling with innocent mischief, he was talking with a slender, tall and well groomed man whose back was to her. As soon as Mohsen Mirza caught sight of his aunt and cousin, a quick frown appeared on his forehead and then turned into a smile. Appraising their appearances which at that particular moment mattered, he wondered why they wore hats to a soiree. The intelligent man that he was, he immediately realized that Western sense of elegance had not as yet matured amongst the ladies who were just out of Islamic Hejab. Ashamed of his own rash judgement, he bowed to his aunt and while kissing her cheek whispered: "Aunty, no one wears a hat coming to a soiree. Just act as normal as possible now and then go inside and take it off. No one will notice."

Too excited to feel embarrassed, Afsar whispered back: "Shall do, Agha voila." She returned his kiss and stood erect waiting for the introduction. Mohsen Mirza turned his bright eyes to his cousin who looked exceptionally beautiful, bent low and kissed her rosy cheek. She blushed. Then he turned his playful eyes to his companion and introduced the ladies.

Mohammad, distinguished looking in every sense of the word, and as proud as a peacock, abstained from the usual bow. Instead he stretched his hand and Afsar Khanum took it, in her heart praying for him to become her son-in-law. Then their eyes met and instantly they became friends forever. Mohammad turned his attention to the petite, pretty girl with the largest eyes he had ever seen. Mesmerised, he drank in with glad eyes, her shy smile, the slope of her shoulders, the poise of her head; and at once a thrill ran through his body like an electric current. With new intensity he felt conscious of himself from the elastic spring of his legs to the rise and fall of his lungs as he breathed. She was close enough for him to smell her scent which he immediately recognized. At that moment, he knew he must have her. He took her hand. Shamsi, eyes downcast by modesty, sensed the shiver that ran through him. It made her uncomfortable. Quickly she withdrew her hand, threw a guilty glance at her cousin and wordless, glided away, aiming to join her sisters who were standing near the artificial waterfall, busy speculating about Mohsen's handsome friend they had never seen before. Usually, strangers were not invited to the parties of the nobility, as their uncouth behaviour, very often, disturbed their sense of decorum and made them feel uneasy.

As they saw Shamsi leave their mother, Farideh, her eldest sister, with her hand beckoned her to join them. "Who is that good looking man Shamsi?" Farideh asked in a hurry. Disinterested, Shamsi shrugged her shoulders. "I assume Mohsen Mirza's friend."

"He is handsome." Farideh commented wondering at her pickling sister's naivety.

"I do not think so. He seemed very arrogant. He didn't even bow to Madar, let alone kiss her hand."

"It seems Madar didn't take any offence. Look at the smile on her face. She is enchanted by him." Farideh remarked in a teasing tone.

Afsar was indeed in an elevated mood. She had already sensed Mohammad's interest and noticed the flicker of disappointment pass over his face when the stupid girl parted so abruptly. To sow the seed, she set to work. "Does Dr Amiri reside in Shemiran?" She asked of her nephew.

Guessing the reason for the question, and too proud to let his lack of wealth tarnish his image, Mohammad took the words out of Mohsen Mirza's lips, "Khanum I have just rented a very small apartment near the University. It is big enough for a bachelor and allows me to walk to work."

"You have chosen sensibly doctor, and where do your respected parents live?"

"I am from Isfahan. My parents passed away when I was a child. My siblings and their families still live there."

Thank God for that she thought, believing in-laws are pests, especially if they come from a province where most folks are traditional and narrow minded. The man she liked and he certainly was presentable, but were the members of his family? On this issue she reflected with great sensibility. But no one better had yet asked for Shamsi's hand. With that reality in mind, she gave him an affable smile and exclaimed: "Oh – so you are alone in Teheran. Therefore we must look after you." She swung her head to Mohsen Mirza. "Must not we Mohsen joon?" Smiling at her wiliness, Mohsen Mirza shook his head, threw a congratulatory glance at his radiant friend and replied: "Of course Aunty."

Afsar shook her head in delight and turned her shining eyes to her 'already' son-in-law, "doctor, if you have no prior engagements, would you like to join our family lunch tomorrow. It is Friday, and you would have no classes to attend to. Mohsen Mirza is coming, so you won't feel alone amongst strangers." Afsar turned her eyes to her surprised nephew and gave him a quick wink.

My aunt should have been a diplomat and not a house wife. Mohsen Mirza mused with a wondering smile. He was thoroughly enjoying her conniving manoeuvres.

"Khanum Aziz, I would be honoured to join your family circle. I am staying the night here and we will come together."

"Fantastic. Now I must leave you young men to those of your own age and join my friends." Afsar said with a sweet smile while offering her hand to the doctor to kiss. He took it, gave it a tender squeeze, slightly bowed his head and then released it.

Wounded by his arrogance, Afsar threw a cynical glance at her nephew and walked away – sure that her daughter wouldn't pickle. Suddenly she became conscious of her hat. She changed her direction and hastened towards Shamsi, still chatting with her sisters.

When Afsar left, Mohsen turned to Mohammad. "What do you think – she is very pretty, isn't she?"

"Indeed! I also like your Aunt – she is a lady with a head on her shoulders."

"A bull, my aunt is – but a reasonable one. If you want to ingratiate yourself to her, next time, do kiss her hand!"

Smiling, Mohammad nodded his head and teased: "If you insist I will."

At that moment one of the waiters approached with his tray. Salubriously, they each abducted a glass of whisky on ice, touched glass; chin chinned and drank to happiness. HAPPINESS!

Two months later Shamsi became Mohammad's wife. The wedding took place in style, at Mohsen Mirza's house with only the closest relatives of the bride in attendance. To Afsar Khanum's delight, the Isfahani relatives were prudent enough to provide ample excuses for their absence – not because they didn't want to celebrate Mohammad's happiness; but because the class difference was too intimidating.

The couple moved into an apartment prepared for them at a separate wing of Afsar Khanum's large house which neighboured her other daughters' private homes. Mohammad, too proud to be called a 'damad sar khaneh' literary meaning 'a homeless son-in-law', became even more thrifty. He had to save enough money to buy a house for his grumpy wife. He loved her passionately and wanted to make her happy.

From the start of their union Shamsi, her dream of marrying her cousin dead, objected to her fate and closed her heart to Mohammad. She looked down on his background, his occupation and his inability to make as much money as her brother-in-laws; even though the man had almost abandoned his relatives and was endeavouring to the end of his wits, to provide her with a secure and comfortable life. Resentment and jealousy blinded her to all of his admirable qualities and efforts to make her happy. She shunned his relatives whom she met in Teheran; and detested his shy aloofness that she took for lack of attention. She never realized that, having been orphaned at infancy, he had never learnt how to pamper and show love. She knew her brother-in-laws were spoiling their wives with gifts and expensive European holidays; but was unaware that the gifts were to shield their infidelities. It had become fashionable for men of means to sleep around and keep mistresses now that they could not maintain an andaroon (harem). As the saying went, 'a man could not be fed kebab every day.' Only a few men were content having Kebab daily and Mohammad was one amongst them. Even though surrounded by beautiful and willing students he had eyes for none save his petite Shamsi who envious of others' felicities put his behaviour under a microscope and found fault where there was none. She never had a smile for him and he kept wondering why. Gradually brooding gave her permanent frown and her sense of inferiority in marrying below her rank, diminished her desire to socialize.

Mohammad was a fun loving man; fond of his glass of whisky and an affordable game of bridge or poker; habits his wife detested and avoided.

Those days, the babies of the rich were weaned by wet nurses or Naneh's who acted as surrogate mothers and often lived with their charges until their dying days. Unfortunately, Shamsi's Naneh was an ignorant, mean and money-minded individual who had made it her business to interfere in Shamsi's marital relationship. Out of spite for her thrifty Master, she endeavoured to add fuel to fire whenever possible. As much as Shamsi was envious of her sister's prosperity, her Naneh was of the Nanehs of her sisters, who were being pampered by their generous masters. Therefore, their home, instead of being a castle was a battle ground. Thus Shamsi, moaning and groaning wasted two years of her youth while Mohammad saved enough money to buy a four bedroom house with a small yard, close to Afsar Khanum's. This acquisition enchanted his wife and made her feel equal to her sisters. Once again, she began to socialize and smile at life.

It was a Thursday evening and they were going to dinner at Mohsen Mirza's. In the sitting room, Mohammad kept glancing at his watch. She was late as usual and he abhorred this habit of hers. He hated unpunctuality and thought of it as a lack of respect for people's time. But tonight, he already had one shot of whisky and the alcohol had subdued his rigid standard. He was about to pour himself another drink when Shamsi appeared in a new black satin dress with a low cut neck exposing her creamy flawless skin and the cleft of her large breasts. Even though her infatuation had turned into friendship for her cousin, she still wanted to impress him by her beauty. Thus she took extra care of herself when meeting him and tonight she really looked very sexy.

Enchanted by her appearance, Mohammad's irritation turned into pride. Smiling at her, he placed his glass on the table and exclaimed: "Wow! You look absolutely ravishing ma petite."

She threw her arms up like a ballerina, swung around, stopped and fixed her questioning eyes on his shining face, fishing for more praise. "You are just beautiful!" He said and then stepped closer, softly brushed his fingers around the front of her neck and added: "A necklace would enhance the elegance of your ensemble." Shamsi frowned, pouted her lips, looked straight into his flirting eyes and complained: "I have no worthy necklace to wear Agha."

He lifted her chin up with his index finger, stole a quick kiss from her lips and in a tender tone assured: "Tomorrow I will buy you one, ma cherie." Thrilled, visualizing a pearl necklace just like the one Farideh had worn the other day; she gave him a bright smile, locked her hand in his arm and led him to the door.

That evening, Shamsi, glided in the air. She engaged in conversations, laughed at the jokes she often had found insipid and kept glancing at her image on the wall mounted antique mirror, forgetting all about impressing the host. Surprised and delighted by her sociability, Mohammad wondered what had caused the change.

At home she wore a clean night gown, perfumed the zones she knew he loved to kiss and gave herself to him willingly – without closing her eyes and counting the minutes for the end of the intimacy.

The next morning she made an effort to rise early so that she could have breakfast with him. At the table, the smile did not leave her lips. She ate with appetite and when he rose to leave she kissed him goodbye – something she had never done before.

For Shamsi, the day dragged on, and when it began to dissolve into dusk, she went out into the court yard and sat on the garden chair staring at the sun languidly sink beyond the crimson horizon letting the stars glitter their existence and crescent of a moon announce the change of the lunar month. Down below, Shamsi could sniff the odour of cooking wafting out of open kitchen windows, making the air welcoming for the hungry husbands returning home. She kept glancing at her watch. Mohammad was late. She rose and headed for the kitchen, her mind on the gift she would be showing off, particularly to her sisters who had been looking down on her. She hated their sarcastic tone when referring to his treatment of her and their repeated remarks that husbands had to clothe and bejewel their wives, not just feed them! Thanks to the Lord, now she could prove her husband was like theirs – generous and thoughtful.

Much later than usual, Mohammad arrived, gift in hand. He found Shamsi in the kitchen helping Naneh with the preparation of the dinner which was chateaubriand with French fries and salad – his favourite dish. He took a long sniff, almost tasting the meat in his nostrils and shook his head in approval.

"I see you have decided to spoil me, ma cherie?" He said beginning to believe in miracles. She threw him a bright glance and a shy smile. He bent and kissed her forehead before offering her the beautifully wrapped box she was eyeing.

Childlike, she snatched the gift, unwrapped it quickly, and opened the box. Her hungry eyes fell on a smart necklace of black crystal beads. Her smile turned into a frown and her colour faded. She raised her disillusioned eyes to him and whined: "This is not real." "No, it is not. But it will go well with all your décolleté robes." He replied with a broad smile.

A sneer deformed Shamsi's countenance. She threw the necklace in its box; ran up the stairs to her room, contemptuously threw the box into the garbage bin, dropped on her bed and began to cry. In the kitchen, Naneh turned her myopic eyes to her bewildered master, "khanum deserves real gems not fake ones." He shot her a derisive glance and retorted: "Both you and your Khanum know well that on my wages I cannot afford gems." Then he turned his back to her and walked out of the kitchen, banging its door on her malicious face. In rage, he climbed the stairs, two at a time, and barged into their bedroom to change. He found her sprawled over their bed crying. He sat by her, stroked her curly hair and gently asked: "Why are you so upset – you needed a necklace and I bought one that I know will go well with your clothes. You, my love, are so beautiful that you do not need gems to turn heads?"

"Shut up you stingy man. If you could not afford me, you should have not married me – you have made me miserable and an inferior in front of the whole world. You...." She stopped and started hitting at the mattress with her clenched fists. Shocked and hurt by her rudeness and unkind words he withdrew his hand and brushed it over his pants as though cleaning it from dirt. He rose to his feet and whispered: "Khanum I took a wife and not a whore." Head up, he walked to his side of the bed and in silence, undressed, pulled out his pyjamas from under his pillow, put them on, hung his clothes in his closet, extracted his navy blue satin dressing gown from its hanger, put it on and head up walked out of the room. With measured steps he descended the stairs, entered his study and closed the door behind him. He picked up his evening paper from the coffee table, sat and tried to lose himself within the folds of its pages. To his chagrin, he couldn't make sense out of the simplest sentence. He threw the paper down, leaned on the back of the sofa, swallowed the lump that was choking him and closed his eyes.

Naneh, hitherto spying on her Master from the adjoining room, tip toed to her khanum's bed chamber; sat on the edge of her bed and rubbing her shoulder whispered: "Dear child, he doesn't deserve a wife like you. He should have married a woman from his own rank not a lady like you." Shamsi turned around, sat up and fell within the fold of Naneh's arms. Her warmth was still as comforting as when she was a little heart-broken child seeking the love her mother had denied her. Naneh kissed her long curls, patted her back and whispered in her ears the words she knew would heal her wound. They remained engulfed until Naneh's sharp nose smelt burning meat. She unfolded her arm, looked at Shamsi's haggard face and said: "Come child, we don't want to waste good meat because of an undeserving man." Shamsi wrinkled her nose, shook her head in disgust; pulled a tissue from its box, cleaned her eyes, blew her nose and clenched the wet tissue. Slowly she rose and with slumped shoulders ambled to the door and out. Naneh followed her and then as though remembering something returned inside, went to the garbage bin, lifted the box out, extracted the necklace from it, threw the box back and secured the trophy in her pocket. Her daughter would love it. It was very pretty and foreign made.

In his study, feeling less than an ant, Mohammad chewed his tough, burnt meat, tasting nothing but the dirt thrown at him. "Disgusting" he murmured and threw the fork with the beef piece dangling from it, onto the plate, chipping its rim. He pushed the coffee table away, stretched on the couch, closed his eyes and hoped to die.

As time passed and Iran became more prosperous the entrepreneurs became wealthier and the wage earners struggled to pay the rising cost of living. Shamsi's brother-in-laws climbed the ladder of financial success, each on his own merit, while her husband's rapid academic achievements brought in nothing but prestige and a slight salary augmentation. By now a full Professor, to meet the demand of rising living costs, Mohammad taught evening classes and summer courses, at various universities. Work had become the focus of his life and he enjoyed it.

In the absence of any means of birth control except withdrawal, Shamsi, became pregnant and gave birth to a son his father wanted to name Datam, an ancient Persian name belonging to one of Iran's most famous commanders of the Achaemenian era. Shamsi hated the name for its unusualness. Nonetheless, the first born son was to be christened by the father. Mohammad was an atheist and a nationalist. He did not want to give his children any Islamic names which were Arabic. So his son was called Datam and that name made Shamsi pour out her pent up resentments for the father on the baby who was gifted with the sweetest of tempers and the milkiest of skins. The boy was so lovely that everybody except his mother adored him. Two years later, a second son was born. He was named Tirdad, another Persian name. But, by now, these sorts of names had become fashionable and both Shamsi's nephews bore names of Iranian heroes. Tirdad became his mother's apple of the eyes. She doted on him all the love and attention she had refused Datam and Mohammad.

The Second World War spread its bloody wings over Iran. Allied forces occupied the country, exiled the pro-German Shah and put his young son on the Peacock throne. It took years before peace and stability returned to Iran. Mohammad managed to buy another property which he rented quickly. He also bought a car, engaged an instructor to teach Shamsi and when she received her licence allowed her to drive the vehicle during the weekends. This was a huge success for her. Now she acted like a European lady, sitting behind her own car and going wherever her fancy took her. There were only few women behind the wheel those days and Shamsi was one of them. Nevertheless her happiness vanished when a jealous friend told her that her husband had allowed her to drive because he could not afford the salary of a chauffeur. Suddenly Mohammad's rational and broadminded act turned into a punitive, self-centred deed. Angry with him and feeling demeaned she became more resentful of her fate. For days and sometimes weeks, man and wife did not speak and then when they did, it was with half sentences and catty remarks. Mohammad kept his cool and increased his night outs. Shamsi refused to accompany him and was left alone knitting away her bitterness towards the entire world. Afsar Khanum, concerned about her state of mind, summoned her for a discussion.

It was spring and her garden was filled with flowers of different kinds, over which fervent bees buzzed ceaselessly. The fruit trees were dressed in pink and white and the air sweetened by their blossoms' fragrance. The fish in the pool playfully swung their tails under the droplets of the fountain that danced joyously to the whisper of the breeze. Beauty of nature had absorbed everything in its captivating power, creating an atmosphere of tranquillity in which even the gloomiest heart would light up. Under her weeping willow Afsar Khanum was taking tea when Shamsi, her murky aura disturbing the existing harmony, arrived, followed by Mariam carrying her tea tray

"Salam Madar." Shamsi greeted, taking her cup and sitting on the chair facing her mother. Mariam, took Afsar's empty cup, put it on her tray and walked away.

"Salam dear and why are you in black and looking so glum?"

"I am mourning my fate." Shamsi murmured, sipping at her tea.

"Rubbish, you should be in white and celebrating your fate. You have a wonderful, loving husband and two healthy, gorgeous sons. You have your own roof over your head, a car and your husband earns good money. And above all, is well respected in society. What else do you expect from life?"

"All that my sisters have and I do not." She replied banging her empty cup on its saucer.

Afsar, well informed of the infidelities of her two millionaire son-in-laws, threw her a piteous glance, shook her head in wonder and said: "Dear, grass is always greener on the other side of the hedge. A wise wife never compares her marriage with that of others and God hardly ever gives one everything at the same time. So, to be happy one has to find contentment within one's own means."

She shook her head again and then continued, "Child, life is too short to be wasted in umbrage. Try to appreciate the gifts that surround you. Smile and let the world smile back at you."

"Madar, why do you never support me – Why?"

"I cannot support you when you are unreasonable child."

"I am not unreasonable. My husband is parsimonious, uncaring and selfish. He never buys me anything of value and he is out playing bridge or poker most of the evenings. I have nothing, nor anyone to smile at. Do you call this a happy union, Madar dear?" She leaned back, "I wonder what your reaction would have been if one of my sisters was in my situation?"

Afsar groaned; slapped the top of the table and shouted: "You are filled with envy. It has blinded you to all the good things you have and your sisters don't. How do you know what goes on in their homes? You only see their smiles which makes you pity yourself because you are unable to smile. Do you know why they are able to smile and you are not? Because they are wise enough to take the good with the bad. If you had half of their wisdom you would do the same. But no! Shamsi has to have everything her own way!" Exasperated, Afsar threw her arms in the air with her palms flapping. The sudden movement frightened Shamsi. She moved back, her eyes darting hostility at her mother. Afsar picked up the napkin on her knee and wiped off the foamed saliva from the corners of her mouth. She threw the napkin on the table, leaned back, fixed her softened gaze on Shamsi's flushed face and tamed her tone: "Khanum joon, you are married to a man who loves you and that my dear, by itself is sufficient to make any woman happy. Besides, he is handsome and elegant. He gives you an adequate pocket money with which you can buy what is necessary and when he goes to his gambling sessions why do you not, like the wives of his friends, accompany him?" She paused for a breath and then shaking her head added: "It is because you are stubborn, pig-headed and self-absorbed."

Shamsi narrowed her eyes and peering at her nodded her head left to right and right to left. Then she stopped and in an icy tone said: "As ever, you are so wrong Madar. I do not go with him because I hate gambling, not because I want to force my agenda on him. What is my AGENDA?" She glanced skyward, "I wish I did have an agenda to force on him." The lump in her throat burst and tears rolled down dropping off her quivering chin. Afsar leaned forward and gently patted on her limp, cold hand.

"My dear don't cry. Crying doesn't solve any problems. Just be wise. You do not have to play cards. Some of the other wives don't gamble either. From what I have heard from Mohammad, these ladies chat, joke and enjoy the evening together. He loves to have you with him and show you off. He is so proud of you my dear and it breaks his heart to see you prefer Naneh's company to his." Afsar stopped tapped Shamsi's hand again, looked deep into her glistened eyes and added: "Besides, they don't gamble as such. They just play for distraction and you cannot deny a man for wanting to have some innocent fun!"

Shamsi pulled her hand away and scoffed: "So the two of you have been back-biting me?"

"No my dear, not at all. In fact we have been trying to find a way to make you happy. I personally think you are unhappy because you have no friends, you do not socialize with anyone and do nothing that occupies you except knitting and chatting with that malicious Naneh of yours. Perhaps it would be a good idea for you to take a course in something that pleases you. Now-a-days many ladies have classes in their homes where they teach others what they are good at. You can take a cooking course or learn a language. Amongst my son-in-laws your husband is the most educated. He values education and loves to see you learn what you wish."

Shamsi leaned back, pondered and then let the muscles of her contorted face relax.

Afsar Khanum noticed the change and sent a silent prayer.

"Madar, I think you are right. I should break the monotony of my life by learning something, perhaps cooking. I will talk this over with Mohammad and I hope he won't say no because he has to pay for the course's tuition."

"Do not be too harsh on him. He will do anything to make you happy – I know that for sure, child. You really are very lucky to have a husband like him. Not only he is handsome, he is also a fine man, wonderful father and a loving husband – very rare indeed. Lucky you my dear – I wish I had your luck."

Shamsi leaned back and let the breeze tease her long hair.

Two weeks later she enrolled in a course given by a lady at home and subsequently became an excellent cook and baker. The qualification provided her with the opportunity to become financially independent by teaching Domestic Science at a high school near home. For a while her relationship with Mohammad improved. Proud of her new skill, she prepared for him all the French dishes he was missing and in return he praised her talent, reduced his night outs and took her and his sons to the newly inaugurated Kafeh Shardari, a large entertainment complex with a cinema and several indoor and outdoor restaurants. For once their home became happy and their children began to laugh. Neither parent had realized how traumatising their interactions had been for their sons. A year passed in blissful contentment and both children did very well at school. Then Shamsi's younger brother-in-law doctor Farahi became a deputy Prime Minister. A distinguished gentleman and very sociable, he charmed his way to the Pahlavi Court. The Shah married his third wife, Farah Diba and Shamsi's young niece, Safoura Farahi became a bride's maid. The wedding was televised and she saw Safoura standing behind the Queen. The sight was like a sting of an asp on her ego, the pain of which resurfaced all the subdued bitterness she bore against her fate. She had to get rid of the perpetual pain in her heart and mind, caused by being married to a non-entity without any connections, or back bones. But how? Her restless mind began to search for a way, albeit without success. For days sleep was lost to her, her appetite vanished, her dreams turned into nightmares and life with Mohammad became absolutely intolerable. She could bear it no more. So one morning, when he had left for the University and the boys for their schools, she packed her suitcase, wrote him a brief note informing him of her decision and together with Naneh left home for her mother's.

Afsar Khanum, stretched on her sofa, was enjoying her program on the television when Shamsi appeared case in hand, tailed by Naneh carrying her own bundle. Astounded, she glared at them for a minute or two and then asked: "What is this?"

"I have left Mohammad and have come to live here, with you Madar."

"Don't joke with me, dear. I am too old and might have a heart attack."

"I am not joking at all. I am dead serious. I can no more live with a man I do not love or respect."

Afsar turned the TV off, sat up and asked: "What does love has to do with marriage Khanum? I lived with a man I did not love for twenty five years. This I did because he was a decent man and a good father."

"That was your mistake Madar. You wasted twenty five years of your life senselessly. I am not you. You forced me to marry Mohammad just to get rid of me. Now you have to do with me until I find someone worthy of me – who will make me laugh, instead of frown all the time."

"Who do you think, of your own rank, would marry a divorcee with two teenage boys?"

"Someone will."

"Yes, someone with a leg in his grave."

Shamsi let go of her case, dropped on a seat and burst into tears.

"Azizam, you are making a gross mistake. Please wise up and don't ruin a good marriage. Here is your home as much as mine. Stay until you are over your anger. Then return to your family and be a good mother to your children – as I was to you."

Shamsi stared into her shrewd eyes and mocked: "To me Madar?"

Afsar, conscious of her own discriminating behaviour dropped her eyes, ignored the question and asked: "Which room would you like my dear?"

"My own room, the one I grew up in and not the quarter I shared with that man."

"You shall have it. But Naneh has to go"

Naneh, listening to every word exchanged, looked at Shamsi with enquiring eyes, believing that she would insist upon keeping her. But, Shamsi was not in a mood to fight her mother for an additional mouth to feed. So she avoided her eyes and remained silent. Let down, Naneh turned her spiteful eyes to Afsar, "thank you Khanum for your appreciation of my diligent care of your daughter all these years. She 'was' dearer to me than she ever was to you." Naneh pointed at Shamsi by a half turn of her head and toss of her chin, "I am the only mother this khanum ever knew, and, I hope you can live with your conscience for having been such an unfair mother."

Astounded by Naneh's audacity and the venom in her tone, Shamsi opened her mouth to rebuke her, when the woman picked up her bundle and walked out of the room leaving behind an air of petulance.

"What an ungrateful bitch?" Afsar whiffed before summoning Mariam to come and carry Shamsi's case to her room.

That day, Afsar waited until dark, when she knew Mohammad would be home. Then under the pretext of having to visit Farideh left for his house. Lingering by the gate she took a deep breath, sent a silent prayer and then pushed the bell button.

At that moment desolate and despondent, seeming as dead as a corpse, Mohammad was unconsciously paging the evening paper without being able to read a single line. His mind was a bowl of fire and his eyes clouded by the agony that was kneading his heart. Impatient he threw the paper on the table and was about to pick up his whisky glass when he thought he had heard the buzz of the bell. His ears pricked up.

Afsar pushed the bell button again.

He heard it. He jumped up and rushed to the gate, hoping to find her returned. With quick movements of his shaking hand, he unlatched the lock, and opened the door to a miserable looking Afsar, staring at him with gloomy eyes. Trying to hide his disappointment he stepped aside for her to enter. "Salam Khanum." He greeted her in a whisper, as though guilty of some misconduct.

"Salam son, am I still welcomed here?"

"You always will be welcomed here Khanum Aziz."

Afsar stepped in and looked around. "Where are the children?"

"I have sent them to the cinema."

"Do they know?"

"Yes, I told them. Tirdad wouldn't stop crying. But Datam took it with his usual calm."

For support, she seized his arm and together they sauntered to the familiar table, under the persimmon tree. Afsar's eyes fell on the three red fish that aimlessly floated in the green water of the pond. To her, they seemed as lost as she was in the larger scheme of affairs. Pulling a chair out for her, Mohammad asked:

"Is she with you?"

"Yes son."

Relieved, he sighed. "Can I make you a cup of tea Khanum?"

"No thank you. I have just had dinner. It has given me indigestion." She sat down. "Son, I don't know what to say to you. I am so sorry for what that stupid girl of mine has done – in fact shattered." She extracted a handkerchief from the pocket of her dress, wiped her eyes, blew her nose and clutched at the wet cloth. Looking at her with affectionate eyes he realized her anguish was as profound as his. He crossed one leg over the other, tilted towards her and trying to console her said: "It is not your fault that my wife has left me." He sighed, "It must be mine. But I really do not know what I have done to deserve this abrupt abandonment."

The specks of his sorrow waved in the air and settled on Afsar's arms as goose pimples. She grabbed his cold hands that lay limp on the table and pressed them with all the empathy in her heart.

"Son, you have done nothing at all. You are a fine man, good father and understanding husband. It is her and not you at fault. I should not have let her be weaned by that dreadful Naneh whose milk has poisoned her mind." She blew her nose again, tucked the kerchief into her pocket and continued: "My daughter is blinded by envy and cannot see the blessings that are within her grasp." In regret, she dropped her head and saw a strand of black hair curved on her white dress. She nervously brushed it away with her fingers, and then looked up into Mohammad's eyes. In them she read a deep sense of loss which made her mad at her daughter. Gently patting his bony thigh she asked: "My dear, is there anything you want me to do or say to her?"

"You are a wise lady. I am sure all that has to be said, you have already said. I will try to adapt to my empty life, but it is the children I am concerned about. I do not want them to become delinquents because they do not have a proper home."

"With a father like you, they will never become delinquents. Besides, we are all here for them. You know that, don't you?"

Nodding his head Mohammad lifted up the glass he was fiddling with and greedily drank its entire content. He put the glass down, threw Afsar a loving glance and teased: "You should start drinking whisky. It will calm your nerves and make you sleep well."

Afsar huffed at his joke and rising to leave wistfully countered: "Nothing at all can calm me down. I am just exasperated. You know that among all my son-in-laws I love and respect you most, don't you?"

He rose and gave her a warm hug, patted her back and whispered: "Yes, I know and you are the mother I never got to know and love."

She gently moved back, held him at an arm's length, looked deep into his sad eyes through which she reached his soul and infused it with the warmth of her affection and respect. For a few minutes they stood as one soul in two bodies sharing the same grief. They each were scared to let go, in case it might be their last encounter as relatives.

"Thank you my son. You are the finest man I have known in my life."

He gently squeezed her arms before letting them go. Then he took her hand, brought it to his lips and kissed it. She smiled and taunted: "How come, you never kissed my hand before!"

"Kissing is an act of love for me and not a show of finesse."

She smiled at his ingenuity and followed him to the gate which he opened for her.

Soon the news of the separation gave the gossipmongers plenty to mull over. It made the foes happy and put the friends in a difficult situation. They had to choose between the two and needless to say most sympathised with Mohammad. No one could understand why Shamsi had left a perfect husband, two lovely children and a respectable life.

Practically ostracized, she became more self-centred and deeply self-righteous. She asked for divorce. Mohammad kept the children and granted her request. When the divorce document arrived for her signature, she took it to her lips and kissed it as though it was her key to happiness. Triumphant and exuberant she began to pamper herself. She bought beautiful outfits, changed her hair-style, rouged her cheeks, perfumed her wrists and enrolled in an English class.

Mohammad asked his eldest sister, a widow, to move to Teheran and take care of the teenage boys. The divorce affected Tirdad more than it did Datam. Hugging and smelling his mother's pillow, he cried at nights until he fell asleep. At school, he became a dangerous truant fighting with other boys, breaking windows he blamed on others and one day he crept into the college gardener's truck, put the gear in neutral, jumped off, gave it a push and watched the vehicle slide down, cross the street which fortunately was without any traffic and collide into the facing shop. Luckily it was siesta time and the shop was closed and shuttered. Had it not been for the friendship between doctor Mojtahedi, Alborze's Head Master and doctor Amiri, the boy would have been expelled.

Nevertheless, he was suspended from class for two weeks. Instead of feeling ashamed he felt superior to his peers, cousins and emotionless brother.

Unlike Tirdad, the introvert Datam, ashamed and forlorn wore a mask of tranquillity. Angered by his mother's desertion, he felt for his father whom he knew had locked his shame in his chest and was putting up a brave face. He grew closer to him and adopted his habit of gambling at nights. Kind and calm, he was liked by his friends and domestics. Since Dr Amiri's bridge nights had become regular, the boys' poker games became regular too. The house-boy for ten rials a night acted as a gatekeeper in case the doctor arrived earlier than expected. One evening he did and the boys, engrossed in their bidding, did not hear the warning coughs and whistles of their watchman. They heard the doctor's footsteps too late to put away the cards and the chips and pretend to be studying. The door opened with a yank, Mohammad entered into a room cloudy with cigarette smoke; littered by filled ashtrays, sandwich crumbs and empty beer cans. The boys froze in their positions, none daring to look up at the doctor who was seething with anger. A terrifying silence reigned until the doctor overcame his initial shock. Raucously he ordered the four boys to get lost and never appear in his sight. Datam burning with shame dropped his head and fixed his eyes on the paisleys of the Isfahan carpet. The players, without bothering to pick up their cigarette packs and matches or lighters, collected themselves, forgot about changing the chips, swept their money from the floor with shaking hands, rose and hastily whispered their apologies and head downcast, one by one, brushing against the towering doctor, crept out of the room, ran through the yard and disappeared into the darkness of the night.

"Look at me you idiot." Mohammad shouted.

Datam raised his head and with eyes that implored forgiveness stared at the twitching face of his father.

Searching for the right words, neither broke the silence that was choking them. The boy knew he had done wrong and the father knew he could not rebuke his son for doing what he had just been doing himself. It would be unfair to teach the boy to have a double standard and yet gambling at that age was not an appropriate habit to form. 'What then?' Mohammad asked himself. And then he heard himself say: "Son I am sorry for my nights out. They are just to divert my mind from seriousness of life. We do not gamble to win money; we play to have fun. Besides, bridge is like yoga for me. It relaxes me. Please forgive me for this indulgence – and my silly outburst just now."

Caught by the flames of his father's blazing sense of desolation and his own guilt, Datam let out a loud cry, covered his distorted face by his quivering palms and let his pent up tears pour out. He had been holding them for too long.

Mohammad knelt by him, hugged him tight; pushed his hands away; kissed his wet cheeks and gently rubbing his back murmured: "I love you Son – I love you very much and tomorrow invite your friends to come and have dinner with us."

That night Datam could not keep his eyes closed at all. With every attempt he saw his mother turned into a witch trying to scratch his father's heart with her long dagger like nails. The sight was so frightening that he once sat up in bed and turned the light on.

The broken home affected both boys' behaviour. Scholastically they suffered to the extent that Mohammad planned to send Datam to the United States, hoping a new environment would improve his studies. In spite of finding concentration difficult, Datam managed to graduate from high school and by a stroke of luck, was accepted at New York University to study economics. The same was planned for Tirdad, after he finished his high school. In the meanwhile Shamsi's wandering soul kept searching and searching. Eventually, a tall and bulky Romeo by the name of Ramezan Afati materialized in her English language class. At first, he threw her inviting glances which made her blush. Then he began following her home and standing at a corner watching her disappear inside the house. This routine lasted a month and then stopped. Flattered by the attention she began to miss it. Then one afternoon, she noticed him again. This time she purposely stopped by a shop window hoping he would join her and say something. She lingered on until she saw his reflection on the glass. She turned and came face to face with him. A happy smile lit his round face and his narrow, grey eyes began to sparkle with triumph. Shamsi collected her courage and asked: "Why are you following me Agha Afati?"

"Because your beautiful eyes have captured my heart. I want to be near you and know all about you, Golam (my flower)."

Shamsi's starving heart began to palpitate.

"You cannot find out much about me by just following me."

"Then may I walk you home – we can talk and walk?"

Scared to be discovered, Shamsi refused his request with a negative nod.

"Then how can I get to know you my beauty?"

"We can get to know each other during our lunch hour; only if you promise not to follow me home again."

"And why should I promise that Golam?"

"My sisters live in the same street as my mother and I do not want them to see me being regularly followed by a stranger. It is not good for my reputation."

"I am sorry. In my selfishness, I did not think of your reputation."

"I forgive you. Now please go." Shamsi said giving him a glance full of promise.

"I will go, but I will take you with me."

Frightened, Shamsi replied: "No way. I am going home right now."

"You may run away from my sight, but not from my heart azizam."

These words, she had been dreaming to hear were music to her ears. A desire to touch him rose in her. Unconsciously her hand moved but she managed to control the impulse.

"Till tomorrow then." She whispered turning and walking away.

He stood there watching her until she turned left and vanished from his sight.

That night Shamsi's dreams were sweet and his lascivious.

Tomorrow came and passed away, leaving Shamsi's mind in a euphoric state. For once she had felt totally and absolutely happy in the company of a man who had made her laugh the entire lunch time. What bliss that had been?

What bliss!

Happy days passed swiftly. Amusing conversations during lunch-time led to afternoon tea at secluded coffee shops and then strolls to Ramezan's nearby flat and eventually his bed.

Then her liaison was discovered by Farideh's chauffeur who had seen them regularly having tea at a tea-house near Shamsi Khanum's language school. Hoping for a salary augmentation, he made up a juicy story and pretending to aim to preserve the honour of the family he whispered it to his mistress, in private. That same day the news was delivered to Afsar Khanum and its resultant shock sent her to bed with shingles. Soon the information reached most ears and Shamsi was ruthlessly attacked for dishonouring the family name. However Mohammad turned a blind eye but he couldn't stop tongues waggling about a woman he still loved. Gossip became so hot that the lovers were forced to marry at a notary office.

A business man from an ordinary background, Ramezan appeared to be everything Mohammad was not: flattering, charming, attentive, generous, and selfish. Together, they went through life as though there was no tomorrow. They dined out, took vacations to Ramsar and made love to their hearts' desire until Shamsi became pregnant and the novelty of the relationship wore off. Ramezan turned inattentive, selfish and cruel. The day he beat her, she packed her case and once again knocked at her mother's door. She was allowed in but albeit reluctantly.

Dejected, remorseful and ashamed she kept silent and became more reclusive and bitter towards the world. One day it was her mother to blame because she had paid more attention to her sisters than her, and the next, it was Ramezan who, with his lies had conned her to marrying him. As her tummy grew the list of the culprits extended to include even those who had once said 'Salam' to her.

Her family was furious with her. One divorce was bad enough – two was unacceptable. No one more than her mother suffered. Still in bed, she kept scratching at her spots and murmuring: "Pregnant from that bastard! What shame – what disaster?" The situation was more intolerable, because Mohammad had maintained a civilized relationship with them all. The man was more of a gentleman than all those with blue blood running in their veins. Embarrassed beyond measures Afsar didn't dare to telephone him anymore. How she wished Mohsen Mirza was alive! The poor fellow had died in a car crash. What a waste of life – of such a kind, generous and useful man! Now she had no one trustworthy enough to use as a go-between to see if Mohammad was forgiving enough for reconciliation. In that stuffy room, with the itch of those red spots on her tummy driving her crazy, she kept wondering and wondering until she remembered Datam was returning home for the summer holidays. She could talk to him. The boy loved his father dearly, and he would be able to persuade him to take his mother back, even though pregnant. Datam was so gentle that no one had ever been able to say no to any of his requests. "Voila." She heard herself exclaim. Suddenly she felt invigorated and well, as though there had never been any itchiness. Within a week the spots vanished and five kilos lighter, she became her active and spirited self again.

July arrived sooner than Afsar had expected. Gardeners began to irrigate their territories so that they would be verdant and colourful for the parties to be held, in honour of the overseas students returning to spend their vacation at home. Persian gardens are famous for their beauty and lushness. The word 'paradise' comes from 'paradis' which in the language of the ancient Iranians means 'garden'. Depending on their size, these paradises are cultivated with various kinds and colours of roses, jasmine bushes, and fragrant bulbous, violas and fruit trees. However, the main feature of all these lush areas is a pond or a pool in which a fountain rejoices the gift of life. For Iranians 'water' symbolizes light which is the source of life.

One cool evening, Afsar Khanum and Shamsi found themselves in Mohammad's car heading for the airport. It was well past the rush hour, so the long drive was fast. Shamsi withdrawn and sombre sat on the back seat. Her posture was tense, as though expecting some sort of calamity. Oblivion to the presence of the other two, she was gazing at the advertisement posters that ran away from her inattentive sight. There was no joy in her. The second divorce had shaken her hard and killed in her any hope of happiness. In fact she felt nothing except the occasional movements of the life growing inside her.

Mohammad aware of her presence monitored her movements through his rear view mirror while engaged in conversing with a cheerful Afsar Khanum, sitting next to him. Their talk was light and mainly concerned the plans each had to make the vacation enjoyable for their visitor. It was the first time he was returning home and they both wondered whether he had become totally westernized or had maintained his Iranian grace. Every time they mentioned Datam's name, they heard the sound of a sigh coming from the back seat.

It was a pleasant evening. Above the clear sky was smitten by a canopy of shimmering stars and a pleasant mountain breeze fanned the carelessly happy folks who had already heard the Pan American's landing announcement. As the passengers started arriving, the hustle and bustle increased in intensity and suddenly Afsar Khanum spotted Datam, smart in a white shirt, navy blazer, grey pants and a bright smile. "Here, he comes." She announced waving at him vigorously. He saw her and then his eyes fell on his mother and her protruding belly. The joy in his heart turned into bafflement. No one had told him that she was pregnant. Yet, as calm as ever, he opened his arms and hugged and kissed her first and then the others. Mohammad had sent an adolescent away and now to his delight he found a man returning. Eyes glowing with pride, he took hold of his trolley and they negotiated their way, amongst the crowd, to the car. Datam fitted his suitcase and travelling bag in the car boot his father had opened for him and then closed the top and took the front seat which his grandmother had relinquished. Men always sat in front and women in the back. That was the most respectable sitting arrangement in cars, which Afsar often ignored when travelling in Mohammad's vehicle.

"How was your flight son?"

"Long and uncomfortable, but the food was good. Where is Tirdad Baba joon?"

"I got him a summer job at the University in Rezaieh. Unfortunately you won't see him on this trip."

"I am happy to see you look fine son." Shamsi interrupted Mohammad.

"Fine is not the right word. He looks irresistibly handsome."

"Thank you Afsar joon." Datam said turning his head back and giving his grandmother a loving smile.

"I am so proud of you Azizam; with your education, handsome face and athletic built, you are going to win the hearts of all the eligible girls in Teheran. Enshallah I will be alive to celebrate your wedding."

"Khanum he is too young to even think of marriage." Mohammad remarked, glancing at his mother-in-law, through the mirror.

"Do not contradict me doctor. I am not going to live a hundred years. My grandson must marry and produce a son like his father-while I am still alive."

Shamsi's jaw dropped. Here was her thoughtless mother at work again. How she resented her stupid remarks! She sighed again.

"Afsar joon, I will marry when I fall in love."

"Son – love has nothing to do with happiness in marriage. You must marry a girl who is prepared to accept you for who you are, is wise enough to appreciate your good qualities and is willing to become your partner for life."

"I hate you, Madar." Shamsi's inner voice screamed. She turned her back to her mother, closed her eyes and prayed for her death.

"Grandma, I will only marry for love – only in love one can find happiness, for better or worse."

Afsar sighed. The boy was right. How she had longed to feel love and how disappointed she had become to have to close her eyes and fantasize when her husband made love to her – how could anyone call that physical torture lovemaking? How?

Mohammad parked the car in front of Ghamar Khanum's house and hooted for Karim, the new domestic, to open the door.

The entrance door slit open and Karim's head protruded out. He opened the door wide, came to the car and bowed. "Is our dinner ready?" She asked in a harsh voice.

"Yes Khanum."

"Serve us immediately. We are famished."

"Chashm Khanum." Karim announced his obedience, opening the car door for her. She stepped down and the rest followed. Inside they went through the corridor that led to the veranda. There, they descended a set of steps to the garden where the dinner table was set by the rippling pool on which the face of the moon waved. A few frogs sang their songs and from the neighbour's house noise of a party in progress whiffed through. They took their seats. Staring at her mother, Shamsi frowned and complained:

"They always have parties in that house and sometimes the loudness of their music drives me crazy."

"Why do not you put some cotton wool in your ears – then you won't hear them." Afsar rebuked with a wink at her grandson.

Shamsi was about to say something when the appearance of the servants shut her up.

Karim hastily placed the rice dish in front of his mistress and his wife the bowl of lamb stew.

"Why there is not sufficient saffron on the rice Karim?" Afsar asked her tone intimidating.

"Khanum I put as much as I always do."

"Afsar joon, the rice is practically gold with Saffron and it smells delicious." Datam remarked feeling sorry for poor Karim.

"No, it is not, and this stupid man always makes me lose face in front of my guests."

"Khanum there is sufficient saffron on this rice. And besides, we are not strangers at your table and know what a generous hostess you are." Mohammad remarked, while offering his plate to the old lady to dish for him. Busy serving, Afsar forgot about Karim who lingered on for a few more seconds before turning his back and fleeing away. For posterity's sake he had learned to accept his mistress' unreasonableness with a pinch of salt and turn a deaf ear to her reprimands. He was young and intelligent and besides his wife was pregnant. They had replaced Mariam who had eloped with the neighbour's gardener.

Taking delight in the presence of his son, Mohammad flooded him with all sorts of questions regarding his studies. It was of utmost importance for him that Datam excelled. A good education was the only inheritance he could leave his sons. Afsar Khanum listened to the exchanges with joy and Shamsi sat mute, plunged in remorseful thoughts. With every fibre of his entity, Datam was conscious of his mother's movements. He loved her dearly even though wounded by her selfishness. Never judgemental, he was trying hard to find an excuse to exonerate her for abandoning them. But with a father like his, he could find none.

Dinner was followed by a large bowl of summer fruit brought in by Karim's wife in a loose gown that hid her belly. They did not know what their mistress's reaction would be to her condition. So they were hiding it for as long as it was possible and diligently saving money in case they were sacked.

Dessert consumed Mohammad didn't wait for tea. He politely asked the hostess for permission to leave. They all rose and at the door Afsar Khanum hugged Datam and in his ears whispered, "Dear, can you come here first thing tomorrow morning?"

"Of course I can – Granny."

That night Granny hardly slept – the thought of Shamsi giving birth to that man's child, under her roof, was eating her heart like a mass of maggots on a corpse. How could she ever raise her head in front of her equals? Sometimes she couldn't even look into her closest friends' eyes so humiliated she felt.

At the crack of dawn she rose, went to her bathroom where she performed the ablution ritual; returned, took her prayer mat from its place by her bed, spread it on the carpet, covered her head with her chador, tied the ends under her chin and stood to pray to Allah who seemed to have forsaken her. She begged and begged him for an end to her torment – even death would be better than what was awaiting her family. Eventually calmed by the power of prayer, she took her breakfast of goat cheese, bread and cucumber in the garden where the breeze was fresh and the dews sparkled on the lawn like diamond studs. Pensive she sat alone, looking at the jasmines that were in bloom and the climber roses that had invaded the entirety of one long wall. Her annuals were surviving the heat but their beds were as dry as desert sand. Why had the gardener not irrigated them yet – the lazy idiot? She thought, shaking her head in despair.

The train of her thought was broken by a hug from behind. The suddenness of the embrace rushed a cry of fright out of her mouth which was drowned in Datam's happy laughter.

"Sorry Granny, I did not mean to scare you." Datam said kissing the crown of her head.

"Son, next time you will kill me."

"Granny love never kills anyone." He pulled a chair away from the table and sat on it, his smile as bright as the sun above.

Then he remembered the gifts he had put on the floor. He rose, picked them up from behind her chair and placed them on the table.

"Who are these for?"

"You and Madar."

"It is your mother that I want to talk to you about."

"My mother?"

"Yes your mother. I want you to become the instrument of reconciliation."

"How Grandma? My mother has broken all the bridges behind her. She left us without a good reason. She married a man none of us ever met, and then left him pregnant. No abandoned husband with any pride can take back such a woman?"

"Your father will. He is an extraordinary man with a heart of gold. And I know he still loves her. He loves his sons even more and wishes them to have a normal family life. He is a forgiving man. I know with all your smiles and pretences you have not forgiven your mother. Please remember we all make mistakes and those who love us must be generous enough to forgive us. What kind of a future will your mother have with a baby and no breadwinner? People will look down at her – they already do. Most of her friends have discarded her like their dirty clothes. No one will ever want to marry her again. She is worse than a pickled virgin!" Shaking her head in pensiveness she paused.

In thought, he remained silent.

"I want you to talk to your father and persuade him to take your mother back. She wants to reconcile but does not know if he will take her back. Will you do this for us all, my child?"

Datam stopped fidgeting with the edge of the table cloth and looked up at her.

"Certainly I will try Granny. But will my father listen to me?"

"Yes he will listen to you – he loves you more than anyone else in this world. Of course he will listen to you."

"Enshallah Granny. I promise I will do my best." He picked up one of the parcels and placed it in front of her. "This is just a little souvenir from America."

"You shouldn't spend your money on me son."

"Who is better than you, Granny? It is only a black cotton shirt – I have got the same for mother, in cream."

Afsar, inquisitive like a child, tore off the wrapping and pulled out her present; shook its creases out and smiled her approval.

"You have inherited your father's good taste. I will put it on this afternoon when I am going to Mrs Mansour's house. You know that her son has become the new Prime Minister. They live at Avenue Ehteshamieh, near where late Mohsen Mirza's villa was. How I miss him! He was like a son to me."

"How did he die Granny?"

"On the way to Chalous a bus collided with his car. Fortunately he died instantly – the dear soul."

"He was my father's best friend. They were like brothers."

"Yes. And his matchmaker."

"I did not know that."

"No one did except him, me and your father."

"Perhaps if he was still alive, he could have prevented the divorce."

"Perhaps – he had a persuasive way with people."

"He was handsome, charming and so rich; why did he never marry Granny?"

"He had a French girlfriend he loved very much and his father did not permit him to marry her. She married someone else and he could never get her out of his system. That is what we were told. There were also malicious rumours, but one can never believe rumours. Of course your father would know the truth, but one can never get a word out of him."

"You are right Granny. My father hates gossip. Pity about Mohsen Mirza's love affair and I certainly am glad norms have modified now. I would hate it if my father stopped me from marrying the girl I love."

"It is always good to listen to your parents and benefit from the wisdom they have earned through experience."

"Granny that is a different story from being forced to marry someone you hardly know because your parents have chosen her for you."

"Son, whichever way you look at marriage – it is a gamble – arranged marriages are less risky than love marriages because investigations are made, matters are discussed and problems resolved before the commitment that should be for life is made. Some people are lucky and some are not. I hope you find a woman who will make you very happy son; and I hope I will be alive to put your hand on hers."

"Enshallah, and Granny I will drive you to Mrs Mansour this afternoon myself. At what time shall I pick you up?"

"That is a treat son! Come at four. Now go to your mother, but not a word of what we have discussed."

"That will be our secret my lovely Granny." Datam promised standing up.

"Go now and God be with you."

Datam crossed the roofed veranda, turned right into a narrow passageway at the end of which was his mother's quarters. He opened the door and was hit by a heavy stale air. She was still in bed. He went to the south-facing window and opened it. She tried to rise. He gently pushed her back; sat on the edge of her bed, kissed her face, stroked her untidy hair and gently patted her belly. Their eyes met and she read forgiveness in his. A serene smile illuminated her sunken countenance and her eyes began to glitter with tears. He bent and kissed each one of them. She hugged him tight and began to cry.

"Hush Madar, it is not good for you to get upset."

She released him from her hold, pulled herself up a bit, and leaned against her cushioned headboard.

"Madar, I am taking Afsar joon to Avenue Ehteshamieh this afternoon. Would you like me to take you to Darband for an ice cream by the waterfalls?"

His words were like running water, its current sweeping away her fears of rejection. Suddenly she felt light. Her breathing became easier and more regular. Her face relaxed and she enjoyed the freshness of the air that had invaded the room. It was soothing. It was in fact just divine. She smiled. He smiled back at her. She stared at him with eyes glimmering with the joy of returning to the world of the living.

"No, thank you son, motion makes me sick. But you can buy a barbequed corn dipped in salt water for me." She requested like a spoilt child.

"I will, but by the time I get home it will be cold and stale."

"You are right my love. Never mind. Just come and visit me every day."

"Shall do Madar joon. You do not have to ask me for that!"

She dropped her head and murmured: "Son, are you able to forgive me ?"

"Yes Madar, because my love for you is unconditional – never doubt that."

She raised her grateful eyes to heaven and uttered, "Thank you my God for returning my son to me." He bent and gave her a huge hug.

Sharp at four, Datam parked his father's blue Peugeot in front of his grandmother's gate; got out and rang the intercom. A few minutes later, smart and without a hat, Afsar appeared smiling at her favourite grandson.

"Afsar joon, what have you done with all the hats you had?" He asked opening the door for her. "They went out of fashion as quickly as they had become fashionable," she got into the car, "they are gathering dust in the storage room."

"Overseas, ladies still wear hats but mostly in winter when it is really cold or during church ceremonies." He started the car.

"Here we wear scarves."

"The next present I bring for you, will be a woollen scarf Granny." Afsar smiled at his profile, her eyes admiring the modern buildings that had grown on both sides of the asphalted road on which cars, taxis and buses raced against each other.

"This is a luxury to be driven around in a private car – much better than the wobbly Doroshkeh's." She commented, affectionately patting his thigh.

Their drive was pleasant and their talk light and amusing. As Datam turned right from avenue Marvdasht into Avenue Ehteshamieh, a pleasant feeling gripped his heart – as though somehow his life was connected to this road. Facing him was the majestic Alborz range reaching heaven. The avenue was tree lined and moderately wide. It ran North South from avenue Doulat to Old Shemiran road. Adjoining this Avenue's pedestrian pathways, were stately homes secured behind high brick walls, some capped by flowering creepers. As he was driving up hill, on his right, a large square blue tile caught his eyes. On it was etched Rose cul-de-sac. What a beautiful name to give a cul-de-sac he thought.

He stopped the car by the impressive gate of Mrs. Mansour's house. The presence of rough necks in cheap suit and tie meant SAVAK (Iran's secret service) vigilance, signifying the presence of the Prime Minister at his mother's home. He got out of the car, opened the door, helped his grandmother out, jumped back and hurried to meet his friends. The tea party was the last joyous event for the Prime Minister. The following week he was assassinated by a member of a fundamentalist group who opposed his progressive plans for Iran.

The afternoon turned into dusk, the setting sun dusted the horizon with gold and the air became pleasantly cool. Datam arrived home from having met all his school friends, at the new Ice Palace belonging to a famous millionaire. The establishment had a huge restaurant and an enormous ice-rink. Being the first of its kind, it had become the place of rendezvous for the well-to-do and a place to see and be seen.

He found his father in his study, lying on the couch, his face hidden behind the double page spread of his Keyhan newspaper.

"Salam Baba."

"Salam son." He replied, his bespectacled face becoming visible from above the pages he lowered.

"Baba, can I talk to you please?"

"About what son?"

"About Madar."

Mohammad threw his paper on the floor, took off his spectacles which he secured on the arm of the settee, sat up and then with his hand gestured him to sit. Datam, his heart hammering hard, dropped on the comfortable chair opposite the couch. Staring at his father he noticed the sudden colour change on his face. A sense of panic rippled inside him. He sent a silent prayer and quickly asked:

"Baba joon, do you still love Madar?"

Mohammad threw him a pensive glance, his mind racing to find an honest answer. A poignant silence fell and dragged on. Datam kept his anxious gaze on his father's tight face, praying for a miracle and Mohammad, his eyes closed, fought against his injured pride. Memories rushed in and out swiftly – good and bad, each competing for dominance. Datam noticed the quivering of the veins on his neck and the slight tremble of his hand. Now worried about the state of his health, he sent another prayer, this time asking forgiveness for his interference.

Mohammad opened his eyes, moved in his seat so that Datam was in his direct line of vision; licked his lips, shook his head and replied: "Yes – I love her, because she is my sons' mother."

Datam released a sigh of relief loud enough to make his father laugh.

"Thank you Baba joon, and for our sake will you take her back?"

"Yes I will – if it will make you happy." The phrase flew out of his mouth like an imprisoned butterfly.

Datam rose, took a step, knelt by the couch, took his father's moist hand and kissed it several times.

"Father, I am so proud of you. You are a wonderful human being. Thank you, and thank you a thousand times."

Mohammad broadened his smile, squeezed Datam's hand and together they rose.

"Now let's go and have dinner. I am famished."

"Baba you are the kindest, most forgiving man I have ever known. I am so proud to be your son and bear your name."

"Well well now! What about a bottle of Shiraz?"

"Indeed why not!"

Three weeks later Mohammad remarried Shamsi at a notary office.

Datam returned to New York, a happy man.

Overjoyed more than anyone else, Tirdad celebrated the reunion with his friends at a restaurant in Tabriz.

And Afsar Khanum fed the poor at the local mosque.

Chapter 3

The Whirlwind of Change

It was a beautiful August day and the streets were empty of cars and people. The Parisians had deserted their city and gone on vacation. An Air France bus from Charles de Gaulle delivered Tirdad and Mohammad to Place de l'Etoile. They descended its steps and with the assistance of the bus driver collected their suitcases from its trunk. Awestricken and totally absorbed by the architectural magnificence surrounding him, Tirdad's eyes wandered from Arc de Triumph to Champs Elysees and all the other wide avenues that fed into Place Charles de Gaulle. He felt like a child in a dreamland. Suddenly a pang of pride assailed him and he immediately straightened his back and elongated his neck. Without being conscious his lips murmured a Khodaya Shokret, a rare occurrence. Hardly ever he had thanked God before. But being here was like being in paradise. He had never imagined a city could be so grand and he, able to live in it!

Mohammad, delighted by the joy radiating from his face, gently took his arm and in a cheerful tone said: "You have plenty of time to get to know Paris. Let's go now. We have a metro to catch. Our hotel is in the 6th arrondissement, a good distance from here, on the other side of the River."

"A river runs through this city?"

"Yes. River Seine divides it, to a left and right bank. Here, we are on the right bank."

Conscious of his father's thriftiness, he asked: "Is the left side as chic and beautiful as this one?"

"Yes, and in fact more elaborate and exciting. It is the old side of the city."

"This place seems like a paradise!"

Remembering the hard days he had endured as a student, Mohammad didn't want his son to be deluded to think that all was going to be rosy for him. So he looked at him with kind eyes and said: "Son, Paris is just a beautiful city, but that doesn't make it a paradise, in fact, sometimes it can be hell. Remember our proverb: 'Where is paradise? There, where the heart is content." Then smiling he lifted his luggage and aimed to cross the avenue that led to the metro station. Tirdad was so entrenched in his euphoria that didn't hear a word of his father's preaching.

Mohammad crossed the street thinking Tirdad was following him. Then he turned back and saw him still standing on his spot smiling at the world. He waved him to come. Tirdad didn't see him. "Tirdad!" he yelled, surprising the pedestrians, unaccustomed to screams. Mohammad's voice jolted him out of his trance. He lifted up his luggage and hurriedly crossed the street almost being hit by a car. Together they traversed another Avenue before descending the steps to the metro station. Tirdad had never travelled by metro. The experience at first frightened and then thrilled him. This new world was definitely different from the one he had left behind. It offered so much to enjoy and so much to learn.

Their hotel was small and their room clean. They had a shower each and tired Mohammad lay on his bed for a little rest only to face Tirdad's objections. He was so restless that he couldn't even sit for a moment. Not to disappoint him, Mohammad, reluctantly rose, changed and took Tirdad out for a walk by the river on which sparkling leisure boats calmly navigated.

That night, lying in bed, too excited to sleep, Tirdad recalled all the scenes he had imbibed and concluded that Plato's Utopia could not possibly be better than Paris. To his astonishment, for the first time in his life, he found sharing with his father, the same sentiment, for the same thing. This was a miracle indeed. Perhaps, in this marvellous city, not haunted by bad memories, he could get close to him and learn to love him again. He hoped.

In the coming days, Mohammad, in the only place in which he had tasted happiness, forgot why he was there. Like a lost soul in search of redemption, he took Tirdad to all the places of his dreams, where he, once, had felt alive and free: Quartier Latin, Montmartre, Pigalle, Marais and Champs-Elysees; recalling Mohsen Mirza and all those who had made life worth living. The experience was so fine, so rejuvenating, so ethereal and at the end, so sad.

The next morning was another bright and warm day and the terrace of their hotel jam-packed with tourists taking breakfast. All smiles, having enjoyed their warm croissant and café au lait, Mohammad paid the bill and the two headed for the Real Estate agency they had spotted nearby. There, Mohammad told the agent they were looking for a studio close to Sorbonne University. The man consulted his list of rentals and found one just around the corner. They walked to the studio, found it acceptable, returned to the agency, and completed the paper formalities. Then, they walked to Sorbonne's language school, where Tirdad had to take a language test. Nervous he was taken to a classroom where a group of foreigners were sitting behind their desks, pen in hand. The examination took two hours, during which Mohammad lost himself within the familiar buildings of the University. Much had changed since his days. But the aura had remained the same.

Two days later they received the test result which was better than the University's required skill level. They delivered it to the University's Admission office, and thus having met all the requirements Tirdad was officially enrolled. To celebrate his son's accomplishment Mohammad treated him to a dinner of Entrecote which Tirdad had never tasted before. The evening passed merrily and the two walked to the hotel rather tipsy.

That was Mohammad's last night ever in Paris. The next day, a proud father he flew back to Iran and Tirdad commenced his new life.

Charming and sociable, it took no time for him to make friends with his peers both foreigners and French. He joined their home gatherings during which they debated social, political and economic issues, smoked pot and returned to their lodgings, filled with antipathy for capitalism. As Tirdad became more familiar with the French egalitarian political and social system, he became more resentful of monarchy and the class system. A vulnerable soul, he blamed his parents' divorce on the social injustice that he believed prevailed in the Iranian society, particularly among his maternal pomp and pompous family members. Had it not been for the wealth his undeserving uncles had accumulated through illegal means (perceived by him) his mother would never have had any reason to bear a grudge against her husband and leave him. During his high school days, he had several friends whose parents belonged to the Tudeh party, the first Iranian political entity, created in 1942, by the Bolsheviks in Azerbaijan. Although their control of the Province was short-lived, the seed they had sown before being driven out grew to a well-organized group of educated and dedicated comrades, aiming to challenge the monarch for control of the country. Their vision was to install an egalitarian system, like the one in the USSR. They detested the British economic control of the country. They believed the Shah was serving British interest more than the interest of his own nation.

In 1949, surviving an assassination attempt against his life, the Shah banned the Tudeh party and rigged parliamentary elections. A few years later, during the premiership of Dr Mohammad Mossadegh, when the Iranian economy was at its lowest ebb, they resurfaced and flourished. Mossadegh's nationalization of Iranian oil antagonized the British enough to impose a full-scale trade embargo on Iran. The British began to explore ways to get rid of the old menace as they called Mossadegh who relentlessly continued to assert his power and authority, including challenging the Shah for control of the Iranian military. When the Shah tried to rein him in, Mossadegh became obdurate. He pressed the Shah with demands for political democratization and economic reform. When the Shah refused him, Mossadegh resigned. The Shah elected a 'yes man' as his Prime Minister. Riots broke out and Mossadegh was reinstated. Rumours of a planned coup began to circulate. Mossadegh reacted by breaking diplomatic ties with Britain. He forced the removal of all British intelligence personnel from Iran. Mossadegh's nationalism and his willingness to stand up to Britain made him a national hero. But by alienating Britain, he paid a tremendous political price with huge ramifications for the political future of Iran.

The intrigue in Tehran coincided with the 1952 presidential election in America, taking place against the background of the Cold War with the Soviets. As soon as Dwight D Eisenhower was elected president, the British government sent a top intelligence officer to Washington. Monty Woodhouse, informed U.S intelligence about the political situation in Iran, the economic vulnerability of Iranian oil, and the unreliability of Prime Minister Mossadegh in the effort to contain international communism, particularly as Iran shared a large border with the Soviet Union. Woodhouse met with his U.S counterpart and managed to persuade him that a political and economic disaster for the West was unfolding in Iran.

Convinced by the CIA that Mossadegh was a pro-Soviet and anti-American leader, President Eisenhower, on June 25, 1953 gave the green light to Operation Ajax. Through a combination of paid political propaganda, paid street agitators, fomented street protests, and a rebellion organized by pro-Shah military leaders, Kermit Roosevelt, director of the CIA's Middle East Bureau, succeeded in flaring up chaos all across Iran. The anarchy and turmoil created a political environment that allowed the Shah, having fled the country, to return, sit on his throne and immediately sack Mossadegh and imprison him for life. This covert

CIA coup against a democratic government, in favour of an autocrat, aborted the development of democratic infrastructure and civil society – political parties, a legitimate and functioning parliament, an independent judiciary, and an uncensored media in Iran. The crushing of these basic building blocks of democracy and pluralism that undermine extremism and fanaticism was, in future, to plague the West and create chaos in the Middle East.

Subsequent to the Coup, a prohibitive intelligence service named SAVAK was created jointly by CIA and Mossad to hold Mohammad Reza in power, serve the belligerent powers' interests in Iran and crush the Tudeh Party. The comrades either fled to the USSR or went underground waiting for the right moment to resurface again with a greater vengeance against a pro-Western monarch who to preserve his power kept a closed eye to the gap between Western rhetoric and Western actions . The intellectuals and the nationalists in Iran realized then, and remembered it for almost thirty years, how the West trumps basic democratic and human values to address its short-term political and economic goals. Had Iran been allowed to remain a democracy, the Islamic Revolution of 1979 would have not even had a chance to germinate, let alone succeed!

Already influenced by the leftist ideas of his Iranian friends, once settled in Paris, association with young leftists, together with study of accessible literature by communist philosophers, turned Tirdad into a dedicated communist ready to strike at anything that smelled of social injustice. He became convinced that it was his duty, as a conscientious social entity, to try, to bring justice to the society in which he had been victimized.

In the summer of 1966, both brothers returned to Iran; Datam having graduated and Tirdad having two more years left of his studies. To their relief, they found their home peaceful and their mother happily occupied with her four-year old daughter, she had named Kobra. To their surprise and admiration, they each, in his own way, noticed their father's genuine affection for the child. The little girl, with jet black hair, large black eyes, olive skin and a grim air, looked very different from them. They had fair skin, amber eyes, brown hair and bright smiles. Their little sister was rather reclusive and appeared to have a brooding nature. At first she seemed intimidated by the presence of the two intruders who had invaded her space and were stealing her parents' attention (no one had as yet told her about her real father). However, after a few days of being pampered and spoilt by the two, she lost her antipathy and somehow gravitated more towards attentive Tirdad than reserved Datam. This pleased her mother.

After years of hard work, doctor Amiri had become the President of Rezaieh University in Azerbaijan. This meant he was away from home three days a week. However, when the boys arrived, the classes were closed and he had ample time to spend with his sons. Before their arrival he had worried about their behaviour towards Kobra. But, when he saw their acceptance of her, he breathed with ease, for it meant his home would remain a happy one. Only God and Afsar Khanum knew how hard he had worked to achieve that goal.

Datam, amazed by the change of their home's atmosphere, yearned to discover how the miracle had happened Remembering that his grandmother's regular tea-session at Mrs. Mansour was on Thursday afternoons, he called her on a Wednesday evening and offered to drive her there.

During their drive, he engaged Afsar with some domestic gossip he knew she would enjoy. Then when he felt she was completely relaxed he fell silent. Afsar waiting for more amusement diverted her eyes from the road to his pensive profile.

"Why, all of a sudden you look so serious?"

His eyes on the road, Datam changed gear and replied:

"I want to ask you a question about my parents?"

"About your parents?"

"Yes. Please tell me what happened between them after I left?"

Afsar was getting over her surprise when Datam added: "I am so proud of my father. You cannot image how happy Tirdad and I are."

Afsar leaned against the door and faced him. He gave her an affectionate glance, stretched over and pushed the door's lock button down.

"You do care for me, don't you?"

"Of course I do."

"Good. That pleases me enormously."

She smiled and then started:

"When Kobra was born, Mohammad drove me to the hospital. In the back seat was a huge basket of flowers. Knowing how careful he is with money, frankly, I was surprised. During the drive he couldn't stop bragging about the baby and how its existence would bring them happiness." She paused, nodded her head in bewilderment, released a heavy sigh and murmured: "Your father is truly an exceptional man Datam."

"I agree with you Granny and I wish I had inherited some of the goodness in him."

"You have son. It was you who brought them together."

Datam smiled. "Afsar joon, it was you who asked me to do so. You are also an exceptional mother."

Delighted by the compliment, she stole a quick kiss from his tanned cheek. He looked at her from the corner of his eyes and smiled. She gently patted his lap. "Son, thank you. I hardly ever receive any compliments. They are scrumptious and it is such a pity that people don't pamper each other with them more often."

"I agree with you Ghamar joon, and now let's return to the hospital?"

Afsar leaned back again and continued:

"There he kissed her, took the baby into his arms, examined her with the curiosity of a real father, kissed her wrinkled red face and played with her curved, plump fingers and then returning her, said that he wants to adopt her. Instead of thanking him, my silly daughter, grabbed the bundle of black hair from him, pouted her lips like a spoilt brat, stared at him with unkind eyes and shaking her head cried no – I won't allow that. She is mine and mine alone." Afsar noticed the thumping of a vein on Datam's temple and paused.

"Then what happened?" Datam asked in his usual calm.

"I almost fainted when I saw the hurt on his face. At that moment I was so angry with your mother that I could have strangled her. But your father was more understanding than me. Later, to keep face, the two of us concluded that at the time, she was not mentally ready to make any rational decisions. But I am sure your father shared my opinion that the silly woman had thought he wanted to adopt her child not out of love but out of the selfish purpose of impressing people by his heroism. Well, your mother was wrong again. All he wanted was to save her face and by doing so maintain respect for the family."

Afsar took a tissue out of her bag, blew her nose and then asked: "Do you know what a Sismoney is?"

"It is a ceremony to celebrate a birth and the hidden reason is for people to provide for the basic needs of a baby."

"Yes. But in my long life I have never known a financially secure husband to want to celebrate the birth of a child not his own."

Datam diverted his eyes from the road to her. "Afsar joon, we both have agreed my father is an exceptional husband."

Afsar lowered her eyes, shook her head. "Yes. And I am sure his aim was to suffocate gossipmongers and stop malicious tongues from wagging. I have never seen anyone so concerned about the reputation and respect of his wife. He is just a very unique man."

"I know that Afsar joon and from our home atmosphere I am sure that my mother has finally acknowledged it too. At least I hope so."

"Well, she wasn't very happy with the notion of your father organizing a Sismoney."

"And why not?"

"I do not know dear. What goes on in her sick mind is beyond my comprehension. Nevertheless, Mohammad went ahead and organized the Sismoney. He invited everyone on the list I gave him and we planned it for the first Friday after her return home. I was very much looking forward to the event. His acceptance of her child, in a way, was returning respect to me. You know how people are – often, more malevolent than kind and understanding."

Datam sighed and acquiesced.

"Anyway, between the two of us, we did everything, almost to perfection. Early in the morning of the event, Akbar and his wife went to your house and by the time I got there all was clean and spotless. I thought Shamsi would be downstairs telling them what to do, but no, they had done it all by themselves and her ladyship was still in bed with her baby. So I went up, gave her a big piece of my mind and managed to get her down acting like the lady of the house. You cannot image how happy your father looked when he saw her dressed up and pretty. I think his smile tickled her conscious, for she smiled back, turned her eyes to the bundle she was cuddling and then back at him and asked: 'she looks cute doesn't she?' He went to her, kissed her face and the baby's and then left us to take care of our female affair." Afsar took a deep breath, swallowed her saliva and continued: "Soon the guests began to arrive with presents for the baby. Within an hour, the rooms were filled with the nobles of our society. Needless to say, that I had made sure the tea table teemed with the best from Behjatabad fruit market and Fard Pastry shop. Akbar served tea, Turkish coffee and soft drinks. It seemed the ladies were enjoying themselves and Kobra, in Shamsi's arm, bathing in the existing gaiety, gurgled nonstop. Then, my thoughtless sister, Ashraf, turned to Shamsi and said this is a really lovely party and you are so lucky to have a husband like Mohammad. Then she added: I was so surprised when he called to invite me. None of our husbands would have done it, even though it would have been to present their own off-spring. Suddenly realizing her guff, her chin fell, she stopped, not daring to look at me in the eyes. An oppressive hush fell; colour drained from Shamsi's face and a smile froze on everyone else's lips. No one knew what to say or do. All eyes were fixed on Shamsi's colourless face. After a few seconds of staring at the baby, she raised her head, and facing Ashraf said: for your information aunty dear, Mohammad wants to adopt Kobra, but I won't let him, because as you said, she is not his and never will be. She is mine, and mine alone. I will get a job and provide for my daughter myself.

"Did she really say that?" Datam asked, astonished.

"Yes. That is what she said. You should have seen the expression on the guests' faces. Well, her words made them so uncomfortable that soon the house became empty. The first to leave was my thoughtless sister who didn't want to be left alone with me. But one cannot blame people for telling the truth. Anyway the worst was that Mohammad, who had returned home and stayed in the TV room, had heard everything."

Datam suddenly swivelled the car towards a curb and stepped on the brake. Afsar's head almost hit the front window.

"Afsar joon sorry for this. Let's just wait until I can collect myself."

"Son, you almost killed me. Never mind that, we are getting to the good part now," she smiled, "the next day Mohammad called and invited me to have dinner with them. I knew he had a plan so I agreed and went. After dinner, when we were having tea in the sitting room, he turned to her and said: "Khanum joon I just want to explain to you why I offered to adopt Kobra. It is purely to save her from malice. You must realize that in a traditional society where everybody knows everybody else's secrets, a few unkind remarks could poison a child's mind and lead to the inception of many complexes that in turn could lead to low self-esteem, depression or God forbid some kind of mental disorder. If you love your daughter you must think of her future. She must grow up in a happy home, where acceptance and respect are norms to follow. Here, Afsar Khanum is my witness that I am doing my best to make our home a happy one and I expect you, if you wish to continue living with me, to do the same, if not for my sake, for your own and your daughter." It took your mother a good few minutes to comprehend and digest the depth of his logic and the alternative that faced her. You cannot imagine what anxiety I went through until she looked up at him, smiled and promised to behave. I am glad to say that up to now she has kept her promise."

Datam leaning on the car door smiled, nodded his head and whispered: "It is really true, that no one can say no to love." Afsar shook her head in acquiescence, glimpsed at her watch and said: "That is very true son. Now start the car, I am already half an hour late."

The year 1966, was an auspicious year not only for the Amiri's, but the whole nation. Peace, general prosperity and a semblance of political stability initiated a period during which life, for most Iranians, became dream-like.

Restaurants, nightclubs and cabarets catered to all levels of income: the rich who lived in the north of the city, frequented night clubs and chic restaurants; ate chateaubriand, drank whisky and danced Twist and Cha Cha Cha. Movie houses, theatres and concert halls were packed with spectators. In the south of the city, famous musicians performed in cabarets, like Shokofeh-no. There, those of lower income spent their evenings enjoying kebabs, drinking vodka and listening to their beloved singers like Mahvash and Sousan. During winter months, ski resorts hummed with excitement and in summers, the beach at Ramsar was colourfully shaded by huge umbrellas under which lay women in their bikinis, drinking pomegranate juice or sour cherry syrup. In the evenings they gambled at the Casino Ramsar or danced in the hotel's nightclub. Ramsar remains the most beautiful city in the north of Iran, where the Alborz range frames the Caspian coast. Its wide, verdant breast tilts down, crosses the city and melts into the Caspian's sandy shore. Citrus trees ornament the sidewalks and palm trees divide the roads. As though the Caspian beaches that run for miles and miles were not enough, there was a plan in progress to make Kish Island a free port, with five star hotels and casinos. The Shah and his cronies already had villas there and if one knew the right person, one could be invited to spend a winter weekend there, swimming in the warm waters of the Persian Gulf and boast about the privilege until one's dying day. The cost of land was rising and landowners were selling their old mansions to developers who were turning them into modern complexes more lavish than anything found in Manhattan.

At the time, Iran was one of the least extremist of the Muslim nations. Despite the Shah's autocratic rule, social tolerance was widespread, and exposure to information and technology possibly greater in Iran than anywhere else in the Islamic world. Had democratic institutions been allowed to develop, they might well have saved the monarchy from fall.

Life was really agreeable in the Iran of those days, and the students back for their summer holidays from abroad, were having fun which was also clean. Consumption of alcohol was limited to a glass or two of Whisky and drug use rare. Girls socialized with boys and the maximum intimacy was a goodnight kiss or a tight hand grip. The institution of marriage was highly respected by all and having a Sigheh (temporary wife) forbidden. Everyone, from the prince to the pauper, had the privilege of enjoying freedom of choice – that precious gift we often take for granted.

There was work. There was bread. And there was plenty of laughter.

It was during that summer, at a dinner party that Datam met Rose. The same Rose whose name he had seen etched on a blue tile, stuck on a wall of a cul-de-sac, off Avenue Ehteshamieh. Standing erect, a black Hermes crocodile clutch tugged under her slender, tanned arm, she was attentively listening to her friend, Nargess bragging about how she had rejected Ferdous's indecent insinuations and left him cold with surprise. Rose knew them both well. Nargess was her school friend and Ferdous her naughty cousin who apparently had not as yet matured. The evening was too good to waste in bitter talk. So, smiling brightly, she interrupted her friend: "Nargess joon, obviously he has remained the spoilt brat he used to be and doesn't deserve someone as beautiful and nice as you." Rose swept her eyes around and then turned them back to her friend. "Tonight we are surrounded by so many fantastic prospects against whom Ferdous wouldn't count a rial. Get him out of your mind, smile and look for someone worthy." Rose's logic planted some sense into Nargess's blocked head and she began browsing. Her hitherto serious eyes lit when they fell on a young man in a smart grey suite. Indeed they were encircled by handsome, chic men, some of whom she already knew of. Her face lost its gloom and a bright grin enhanced its charm. She turned to her friend and asked:

"Tell me Rose, are you looking too?"

"Of course I am. I do not want to pickle."

"What? With your looks and background you will never pickle."

"Do not bet on it. Men are funny creatures and I do not want to marry just anyone."

The band began to play Frank Sinatra's 'Stranger in the night'.

They both loved the song. So they stopped talking and listened to the music, humming the words and gently tapping the ground with their feet. Under the moonlit sky their silhouette danced on the surface of the pool by which they stood. A gentle wind teased Rose's dark brown curls. In her simple black Chanel evening gown that accentuated her perfect shape, she looked like a model from the pages of Vogue magazine. No one passed her without admiring her elegance and dignity. Of medium height she was extremely beautiful. Her flawless skin was ivory, her mesmerising black eyes large and glittering; her small nose sculptured and her mouth round, rosy and parted with a serene smile. She had a presence that no one could deny – even those envious of her grace. One amongst the captivated guests was Datam who stood a short distance away. He could not remove his eyes from her face. Ferdous, his best friend busy telling him how he had broken off with his girlfriend, noticed his lack of attention. He turned his head towards the direction of his gaze and when he saw Rose's face above the back of a girl's head, he smiled, raised an eyebrow, grabbed Datam's arm, and shaking it said: "Do not look at her like that; she is my cousin."

"God she is beautiful! What is her name?"

"Rose Qajar; just back from England, working somewhere as a bilingual interpreter."

"Hurry, introduce me to her?"

"Only if you promise to behave like a gentleman."

Datam hastily nodded his consent and the two found their way to where Rose and Nargess were standing. An alert girl, Rose had felt the young man's eyes on her. He was good-looking, tall and elegant. She admired elegance in people. She sensed their approach without turning her gaze to them.

Ferdous, walking ahead and waving his hand in the air, tried to attract her attention. Because of Nargess, whose back was to him, Rose was reluctant to respond until they came face to face.

"Salam cousin." Ferdous said smiling. Hearing his voice, Nargess's heart sank and blood rushed to her cheeks. She waited a few seconds before swinging around. At that moment Ferdous was kissing Rose's face. Then he turned. Their eyes met, just for a second and in that second they each felt a dreadful pain. As egoistic as ever, he did not offer her a greeting. The wind lost its gentleness and the four felt uneasy. Nargess turned to Rose, "I cannot bear the polluted air here. I am going to make a round of the garden."

Rose winked her understanding.

"Ok, I will be leaving at my usual curfew hour of twelve. If you want me to give you a lift, meet me by my car and do not make my chauffeur wait for you."

"Ok madam boss." Nargess replied with a wicked smile, and glided away, like a mannequin at a Chanel defile that had become a regular occurrence in Teheran grace of Empress Farah, a Francophile.

Ferdous, turned his nose up, lifted an eyebrow and shrugged his shoulders as though he didn't give damn about the insult. But the flush of embarrassment that coloured his countenance crimson betrayed him. Sensing his discomfort Datam turned his head skyward and exclaimed: "Tonight we have full moon."

Indeed there was a full moon smiling at them. Ferdous diverted his attention from the moon to his cousin, "Rosy, I want you to meet my friend here, Datam."

Rose turned her brilliant eyes to him, smiled, demurely stretched her manicured hand, and in her soft, husky voice corrected: "I am Rose and not Rosy, nice to meet you Datam." They clasped hands. The contact electrified their totality and inflamed it with such a delicious passionate fire that could do nothing but solder their fate forever and settle as ash over their graves – a lifetime later.

Frank Sinatra sang along.

Eyes glued on the girl, Datam felt hypnotized. As he sensed her hand slipping away from his, he tightened his grip and asked: "Would you like to dance?" She smiled her acquiescence and turned towards the dance floor pulling him behind her. They spent the rest of the heavenly evening in each other's arms, meandering to the rhythm of the music – sometimes fast and sometimes slow.

From a distance, Ferdous watched them with a tinge of jealousy. And then, he saw Nargess being led to the dance floor by a very handsome fellow in a grey suite. A frown of regret set on his narrow forehead and he heard himself murmur: "Well, that is the end of her now – all my own bloody fault."

After that memorable evening, Datam and Rose regularly met at parties thrown by mutual friends. In Iran of those days, the country was ruled by one thousand and one, prominent families. Their social circle was guarded and the socialites mostly related, were intimate and caring. When an attachment was noticed a wave of matchmaking activities followed. So peers made it their business to create situations in which Romeo met Juliet. No liaison ever remained a secret. And as soon as the rumours reached the ears of the couple's parents, they began a series of background investigation, a paramount necessity before a Khasegari (asking for a hand in marriage). The Amiri's were delighted their son had met a girl from such a distinguished and wealthy family. But Rose's parents although they approved of Amiri's background were concerned about Datam's future. He had no occupation as yet and was eligible for Compulsory National Services that would render him unemployed for at least two years. Besides, men superior in standing to Datam were after Rose's hand in marriage.

Rose was the only child and rather spoilt. She was also obstinate and determined. She had made it clear to her parents that she would only marry for love and nothing else. Prince and Mrs Qajar (In Iran, the wife of a prince is not addressed as a princess) did not want to talk to their daughter about this Datam lad, before they had met him themselves. They had heard all sorts of things about the man and his family except information about Mrs. Amiri's divorces. And that was because they had not dug enough into Amiri's private affairs. So to be fair, they resolved to create a situation in which they could meet this prospect in person and evaluate him for themselves. They did not want to just rely on their investigation because people always exaggerated or omitted information depending on their relationship with the party being investigated.

Rose's birthday was approaching fast and her parents decided to celebrate her 21st, in a lavish party to which she could invite whoever she wanted.

Their house at Rose Cul-de-sac was grand and the garden huge and well designed. A large rectangular blue swimming pool shimmered like a huge aquamarine, particularly in the evenings when lit curved fountains jetted into its midst from its length and breadth, creating four luminous domes. Tonight, plenty of rose petals undulated on its rippling surface. The pool was constructed in the midst of a velvety lawn dotted by small flowerbeds packed with colourful annuals. There was a well-defined herb garden just before a wide cherry orchard rich in juicy, pink fruit. Climber roses and white jasmines crawled up all walls making them invisible and verdant. At one corner, near the veranda, a round travertine dance floor was constructed for summer festivities. This evening, plenty of chairs and tables were meticulously arranged at different corners of the lawn for the expected hundred youngsters to occupy when exhausted from dancing. A bar was set by the dance floor. Waiters, tray in hand offered Caviar on toast and Rose, in a green silk dress, embroidered with gold threads and fresh- water pearls, shone like a huge emerald. She stood near the gate, greeting her friends and anxiously waiting for Datam. Punctuality not being one of his virtues, he arrived half an hour late; dressed in a smart dark grey suit, bearing a smile that immediately captivated Mrs Qajar and brought an admiring glow to the Prince's appraising eyes for the stranger. Both in their hearts hoped he'd be Rose's lad. As Datam's eyes fell on Rose, his heart lost a few beats and a feeling of joy invaded his totality, illuminating his face with the glow of love. She offered him her cheek. He kissed it and felt ebullient. She took his hand and directed him towards her parents who were watching them from a short distance away. The halo of love that crowned the two removed the doubt about the identity of the stranger and fed their hearts with a palpitating divination. When close enough Rose turned to her parents and said: "Mamman, Baba, this is my new friend Datam. We met at aunt Nayer's house. He is Ferdous's best friend."

"Welcome Datam." Prince and Mrs Qajar said almost in unison. They shook hands and before they had a chance to utter another word Rose pulled Datam away and guided him to the dance floor.

The merrymaking continued until the band stopped and announced the readiness of the dinner. The crowd headed towards the building and the dining room at the entrance of which stood two waiters offering the guests Limoges porcelain plates and Sterling silver cutleries. Iranians are not accustomed to seated dinners. They like to serve themselves and mingle amongst those whose company they prefer. This informal manner of consumption gave the parents, each, an opportunity to talk to Datam and extract from him some useful information about his character and his future aspirations.

Mrs Qajar was a good natured, down to earth and sensible lady. All she wanted for her daughter was to see her happy with an honest, loyal man. However, the Prince was more cautious. He knew wealth could be lost but not education and to succeed in life, ambition and determination were essential. Therefore, these merits, besides backbone and a solid, likable character had to be present in the man he would allow Rose to marry. He also trusted his own first impression of people. Fortunately, so far, he had liked what he had observed in the young man about whom he had been so worried. He believed fate was in the hands of God. Yet God had given man the power of rationality to make the right decisions. Blissfully it seemed his Rose had chosen well. This thought helped to make the rest of the evening enjoyable for him.

The guests, having part-taken of a sumptuous meal, were chitchatting and laughing, when a huge birthday cake, shaped as a Qajar crown, set on a round silver platter, carried by none other than the chef himself, appeared in sight. Instantly the band began to play the 'happy birthday' music. The crowd joined in by singing the verses. The chef, dignified in his spotless white uniform and long white hat that gave his punitive stature some height placed his masterpiece on the desert table. Proud of his artistry, a shining smile tilting on his round lips, he stood erect, enjoying the expression of amazement flickering on the guests' happy countenances. Indeed they were all awestricken by his creation of a white crown, adorned by pearl-shaped cream rosettes, glazed cherries, shredded pistachio and almond marinated in saffron and gold threads of crystallized sugar. He turned his soft blue eyes to his mistress and read a 'well done' on her lips. Pleased, he left to hear the praise of the cake's taste later. It was Mrs Qajar's habit to thank her domestics for their contribution in making her parties the talk of the town.

Rose closed her eyes, wished for happiness, and opened them to Datam's smiling face. Their eyes interlocked for a second and then, she inhaled a deep breath and with one long exhalation blew out the playful candle flames – twenty one of them.

Kisses were in order but Datam did not dare to approach her. It would have been very improper. The Prince noticed the abstention. His respect for the young man increased.

The band resumed its joyous music; the floor became packed and the two lovers danced away the night till darkness dissolved into dawn.

Late, in the morning, when the servants were clearing the mess in the garden, Rose joined her parents, at the breakfast table on the veranda. She kissed each of them on the cheek before sitting down. The maid brought her a cup of freshly brewed coffee and a small pot of boiled milk. She thanked her with a smile, unfolded the white napkin in which warm sangak bread was wrapped, took a piece, spread it with butter and quince jam and was about to munch at the crunchy bread when her father fixed his concerned eyes on her radiant face and softly said: "Rose we know you are attracted to Datam." He paused for a second and then continued: "He seems a fine fellow and educated enough but do you know that he will never give you the lifestyle you are accustomed to?" Blushed, Rose turned her eyes to the bread crumps sailing on her white silk dressing gown. Annoyed, she teased them away with a finger, looked up and caught her father's waiting eyes.

"Do you love this man?"

Shyly she whispered: "Yes Baba."

"Will you have him without looking down on him?"

She looked into his wondering eyes with respect and replied: "I will have him for who he is and not for what he can give me. Baba joon, you have given me enough not to have to marry a man for money – and I am eternally grateful to you for this independence."

"Good. So you will be marrying for the right reasons!" The Prince said with a smile. He took a piece of bread, spread it with honey and began to eat it with joy.

Mrs Qajar, who had so far kept her counsel, produced a frown. "My daughter is wise. Did you think she would ever marry for the wrong reasons?"

The Prince finished eating his bread and replied: "Khanum I just wanted to be sure that you have been a good enough mother to install the right values in my daughter's mind."

His wife, familiar with his peculiar sense of humour, threw him a bemused glance, turned her soft eyes to Rose and said: "I feel good about him child – but before I express further opinion I like to meet his parents."

"Thank you Mummy; if he is serious about me, they will be at our doors soon."

It was a Friday afternoon when they came for Khasegari: an official meeting during which the father of the groom asks the father of the bride for her hand in marriage with his son. If the proposal is accepted, practical matters regarding the union are discussed and agreed upon.

Standing on the veranda, the Qajars, with their habitual cordiality welcomed their guests that included Afsar Khanum almost hidden behind the huge basket of white roses Dr Amiri was carrying. A uniformed servant took the basket from him, took it to the sitting room and placed it at an appropriate corner. Datam politely introduced the members of his family. They shook hands and then Mrs Qajar ushered them to the main sitting room. One step inside and they had to stifle the exclamation of awe that was forcing itself out of their mouths. The room resembled a grand lounge in a palace. Mrs Qajar noticed their admiration and appreciated it with a modest smile. Shamsi and Mohammad took the pale green satin sofa while Afsar Khanum sat on a matching armchair, by a huge fire-place the mouth of which was hidden behind a peacock's colourfully-bejewelled, spread wings; its eyes two huge jades. It was sculptured in solid brass and when it caught a ray of light fluttering in through the south facing window, it glittered like a rainbow. The room was brilliantly lit by natural light. Several vases packed with tuberoses and white gladiolas sat on antique tables and consoles that were standing at different corners, each serving a practical purpose. A moderately large square glass rested on curved, polished brass lion's legs, its surface decorated by crystal dishes of freshly baked pastries, salted pistachio nuts, Baklava and a large bowl of fruit. Soon after the guests made themselves comfortable on their seats, tea on a silver tray was brought in by a domestic in a smart black suit, white shirt and a tie. The aromatic concoction was sipped over small talk, forged smiles, and plenty of Tarof (meaningless pleasantries and flattering remarks) which Iranians are masters of. As soon as the last empty cup was set in its saucer, the waiter arrived and cleared the table. When he left the room, doctor Amiri, sat upright, gave himself a proud air and turned his serious eyes to the Prince.

"Excellency, I am sure you know that my son, Datam, is highly educated; comes from a respected family and has not an iota of blemish on his reputation. He is a man of honour and honesty. There are several girls who dream of marrying him and we have received a few messages from prominent families wishing to give their daughters to my son (all lies). It is fortunate for you that he has fallen in love with Rose Khanum who is beautiful and seems charming – and above all the daughter of such illustrious father. Sir, we are here to ask you to give her hand to our son in marriage. It seems they have been made for each other."

Datam's tense countenance was changing hue with each wrong word that flew out of his father's mouth: so embarrassed he felt.

The women sat silent; their eyes rotating from Dr Amiri to the Prince and back to him.

Rose watching Datam was amazed at his sensitive nature.

Mrs Qajar seemed listening to the doctor, but in fact was deciding whether she should have the wedding gown tailored in Teheran or take Rose to Paris. Of course, all depended on the date of the wedding.

Afsar Khanum who had never expected to find Rose so charming and sophisticated was praying for a 'yes' from the Prince. The girl was a godsend for her Datam. They would make an excellent couple. Besides, this marriage would enhance the dignity of her family. That pleased her enormously. And, Shamsi sat like a cat waiting for a mouse to catch.

The Prince, removed his gaze from the doctor, turned it to the eyes of the peacock that were glowing green and remained silent. The serious expression on his face gave the impression that he was in deep contemplation regarding the issue at hand. In fact he was not. He was thinking about the father and not his son. Amiri's approach had amused him and he was evaluating what calibre of a man he was. He recognized that the man was shrewd and prudent. That was good. He was proud of his son. One couldn't blame him for that. But he lacked finesse and class. That was unfortunate. They could never become friends. He would have loved to be able to socialize with Rose's in-laws but it seemed that was not to be. He crossed his leg, licked his lower lip and deciding not to be egoistic looked up at his wife and smiled. She took it as a good sign. So to return cheerfulness to the sombre ambiance, she rose, went to the table and asked each of her guests what they would like to eat. Afsar Khanum wanted a piece of cream puff- pastry, Shamsi a piece of Baklava, to try to see if it was as good as those she baked. To her astonishment, it was even better. Doctor Amiri wanted a branch of seedless grapes, and the Prince nothing at all. He was health and weight conscious. He had a slim figure that looked smart even in rags and he intended to keep it that way. He believed the only possessions which totally belong to us, from the beginning to the end, are our soul and the frame in which it dwells. Therefore they have to be kept clean and in good condition.

Not knowing what to say the guests kept busy eating, smiling and nodding at the delicious taste of their pick.

Mrs Qajar, back on her seat, focused her eyes on her daughter and when she caught her gaze, with a quick head gesture made her realize that they should leave the room.

Rose acknowledged her understanding with a wink and communicated it to Datam. It was time to let their parents, without having to look into their eyes, decide their fate. As per tradition, bride has a price or Mehr which is her security in case of a divorce and must be paid by the groom upon request, even if there is no divorce. In return, the bride must bring a Jahizieh or furniture to the home they will be sharing. The Jahizieh remains the possession of the bride forever.

Datam turned to the Prince and politely asked: "Shahzadeh (prince) will you permit us to leave the room?"

The Prince smiled at him and nodded his permission. The two rose and walked through the door which Rose quietly closed behind them. Outside was warm. She took Datam's arm and led him to her favourite bench, placed under the shade of a huge weeping willow.

In the absence of the two youngsters, the room's atmosphere became formal again. The Prince moved in his chair so that he could directly face doctor Amiri. Then he cleared his throat and in a very relaxed tone said: "Doctor Aziz, I am sure you know that my daughter has also refused several marriage proposals from men of substance, (true). We respected her decisions because we were sure she would ultimately decide wisely. Her choice has fallen upon a man that my wife and I respect and hope, Enshallah, will make her happy." Afsar Khanum looked skyward and exclaimed an Enshallah.

The Prince kept his smiling eyes on the Doctor whose serious facial expression warned of his determination to negotiate whatever sum the Prince demanded. All that was concerning him now was that sum.

Mohammad who had remained partial to class differences and shunned from acquiring, even a semblance of fineness, ignored the Prince's compliment and asked: "Sir, what do you demand as Mehr for your daughter?"

The Prince, took no offence from his improper manner, and in a casual tone replied: "Agha doctor, my daughter is priceless." He paused, fixed his teasing eyes on Mohammad, expecting to hear: 'we all know that'. And when he did not, he realized his counterpart definitely lacked proper manners, and didn't know with whom he was dealing. In his silly mind the man was trying to strike a deal, as though money mattered when one's child's happiness was involved. So to prolong, his agony, he made himself more comfortable on his chair, changed the position of his legs, cleared his throat and let an anxiety-ridden silence fall over the room. No one moved, except Mrs Qajar who had guessed what was going on in her husband's mind and rightly so. She rose, put a bunch of grapes on a plate and handed it to him. The Prince, took the plate, thanked her and gently picked a few grapes, ate them one by one, his eyes on the colourful patterns of the Tabriz carpet. The silence was getting tenser by the second. Afsar

Khanum, thinking that the deal was off was almost choking and Mohammad was beginning to regret his offensive manner when the Prince put the fruit plate on the side table, raised his gentle eyes to him and in a matter of fact tone said:

"Doctor, since there are not enough zeroes to put in front of the sum worthy of my daughter's value, I demand a volume of Koran to bring them luck and for her Jahizieh I will give her a furnished house in which your son and my daughter can live with dignity and in utmost comfort."

Mohammad's posture suddenly relaxed and to his surprise, he felt the softness of the cushion against which he was leaning. The generosity was beyond his comprehension. Confronted with such unbelievable largess he could say nothing but a very polite: 'Thank you shahzadeh.'

This was the first time he addressed the Prince by his rightful title.

The gesture pleased the Prince, at last the man had realized with whom he was dealing.

Mrs Qajar threw her husband a loving smile, rose and went outside in search of the couple. She found them absorbed in their own world. They did not even hear the click clack of her heels on the stone pathway. She looked at them with love and remembered the time she couldn't get enough of her own beloved and sighed. If one could grab the happy moments of life and hold them forever – what joy that would be! She thought before saying: "Congratulations my beloveds. Now I am going to have the son I have wished for all my life. Am I not lucky?" Her soft voice brought them out of their daze. They stood up in her respect. She opened her arms wide and they both fell in to them. Then, hand in hand they walked to the lounge.

Afsar Khanum could not stop herself from smiling and eating. She turned to Rose, and opened her arms, "Azizam, come let me welcome you to my family with a kiss. I am so thankful to God that my Datam has had the sense to choose a lady like you. Enshallah you will reach the autumn of your lives together – in happiness."

"Thank you Afsar joon." Rose whispered before bending to fit within the fold of her arms.

"Enshallah." Murmured, an excited Mrs Qajar whose eyes blazed with the light that fulfilment of a wish ignites. She couldn't remove them from the happy face of her excited daughter who was bending to embrace her future mother-in-law. Shamsi twisted sideways and offered her cheek to her. Rose dropped her arm, ignored the cheek and stole a meritless kiss from the tip of her head. As she was about to move back Shamsi clutched her arm and shaking it said: "Rose Khanum, I hope you will make my son happy."

"Enshallah Shamsi joon." Rose replied, turning her marvelling eyes to her mother who had observed it all. Mrs Qajar slightly knitted her shapely eyebrows and gave an indiscrete shake to her head. To Rose it meant: 'Do not take it to heart.' Then she heard her mother say: "Shamsi Khanum, let us hope they will make each other happy."

The Prince threw his wife an approving glance.

Mohammad cursed his wife's folly, left his seat, walked to Rose and putting his arms around her murmured: "Azizam, Enshallah my son will prove a worthy husband. We are so proud to have a bride like you."

"Agha doctor, I am sure he will." Rose replied with a radiant smile. Then she turned her eyes to where Datam had been sitting. He wasn't there.

He had left the room to hide his embarrassment. His mother's words had shocked him.

Exactly four weeks later, to the delight of all except Tirdad, Datam and Rose exchanged vows in a spectacular wedding reception given by the Prince, instead of the groom's father whose responsibility it was. The famous singer, Mahasti entertained the three hundred of the crème de la crème of the society who were fed Champaign, caviar and a cornucopias dinner that was talked about for weeks and weeks. The bride in a long, simple embroidered white silk gown and her groom in a white evening jacket, black pants and a black bow tie were remembered as one of the handsomest couples wedded that summer.

To shut up gossipmongers who were already whispering that Datam would become a 'homeless groom', Rose moved to the Amiri residence until September when it was decided for them to return to the States for Datam to study for a PhD degree and make the Prince feel secure in his ability to provide a respectable life for his daughter. To be certain that his daughter would not suffer the hardships of student life; he promised her a hefty monthly allowance and gift of a car of her choice. Doctor Amiri, in order not to lose face in front of the Qajars, promised to subsidize Datam's scholarship with what he could afford which was not much. Both fathers knew the value of a good marriage and wanted to contribute to the happiness of their children. Mrs Qajar was delighted with her husband's decision, as she wanted nothing but the happiness of the couple.

But alas – in the Amiri residence, flames of jealousy had already turned the joy of the union into ash. As soon as Tirdad heard of the promise he decided to confront his father with his objection. Patiently he bided his time until an afternoon, when, having had their tea, Datam and Rose went out for a walk. Once he heard the gate close, Tirdad turned to his father and burst out: "Baba, you have no right to volunteer to support your spoilt Princess's life. Her father is rich enough to do it for her and besides by helping them you will be taking bread out of our mouths."

Mohammad, conscious of his dislike for Rose who represented all that he detested: aristocracy and wealth threw him a stern glance and replied: "No one will take any bread out of 'your' mouth unless you mean yours and your girlfriend's."

He paused again, raised an eyebrow and fixed his disdainful eyes on Tirdad.

"So you know?" Tirdad asked in a reflective tone, the sour feeling of shame flaring up inside him.

"Yes and should you have told me the truth I would have helped you anyway. But no, you had to lie. Did you think I wouldn't check with the University bursar if your tuition had been increased or not?"

Caught as a cheat, Tirdad kept his head down and remained silent.

"Even though I knew you had lied to me, I obliged your request. This I did so that financial worries wouldn't affect your studies. Now you dare to question my judgement?"

Swarmed by a wave of contradictory emotions Tirdad remained tongue-tied.

Mohammad looked at his wife. From the sheepish expression on her face, he realized she had been privy to Tirdad's secret. He shook his head in disgust, turned his eyes back to Tirdad and added: "Supplementing the cost of their living, with the little that I can, I will be helping your brother and his wife, whose father's generosity has put me to shame. I am doing this not for Rose, but for my own son and my own honour."

Combing Kobra's curly hair Shamsi stopped, pushed the girl away, turned to her vernacular husband, narrowed her eyes, waved the comb at him and, dragging every word said: "If you think we have been honoured by this marriage, you are very wrong Agha. Nowadays, men like Datam are rare and the Qajars should thank their lucky stars they have found such a husband for their daughter who I am sure is about to steal our son away from us. Look at him now. He has only few days left in Iran and instead of being with us, is running after her like a dog."

"Do not be ridiculous woman, 'stealing our son from us'! What do you mean by such nonsense? She is his wife. They have just married; for heaven's sakes woman, they are honeymooning in Avenue Shadman instead of being in a beautiful resort, away from us, like all other newlyweds. What do you expect him to do? Come and sit by you and drink tea!"

"Baba, I do not like Rose at all." Kobra interrupted.

Taken by surprise, Mohammad looked into her large eyes and asked: "My dear, why do you not like Rose?"

"Because she doesn't like me. If she did, she wouldn't have thrown her wedding bouquet to cousin Fafi. She should have thrown it to me."

"Azizam what she did was not intentional at all. She doesn't even know Fafi well. A bride just throws her bouquet to the crowd; she has no control over who catches it."

"That is not what Madar told me." Kobra said turning towards Shamsi who did not dare to lift her eyes from the strings of hair caught between the teeth of the comb.

Disgusted and tired of confrontation Mohammad rose and walked out of the room banging its door. "How petty can an adult be to backbite such a lovely lady to a child?" He said shaking his head. His loud voice echoed in the corridor and reached the intended ears.

Rose's ladylike behaviour had already won Mohammad's respect and as her qualities revealed themselves, his affection for her increased. She proved to be a deep, honest, clever, active and intelligent girl; truly in love with his son. The two complemented one another: Datam was shy, Rose was shrewd; he was calm, she was vivacious; he was lacklustre, she was vibrant and when he was negative she was positive and it was this last quality he admired most in her – the quality he had wished his own wife had possessed.

Summer expired. Datam and Rose went to Champagne where Datam was to continue his post graduate studies at the University of Illinois, and Tirdad returned to the studio, at the Latin Quarter, he shared with his Austrian girlfriend and class-mate. Jill wasn't anything to look at but she was capable, clever and understanding. She loved him dearly and bore his sudden unreasonable outbursts of anger with patience. Thus, in a blissful contentment they lived together until they finished their studies with good results. Secure in their love and commitment to each other, they parted for their respective countries, knowing that the separation would not be for too long.

In Iran, Tirdad, a political scientist, found a job at the Plan and Budget Organization with an adequate salary for a bachelor living under his parents' roof. Prices were rising and rent had skyrocketed. He corresponded with Jill regularly. And one evening, after dinner, when the family had settled in the TV room he addressed them with a happy smile: "Baba and Madar you are going to become grandparents and Kobra, you an aunt."

Shamsi rested her knitting needles on her lap and stared at him with open mouth.

"What? Am I hearing you correctly?" Mohammad blurted out, his eyes bulging out of their sockets.

"Yes Baba; you are going to become a grandfather. Jill, my girlfriend, who you generously fed, is pregnant."

"So?" Mohammad asked in a derisive manner.

"So what Baba?" Tirdad asked his voice shaking with indignation. "We lived together for four years like a man and wife and now she is carrying my child!"

Shamsi, frozen on her seat glued her startled eyes on her son, who had turned into a roaring lion. She had never seen him so resolute, so single-minded and wild. It frightened her. Suddenly it dawned on her that she really did not know him at all. The thought made her heart sink and she whispered a: "Ya Allah. (Oh God)"

The frown on Mohammad's forehead stiffened. He contemplated for a while and then tightening his brows asked: "How do you know that I am the rightful grandfather?"

"I know it, because I know her." He snapped back.

"And why did you not use protection?" Mohammad asked in an icy tone.

"You are a scientist; you should know that accidents do happen. Besides, you taught me to be responsible for my actions. Now that I want to follow your advice you are angry with me. Is that right? "

Faced with a fact, Mohammad fell into a deep pensive silence. Shamsi remained still and Tirdad, seething with anxiety kept his penetrating eyes on his father's furrowed face. His stomach was churning and the veins in his neck hammering so hard that Shamsi thought they might burst. 'Why is he so worried?' She kept asking herself without realizing that he could not afford a wife and a child without their support. Then she heard Mohammad say: "How do you know that she is bearing your child? How do you know that at the same time she did not sleep with others?"

"I know that because she loves me." He paused, lifted an eyebrow, produced a sarcastic smile and resumed: "I wonder if you understand what that means?"

Deeply offended by Tirdad's audacity, Mohammad rose, came close and raised his hand to slap him on the face when Tirdad anticipating the strike, moved away, jumped up, caught his hand in the air, twisted it hard, threw him a hateful glance, dropped his hand and ran out of the room, slamming the door behind him.

The old man stood in the middle of the room cursing his luck. Shamsi remained seated, silent and disillusioned, staring at the retched form of her husband who had cupped his hands around his throbbing temples and was murmuring: "Please God, let me know what to do with this imbecile."

Kobra frightened by the violence began to scream.

That night neither Mohammad nor Shamsi exchanged a word. It was not their way to consult or lighten each other's heart. Their views were so different that when discussing an issue, instead of resolving it, they finished by arguing and creating more issues, that left unresolved, turned into grudges that neither let go.

Tirdad disappeared for several days. Then one evening, when he knew his father would be home returned and with his key let himself in. He climbed the steps to the front door which was open and stepped in. Like a thief, he lingered with his ears pricked up. He heard the familiar voice of the news-reader waving out of the TV room. He tip toed to its door, noiselessly slit it open, peeped through, and when sure they were alone, stepped in. Neither parent heard him enter. Mohammad was hard of hearing and Shamsi drowned in her own world.

"Salam. I have come to apologize for my rudeness."

The echo of his voice lifted Shamsi's spirit out of its doldrums. She turned and greeted him with the sweetest of smiles.

Mohammad heard him but didn't turn.

"Baba, may I have a word with you in private please?"

Maintaining his gaze on the screen, Mohammad replied: "Not if you want to act like a beast." His tone was authentic but void of animosity.

"I am sorry for my outburst. Please Baba – you must hear me out."

Mohammad switched the television off, turned his grim face to him and with his hand invited him to take a seat. Then he addressed his wife and in a mellowed voice asked her to leave.

Shamsi nodded her rejection and did not move.

"Khanum, please?"

"Why? I am his mother and have the right to hear him too."

Irritated by her obstinacy Mohammad snapped: "Did you not hear his request for a private talk with his father?"

Wounded by her husband's forever insensitivity, she turned her pleading eyes to Tirdad and waited.

"Madar, please let me have a private moment with Baba. Please?"

Dejected, she rose and walked out without closing the door. Tirdad aware of her tendency to eavesdrop got up and shut it. He returned to his seat and faced his father. Shamsi squatted behind the door, sharpened her ears like Matahari, and heard: "Baba you were noble enough to remarry my mother while pregnant with someone else's child and yet you are prohibiting me to claim my own offspring? Is that fair Baba?"

The words sent a shiver down Shamsi's spine and she began to tremble. To stop the shake she hugged her knees, rested her head on them and began to rock.

Inside the room, even though the window was open, beads of cold perspiration glowed on Mohammad's wide and deeply lined forehead. Ashamed of his own unfairness; unconsciously shaking his head and biting his lower lip, he stared at the dead autumn leaves that were heaped beneath the persimmon tree, in the lit courtyard. When the silence engulfing them became too oppressive, he turned his eyes away from the autumnal debris and focussed them on Tirdad who was watching him with intense eyes. The tension inside him was churning his intestines causing painful spasms.

Mohammad leaned towards his son, put his hand on his lap, looked him in the eyes and said: "I remarried your mother for your sake more than Datam's, and it is for your sake I am advising against this marriage. If you believe in Jill's sincerity invite her to Iran; let her live with us for a little while so that she realizes what is in store for her living in a foreign country with a totally different culture and value system and then, if she still wants to become your wife, marry her. Besides, from what I hear abortion is easy and in certain countries legal these days."

Mohammad's voice was soft and his tone matter of fact, as though he was advising the son of a friend and not his own. The considerate cautiousness in his suggestions eroded Tirdad's fear and settled his stomach. He released a sigh of relief, leaned back and relaxed.

Behind the door, Shamsi was so busy tracing dark shadows that she could not hear what was being discussed – nor did she care. Their voices sounded like howls of wolves: loud and frightfully threatening. She felt like a lump filled with pain.

"Baba, I know Jill, she loves me unconditionally. She comes from a solid middle-class, rural family accustomed to hardship. She will make me a good wife and will be a good mother to my child. Moreover, she is a Catholic and will never abort."

Mohammad pondered for a moment and then said: "Ok, if you are this sure, send her a one way ticket." The glow of happiness that exuded from Tirdad's eyes lifted Mohammad's spirit. "Congratulations son." He said in a tone void of joy.

"Thank you Baba. Thank you."

That evening the father and son went through a bottle of Shiraz while Shamsi tucked under the folds of her heavy eiderdown felt as isolated as a corpse buried under heaps of earth. Neither knew why she had refused to partake in their celebration – nor did they care.

A month later, a cheerful Jill, arrived to embrace her future in a country where she knew no one except her lover. At first everyone was surprised at Tirdad's bad taste in comparison to his brother's. But soon Jill's politeness and willingness to embrace Islam endeared her to some of her critics. However the staunch ones remained laughing at her broad Austrian accent, thick masculine voice and large built.

Iranians are a hospitable nation and respectful of foreigners whom they look upon as their guests. Thus doors opened to the Austrian and she began to feel at home.

Within two weeks of her arrival the couple married; their wedding costing the poor doctor a year's salary, just because Shamsi wanted Tirdad to have as grand a wedding party as Datam had. Even though the wedding party was respectable it lacked the princely touch of Datam's. For better or worse, the couple took their vows and settled on the second floor accommodation allocated to them at the Amiri residence. This was the best Tirdad could offer his wife. With his meagre salary he could not afford to rent even a one bedroom flat. Inflation was rising and with it rent. To please her husband, Jill set to learn Farsi and make friends. Her sincerity endeared her to the family and everyone went out of their way to make her feel at home. And at home she felt.

Seven months later she gave birth to a beautiful girl the couple named Yasmin. To save face, society was told that the baby had come two months early. Yasmin, with her large blue eyes, milky skin and wrinkled plump face stole everyone's heart, specially her grandmother's, who volunteered to nurse her while Jill worked at the Austrian Embassy.

Life went on – as it always does.

Tirdad kept his involvement with the Tudeh party a secret, both from his wife and parents. At work and home he was kind, obliging and agreeable – during party meetings he was vociferous and impatient for change – totally a different man.

As time went on, Teheran became larger, uglier and more polluted. High-rises went up, bridges and roads crossed each other and people prospered.

Datam and Rose returned from Illinois. They took up residency at Rose's elegantly furnished house given to her by her parents, (her promised Jahizieh), at Rose Cul-de-sac.

Datam, with his PhD degree, making his father and the Prince very proud, found a prestigious job, the income of which met with the Prince's approval. To fulfil her responsibility to society Rose delved into charity work.

The difference in lifestyle antagonized Tirdad to the point of bitter animosity and made the Thursday lunches at the Amiri's hell for all, particularly Rose – the culprit. To annoy her, Tirdad purposely talked politics, criticising monarchy in general and in particular the Qajar Shahs, one of whom was her great grandfather. During these disputes Datam kept quiet, Shamsi took Tirdad's side, Jill and Dr Amiri tried to shut him up. The sessions became so disagreeable that Rose stopped accompanying her husband. However feeling sorry for the Austrian, she maintained her friendship with her. She knew Jill loved swimming. So she invited her to come and swim in her pool. As a trust bloomed between them, Jill began to tell Rose of her frustrations regrets and hopes. Rose listened with care and tried to console her by praising her patience and admiring her endurance. She had great sympathy for her and it made her sad to see her disillusioned with life in Iran. The girl, efficient and hardworking, was climbing the ladder of success fast yet she seemed very unhappy.

One afternoon when she had had her swim and they were having tea together by the pool, she turned to Rose and said: "I envy you Rose."

"What is there to envy Jill?"

"Your Husband – he is such an understanding and loving person, very unlike mine."

"What has he done to you Jill?"

"Nothing short of making my life miserable. He is even resentful of my promotions. To belittle me he keeps criticising me in front of our friends and finding fault with everything I do or say. He thinks by doing these awful things he is elevating himself in their esteem."

"What an idiot. Have you talked to Shamsi about this?"

"Shamsi is no one's friend. What Tirdad likes, she likes and what he doesn't like she hates."

"That is very true. But I thought she always liked you."

"That is pretence to make you jealous."

"That is ridiculous. Sometimes I think she is not in her right mind. I really feel very sorry for her. But I don't live with her and you do and that must be difficult."

"You know Rose, I am exercising a lot of tolerance and I am afraid one day it might reach its ebb."

"Don't say that Jill. Perhaps once Tirdad is promoted, his wounded ego will heal and his behaviour change?"

"With his big mouth and arrogance he will never be promoted. He will be lucky to keep his job."

"That is sad to hear."

A car honked a couple of times.

"This must be Datam back from work." Rose remarked turning her head towards the gate. A second later she saw her maid rush to open it. Smiling she turned her head back.

"Please don't tell him anything of what I said to you." Jill begged.

"Of course not."

"I'll go now and will come on Thursday, if that is OK by you?" Murmured Jill, picking up her beach bag.

"Of course it will be OK by me. Just don't think that you are the only one on Shamsi's black list. I don't believe she has ever smelled the scent of love. She is nasty to the bone. It is true that mother-in-laws don't often like their daughter-in-laws but there are only few set to destroy their children's marriages and ours is one of them."

They walked to the gate. Jill said a hello and goodbye to Datam, got into her car and drove away.

Gradually Rose, too, became weary of her mother-in-law's enmity. The woman had made it her business to interfere in her social activities, charity work and even dared to criticise the way she dressed. Rose was recognized as one of the smartest ladies of the Capital.

Her interferences and venomous tongue were affecting her relationship with her mute, non- interfering husband who detested confrontation. One day, after some ugly disputes with Datam over minor issues, her patience faded and she decided to confer with her mother.

It was a fine afternoon when nature was at its calmest. There was no wind and no clouds to stain the blue sky. Joyously playing in the midst of tree branches the birds chirped and the bees buzzed around the roses that were in full bloom. The air was fresh and the sun benevolent. Mrs Qajar was monitoring her gardener trimming the branches that had overgrown. He had a habit of trimming them too much which was both ugly and harmful to the plant. She knew why he did it. But instead of reprimanding him she supervised him. Gardening was one of her passions and she was proud of her green fingers.

Rose drove her Mercedes through the open gate, parked it in the visitor's space and ran to her mother's open arms. They embraced, one smiling and the other brooding. Safe within the loving folds of her mother Rose burst into tears.

"What is it my love? Have you had a row with Datam?" Asked Mrs Qajar concerned.

Rose murmured a husky 'no' and continued weeping. Mrs Qajar removed her arms from around her, gripped her hand and led her to the sun-lit family room almost certain of the cause of her distress. Zahra, the maid, saw them come. She offered her Salam and asked if any of the ladies wished for tea.

"Zahra Khanum make some strong Turkish coffee for us." Mrs Qajar ordered.

"Chashm Khanum." Zahra replied and hurried to the kitchen.

"Now, tell me what is bothering you child." Mrs Qajar asked taking a seat.

Rose dropped on the sofa and blurted out: "Mummy, I am so unhappy. I do not know what I have done to Shamsi Khanum to deserve her animosity. Her comments are unkind, at times rude and insulting. And worse of all, she backbites me to Datam. Every time he returns home from their house he finds something to criticise about either my clothes, behaviour or what I have said to Shamsi or Tirdad or Kobra. On the very rare occasions that I see them, I hardly ever talk to anyone of them. I am always courteous to them even when they do not deserve it." She pouted her lips, shook her head in distress, "I am just tired of all this and want to return home. I cannot bear it anymore Mummy joon. I cannot!" Rose pulled a tissue from the box on the coffee table, blew her running nose and wiped her eyes, smudging the mascara dissolved by her tears. She looked a mess.

Her mother went to the guest's toilet, wet the hand towel she found on its rail, returned, knelt and gently cleansed her face. "Now this looks better my love." She said before throwing the towel on the coffee table and returning to her chair. "Mummy I love you so very much."

"I know my love and me you too."

In the hallway the telephone rang. Rose moved to rise.

"Sit down. Zahra will take it in the kitchen."

"It might be Datam."

"He can wait. Please listen to me Rose. You are married to a fine man, and must take his mother's nastiness with a pinch of salt. I suggest you remember these verses from Rumi before you utter a nasty word to your beloved:

"Love is an emerald.
Its brilliant light wards off dragons
on this treacherous path,
only for those who are truly in love."

You my dear are a good human being which means your heart is illuminated by the rays of love. Forgive and forget. If you react you will become one like her. You must solve your in-law problems with discretion and prudence. Your husband is a decent man. Do not let petty incidents ruin your relationship with him. It is not his fault that his mother or the others are unreasonable."

"I love my husband. But, he makes me mad at times. Why doesn't he reprimand his family when he sees them so unreasonable, unduly rude and unkind to me – why?"

"Calm down dear, and listen to me. I know Datam well. Out of respect for his mother, he doesn't take sides. But most probably, he does reproach her behind your back. He knows her well, and doesn't want to have a family feud on his hands. You must appreciate his wisdom and concern."

"It is hard to see your husband remain mute when his family are tearing you apart – isn't it?"

"Hush child. Now you are exaggerating, are you not?"

The door opened and Zahra entered tray in hand.

"Who was on the phone Zahra Khanum?" Rose asked hoping it was Datam.

"It was Datam Khan. He wanted to know if you were here. And when I told him you are, he said I shouldn't disturb you."

A glow of satisfaction nipped out of Rose's puffy eyes. Mrs Qajar caught it and smiled.

Zahra offered each their steaming cups, placed a dish of pastry on the table and carrying her tray, vanished to her pantry.

Her heart unburdened, Rose found solace in chatting with her mother and enjoying the bitter sweet taste of her coffee. Once she finished, she put the saucer over the cup, turned the cup over and returned the saucer to the table. She leaned back, a pleasant smile shining on her relaxed face. As Mrs Qajar leaned to pick up her cup she realized she was still wearing her gardening gloves.

"Look, you with your problems have made me forget to take these off. Lucky they are not muddy." Nodding at her own absent-mindedness, she took them off and neatly put them on the carpet. "Let's see what lies ahead of me Mummy." Rose said, picking up her cup.

"I do not believe in any of these nonsenses." Mrs Qajar remarked and bent to look into the cup that Rose had turned up and was staring at. To her disappointment Rose could see not a single path that led to light. Most of the coffee residue that usually slides down the sides of the capsized cup forming meaningful shapes had settled on the bottom of the vessel in a macabre design from which the only discernible shape was of two clasped hands protruding out of a mud heap. As she kept staring at the shapes a sense of trepidation ran through her. She immediately realized that a fortune teller would interpret the mud heap as a grave. As though wanting to distance herself from the thought, she returned the cup to its saucer and pushed it to the far end of the table. Mrs Qajar noticed the darkness that clouded her features and asked: "What did you see that has upset you so much Rose?"

"Unhappiness and trouble Mummy."

Curious, Mrs Qajar picked up the cup; stared inside it, trying to make sense out of the shapes. Suddenly her tense features relaxed. She smiled, raised her head and said: "The heap that you interpret as problem, I see as a mother's bulging stomach. A baby my love – a baby! "

Rose knew she was barren, but her parents did not. So she feigned a smile and rising to leave said: "Enshallah Mummy joon. You will make the best grandmother in the world."

After Rose left, Mrs Qajar, reflected upon her complaints and wondered why those three disliked her so much. Had she had a daughter-in-law like her, she would have thrown gold coins at her feet and sacrificed a lamb in gratitude for the blessing. The girl loved her husband, demanded nothing from them or her husband who actually was living under her roof – a homeless groom! Informed of Mrs Amiri's past, she thought of her as most unfortunate for having made so many bad decisions, the outcomes of which had turned her into such a bitter person. A deeply religious lady, she believed in tolerance and forgiveness. So the next day she called Shamsi and invited her to lunch at the Cellars restaurant, renowned for its chateaubriand which she knew Shamsi loved. The restaurant was famous for its French cuisine, tender meat and chic and well-connected clients. She picked up her guest from her home and they drove to the restaurant. When they disembarked from the car, Mrs Qajar, took two hundred rials from her purse, gave them to her driver and told him to buy a sandwich for his lunch and not wait to eat at home, in the middle of the afternoon. Ahmad Agha thanked his mistress with a smile. He loved her. She was so understanding and benevolent. As the two elegant ladies approached the restaurant the doorman in his grey uniform with gold buttons made a deep bow to Mrs Qajar and opened the door wide for her. She thanked him with her usual serene and friendly smile. They graciously descended the steps and entered the restaurant that was crowded by people, most of whom they knew. This thrilled Shamsi: to be seen in such a famous establishment accompanied by the mother of her daughter-in-law would have tongues wagging. The next day she would be telling her friends that she had invited Mrs Qajar to lunch at the Cellars. They would all go green with envy. It was about time for people to become jealous of her too. She grinned at the prospect, straightened her back and put her nose in the air.

Their reserved table was in a discrete corner, preferred by Mrs Qajar, a very private person who shunned publicity. The Manager presented himself, bowed to his charming regular client and handed them each a huge glossy menu card. It took them a while to go through the choices and finally they each ordered chateaubriand, well done, accompanied by potato soufflé, and chocolate mousse to follow. For drinks they ordered coca cola. While waiting to be served they engaged in a bit of gossip and a bit of grumbling about the rising prices of everything. Their conversation was halted by the arrival of the waiter carrying their main course.

Mrs Qajar cut a piece of meat, took it to her mouth, tasted the sauce and then chewed it with delight. A smile of satisfaction formed on her beautiful face. Rose had inherited her soft, creamy skin and chiselled nose but not her amber eyes. They ate in silence and when finished Mrs Qajar asked:

"Shamsi Khanum, my meat was excellent. How was yours?"

"I am sorry to say mine was not tender enough. Often, some pieces are not as good as others and it is my bad luck to end up with a piece hard to chew."

Mrs Qajar threw a quick glance at Shamsi's plate and found it cleaned out.

"I am sorry Shamsi joon. You should have complained as soon as you found the meat tough. They would have changed it for you."

"Well, I did not want to embarrass you."

"Thank you for your consideration, but that would have caused me no embarrassment whatsoever. This is a restaurant famous for the quality of its meat and rest assured that they do not want a single customer leave unhappy with the food or the service. In fact they would have welcomed your complaint, and delivered it to their butcher with a goodbye note!" Mrs Qajar stopped and smiled. Shamsi did not return the smile. She just pushed away her empty plate, threw her a cold glance, as though it was her fault that her meat was not tender, and remarked:

"Let's hope the mousse is good."

"I hope so. I love chocolate mousse."

"I do too. In fact I make very good mousse myself."

"Shamsi joon, we all know how good a cook you are, probably one of the best in Iran. Both Rose and I love your cooking, particularly your cookies. They are excellent."

The compliment boosted Shamsi's self-confidence. She smiled and made herself more comfortable on her chair. Then she turned her criticising eyes to her host and asked:

"Why did you never teach Rose the art of cooking? Datam always complains about her lack of cooking skill."

"Then Datam should have married a cook." Mrs Qajar replied and then burst into laughter.

"He married your daughter."

"Lucky him," Mrs Qajar replied with another laugh. Under no condition was she going to allow Shamsi ruin their lunch. It was apparent that the poor soul had a lot of chips on her shoulders. Therefore one had to laugh her malice off.

"Shamsi joon, Rose is not a good cook because food doesn't interest her. So she has hired a cook to take care of my lovely son, Datam."

Shamsi was cornered and couldn't repudiate a valid point. "Khanum Aziz my point is that all house wives should know how to cook."

"Here I agree with you Shamsi joon."

The mousse, topped with cream rosettes, arrived.

Mrs Qajar, toying with her dessert, fixed her eyes on Shamsi to see if lines of objection would form on her forehead. When they did, she raised her hand and summoned the waiter passing by. The man stopped and very politely asked: "How can I help you Madame?" Mrs Qajar looked up at him and politely commented: "My guest is not happy with the mousse. Could you please give her the menu to choose something else?"

Surprised, Shamsi hastily put her left palm over the glass vessel and protesting said: "No, No. I love it."

"I am sorry Shamsi joon. I thought you were not enjoying it – like your chateaubriand."

"The mousse tastes fine but it needs a little more brandy."

Mrs Qajar turned her mischievous eyes to the waiter and smiling said:

"My guest here is a master cook. Could you please deliver her suggestion to your chef?"

"Of course Madame." He replied with an understanding glow in his black eyes.

"Then, could you please also tell him to reduce the amount of sugar and increase the amount of black chocolate in his recipe." Shamsi added in an authentic tone, giving herself the air of a connoisseur.

"I will Madame." Replied the waiter and hasted away before being detained any further.

Mrs Qajar dropped Shamsi home, realizing no truce could ever be made between her and poor darling Rose!' So in her heart she prayed for her daughter's salvation.

As though God heard her prayer, a wave of strange, unpredictable occurrences turned into a cyclone that destroyed everything in its path changing life in Iran forever.

The Shah was at the pinnacle of his power and his Prime Minister boasted of zero unemployment. However, hidden from the larger society were various active factions aiming to topple him. One such faction was the Tudeh party of which Tirdad was a leader. Advised by Moscow they had increased their underground activities.

The murmurs of discontent against the Shah's haphazard decisions began to be heard as early as 1977, by all except the Monarch himself. Faced with an ineffective government that dared not take a step without his Majesty's consent, murmurs turned into sermons at the mosques and open letters written by intellectuals, published in newspapers. At the same time America elected a democratic president dedicated to the concept of democracy and human rights. To please Carter the Shah allowed a limited freedom of speech, introduced minor changes to the government and made certain concessions. The opposition took the changes as a sign of weakness and became more aggressive in its demands for democratization. The British and the American ambassadors, who had been the Shah's most active advisors hitherto, abstained from guiding him. He had surpassed his usefulness for their nations. He took their abstention as abandonment. Isolated and indecisive, he gave in with one hand and took away with another. As he showed weakness in crushing the opposition the dissent movement increased in momentum. To solidify their power, the different factions deemed it necessary to unite under the banner of Ayatollah Khomeini, a vociferous leader with a heavy grudge against the Pahlavi father and son.

Khomeini lived in France at the time but his lieutenants in Iran were restlessly active on his behalf. Gradually demand for reform turned into a cry for regime change. Industrial strikes paralyzed the nation. To pray for stability, Prince and Mrs Qajar decided to take a pilgrimage to the shrine of Emmam Reza, the eighth Shia Emmam, at Mashhad. On the eve of their return the staff at Mehrabad Airport went on strike. The air traffic control zone was left without any operatives. That winter night was pitch-black and the sky pregnant with snow clouds. A thick blanket of fog veiled the Alborz range and its environs. About ten minutes before landing the pilot lost visibility and the plane nose-dived into the breast of the mountain at Galandoak village, near Teheran where the Prince had a country house. Blissfully, the passengers' fear only lasted for a few minutes during which time the Prince gripped his wife's hand and for once forgot about protocol, putting his lips on hers; kissing, they met their end.

The blast of the explosion was heard as far as Shemiran and its flames seen by the petrified villagers who at first thought Iran was attacked by the Russians. After several dull moments of hushed and panicked confusion many gathered courage and rushed out of their homes, amongst them, the forever curious Gholam Reza, the Prince's gardener. The roaring flames pulled them to the scene of the tragedy. There, just outside of the village, by the sloping breast of the mountain, an inconceivable scene transfixed them to the ground. Mesmerized they stood watching the savage flames roar thunderously, luminous tongues wrathfully licking the snowflakes that floated in the air. Blazing airplane parts were scattered around and the icy air was tinged with the smell of burnt flesh and metal. Suddenly a youth found his senses and yelled: "We must seek help. There might be survivors." Then he ran back to the village.

At dawn, when the rescue team from Teheran arrived, all they found was a deep hole in the side of the mountain, the charred carcass of the aircraft and, many frozen, scorched body parts scattered around. The vultures had not as yet arrived.

The snowflakes floating in the air continued their fall, painting the crystallized earth white.

Early, that morning, the Iran Air Manager, having consulted the passenger-list called the given phone numbers, broke the news, and asked the relatives to go to the site of the accident.

Rose and Datam shocked and disconsolate hurried to the gruesome location where a thick layer of snow had covered the area, making the task of finding anything almost impossible. Fortunately the downpour had stopped and a pale sun was fighting the clouds for dominance. Trembling with grief and shivering from the biting mountain gust lashing at their faces, searchers went around breaking the smoothness of the ice upon which they stepped with a crunchy sound that absorbed the noise of their hammering hearts. Then, when a mound caught their attention they knelt by it and eagerly brushed the snow away hoping to discover the remains of a loved one. At a distance, Rose, her rapid breaths steaming the air, spotted something glittering under sun light. It seemed to resemble her father's spectacles' frame. She took hurried long strides, her boots crushing the snow and leaving behind a trail of deep foot prints. She stopped, stared at the shining object, and then dropped on her knees. She picked the frame that remarkably had remained intact, looked at the inside of the right handle and recognized the brand. Sure that it was his, she took it to her lips and kissed it several times before fitting it in her coat pocket. Then she began to dig into the snow heap that was wavering in her sight changing colour, from white to brown and white again. It was the mound of coffee heaped at the bottom of her cup into which she was digging. Faster and faster she dug with one hand and swept away the snow, mud and whatever it was, with another, oblivious to the painful stings of ice. Suddenly her fingers touched something solid. Excited, and with an increased zest, she dug around the seemingly impenetrable 'thing' until her hand was able to grasp it and lift it up. It was a shapeless lump of ice. She kept shaking it, blowing at it and wiping it against her coat again and again, until the silhouette of a pair of clasped hands became visible. She let out a scream and dropped the find. A ray of sun fell on it and she caught a diminutive sparkle like that of a diamond's. She picked up the lump again, stared at it. On one of the fingers seemed to be a ring. She pinched the edge of her sleeve and began rubbing it vehemently over the ice lump that seemed to resist melting. Eventually droplets of water fell until, within the ice frame, she was able to recognize her mother's wedding ring. She raised the lump up and whispered: "Datam look." Then she took the lump to her trembling lips and kissed and kissed it again with the ice bruising her skin but she didn't feel it. She felt as icy as the ice that was melting in her grip – such was the state of her mind: more lifeless than the hands she was holding.

Towering over her, Datam stood still.

Then when it became too cold to tolerate, he gently took her arm and lifted her up. She held to the hands as though her life depended on them. The warmth of her inflamed, stiff fingers was now dissolving the ice fast and pinkish droplets were slipping down her bruised palm to the ground. Datam holding her hand bent and picked up the golden frame that had slipped out of her pocket. He tucked it into his own coat pocket and the two walked over the snow to where several ambulances and a truck stood; their drivers offering large and small plastic bags to those lucky enough to have found something to cherish. Datam took one, gave it to Rose. She refused to part with the hands. "Please darling, put them in the bag before the ice melts completely." Numbly she obeyed.

"Shahzadeh what are you doing here?" asked a familiar voice.

They both turned and saw Gholam Reza wrapped in the Prince's old heavy parka coat. Rose gave him a sad look, lifted the plastic bag up. "This is what is left of your Master and Mistress my man – this." Crying and dangling the bag, she fell into the gardener's embrace and in unison they wept.

Gholam Reza had grown up with the Prince who was not only his Master but best friend. His loss was as great as Rose's. He knew Rose for the lady that she was. But he never trusted Providence. With the Master gone, what would happen to him and his wife? What? And during these awful times!

It was getting unbearably cold now that thick, dark clouds had covered the celestial dome. It seemed as though the sun had decided to join the mourners and hide behind a black veil. Datam gently tapped on Rose's shoulders.

"We should go now."

Rose let go of Gholam Reza and said: "I am going to bury my parents here, in their own garden, where Gholam Reza can look after them." Then she clasped the gardener's arm and shaking it asked: "Won't you?" The flow of his tears accelerating, Gholam Reza nodded and murmured: "Yes, of course Khanum joon. With them near us Behjat and I will feel secure and content."

"True. True my man." Rose answered with relief and let his arm go. The fact that her parents would rest in their own home, tended by those who loved them and away from all the insanity that had overwhelmed the country, returned some life to the grieving girl. "Gholam Reza did you walk here or come by your bicycle?" She asked in a matter of fact tone.

"Khanum joon I walked here." "Good, then you can come with us in the car." Rose said hurrying to their vehicle.

Datam stopped by the gate. Gholam Reza opened the door, jumped out, ran to the gate, unlocked and opened it wide. Then he hastened to his quarters.

Datam drove in, parked the car in the garage, opened the door for his wife, who, holding the dripping bag, stepped out and walked into the arms of a weeping Behjat. Datam gently pulled the bag from her grip and placed it on the plastic tray Gholam Reza offered him. The two of them walked to Gholam Reza's apartment and headed for his kitchen. There Gholam Reza lifted the bag from the tray, took it to the sink; turned the hot water tap on it until all the ice completely melted. Trembling with emotions, he pulled the hands out and kissing them noticed that the intertwined fingers were soldered together. Fortunately Mrs Qajar's ring was sitting above her finger's knuckle. With gentle manoeuvring he managed to take it off. For a few seconds he clasped it tight, as though trying to capture part of her to lock inside his heart. The sensation was so soothing that he took it to his lips. Suddenly, as he kissed it, a strange awareness set upon his soul and he felt as though it was her flesh his lips had touched. He was not a superstitious individual but at that moment he was sure that he had somehow connected with her. Smiling he turned to Datam and offered him the talisman. Staring at him with mournful eyes Datam took it, rolled it within his palm and closed his eyes. In his inner vision he, too, saw her smiling with the serenity that was always hers. Squeezing the ring he whispered: "I will never forget you Khanum joon – never."

Rose, followed by Behjat arrived and as she saw Gholam Reza holding the hands and whispering something, she screamed: "What are you doing with my hands?"

"He is preparing them for a proper burial. Darling, do not interrupt his prayer."

Hearing this Rose dropped on one of the two chairs that were by a wooden table, rested her elbows on the table, cupped her face with her hands and continued crying. Then she heard Gholam Reza say: "Behjat, please give me one of your white prayer wraps; a clean one."

His wife, quite confused, hurried to their only other room; pulled out a drawer and from amongst the neatly set items picked up a folded white cloth infused with rose water. She hurried back to the kitchen where her husband had already dried the hands and put them over a towel covering a plastic tray. She handed him the cloth, walked to Rose and began stroking her quivering shoulders, like the time when she was a child in a tantrum and needed affection to calm her down.

Gholam Reza took the cloth and spread it on the table; whispered another prayer and blew it over the cloth and then respectfully solemn, stood still. Datam stepped close to his wife and whispered: "Would you like to shroud the hands yourself?"

She looked up at him, her blurred eyes swollen and red. Everything had been so unexpected that she didn't know whether all was real or a bad dream. The cloud in Datam's wet eyes assured her that this was no dream.

He offered her his handkerchief. With it she wiped her face, blew her nose and rising, tucked it inside her sleeve. At first she kept staring at the clasped hands. Then with utmost respect she picked them up and kissed them several times. Gently she placed them in the midst of the so-called shroud and then turned to Behjat and asked for her Koran. The woman walked to where her prayer mat was. There, next to it sat her Koran. She picked the holy book up, kissed it; returned and with care handed it to Rose. She thanked her, hugged the holy book; closed her eyes and whispered: "Lord, have mercy upon my parents and grant them thy salvation." She kissed the holy book again, put it next to the hands and wrapped the cloth around them. Thus shrouding her parents' remains she turned to Gholam Reza and said:

"I want you to bury them under their beloved weeping willow."

Gholam Reza ran out to prepare the grave while Behjat brewed tea.

Datam staring at his wife with love opened his palm. The sparkle of the diamond caught her eyes and she remembered its existence.

"Mummy always wanted me to have this ring." She remarked before picking it up and kissing it. Then she tried to fit it on her finger which had doubled in size.

"They are swollen because of the frostbite my love. Try it later."

She didn't hear him. She kept pushing and turning until the ring fitted.

"This will remain on my finger until my dying day." She remarked showing her hand to him.

Datam put his arms around her, pulled her to himself, and kissed her forehead while soothing her with his love.

Half an hour later, when she threw the first handful of earth over the shroud she smiled, thinking that even death had not been able to separate the two lovers. They would go to heaven together and one day she would join them wherever that heaven may be. She had learnt it from her mother that death was not the end. It was entrance into another dimension of life. She had also learnt from scripture, that God made man of mud, and then blew into it of his soul that gave it life. If we are to believe God is omnipresent, then our soul must be too. God never ceases to exist, than how can we, who are part of him?

Her parents away with God, her friends scattered around the world, the only family left for Rose were her in-laws, Gholam Reza and Behjat.

Shamsi, unsympathetic towards the bereaved girl, was grossly occupied with the problems Jill was having with Tirdad. Kobra, siding with Tirdad, seemed to be at war with Jill as well as Rose. And, worse of all, the nation was at war with itself. To the chagrin of Dr Amiri and Jill, every night, Tirdad, his mother and sister climbed the stairs to their roof top, screaming Allah Akbar, "God is great" the motto of the revolutionaries, serenaded every evening at eight o'clock from their roofs. It was their message of unity against the Shah who was hiding in his palace.

Out of frustration, sometimes when Mohammad could spare a few litres of petrol (the refineries were on strike) together with Jill, they escaped their home that had become a political battle ground and visited Rose and Datam. At their home, they could relax, forget their troubles, drink a glass of whisky, dine in peace and enjoy the aroma of jasmine and the song of the frogs.

Long days and sleepless nights passed in fear, tension, and prayer for a peaceful resolution to the political upheavals. Due to the Shah's indecisiveness the political situation deteriorated hourly and then one day Rose heard the familiar sound of the royal helicopters passing over her roof. She ran to the garden, stood still, wondering where they were going. Then she remembered his speech in which he had announced his plan to go overseas for a short rest. Rest my foot. He was running away again, she thought, her eyes moist with desperate tears. He was deserting them again and yet she felt she still loved him. Her heart tight, she fixed her eyes on the choppers until they became inconspicuous dots, as all the Pahlavi achievements would become soon. Tearful, she ran to the television room, turned the TV on, dropped on the couch and witnessed the ignoble end of a dynasty and of an ancient Monarchy.

"Cyrus, rest at peace as we are here to guard your Empire." Mohammad Reza Pahlavi had proclaimed at the tomb of the greatest Emperor in the history of mankind; in front of his noble guests, at the ceremony celebrating the 2,500 years of monarchy in Iran.

What happened to that promise? Rose kept asking herself and biting her lip.

Within days the whirlwind of revolution swept over the country blowing away all obstacles on its path. The exiled Ayatollah returned home to a welcome fit for the prophet himself.

Wealth and the wealthy sought safer shores, while the vengeance fever spread throughout the nation devouring the innocent as well as the guilty. Photos of executed members of the hated regime occupied the front pages of daily papers with new editors. At dawns, in Evin prison, the shattering sound of machine guns replaced the chirping of the birds which had migrated to more peaceful habitats.

Avenue Ehteshamieh with its aristocratic population became a ghost district.

Jill asked for divorce. Tirdad, against all advice, kept Yasmin and let her go.

Datam and Rose left Iran for London where Rose had an apartment. Due to Datam's various government positions, he sought political asylum and in due course it was granted. With his PhD degree he found a teaching job at the London School of Economics and prayed for the soul of the Prince who had put the idea of post graduate studies into his head. Rose heard that everything she owned, except the house at Galandoak was confiscated by the Foundation of the Emmam. No one could figure out why this property had remained secure except Rose. In her heart she was sure that the spirits of her parents were guarding the property for her.

Being a jack of all trades, with what her parents had left under her name in a London bank account, she began buying dilapidated apartments, renovating and selling them. In order not to go insane, she kept herself busy at all hours. But she had no control over her dreams. At nights she dreamt of the life she had lost and the hands she had buried. Her mother's ring never left her finger.

Datam shared her love of Iran and missed his parents. An introvert he allowed his grief to eat him up and turn into cancer.

As time passed the Iranian community in London enlarged; those with cash lived off their interests, at the time 21%; the educated found jobs and the unlucky depended on the magnanimity of the others. The community proved itself considerate and charitable and as it prospered, charity organizations bloomed and helped those without means, mostly from the military, the backbone of the Pahlavi strength deserted by a Shah they had remained loyal to and forgotten by an Empress who had chosen to become non-committal.

The Shah was dead and his family settled in the America that had closed its door to him when in need of urgent medical treatment. That same America now sheltered his family, not out of loyalty to an old ally who had served their interests for almost thirty years, but because his heir, Reza the Second, had become the symbol of opposition to the Regime in Iran – another pawn in the political chess game the great powers engage in to safeguard their own interests.

Chapter 4

Kobra

They had returned from their Friday lunch at Afsar Khanum's, where the family had gathered to evaluate the proficiency of her new cook. He had proved worthy of being employed. Kobra having had far too much to eat felt exhausted. She was relieved to be back at home and was looking forward to a relaxed lay in front of the TV watching her favourite serial, Uncle Napoleon. Already in her dressing gown she was hanging her party clothes when the door slit open and Shamsi's head popped through it. Kobra closed her wardrobe's door and as she turned, her eyes met those of her mother's. They were overcast with gloom.

She is again troubled by something someone said during the lunch. Kobra assumed crossing the room to where she was standing.

"Are you coming down to watch Uncle Napoleon?" Asked Shamsi, her tone unusually affable.

"Madar, that won't start until eight o'clock. It is only six now."

"I know, but before it starts, I want to talk to you about something important."

The ceiling light was shining on Shamsi's grim countenance and as she breathed her large nostrils quivered. Kobra did not like that expression on her face. She found it rather morbid. Pensive, she followed her down the stairs and into the TV room.

"I hope Baba will arrive soon. He loves the show."

"An hour ago he called to say he is on his way. I think he will get here before the show starts."

"Good. And are you going to complain about Baba again?"

"No, no."

"Then if you are going to counsel me, please do it in front of him." She demanded, knowing that her father was far more impartial than her mother.

"No. I want to talk to you about something that only concerns you and me."

"And what can that be Madar joon?" Kobra asked in a teasing tone, sure of the triviality of the issue, whatever it may be.

Shamsi settled on the sofa and with her hand tapped on the space by her. "Sit here, by me, please." Running out of patience, Kobra, pouted her lips, dropped on the sofa, turned her curious eyes to her mother, "for heaven's sake what is it Madar?" Shamsi clasped the edge of her sleeve and twisting it began:

"For many years, before you were born, I lived with Baba without loving him. I was stupid and naive. I thought by changing my life I could find happiness. I asked for divorce and was granted. I met and married a man whom I thought would make me happy but he did not. That man is your father."

A bomb blasted inside Kobra's head, setting fire to every fibre of her being and turning to ash her self-respect and identity. Cold sweat set on her tightly furrowed forehead and her heart palpitated so hard that she became breathless. Her face turned grey, her chin dropped, her mouth opened and she shrank in her seat. The room swirled around and around making her dizzy. If she kept her eyes open any longer she would vomit. She shut them and wished to die.

An oppressive silence followed. It was broken by the sound of the neighbour's car horn. Shamsi crossed her legs and recommenced. The echo of her voice pounded on Kobra's head like mallet, giving her an excruciating headache. "Oh God", she moaned in her heart, "I don't want to hear anymore. No more, please!"

"I divorced your father. Baba took me back, even though I was pregnant with you. When you were born, he wanted to adopt you. I did not let him. That would have deprived you from inheriting from your father who is better off than Baba."

As she listened, the pain inside her, exacerbated. The words she was hearing were like stabs of a sharp dagger into her heart, mind, soul and pride. Such cruelty could not possibly exist. How could a mother deprive her child from the sense of belonging that is the essence of mental stability, just for money – how? Kobra marvelled biting her lips until she tasted blood. She rose, pulled a tissue out of its box and wiped the blood. For a while she couldn't even look at that selfish creature who called herself a 'mother'. Then, when she dared to turn her hateful eyes on her, she saw a stranger relaxing on the corner of the sofa glaring at her with innocent eyes. She has unburdened her guilt. Now she can relax and watch me suffer. Kobra thought, a sarcastic grin parting her bruised lips. She narrowed her eyes and staring at her in mockery asked: "It is always money for you is it not? I bet you divorced Baba because he did not have as much as my uncles. You have no heart at all." She nodded twice. Then in anger she pinched her mother's sleeve and twisted it, pulled her towards herself and peering into her wide eyes asked, " who gave you the right to decide for me?" she released the sleeve. Shamsi fell backward, her side hitting the arm of the sofa, "could you not have told Baba to wait until I was old enough to decide for myself? Could you not – you selfish beast?" Emotionally worn out Kobra leaned back, tears running down the side of her quivering face.

Surprised by her unexpected hostile reaction, Shamsi moved closer and opened her arms to put around her shoulders. With an assault of her hand Kobra pushed her away and whispered: "Now I know why my cousins look down on me."

"Do not be silly. No one looks down on you. They all love you. Children are cruel; they sometimes say something hurtful and then forget all about it."

"No. Children are honest, they haven't yet learnt to lie and deceive – like grownups – like you."

"I have not deceived anyone, especially you. I did not tell you about your father when you were a child because I did not want you to feel like an orphan. I do not feel guilty about that at all. I did what I thought was best for you my love."

"You never feel guilty about anything, do you? You are so self-righteous that you cannot see anything in its correct perspective. You only see what you want to see. I had the right to know who my father is from the moment I opened my eyes to this fucking world. Now I know why you never gave me my birth certificate. By the way what is my true surname and does my father know that I exist?"

"Yes he does. He came to the hospital when you were born and saw you. He asked me if he could visit you regularly and I said no. Your surname is Afati. When I registered you at school, I told your headmistress the truth and asked her as a favour to have you called Amiri, and register you as Amiri-Afati."

"You denied me my father and him, his daughter?" Kobra shouted with so much hateful intensity in her voice that Shamsi flinched. She tensed before replying:

"Yes. I said no to him because I did not want to see him anymore myself."

"Here you are – selfish again – depriving a father from visiting his daughter because 'you' did not want to see him." She shook her head side to side; narrowed her eyes and asked: "Mother dear, do you know why you feel so miserable and lonely all the time?"

Shamsi didn't reply, just stared at her with dead eyes.

"Your loneliness is your punishment for your egoism. You really only love yourself. People have noticed it, and that is why they have abandoned you – even your sisters."

Shaken to the bone, Shamsi, lost for words, remained silent. What could she say? Here was 'her' daughter, joining the others in their rejection of her. Was there anyone in this wide world who loved, appreciated and above all 'understood' her? Was there? She kept asking herself and shaking her head in denial.

Just at that moment they heard Mohammad's car horn summoning Sadegh, the house boy, to open the gate.

In that state of mind Kobra didn't want to face Mohammad. She jumped up, left the room and banged its door. She felt faint and her head ached agonizingly. For support, she grabbed the rail of the staircase and very slowly, like an aged woman, climbed the stairs. In her bedroom, she sat on her bed, cupped her aching head in her hands, closed her eyes and dropped backward. The mattress was hard, the room dark and her mind bungled. Everything in her fifteen years of existence seemed to have been strange, sinister and illusive. What else was in store for her? She wondered with great apprehension. Her mother had deceived her. If one could not trust one's mother, who could one trust? No one! That fact became firmly implanted in her mind. She went back in time, remembering the incidents, particularly those that had been hurtful and strange: her brothers had pampered her, surely not because they had loved her, but because they had pitied her – the same with everybody else in the family. They all knew that she had no father. And Baba was always kind and considerate. Yet she could not remember an instance he had paid for any of her expenses. Why should he? He was just being kind out of compassion or perhaps to maintain face. But he had wanted to adopt her. That would have erased the shame and made life so much easier for all. She would have been honoured to bear his name. But no, that egomaniac had to stop the one single action that could have exonerated her from all the mistakes she had made. 'What a shame!' She whispered in desperation.

Kobra hardly slept that night. At first she just lay in bed, her tearful eyes fixed on the ceiling unable to move. She felt as though her mother had murdered her spirit, pulled it out of its carcass and then brought the carcass into life by giving it a new soul. With Kobra Amiri dead, she didn't know who she was anymore. How could she wear this Afati farce – this new garb in which she has to be wrapped for the rest of her life? How could she face her friends and tell them I have been deceiving you for years. My name is not Amiri but Afati? How could she adopt a name which has no meaning for her – the name of a man who bedded her mother, planted his seed in her and after six months when the novelty wore off went his way without an iota of care about his planted seed? What an irresponsible gardener Mr Afati must be? She sighed, wiping, with the heel of her hand, the drops of tears that rolled down her cheeks.

She tossed and turned and asked more questions of herself until she heard Mohammad coming up the stairs. Her throat tightened again and tears streamed down the corners of her eyes. That man she loved so much was not her father. How could she bear this fact? How could she? Suddenly she remembered his advice to Tirdad when he was blaming the world for his failures. He had said to him: "Just remember that man is the architect of his own destiny." She kept repeating the sentence to herself until her muddled mind discerned its meaning. A ray of hope lit her horizon. She sat up in bed and began to laugh. Man is the architect of his own destiny. This new born Kobra Afati is going to be the architect of her own destiny. This orphan is going to design her own fate – a life that will be envied by all, especially those who had pitied her and looked down on her. She kept repeating this until she dropped back and fell into a deep, dreamless sleep.

Early in the morning, a resolute Kobra Afati left her bed with a smile. She took great care of her appearance before descending down for breakfast. In the kitchen, she was polite to her mother at whose face she could not look. Mohammad had already departed, and she did not want to be left alone with her. She opened the fridge door, took an apple, fitted it into her satchel and walked out without a goodbye, leaving Shamsi in awe.

From that day on Kobra studied harder than ever, excelled at all her subjects including French language and finished high school with distinction. Thus qualified, just before the outbreak of the revolution she got herself accepted at the University of Sorbonne. The day she received her letter of acceptance was not only the happiest day of her life but of Shamsi's too. Her daughter had achieved something none of her much older nieces had as yet.

One early August morning, as proud as a peacock, standing by the gate of their home, Kobra , kissed the Koran held by her mother, bent low so that she could pass under it and be crowned by the safe keeping power emanating from the Holy Book.. Having captured the holy benison, she, straightened her posture, picked up her travelling bag from the ground, climbed into the car, squeezing in between Afsar Khanum, and her two cousins. She glanced at their gloomy faces and thought they were drowning in envy. In fact, the girls were mourning the loss of a companion. Together they had passed many pleasant evenings when, due to random curfews, going out had been impossible.

At the airport the farewell was emotional. The two cousins cried. Afsar Khanum prayed to be alive when Kobra returned and Shamsi wouldn't let her move, so tight was her grip.

"Khanum let the girl go. She will miss her plane." Mohammad pleaded, putting an arm around her plump and round shoulders and gently pulling her away. He was sad too. But he knew their sadness was selfish. The separation was to advance her in life and they should all be happy for her. The girl had indeed become the architect of her destiny and he was very proud of her. She had told him everything and he had assured her that in his eyes she would always be his daughter. That had made her very proud.

Without a pang of nostalgia, Kobra, smiling at her future, stepped inside a plane full of those who were seeking safer shores, their hand luggage bulging with valuables while hers was packed with mere necessities. Shamsi had refused Mohammad's financial assistance again. She was going to pay for Kobra's education herself and what she could afford was not enough. So Kobra had to struggle and that she did until her dying day.

Her family never knew she worked as a waitress, a cleaning lady and when tough times hit, an escort. They only heard that she had received a doctorate in Chemistry with which she had obtained a job at a Government institution – a remarkable achievement for a foreigner in France. Shamsi's joy was abundant – not only because her daughter had made her proud but she wouldn't have to send her any more money – rial had devalued and the value of dollar had increased tenfold. However, Kobra continued demanding financial assistance. In the back of her mind dwelt this obsessive suspicion of her brothers aiming to ultimately cheat her out of her inheritance. So she had to take what she could while her mother was alive.

One cold and wet evening, her boots and raincoat soaking, Kobra let herself inside her tiny rented studio in the 12th arrondissement. A letter from Iran was tucked under her door. She picked it up, glanced at the name of the sender and shivered. She threw the envelope on the dining table, shed her coat and boots, took them to the tiny shower room, shook the rain off them, hung the coat on the shower head and leaned the boots against the tiled wall to dry. She pulled a towel off the warm electrical rack, dried her hair with it and then returned it to its place. She glanced at her grim and tired reflection in the vanity mirror and exhaled a deep sigh. Her breath fogged the glass. She kept glaring at her pitiful self and sighing until the fog became so thick that she could see no more. She felt hot, as though some kind of acid was running through her veins dissolving everything on its way. Her cheeks felt as though they had been sunburnt. Why, after all these years, I feel like this? She asked herself. Perhaps it is because I don't want, or, dare not read that letter? Reading it will be like opening an old wound and throwing pepper on it. God, I don't want to be hurt again. I just don't. She felt the warmth of the tears rolling down her cheeks. This is horrible. I am an adult now and must control this ridiculous surge of emotion. Silly, silly me! He means nothing to me. Nothing at all! She took a deep breath that opened her tight throat, tossed her head back and splashed some cold water over her face. The chill felt good. It dispelled the ghosts that were playing hide and seek inside her head. She dried her face with the towel on the rack, and calmly returned to the table. She picked the envelope up, tore it off, pulled the letter out, sat on one of her two IKEA dining chairs and began to read.

She was twenty five and this was the first communication she had received from her father.

The letter was short, concise and as distant as their relationship had been. One more disappointment added to her larger than life repertoire. But, who cared? She shrugged. The tear that had welled up in her eyes didn't even drop. It turned into a sneer lurking at the corners of her mouth. After having gone through three wives, Mr Afati, about to die of cancer had written to acknowledge her existence and wanted to see her. How chivalrous of him? She thought, crumpling and squeezing the paper within her tight fist, as though it was his neck. Oh well! At least now I can recognize him by his handwriting! She murmured and laughed loud. Then she rose, took a few steps and dropped on her bed thinking she would never own him as a father. True he had asked to visit her and Madar had forbidden him. But, if he had wanted, he could have made contact. There had been thousand ways without being discovered. He could have written, phoned or just come by her school and together they could have gone for an ice cream. No one was spying on her and she could have met him, seen his face, smelled his scent and felt his affection if not his love. But no, it was easy for him to abide by Shamsi's order. It cost him nothing in terms of time, emotion and money. Let him die with a load of guilt on his conscience – regrets hurt most when one has no more time to make amends. Let him suffer and suffer and suffer. Thus decided she rose, straightened her shoulders, lifted up her chin, again squeezed the crinkled letter with all her resentment, opened her palm, spat on the paper and then threw it into the nearby garbage basket.

An hour later when Shamsi phoned and gave her the news of his demise, she said: 'I hope he is in the hell he deserves.'

"God forbid girl – what wrong did he do you?" Shamsi asked astonished.

"He planted me in this world." She replied, her voice sourer than vinegar.

"He also gave me a daughter who has made me a very proud mother."

Revolted by her mendacity Kobra shrieked: "Ok Madar, it seems everything is always about you and you alone. So, if it pleases you to turn me into a hypocrite like yourself, I will go on my knees and pray for his salvation."

Here she goes again, Shamsi thought before saying in a firm tone:

"He was your father and it doesn't please God to hear a child talk this way about her father."

"Mother, even though it is your fault that he never saw me, he could have made efforts had he really wished to. No he did not. Therefore, he does not deserve to be called a father and I do not believe in God and I must go now otherwise I will be late for my date."

Shamsi murmured: "Ok, I will call you on Sunday." Marred and bewildered at Kobra's behaviour, she placed the receiver on its cradle, rested her head on the back of the armchair and released a deep, sad sigh. . Everybody she knew had left Iran because their husbands had money, but not hers. The only shoulder left for her to cry on was Turan's. She, too, had gone away. But at least she would return, hopefully soon. Unable to bear the grief inside her, she decided to pour it out. Perhaps the Jennies, who dwelt within the folds of her curtains and moved when the windows, like just now, were open, would sympathise with her. How she craved for a word of assurance, a sniff of love, or a sweet smile, something that would make her feel alive again. How! She turned her eyes towards the open window, through which rays of light splashed over her sofa and a pleasant breeze teased the pleats of the curtains. She smiled. There they were and they would hear her. It was good to be heard – so good. Mohammad never listened to her. They only quarrelled. Dreadful – dreadful!

She kept her gloomy eyes on the curtains and as a pleat shifted she asked: "My heavenly companions, can one of you please tell me what I have done to deserve such animosity from the child I have loved more than anyone else in the world and have done so much for? I worked like a dog to pay for her education and all that she has demanded. I sold my land and sent her the money. What else could I have done for her? What?"

"You should have let Mohammad adopt her." A voice inside her head whispered.

She shook her head in denial and replied: "No. No. If I had done that, I would have become his slave for the rest of my life. He would have thrown it at me at every quarrel and made me feel like dirt. No, there is not enough breeding in him for that kind of nobility. I know that for sure. He is a cheap rat."

"You are wrong again." The voice hurled.

"Let me be. Go away. I am too old for regrets. Go away."

She cupped her head with her palms to stop the invasive pain throbbing in her brows. She took a deep breath, turned her heavy eyes away from the curtains and fixed them on the ceiling, seeking God.

"All I want is for my daughter to find happiness; marry a good man who would love and care for her. After all, she is getting on in age and soon will pickle, if not already. From this far, there is nothing I can do to help her find the right man? Please God, you find her a man who would make her happy. Happy." The pulsating pain in her head took further words out of her mouth. She rose and sauntered to the medicine cabinet in the bathroom. Lately she couldn't live without tranquilizers. She picked up the packet, withdrew from it a sheet of sealed tablets, broke one off its seal, put it in her mouth and washed it down with a palm full of tap water. Then she prepared herself for the evening prayer which she performed only when she needed something from Allah.

Four months later, it seemed God had heard her and was going to grant her wish.

Kobra, as busy as she was at work, finally managed to meet a fine Iranian, from a traditional family whom she hoped to marry and adopt his name! This issue of 'name' had remained nagging at the back of her mind. The harder she tried to obliterate the stain from her pride, the more difficult the task became, particularly now that Iranians were arriving in full planes.

After the advent of the Revolution, close to a million people, mostly members of the upper class and the highly educated dispersed around the world, many landing in Paris where they or their parents had an apartment. Besides that, the French Government of the time was very generous to the Iranian émigrés having caused their misfortune by sheltering Ayatollah Khomeini and providing him with a platform from which he could act. Thus Kobra, to her chagrin, came into contact with people who knew her as an Amiri. To save face and preserve her mother's dignity, she played the game until she became too important a professional and had to lead meetings, with a name tag on her white uniform. It was during one such meeting when she encountered Ferdous, Rose's cousin, now representing an English pharmaceutical firm with an office in Paris. They had been introduced by the company's head executive and Ferdous, assuming she was married now, had congratulated her. She had thanked him coldly and sat as far away as possible from him. The incident had shaken her and impelled her to be ready to divulge the truth about her true identity. After all who cared about her surname beside her? Even though she had passed the level of maturity that enables individuals to accept reality for what it is, when the time came to act, she felt uncomfortable. Thus she wanted to get married and acquire a name with which she could identify and be comfortable.

They had met at the busy office of Iran Air at Champs Elysees where she had gone to book a ticket. Irritated by the long wait, Kobra had voiced her complaint to an unfortunate passing Iran Air officer. Suddenly the rest of the impatient clients had joined in. As a result an argument had flared up. When, eventually, the calm was restored Kobra found herself talking to the shy man sitting by her. He was new to Paris and full of enquiries. By chance their numbers were called one after the other and they finished almost at the same time. The young man, cherishing his luck for meeting a doctor (he thought she was a general practitioner), invited Kobra to share a Pizza with him.

Nader, was a pleasant looking man, with bushy eyebrows, jet black curled lashes and the face of a fundamentalist with black stubble. He seemed very naive and felt lost amongst the non-believers who he had to tolerate until his graduation from the university. Brought up at Qum, he was very proud of the success of the Revolution and his own family background. His uncle Haj Agha Abolfazl was an acquaintance of Emmam Khomeini. It was due to Haj Agha's influence that the Emmam's Foundation had given him a student grant to study Political Science at Sorbonne; otherwise, scholastically he wouldn't have qualified. Now students on government grants were sent to France, Canada or Australia and not U.S or Britain – the enemies of the Regime.

The two dated for almost a year. During weekends and holidays arm in arm they promenaded the streets and the parks, visited the grand museums and palaces, frequented cinemas and consumed hallal food. Still Nader felt like a fish out of water. He longed for home. Had it not been for Kobra, he would have said goodbye to his studies and returned to his own warm, familiar habitat. He never asked Kobra to go to his studio nor did she invite him for an Iranian meal prepared by her. She was not a good cook and this flaw had to be concealed until the knot was tied. During all this time, their physical intimacy was limited to a good night kiss. Nader was brought up to think sex outside marriage was taboo and the wife had to be a virgin. Kobra had guessed this, yet believed that in time she could seduce him – but first she had to get him to drink. Their first intercourse had to happen when he was thoroughly drunk so that he could not realize she was not a virgin. However, to her chagrin, the boy proved stoically true to his moral convictions. The only achievement of Kobra so far was to have him shave every morning. In the absence of any proposal and Nader's reluctance to change, her sense of security towards her hold on him became threatened. He was taking her for granted and that had to be stopped. To this end she masterminded a plan. For two weeks she became totally invisible. He telephoned her at home, on her direct office line, not only once but every hour. No one picked up the phone. Nader kept cursing himself for not remembering the exact name of the company she worked for. Otherwise he would have found its address and gone there. Surely her secretary would have known where she had gone. This devastated him. For the first time in his life, he had become accustomed to female companionship. Desolate and vexed he lost both his appetite and sleep. A good friend suggested a glass of brandy would act as tranquilizer and as such would not inflict any sin. So he went to a liquor shop and bought himself a brand suggested by the vendor. At nights the alcohol sent him to deep dreamless sleep. He liked the remedy and became hooked on it. Then, when his messages went without a response for too long, he decided to go and knock at her door. Anticipating such possibility Kobra had told her friend Nazanin that her apartment was being renovated and she was looking for temporary lodgings. Nazanin had invited her to move in with her. She was Iranian, studying international law at Sorbonne. Even though they were good friends, Kobra had kept her in the dark about her relationship. Nazanin was sharp and beautiful and Kobra didn't want to introduce her to her man in case she stole him from her.

Nader took a shot of brandy before leaving for Kobra's apartment. On the road he drove like a maniac, until he reached her flat in front of which luckily was a vacant spot. He parked his car, jumped out of it without even locking its door. He ran to the gate and knowing the code entered in and ran up the stairs. He halted by her apartment, took couple of deep breaths and began ringing the bell and knocking at the door like a maniac. Disturbed by the noise, the next door neighbour opened her door and poked her head out. The old woman, through her window, had often seen Nader giving Kobra lifts. Retired and semi-mobile, spying on dirty foreigners was her pastime.

"She is not home monsieur."

"Good morning Madame. Do you know where she is?"

"No monsieur. She often travels for work."

"Thank you Madame." He whispered turning towards the stairs.

"Monsieur, if I see her, who shall I say was looking for her?"

Preoccupied with his dark thoughts, her soft voice escaped his ears and dissolved in the chilly air. She shrugged her thin shoulders and banged the door behind her – convinced that she was right in her dislike of aliens. They had no manners at all.

Running down the stairs, he felt nauseous. Suspicious thoughts were giving him a pounding headache. He kept wondering why she had left without letting him know. Where could she have gone and with whom? He did not dare to speculate that there could be a 'who'. Suddenly he felt frightened. It had never occurred to him that he loved her. Yes he did – he had to talk to his parents; tell them all about her and ask their permission to propose to her. The thought elated him and evaporated all his misgivings. He would wait until she returned and then tell her of his intensions. This coming summer, they would go to Iran and have a grand wedding. He was sure her credentials would meet with his parents' approval. She came from a very respectable family while his was a parvenu. His marriage would elevate the social status of his family and he would be rubbing shoulders with members of the old aristocracy and not mere mullahs or the merchants of the bazaar. What joy! So he decided to patiently wait for her return.

On the following Friday afternoon, when he was studying at home the shrill sound of the phone broke his concentration and flared up the perpetual anxiety inside him. Sending a prayer for it to be her, he grabbed the receiver. To his 'Allo' Kobra's seductive voice responded 'Salam Azizam'.

Suddenly his face lit with the glow of thousand shining stars and a delicious feeling passed through him. "Where have you been Kobra Joon? I have been going out of my mind worrying about you."

A triumphant smile bloomed on Kobra's face. "I had to go to Luxemburg on a work mission."

"Why did not you let me know you were going away?"

"I didn't think you cared for me enough to miss me Nader joon."

"What a silly thing to say. Thank God you are safe and sound and back."

"So you did miss me?"

"Of course I did – more than you can imagine."

"I am glad to hear that, because I missed you too."

Her words sent a flurry of joy into his heart accelerating its beats. He had to take a deep breath otherwise he would throttle with excitement.

"What are you doing tonight my love?" He asked in a steady voice.

"Nothing at all."

"Shall we have dinner together?"

"Sure. Shall I book a table at a restaurant I have heard is very good?"

"Yes my love, do just that."

Sharp at 8.30 Kobra heard the ding dung of her intercom. It was him, as punctual as ever. Dressed seductively in a black décolleté gown from Bon Marche, she ran to her bathroom, sprayed herself with his favourite perfume, a habit inherited from the late Afsar Khanum who had peacefully passed away in her sleep; checked her face in the mirror, smiled at the image, grabbed her bag, closed and locked the door behind her and ran down the stairs and out of the building where she found him standing by his brand new black Citroen, eagerness radiating from his large black eyes. At times they glowed like two large black pearls set in snow. As their eyes met, he trembled in gladness relishing the flow of life in his veins again.

'Salam Nader joon,' she murmured, stealing a quick kiss from his lips, something she had never done before. Exhilarated by the warmth of her touch and intoxicated by her scent, he clasped her hand, squeezed it hard and then took it to his lips and kissed it. "You look ravishing azizam." He exclaimed opening the door for her. She smiled her thanks and demurely glided inside, her teasing eyes fixed on his bright and innocent face. Kobra never had thought of him as handsome. What had initially attracted him to her were his simplicity that she thought she could manipulate and his name that she could adopt. Now that simplicity was growing on her and he seemed quite attractive. His Roman nose, though a bit large, complemented the rest of his features. Thank God he had lost a bit of weight which made him look smart in his outfit.

He closed the door, went to the other side, climbed in and before starting the engine turned to her and enquired: 'Where are we going Azizam?'

'To Pigalle, I have booked a table at a restaurant renowned for its cuisine and cabaret.'

A frown formed on his forehead. He looked at her with concerned eyes and said: 'My parents will kill me if they find out I have gone to a joint at Pigalle.'

'Now who is going to tell them that?'

'Someone might see us there?'

'None of your friends will be there, will they?'

'No I assume not. Ok let's go there and sin!'

'I do not believe enjoying oneself will be considered a sin by anyone but a Mullah.'

'Cherie, I wish you were more respectful of the rules of our religion.'

'I am – that is why I am taking you there!' She responded with a naughty smile and a gentle pat on his thick lap.

Overjoyed by being with her again, he inserted his favourite Iranian disc into the player, turned the engine on and drove through the maddening Parisian traffic, being navigated by her, who had to shout over the loud music. After half an hour of search for a space to park, he decided to go into an underground car park.

Back on the street level, Kobra locked her arm within his and gently pulled him towards the entrance of the nightclub above which pictures of topless ladies flashed in colourful neon lights. To the bulky security guy she gave her name that was checked against the reservation list. Then politely the two were ushered down several steps into a large semi-lit room vibrating with Can Can music. Almost naked ladies, with breasts protruding out of their lace cages, carried trays of food and beverages.

Nader's hungry eyes were devouring the nudity in his view with such eagerness that he felt giddy. He had never seen a bare body save his mother's when bathing him while a child.

At their table, they sat side by side facing the stage. It was teeming with tall, seductive performers swinging to the beat of the rhythmic music. Nader was so enchanted that he began rhythmically tapping the table. Kobra put her hand on his, rubbed it gently, leaned her face close to his, looked into his eyes and whispered: "Tonight Nader joon, you are my guest. We are going to start with a bottle of champagne."

"Champagne?" He exclaimed.

"Yes Champagne."

"But that is forbidden."

"Nothing is forbidden if done in moderation. Please don't spoil our evening my love?" Fearful of losing her again he clasped her hand, squeezed it with love and timidly asked: 'Are we celebrating an occasion you have not told me about?'

Kobra shifted a shoulder, tilted her protruding breasts below his gaze, raised an eyebrow, pursed her lips and coquettishly replied: "Perhaps yes." She shifted the other shoulder, "perhaps no – you will find out before the evening is over."

She is playing games with me. That means she loves me. He thought and began to laugh.

"What are you laughing at?" Kobra enquired with wide surprised eyes.

"At you Khanum. You never stop amazing me. It is good, very good."

The waitress arrived with a menu card for each.

His French not good enough to fully discern the menu items Nader turned to Kobra, "Azizam you order for me."

She ordered Lemon Sole for both and a bottle of champagne. Then she turned to him and said: "Here they don't serve hallal meat so I ordered fish for us."

He smiled his gratitude and felt proud of his choice of a future wife.

The waitress returned with a tray on which a champagne bottle rested in an ice-bucket and two flutes. She placed the flutes in front of the guests and presented the bottle to Nader. Shyly he pointed to Kobra who after checking the label smiled her approval. The waitress uncorked the bottle, filled the glasses, and returned the bottle to the bucket which she placed on a nearby table.

The music was pleasant, the atmosphere jolly and the food, when it arrived, was delicious. They ate and drank with delight and when Kobra finished she gently rested her hand on his lap. She waited for him to savour its warmth. She sensed the shiver that ran through him. Her eyes smiled and she began sliding it further and further down until she touched and tickled his bulging genital. A thrill went through him and he shuddered. Bewildered, his eyes roved around to see if anyone had noticed what was going on under their table. No one was paying any attention to them. He gently took her hand and returned it to its original place on his lap. She heard his hard breathing and felt excited. Now she was breathing hard too. It had been a year since she had sex with anyone. Her body ached for it.

She fixed her flirting eyes on his profile. Just like everyone else he was enjoying the show. Champagne must have evaporated his reservations. She assumed with a sense of triumph. In fact she was right. For the first time in his life he was finding himself released from the cage of moral strictures. It felt good. He noticed that the show had stopped and people were moving towards the dance floor. Unchained and free from fear of hell, he captured the music rhythm and began to move to it. It felt exuberant. He rose, took Kobra's hand and pulled her up. Once on the dance floor, she realized it was his first time dancing to Western music. She took joy in leading him and he let her do as she pleased. The Champaign, the music and Kobra's proximity had delivered him to paradise. Someone once had told him that in ancient times dance was a kind of salutation to Gods. Now he realized that it was true – dancing was celebrating happiness and cherishing the source from which it emanates. Eventually the music tamed and they fell into each other's arms. Cheek to cheek, loin to loin, they danced until he found himself having an orgasm – something that had only happened to him in sleep. Instead of feeling embarrassed he let himself enjoy the fulfilment. Kobra detected the reflection of rapture on his flushed, palpitating countenance. She tightened her arms around his neck and began licking the lope of his ear. The sensation sent him to delirium. He closed his eyes and let his senses bathe in ecstasy.

They danced and turned and danced until exhaustion overwhelmed him. He kissed her neck for the first time, tickled it's nape with his nose and stopped. She wiped the sweat beads from his forehead with the tip of her long fingers; took his arm and they returned to their table. Kobra summoned the waitress for the bill which she paid. Then, as happy as a couple after their first nuptial night, they walked to the car and drove to her studio. He parked the car. She coiled her arms around his neck and kissed him on the mouth. Then she got out, went to his side, opened the door and whispered: 'come up with me.'

Still sustaining the delicious sensations he had experienced, he allowed himself to be lured out of the car, up the stairs and right into the partitioned bedroom area. She undressed in front of him: her breasts as round as a large melon with nipples as red as ripe cherries – her slightly large stomach round and her gate to heaven a black bushy triangle that pulsated with desire. He couldn't control himself any more. Savagely he peeled off his own clothes, lifted her up and dropped her on the bed. Skilfully she initiated him into the world of sensuality. He made love to her till dawn when he fell into a deep, peaceful sleep.

It was Saturday and neither had to go anywhere. She rose early – sure that she had hooked him for life. In her kitchenette she made herself a cup of coffee, took out a croissant from its plastic bag that was in her bread basket, warmed it on the toaster, sat behind her small dining table and ate with appetite of an ogre. In her mind reeled pictures of her in a wedding gown holding his arm and smiling at the guests. She would make him happy. Her mother's mistakes had taught her a lot and she craved for a family in which everyone was happy and content, respected and loved. Her croissant tasted delicious, as good as a fresh one out of the baker's oven.

He woke up quite disoriented – blinked several times, massaged his eyes to see well. The cloud disappeared; he stared around the room and suddenly jumped out of bed, pulled away the top sheet searching for blood of virginity. He found nothing except the stains of his own sperms. He paused to stifle the cry of horror forcing itself out of his mouth. He saw his own reflection on the closet's mirror and became conscious of his nudity. Embarrassed, he dressed in haste and finding her in the kitchenette, stood erect in front of her, his wide eyes emanating shafts of indignation and his face twitching like an epileptic's. In his mind he was searching for the most cutting words to stab her with.

Surprised, she rose, smiled at him serenely and in a concerned voice asked:

"What is wrong Azizam?"

"You slut – you Satan incarnate – all the time that I thought you were an innocent virgin you were a nefarious whore, and now I have lost my innocence because of you – you despicable bitch."

Her mouth wide open she stood as rigid as a monument on a grave.

As though words were not enough, he stepped closer, slapped her hard on both cheeks, kicked her table with his foot and then turned his back and ran towards the door. With a quivering hand he unlocked and opened it wide. He turned back, threw her a contemptible glare and yelled: "I hope you die and go to hell – you Salomé." Utterly beaten, Kobra, cheeks crimson, feeling like dirt, froze on the spot she was standing and stared at the door that was left open. She heard him run down the stairs. A few minutes later the door of the building banged closed. She knew he was gone and out of her life.

The neighbour's door slid open; the old woman's head protruded out. She saw Kobra, semi naked in a loose, unbuttoned dressing gown, her eyes awed, lips parted, and standing in a state of utter confusion. The Frenchwoman exclaimed a loud: 'Merde', and closed her door, this time with a bang.

The noise broke Kobra's daze. Like a zombie, she bent down, lifted the capsized, chipped coffee cup from the floor, looked at it with pity, took it to the sink, washed it clean and lodged it on the dish wrack. The chip was not that apparent. She could use it again. She went to the door and closed it. That awful neighbour was a nuisance – always spying on her, with that awful glow in her eyes. She must have a lot of chips on her shoulders. She thought with antipathy.

She returned to the kitchenette, made herself another cup of instant coffee, sat on her chair and began to drink it. The numbness gradually receded and she became herself again. Staring at the stain the coffee had made on the withered carpet she wondered how wrong she had been in her judgement of his character. How could she have been so stupid? Next time she had to be more prudent and careful with her choice. No more fundamentalists. One can never win with them – they all live in the golden coop of their ideology. She heard the concierge push some mail inside through the gap of the door. She turned her head. Two junk mails winked at her. She rose, picked them up and threw them into the garbage bin, and then she busied herself cleaning the flat. Once she got to the bed, she pulled the sheets off with disgust, threw them on the floor, and opened the window to change the air that stank of him. She gathered the sheets up, pushed them into the laundry bag that was near the window, made the bed with fresh linen she extracted from the bed drawer under the mattress, took a shower and went for a walk in the nearby park. There she found an empty bench on which she sat. She looked around. Something in the innocent beauty of nature broke her reserve. She felt the warmth of tears streaming down her cold cheeks. She let them pour. It didn't matter if people saw her crying. Everybody cries one time or other. It is good to cry. It cleanses the soul from the dirt that stains it.

Two years passed without any men in her life. Then during one of her trips to Geneva she met Doctor Hans, a German chemist working for a Swiss company. He was much older than her and wealthy. This was good. Older men made better husbands than young ones. As they dated, they realized they shared many interests and were quite compatible. In love, he asked for a transfer to Paris. The decision made Kobra the happiest woman on earth. Finally a decent, educated, broadminded man with ample money was going to marry her. He was tall, handsome and generous. What luck!

In Paris, they bought a one bedroom apartment together and lived happily for couple of years until Doctor Hans, by nature a Casanova, became tired of her and started a relationship with his very young secretary. Kobra found out and confronted him. He told her the truth, packed his bag and left for his home town of Hamburg, taking his lover with him. From there he took a lawyer to negotiate financial settlements and somehow Kobra became the sole owner of the apartment – how? Even the doctor's lawyer could not fathom that out.

Content with the result of the court case she promised herself never to fall in love with another man. Marriage was not written for her. So she had to concentrate on her work and accumulation of wealth. Sex could be satisfied without love. It was simpler not to be attached to anyone. Attachment entailed responsibility, expectation, disappointment and hurt. Frankly she had had enough of being hurt. Thus decided, she delved into the French epicurean life with a vengeance. She also acquired their manner of speech and gesticulations, like waving her hands while talking and raising an eyebrow and so on. Her gestures seemed ludicrous to Iranians. Only one neighbour was enchanted by her new conduct and that was Homayon. He was tall and well built. The exercises he did at home had toned his muscular arms and tight tummy. His large black eyes were kind and always shining with admiration for her. She liked that very much. With an insatiable libido she had to find a mate on whose discretion she could count – in a country where punishment for adultery is stoning to death, she could take no risks at all.

She lived her life according to her own principles and at times, enjoyed it. Yet the wounds remained sore. As she aged the pain became harder to bear. She had already pickled and it seemed would die with Afati stigma tagged on her. Thus she grew more resentful of her fate. Her jealousy of her siblings, who seemed to be having a fulfilled life intensified. Often she wondered at her own duality of character. Kobra Amiri was a capable, honest and at times amusing person. Kobra Afati was extremely competitive, conniving, and a paranoid. Sometimes she didn't even trust her own eyes. To bring a semblance of contentment into her life, she worked, and worked and climbed the ladder of success but without joy. Even her psychiatrist had not been able to help her find peace.

Chapter 5

Tirdad

Mentally starved and physically neglected, Yasmin turned into a wilted rose bud. Her grandparents, though they loved her very much, had their own compounding problems that like cancer cells were eroding what little energy was left in them. Tension was everywhere even at schools, which were now in a chaotic state. The International and private schools were shut down. Their students had to enrol at public schools, the numbers of which were not adequate enough to cater for the influx, especially now that the classes had to be segregated. To resolve the problem the Ministry of Education halved the study time: mornings for the boys and the afternoons for the girls.

Teachers with the right convictions had replaced those with the wrong ones and those, not discharged had to comply with the new order, curriculum and values without a hint of complaint or criticism. The principles had been handpicked at the Ministry from amongst the zealots prepared to sack any staff not ready to enforce the Islamic values or punish students not in proper hejab. Anything that smelt of the West was banned and any student who looked remotely foreign frowned upon and subjected to cruelty. Yasmin had creamy skin and blue eyes. So even at school she could not find peace. Shamsi, concerned about her health, forced Mohammad to sell their house and buy a duplex which they could share with Tirdad and hopefully his future wife who could mother the girl. The deed done, she furnished the top floor flat so that he could bring to it a wife from a decent family. Yasmin hardly ever saw her father. In the mornings, preoccupied by Party matters, he didn't even notice her sad eyes begging for a smile or a reassuring word. On the one occasion that Shamsi dared to ask him to pay more attention to his daughter, he frowned and responded: "Madar Yasmin is just six years old. She will get used to life without a selfish mother who chose comfort verses humanitarian ideals and goals. Had she truly loved her family, like all my friends' foreign wives, she would have remained in Iran, shared her husband's values, and helped him to overcome his ordeals and achieve his goals. No. She had to run away like a spineless coward – the detestable pig." Concerned that Yasmin might hear him, Shamsi pointed her index finger to the tip of her nose so that he would hush up and whispered: "Then you are punishing your daughter for the sins of her mother."

Irritated Tirdad narrowed his fuming eyes, bent close to her face and without lowering his voice yelped: "Stop pestering me Madar. Don't you know that family matters are trivial within the context of social ideals?"

She wrinkled her nose and tilted her head away from his face. His breath stank of alcohol.

"What has Yasmin's unhappiness got to do with social problems?"

"Madar, you really are very stupid. You do not even know the difference between 'problems' and 'ideals'. Just get on with your cooking and let people with brains and courage turn the hell you live in into heaven." Then he left the kitchen banging its door.

In her room Yasmin wounded by her father's loud outburst, lay on her bed crying.

Shamsi sat down, rested her elbows on the table, cupped her head with her palms, closed her eyes and tried to shut her mind to all that was happening to them. But she couldn't. Her mind was too agitated to rest. It wandered from regret to regret and settled on the most devastating one: why she had not really tried to encourage him to leave Iran with Jill. She could never forget the day Jill had begged him to go with her, promising to become the breadwinner until he could get an Austrian residency. He had looked at her with savage eyes, and yelled: "If you think I will live under your shadow, you are more of a fool than I thought you ever were. I am not my brother. I am my own man and not my wife's lackey." The poor girl, instead of responding to him, had turned her disappointed eyes to her and said: "You know Shamsi joon, none of us matter to him anymore. He has to stay, prove himself a hero and change the system! They have turned him into a monster, those communist bastards." All she had said to her was: "Your husband has his pride. You must respect that." What had made her make that stupid remark? She kept wondering and feeling repentant. But, her ponderings and lamentations never lasted long. She loved him so much that for each and every fault of his she found a convincing justification that exonerated his misconduct – even keeping that poor little girl in Revolutionary Iran. It was this attitude that had barred Mohammad to talk to her about their son.

In his own restrained way, Mohammad was not only concerned but extremely worried about him. He was convinced it was ambition that had blinded him to the reality of the political situation. The fundamentalists seemed in total control of the country and ruthless in dealing with their adversaries. Neither the Tudeh nor the Mujahidin had the slightest chance to usurp their power. Yet, his son could not accept that very transparent fact. He lived in a dream that probably would kill him. Yet talking to him had become like talking to a brick wall. In their house no truce could ever be made. Every evening had ended with some sort of dispute, argument and shouts that the neighbours could hear. This had become too daunting for him to tolerate, so he had agreed to Shamsi's demand to sell the house and buy the duplex in a locality where no one knew them.

The new property, with its two separate entrances, was modern with low ceilings and aluminium framed windows; more like a matchbox than anything else. Medium in size, it had a small, paved courtyard at a corner of which lay a narrow, rectangular patch in which Mohammad could busy himself cultivating herbs and annuals. Gardening relaxed his troubled mind and provided him with the exercise that his ailing heart needed. He kept the yard and the outdoor furniture spotless particularly during the warm months when at dusk he lodged himself on his comfortable cushioned chair; with or without the presence of his wife; enjoying the cool fresh air while perusing the pages of his evening newspaper inundated by gloomy news of executions, war and death. The current events were so devastating that after each read he craved for a glass of whisky he could neither find nor afford. Then he would return inside , lay on the sofa and occupy himself with re-reading French classics that reminded him of his years in Paris – when he had believed youth would last forever. Then when his eyes tired he would close them, rest his book on his torso, and think of Mohsen Mirza, the happy life they had shared, his kindness and his timely death. He was so lucky to have gone when he did – with his background and involvement with the Pahlavi court he would have been one of the first to be taken and shot. The thought of him always burnt his heart. He was the only individual who had been his pillar of strength, a caring brother and a true friend. Mohammad hardly ever prayed but every time Mohsen Mirza's handsome face danced in view of his mind, he sent him a prayer thinking how unfair life had been to him. The poor soul was prevented from marrying the woman he had loved and was unable to come to terms with his own bisexuality. The gentleman that he was, he had carried a heavy load of guilt with a smile on his composed face. Finally a victim of social inhibitions, finding existence too hard to bear, he resolved to die honourably. One white winter dawn, when he knew the winding snow covered mountainous Teheran to Chalous road would be deserted he swallowed several tranquilizers and drove himself to death. Mohammad often wondered why he had sent him that farewell note – why didn't he let him believe that his death was an accident. At the end of each reflection he concluded he had not wanted to deceive his best friend – to the end he had remained loyal. Had he stayed in France he would have been able to practice his profession and lead an ordinary, normal life. But no he had to return to Iran and be his noble father's lackey until the Shah nationalized agricultural land and released him from his burden – but of course that was too late.

Mohammad often visualized that very special evening during which he was ushered into the world of the rich and famous; filled with hope, they had drank to happiness – strangely enough not meant for either of them. Why and why he kept asking himself. What had either of them done to deserve their fates?

He had been preaching to others that man is the architect of his own destiny. But is he? Then refusing to deny the validity of his belief he wondered what wrong decisions he had made to lead his life to such unending, bitter solitude. He had always hoped by the time he and Shamsi reached the autumn of their lives, they would overcome their differences, become friends and good companions. Even in this he had been mistaken. Old couples often enjoy reminiscing together, taking walks and sharing an ice cream in a park. Teheran's mayor was a professional town-planner. He had turned all the barren hills of the city into beautiful parks, with sports areas, artificial lakes and coffee shops – indeed paradises, especially for the aged. It cost nothing to pass an afternoon in the neighbouring park, where they could take a leisurely walk, hear chirpings of the birds, inhale fresh fragranced air or sit on a bench, let the mind relax and the eyes wander from one beauty to another while hearing the soft music transmitted through amplifiers hidden within tree branches. But no, Shamsi wouldn't even agree to do that. She seemed happier lamenting than rejoicing. Unfortunately, they had grown apart with nothing to say to one another except hurtful words.

How he missed Datam and Rose, how! They were the light of his life – always so kind and considerate – only with them he could find peace and joy.

It was a wise decision by Rose to keep her husband's illness from his family. The news would have certainly given Mohammad a heart attack. The couple had made a pact: to live life as though nothing was amiss. The treatment days were a routine they had to follow, and they did it as calmly as possible. Upon their return from hospital, with Datam in excruciating pain, they would each go to a room. He would lie on his bed bearing the pain and the spasms with the patience of Job until the next day when the dolorous reactions to the treatment would subside. Weather permitting, they would take a walk, go to a cinema or do whatever diverted his mind from his discomfort until it settled and he felt normal. Sometimes the pain would persist for days and sometimes just twenty-four hours. Neither his oncologist, nor the urologist knew why. It was very rare to have two independent cancers. Luckily his leukaemia had not progressed enough to need chemotherapy as yet. Although pressed for time, once a week they called and once a month they wrote to Shamsi and Mohammad. Their letters were bearers of good news, interesting gossip, love, affection and concern for all. Even Shamsi missed their letters when late in arriving.

Mohammad, in spite of all the evils surrounding him had managed to preserve some of his positive attitude. At times he went out of his way to create a pleasing chore that took him out of his home into the street where he could see people and feel alive again. A task he particularly treasured was taking and collecting Yasmin from school. Early morning he showered, shaved, put his suit on and waited for her to turn up at the door, dressed in Islamic uniform and scarf, holding her school bag and lunch box.

The activity not only took him out but it also made him feel responsible for something besides caring for the small yard and its new fish pond.

Shamsi, almost a recluse now also relied on Yasmin to make her feel alive and wanted. She doted on her tirelessly, baking her favourite pastries, knitting her jumpers and letting her watch her favourite serials on the TV. Nevertheless, to both grandparents' chagrin, nothing returned a smile to the girl's face, or a light to her eyes, except the buzz of the phone at five in the afternoon of each Friday. At four thirty she would nestle by the phone waiting to receive her mother's call. Jill was punctual and her voice the elixir that helped Yasmin go through the week. Their conversation always ended with: "enshallah, soon we will be together again." And Yasmin waited, prayed and hoped for that moment.

During their conversation Shamsi sat by the girl, patiently knitting and waiting her turn to talk to Jill. She admired her for maintaining a civilized relationship with the entire family. One day she picked up the phone in her room to call a friend and heard her voice. "I have good news for you Agha Doctor. I have found a very good job in Vienna. The income will enable me to rent a two bedroom apartment. Could you please try to persuade Tirdad to send Yasmin here? Please Agha Doctor. I miss her so much." The news made her smile. Then she heard Mohammad's voice: "My dear, we hardly ever see him now that he has become one of the party leaders. I do not know what they are up to but they are very busy. During the days he works at the Plan Organization and at nights only God knows where he goes. He comes home so late that we let Yasmin sleep with us. I agree with you. She should be with her mother. In Vienna she can have a good education and be free of all these tensions that are suffocating us all." There was a long pause and then Shamsi heard Jill reply: "I am sorry to have to say this, but I think he has gone mad. Only a mad or a very selfish individual would deprive his own daughter from the love of her mother and the security of living in peace. He always told me he wanted to make a difference. He can, by being unselfish and a good father."

"Jill dear, you are absolutely right but do you think this cochon (pig) will ever listen to anyone?"

"No Agha doctor. No. I shall call next week. Keep well my dear Agha doctor and give my love to Shamsi joon."

Shamsi put the receiver down and murmured: "Please dear God, hammer some sense into my son's head. Please?"

Months passed in political turmoil. Factions kept fighting the ruling party in vain. Tirdad became more involved in his party's affairs and a ghost at home. And then one Thursday morning, he surprised his mother.

"Madar?" Shamsi heard him call.

"I am in the kitchen." She replied and turned to the door. There he stood elegantly dressed, smoothly shaved and for a change smiling.

"Salam Madar."

"Salam."

He gave her a hug and then said:

"I am going to bring a guest for lunch tomorrow, can you make something delicious?"

Delighted by the demand, she cheerfully replied: "Of course son and what do you want me to cook for you?"

"Why not shirin polo (a rich and slightly sweet rice dish served at wedding feasts)?"

"Shirin polo?" Shamsi asked, surprised at his suggestion.

He stepped closer to her, looked into her eyes, wobbled his head and said:

"Yes Shirin polo. We have not had that for a long time now – have we?" There was something in his voice that tickled Shamsi's curiosity, yet she asked nothing.

"As you wish son."

Unusually amicable, he kissed her head and hurried out without banging any doors. That too surprised Shamsi. She brushed her greasy hands over her dirty apron and ran to the sitting room where her husband had been reading his newspaper. There she found the sofa empty of him and messy with scattered pages. Annoyed she looked through the open window and saw him watering the plants and humming a French tune as though still young and in Paris. She crossed the room to the window and poked her head out.

"Agha, Tirdad is bringing a friend for lunch tomorrow and he wants shirin polo. Hurry up and go and get me a chicken." Mohammad muttered a protest, looked up at her and responded: "Let me finish one chore before expecting me to do another."

"I did not ask you to go down and make a mess of the yard." With both hands banging at her temples she screamed: "Look. You have splashed the mud all over the tiles and stained your trousers which I have to wash. Can you ever do anything properly? No – never!" She slammed the window shut. The bang of the collision made her jump – so nervous she had become. Outside a bird that had peacefully nestled on a branch spread out its wings and furiously flapping them flew away.

Mohammad swept a glance around and then up at the spotless sky. He found the day too beautiful to spoil by getting into any confrontation. So he directed the hose's nozzle over the tiles, towards the flower bed and when his courtyard looked pristine, he turned the tap off, dropped the hose without curling it around the tap's shoulder and sat on his chair taking joy in inhaling the air that smelt of wet earth and herbs. The sun was relentlessly hot and he could see the mist rising from the ground and dissolving in the air. Then to his annoyance he heard her voice again, commanding him to instantly get inside and out, to do her shopping. "Even an instant of peace is denied me – oh God what have I done to deserve this." He murmured closing his eyes. And when he opened them, they fell on one of his three gold fishes, aimlessly floating on the surface of the water. Automatically he rose, stepped forward, bent over the pond and saw his own reflexion wave over the dead fish. He straightened up, shook his head in regret and lumbering up the steps mumbled: "The poor fish, probably died poisoned by the venom in the air of my home."

By the evening, Shamsi had managed to cook and debone her chicken, make a barley soup for dinner and a pomegranate jelly for tomorrow's desert.

Things had gotten very expensive and with their budget limited to their pensions, they had to be very careful. Usually lunch was a rice dish and dinner very basic, sometimes just bread and yoghurt. Mohammad was not a great eater but he did miss his glass of whisky.

The next morning around ten, Tirdad, smart in a white shirt and tight jeans brought Yasmin down and told his mother he would be back with his friend around noon. The girl ran down to the courtyard where she joined her grandfather picking herbs for lunch. His little patch, devoid of any weeds was thriving. Iranians consume fresh herbs with their meals. Their favourites are: mint, basil, radishes, spring onions and chives. And Mohammad's basket was full of them.

Inside, Shamsi locked the door behind Tirdad and hurried to the kitchen – she still enjoyed cooking even without any maids to help her. Naneh had died years ago and the Philippine domestic replacing her, had disappeared with all she had found in her mistress's purse. Now she had the whole kitchen to herself without the slightest objection to the cockroaches and ants that kept her company. No one would ever venture into her kitchen. It sufficed to keep the entertaining area in good order in case someone dropped in and that had become rare.

The clock's pendulum had not sounded its twelfth chime when the door opened and Tirdad entered followed by a young woman clad in black Chador. He helped her take off her veil which he hung on the dresser's peg. "Take off your scarf too my love." He commanded in the sweetest tone. Giggling, she obeyed. He hung the foulard over the veil on the peg, clasped her hand and together, they walked into the sitting room where his parents and daughter were watching TV. They had not heard them enter.

"Salam." The young woman said in a low droning voice. Surprised to hear a female voice, the three turned and saw a young, short and plump woman in grey pant suit, holding Tirdad's hand and staring at them with curious eyes. There was something in her aura that immediately repelled them. "Ya Allah!" Shamsi murmured.

His face as bright as the sun, Tirdad looked at the woman with loving eyes and in a voice sweeter than honey introduced: "This is my wife Nary. We got married at a notary office yesterday. And I want you to welcome her to our family with open arms."

A heavy hush fell in the room. Mohammad looked at his wife, Yasmin, the woman and his son with awestricken eyes and open mouth. No one uttered a word. Surprised and annoyed Tirdad asked: "Are you not going to congratulate us?"

Mohammad, took off his glasses, threw them on the table; faced him with a tight frown and cold, fierce eyes the flames of which burnt his hope for a celebration. Suddenly he realized the enormity of his mistake. He should have asked his parents' permission. Why didn't he? An unconscious shrug went through his shoulders. He bit his lip and stood still, like a dry stick.

In a state of devastation, Mohammad roared: "Congratulate you for getting married without a word to us? Who do you think we are? Asses on whose back you have been riding all your miserable life – shame on you man – shame on you!" Mohammad swallowed his saliva and pointing to the door ordered. "Get out of here before I throw both of you out."

Nary paled, pouted her plump lips, turned her rebuking eyes to Tirdad and murmured: "You told me I would be welcomed here?"

"Hush. Let me deal with them."

Shamsi, who knew her son well and did not want to lose him forever, turned to her husband, "Agha, please take Yasmin to the yard and let me have a word with them."

Standing up, Mohammad retorted: "I cannot stay in the same room as this bastard anyway." He turned to Yasmin and offering his hand to her murmured:

"Come girl, let's get out of here."

Yasmin ready to run away, clasped his open palm and together they trudged out of the room, leaving behind a trail of resentment.

Shamsi went to Nary, kissed her cheeks and whispered:

"Your husband should have informed us of his intention. Had we been consulted, the scene today would not have happened. After all, our only wish is to see him and Yasmin happy."

"Khanum joon, I assure you, I will try my best to make both of them happy. Tirdad's daughter is like my own. I have a son too." Nary paused to measure the reaction to the revelation, and when she saw Shamsi's smile turn into a frown she seasoned her tone with concern, raised an eyebrow and added:

"Khanum Amiri, I hope your son will be a good father to him too."

Not only she is cheap, she is audacious too, Shamsi inferred, staring at the widow with a son while in her stead could have stood a virgin with backbone and a huge Jahizieh. From the quivering of Shamsi's pinched, tightened lips Tirdad read her mind.

"Madar, one of the reasons we have married is because we each are a single parent and want our children to grow up in a warm family environment."

"Enshallah you will be able to create that environment. Now, go to explain the reason for your marriage to your daughter and apologize to your father."

He let go of his wife's hand and sauntered to the courtyard where Yasmin sitting on Mohammad's lap was staring at the dead fish. They heard his footsteps. Neither of the two had the will to pay him any attention.

In his habitual arrogance, he stood in front of them expecting acknowledgement. Neither moved; they remained as lifeless as the paving stones under their feet. The neighbour's cat which often played with the doctor appeared on the top of the wall and with his inquisitive eyes measured his playground; finding it uninviting he turned back without a mew, jumped over the tree branch he had climbed up and descended down to his more accommodating habitat.

Offended by their silence, Tirdad intensified the taunt in his eyes and in a cold, rational tone addressed his father: "I married her without your permission because she is the widow of a Martyr with a son from him. I knew you would try to dissuade me from marrying her. I have a child too. As she is a mother, I believe she will take good care of my Yasmin."

Without glancing at him, Mohammad sniffed and retorted: "Do not lie to me. Had you respected us, you would have explained the situation and like in your previous marriage, we would have understood and accepted your logic. But no, Tirdad is in command and he will do as he wishes – others do not matter. In fact no one really matters in your life except you. Isn't that so?"

"Yes. That is so. I am who I am, because I am your son."

A sharp pain went through Mohammad's heart and drained his face of colour. He fixed his cynical eyes on him and asked: "Are you blaming me for the mistakes you have been making in your life?"

"Yes. It was you and your selfishness that made my mother run away."

"Thank you son – thank you indeed for your clear perception of the incidents of our lives. Go and live with the woman you have chosen. I hope you will find happiness with her – in the face of it all, one way or another you will forget me and your mother, as we have surpassed our usefulness in the cosmic order. We procreated and educated you. Now we can be discarded like dirt."

"Father, I am not your student and do not quote Deepak Chapra to me. I am your son. Love me and accept me for who I am."

"Because I love you, I cannot allow you making mistakes after mistakes. But it is your life. Do with it as you desire and I wish you luck." Mohammad replied in a reluctant tone.

"That is all I wanted to hear from you Baba. Thank you." Tirdad murmured and knelt in front of Yasmin. Her round face long now, she was sank in her own wretchedness, dreading life with that fat, ugly woman who had stolen her mother's place. During the past, lonely years, she had lived with the hope of her parents reconciling. Now that hope was dead – as dead as the gold fish floating on Agha doctor's pond. Suddenly she began to scream and scream. Shamsi and Nary ran to the window to see what had happened.

Mohammad kissed her head and whispered into her ear: "Azizam please calm down. This is not the end of the world. We are all here for you my love."

Tirdad inched close, pulled her to himself and whispered: "Dear, please look at me. Please?"

It took a long moment before the girl turned her sad, puffy eyes to him.

"Yasmin joon, please be happy for Papa. Nary is a good and kind woman. She will take care of you better than Shamsi who is old and impatient. She has a son a little older than you and the two of you can play together and you won't be alone anymore."

Nourished by his attention, Yasmin opened her thin arms and hugged him tight. Between sobs she asked: "What about Mamman – she loves you so much Papa?"

"If she did, she wouldn't have left us, would she?"

Lost for words, the girl tore away from him, her cheeks wet with running tears. He wiped her tears with his finger, kissed her pulsating cheek and declared: "Nary will be your new Mamman."

"No. No Papa. I want my Mamman and no one else."

"Mamman is the one who left you cherie. If she had wanted you, she would have stayed, wouldn't she?"

"No, that is not true. She left us to find a job in Vienna so that we both could go and live with her there. She thought our lives were in danger here. She wanted to save us and not abandon us. That is what she told me and I believe her."

Mohammad, hunched, as though bearing the weight of the world on his shoulders, wondered at the child's presence of mind and in her defence said: "Yasmin is right. Her mother did not abandon her family. She went away to find a way to save it from harm." Tirdad gave him a vile look, turned to Yasmin and said: "Cherie, please, for my sake, give Nary a chance."

Faced with her silence, he lifted her up, stroked her curly hair, took her to the hose-tap, put her down, turned the tap on and gently washed her face, wetting her new white dress in which this morning, she had looked like a beautiful Barbie. Resigned, Mohammad went to Yasmin, took her hand and the three walked back inside where they found Nary and Shamsi setting the steaming aromatic food dish and it's accompaniments on the table. Shirin polo indeed was appropriate for the occasion.

Around the round table Nary sat on the right of her father-in-law and Yasmin on his left. The room's ambiance was uneasy. Intermittent long and awkward silences made it difficult to dine enjoyably. The only person tasting the sweetness of the rice was Tirdad.

Yasmin toyed with her food while throwing side glances at the woman on whose face was glued a faked smile.

Shamsi kept busy offering, at proper intervals, pickles, yoghurt and fresh herbs. These accompaniments are the ornaments of Persian dinner tables. They enhance the taste of various foods.

Mohammad, who so far had been tongue-tied, placed his cutlery side by side on his plate, wiped his mouth with his napkin, turned his sombre face to the new addition to his family and asked: "Khanum tell us about your life?

Nary diverted her questioning eyes to Tirdad, as though needing his permission. He smiled and turned to his father: "Nary lost her husband in a bus-explosion in Tehran and she has a son two years older than Yasmin. Ahmad lives with her. And tomorrow they will move in with me." Mohammad threw him an indignant glance and in an authentic tone admonished: "I asked Nary Khanum and not you. Let her tell us about herself."

"I have nothing to add to what my husband has just told you Agha. He knows me better than I do myself. Your son is a very intelligent man."

"Please Khanum address me as doctor Amiri."

Nary dropped her eyes and whispered: "Doctor Amiri, I meant no disrespect."

Tirdad shot his father a noxious glance, took his wife's hand from the top of the table, brought it to his lips and kissed it. She glared into Mohammad's eyes and smiled her hold over his son.

Shamsi's nostrils' began to quiver and Mohammad sniggered at his inappropriate behaviour. He would never learn! He reflected with great disappointment.

After the guests departed taking Yasmin with them, the beleaguered parents retired to their seats in front of the TV set which Mohammad turned on. They watched the screen without seeing anything or hearing a word spoken. They both, in their own way were busy evaluating the disaster that had befallen their family. From the woman's appearance, voice, gestures and the words she used, it was apparent she was without any education, grace and manners. What had their son seen in the gold digger, their bungled minds could not fathom out. Eventually they gave up speculating and relinquished any hope of him ever making the right decision. Mohammad turned the TV off and went to the window and opened it. A cold breeze rushed in. "Close the window Agha. It is cold." Mohammad took a deep breath and enjoyed it. "I am letting it stay open. I want the ominous aura that snake left in the air cleared out. She gives me the creeps. I saw evil in her eyes. I hope she will not bring us bad luck. We don't need any more misfortune beleaguering us at this stage of our lives." He turned his eyes skyward and exclaimed: "God, please put some sense in this idiot's head before he totally destroys his life. Please!" Above, instead of seeing God's glory shining through the moon, he saw grey pregnant clouds veiling it. Another current of trepidation passed though him. In desperation, he shook his head, kicked the skirting with his shoe, poked his head out of the window, and took several deep breaths. Then, he closed the window with a sharp bang and headed for his bedroom. He knew he wouldn't be able to sleep but at least he could try to divert his mind by reading his book. Shamsi went to the kitchen, took an apple from the fruit dish, sat on her chair and took out her frustration on the fruit. Her bites were so savage that she almost injured the tip of her finger. She never went to bed before eating an apple. An apple a day, keeps the doctor away, she often sang but, not tonight.

The next day, Shamsi was washing the breakfast dishes and gazing at the young leaves of the two acacias that graced their pavement, when a small van parked in front of her window obscuring part of her view. Its door opened and a tall, slender, elderly man with smooth grey hair jumped out, climbed the stairs to Tirdad's apartment and pressed the intercom's button. A few minutes later Nary in jeans and a T-shirt appeared at the door, conversed with the stranger, left the door wide open and then disappeared inside. The man hurried down; exchanged a few words with the driver who had climbed down the van and had opened its trunk. The men lifted out three shabby suitcases and a few carbon boxes which they carried up the stairs to the flat. The driver returned to his vehicle but not the tall man. Shamsi remained spying until half an hour later when the tall man came out, closed the door, and dashed down the stairs and into the van. She heard the engine start. The van drove away. The branches became visible again. But Shamsi took no more joy in their beauty. The van had stolen her peace of mind. What was delivered was her bride's Jahizieh. She shook her head in remorse. For a moment she saw Rose in her beautiful home. She released a sigh, untied her apron, threw it on the kitchen chair and went to the sitting room where Mohammad was reading his newspaper.

"Khanum's Jahizieh has arrived – a lorry full of furniture, Tabriz carpets and a Westinghouse fridge/freezer."

Mohammad, lowered his paper, threw her an amused glance from above the rim of his reading glass and grinned.

"Why are you grinning at me like that? A van just delivered her stuff: a few shabby suitcases and couple of carbon boxes."

"Good. At least we do not have to clothe her."

"It will get to that too."

"Since when have you become a fortune teller Khanum?"

"Since Agha, you became a stupid ass."

Having got used to her bitter tongue, Mohammad pushed his glass frame up by creasing his nose and continued reading the news: twenty of the most active members of Mujahedin had been captured and executed without a trial. The information made him shiver. Soon it will be the turn of the Tudehs, he thought, throwing the paper onto the floor and rising to go to attend to his green patch. He needed a mental stimulator and that he received from his smiling herbs. He loved looking at them, admiring their innocent beauty and appreciating their freshness and the altruistic service they rendered him. Rousseau was right in believing man could find happiness only when existing within nature. How lovely it would have been, if one was able to tear away from social chains, run to a jungle and live with beasts that in fact are friendlier than humans. They only attack when their survival is threatened. Man attacks to preserve self- interest.

From the top floor he could hear movements of furniture and the sound of steps. Well, she must be rearranging the rooms to accommodate her stuff. He thought, shrugging his shoulders. However hard he tried to be fair to the woman; he could not ignore her repellent air. He particularly disliked her cold, conniving eyes that barred any peep into her soul. Only menacing energy emanated from her. He was so uncomfortable in her presence that he was sure the negativism in her would bring the family some sort of disaster. Then regretting his stupidity, he would bite his lip for being superstitious; shrug off the presentiments as prejudice against a choice badly made and feel guilty for hours.

Once settled in her new home Nary opened its door to her family and friends throwing her weight around and snubbing the lesser souls. Her first victim was Yasmin. Far from being a kind and caring step mother, she proved to be inconsiderate and demanding. As there were only two bedrooms, Yasmin had to share hers and her toys with Ahmad – and when they quarrelled over something that belonged to her and he wanted, she had to let him have it or else face ugly verbal and occasionally physical abuse. Once the girl complained to her father, Nary denied her story and he took her word for it and scolded her for lying to him. That hurt more than Nary's pinches and slaps. Alone and unloved, she began to eat out her heart, lose more weight and catch different childhood diseases that had she been vaccinated or properly taken care of would have been avoided. She was so scared of Nary that she did not dare mention anything even to her grandparents. But they were no fools. Shamsi had seen the pinch-marks on her arm and the bruises on different part of her milky skin. She had asked what had caused the bruises and the girl had fibbed. Then, one day, unable to bear seeing her so down, she decided to confront Tirdad who had come to borrow some eggs. They were both in the kitchen. She had already put a box of eggs on the table and was peeling potatoes without looking at him.

"Madar, why are you so grim today?"

"I want to talk to you about Yasmin." She replied raising her eyes to him.

"What is it now?"

"She either moves here, or else you have to pay us rent for your apartment."

"Pay you rent?"

"Yes, rent."

"With what? You know I am unemployed, I can hardly afford to feed my family let alone pay you rent."

Shamsi threw the peeler on the table, gave him a long and meaningful look and asked: "Whose fault is it that you are unemployed?" He tightened his facial muscles and stared at her with detestation. She grimaced and waving her index finger at him, said: "Had you been more careful with your behaviour, none of the members of the Cleansing Committee at your office would have wised up to your love of Vodka. Only an ass would go to office stinking of alcohol, in a country where it is prohibited. Besides, I don't care whether you can feed your family or not. My concern is for Yasmin. She either moves down, here with us or rent."

His eyes bulging out, he clenched his fist, banged the kitchen table, swept the egg container off its surface and ran out of the apartment shouting profanities.

In the evening Nary brought Yasmin's suitcase down with a smile. Finally she had gotten rid of the girl.

Chirping like a bird just out of a cage, Yasmin occupied her own room and decorated it with the toys she had been allowed to bring down. After a few weeks, colour returned to her cheeks and she found joy in waking up.

Dawns turned into dusks, seasons changed, years ended and the sun rose as regularly as ever regardless of the nation's struggle to adapt to the sweeping changes that had affected everyone's life – one way or other.

Besides the war with Iraq, there was an intensified power struggle within the factions. Assassinations, riots and executions haunted the nation and the new Regime fought its adversaries with the vengeance of the Greek Gods. At the same time a Russian master spy defected to the West with a complete list of communist spies and activists in Iran.

The list was delivered to the Iranian Ambassador in London.

It was a gloomy Thursday evening. There were no stars and no moon to brighten the sky – only thick, black clouds hovered above. There were very few cars on the roads. Most restaurants were closed, night clubs and cinemas burnt down and revolutionary vigilantes guarded the cross roads. Randomly they stopped cars to check for arms or alcohol. Occasionally, those who dared the car-checks, ventured to have dinner at a friend's house. And these dinners were simple as the supermarket shelves were empty, domestic help vanished and alcohol homemade. However, prevalent was the cultivation of hemp and use of hashish and opium.

Tirdad and Nary were preparing to leave for dinner at a cousin's house, when a minivan crept close to their building and came to a halt, away from the bright street lamp. Three men, in khaki uniform, left the vehicle, their elongated shadows preceding them as they unobtrusively walked the short distance to the duplex. A single bulb coerced by a chilly autumn breeze lit its entrance. They climbed the stairs and stood by the door. One of them rang the bell.

"Who the hell could it be?" Asked the anxiety-ridden Tirdad already informed of the Russian's defection. Nary looked up at him and replied: "Probably Yasmin come to be spoilt by you." She put her lipstick down on her dressing table and reluctantly rose to go and open the door. On her way, to keep the girl waiting, she went to the toilet, lingered on aimlessly, pulled the flush so that he would think she had relieved herself and then aiming to confront the girl, went to the door, unlocked and opened it to three armed Pasdars who stared at her with dark, malicious eyes. Colour drained from her face. She couldn't open her mouth to ask what they wanted. Her paralysis increased the men's sense of power and their eyes began to mock her. She dropped her head and heard one of them ask: "Is this Amiri residence?" The man's thick, rigid voice cut her hope of a mistaken address. They had come for him. She felt sick.

"There are three doctor Amiris in this family. Which one are you after Agha?"

"Tirdad Amiri." The senior officer, who had been assessing her with lusty eyes, replied. He was tall, handsome and very much in command.

Terrified, Nary sensed the chill of cold sweat under her arms.

"Yes, he is here and what is your business with him? I am his wife." She replied trying to maintain a semblance of calm.

At that exact moment, Tirdad having heard a strange male voice appeared from behind her. A look at the men's faces and the colt case hanging from their belts was enough to make him tremble. His turn had arrived. Unconsciously he took Nary's arm and hung on to it, as though she could protect him from his fate. The tall man threw a quick glance at her and then turned his eyes to Tirdad and in a low voice said: "You know why we are here so do not cause any unnecessary problems for your wife." He turned to Nary. Their eyes met and she shivered. He turned to Tirdad: "Come and let's go."

Conscious of the stranger's interest in her, Nary deepened her frown and in a voice that would melt the hardest hearts asked: "Good Brother, where are you taking my husband? He is a revolutionary like yourselves and a good Muslim."

"Khanum, do not worry, we are taking him for questioning. If he is innocent, he will be back tomorrow."

She stared at him with disbelief and fell silent. A shadow of a smile passed over his well-shaped lips. He turned to one of his juniors and commanded: "Put the cuffs on him." Tirdad turned to Nary, hugged her with all the love in him and murmured: "I love you." Then releasing her, he turned to the Commandant, "can I ask you a favour Brother?" The commandant smirked, turned his eyes on Nary and replied: "For the sake of your wife, whose life you have selfishly jeopardised, yes you may."

"Please do not handcuff me. I will walk down with you. I do not want to frighten my parents. They live downstairs and might see you taking me away. If my father sees me handcuffed he will have a heart attack." The three Pasdars laughed at their fallen peacock. The Commander narrowed his large black eyes, threw him a humiliating glance and in a mocking tone said: "Comrade Amiri, you should have thought about your loved ones before deciding to become a traitor to your country."

Then he turned to Nary. "Khanum my name is Reza Ahmadi. I shall call you tomorrow morning with what news I can gather about the fate of 'this' doctor Amiri."

The disdain in his tone turned Tirdad's fear into hatred for the men in his sight and what they represented. He clenched his fingers so tight that his nails stung his skin. Yet he could do nothing; say nothing except follow their orders.

Nary felt his anger and his fears. She pressed his arm with sympathy and then looked into Pasdar Ahmadi's notorious eyes. They were saying something to her, but she couldn't figure out what it was. His approach to her was civilized and in a way flattering to the wife of a captured communist traitor. The thought of Tirdad being jailed sent another shiver to her numbed body. This meant no bread winner – no bread winner! She swallowed her rising anxiety, maintained her eyes on her husband's captor and replied:

"Thank you Brother, I shall wait for your call, enshallah conveying good news."

Tirdad clutched her hand as though his survival depended on her protection. She turned her eyes to him and suddenly saw a pathetic, defeated, balding man, not at all the one she had fallen in love with years, no, decades ago – when she had needed a decent husband. What a mistake! She thought with a sigh of regret. Pitying her situation, her mind reverted back to the day she had met him – her new handsome boss. With an impressive pedigree, elegant clothes and charming smiles she had thought of him as a perfect candidate for a widow with an orphaned son. To catch him she had monitored his office hours and adjusted hers to his. She had served him tea, the way he liked: with a touch of cardamom brought from home. She had stayed as late as he, knowing he would offer to give her a ride and then eventually in the car, parked in a dark corner of a side street, she had managed to seduce him. There was nothing she wouldn't have done to hook him. It felt so good to play all those games with him. The sex games had been the most enjoyable: one day hot and obliging and another, aloof and disinterested making him beg like a mendicant. His pleas were boosters to her ego. And she would never forget the look on his parents' face when he had introduced her to them. How much she had admired him when he had stood by her, against their demands and – look at him now. Then, becoming Mrs Amiri had seemed a triumph against the accident of birth – born poor – and, now, what? Things had changed overnight. Those with pedigree were sent to the pit of the abyss and in their stead had bloomed a new generation of people with courage and conviction and she needed one of them and not this pathetic man holding to her for security. Slowly she turned her dreamy eyes to Pasdar Ahmadi. He caught them and held them until he read her mind. A shadow of smile flickered over his face. She saw it. It delighted her.

The men and their detainee walked out of the apartment in as normal a manner as Shamsi spying on them could observe. Fortunately from where she was looking, she could not see the van into which her son was unceremoniously shoved.

Inside the vehicle, Ahmadi's assistant handcuffed Tirdad and then pulled out a long white band from the pocket of his parka coat and placed it on his knees. He wrapped his left arm around Tirdad's neck, pulled his head back. With his right hand he picked up the blindfold, passed it over his eyes and using both hands tightly tied it behind his head. For a second or two the prisoner wobbled here and there, as though trying to find a niche in the darkness. "Please tell me where you are taking me to?" He heard himself beg, in a voice not his.

"Comrade Amiri, we are taking you to where your partners in command are." Reza's voice was harsh but his blow to his captive's stomach harsher. Bent with pain, Tirdad felt the warmth of urine damping his skin. In agony, he sat up, locked his legs together and pushed them against the back of the car seat so the urine couldn't leak down and cause him embarrassment.

At the notorious prison, in accordance with his high rank, he was confined into a solitary cell with a mattress on its floor, a pitcher of water, a urine pan and nothing else but darkness. It had no air and stank of ammonia. From then on, he inhaled fresh air and saw light when led to the investigation room where masked men interrogated and tortured him. Unconscious, like the carcass of a cow, he was pulled back and discarded on his mattress until he opened his eyes to more darkness and pain.

Three days had passed without any news from Ahmadi. Nary was in the kitchen preparing dinner for her son and parents who had moved in. Her mood dour, she was thinking bad thoughts: had she mistaken her assumption of Ahmadi's interest in her? Was she going to become a widow again? Was she doomed to rely on her parents support for the rest of her life? Was there no light at the end of the tunnel? Thoughts and thoughts, questions and questions without any comforting answers were making her giddy when the shrill sound of the phone jolted her out of her skin and the spatula from her hand. She picked up the kitchen phone and into it whispered a lifeless 'hallo.'

"May I speak with Mrs Amiri please?"

"You are speaking to her, Brother Ahmadi." Crazed like a teenager, she could hear her own heart beats. "Have you any news of my husband?" She asked in a voice with a mere tinge of concern.

"Yes Khanum. He is at Evin being interrogated and unfortunately placed in a solitary cell without permission to have visitors. However, I might be able to waive that rule – for your sake – such beautiful young lady."

She smiled.

"Thank you Brother and I hope I will be able to repay your kindness one day."

"No thanks are expected. I shall call you soon."

"I hope God grants you the wishes of your heart, Brother Ahmadi."

"Thank you Khanum."

"God be with you Brother." She said before putting the receiver down. Then she heard her step-father yell.

"Who is it Nary?"

"It was the man who took Tirdad away. Tirdad is at Evin confined to a solitary cell." She replied picking up the spatula.

Nary's mother, more interested in her book than her daughter's problems, reluctantly folded the page she was reading, closed and put the volume down. Then, in a derogatory tone remarked: "I assume it means several years of imprisonment. What luck we have had with your choices of husbands?"

Surprised at his wife's unsavoury comment, Agha Azizi, the same tall man who had delivered her Jahizieh, frowned and shook his head in disgust. He was a kind and considerate man. In his youth he had been considered handsome. But the struggles to feed several mouths and tolerate a domineering wife had left their marks on his tanned face and made him look like an old man at the age of sixty. He genuinely liked Tirdad, not only because he had taken two demanding loads off his shoulders but he had also found him pleasant and generous.

In the kitchen, Nary threw the spatula with which she was dishing out the rice, in the pot, hastened to the sitting room, faced her mother, and brandishing her index finger at her said: "You Khanum are the biggest hypocrite in the world. It was you who encouraged me to pursue both of the men in my life. Now, you dare to chastise me for my choices?" She smirked, narrowed her angry eyes and continued: "that really is bizarre. Can't you at least appreciate the fact that I have managed to upgrade your social standing by acquiring an old and respectable identity, which you, mother dear, have been boasting about since the day I married Tirdad – Han?" She took a breath. "Besides, what have my brothers done for you? One is an alcoholic and the other a drug addict. What have you to say to that dear mother?" Her frown intact, she turned to her step-father and pointing at him with her finger said: "and this Agha, out of the goodness of his heart, is supporting them and you too. Now between the two of us, who has been the luckiest? Who dear mother – who?"

"Shut up you dull bitch and never talk to me like this again."

"Stop this nonsense please." shouted Azizi, now in the kitchen dishing out the rice. Neither woman paid him any attention. They continued their verbal squabble until food was brought to the table by the frustrated man whom they treated more like a pawn than anything else.

Here, the house rule was to eat without tension; otherwise food would cause indigestion and foul gas. Once settled around the table, the sight and aroma of the rice turned their anger into appetite. Calm returned and they ate in peace.

Down below, Shamsi and Mohammad aimlessly fretted about Tirdad's long absence. Not daring to question Nary, they, in turn, sat in the kitchen and through its window monitored her landing. Where was he? Why had he not called? What on earth had happened to him? What? The fear inside them was craving to come out in screams. But it couldn't. It couldn't be heard by Yasmin who was told Papa had gone on a pilgrimage to Mashahd. Even the atheist Mohammad had gone on his knees begging God for his son's life.

Dinner finished, Azizi decided to go to the Amiri's and give them the bad news. If he was them, the anxiety would be killing him. It would be better for them to know he is at least alive, though imprisoned. Therefore, having cleared the table, without a word to the women, like a thief, he tiptoed to the door, opened it, stepped out and noiselessly closed it behind him. He knew Nary was intending to prolong the parents' torment. It was her revenge. Revenge against what harm, only God knew. She was more selfish and unforgiving than her mother. He shook his head to get her out of his mind, inhaled a deep breath and pushed the bell button.

Yasmin, watching TV heard the sound. The other two had become almost deaf. Hoping that it was her father, she flew and opened it with a broad smile.

"Salam, Yasmin joon." Azizi said, lifting the girl up and swinging her in the air. He gave her a big kiss, put her down, held her hand and together they walked into the sitting room where he offered his Salam. The two turned to face him. The expression on his countenance took their breaths away, churned their stomachs and hastened their heartbeats. They rose in his respect; welcomed him with lifeless hand- shakes and invited him to sit down. Doctor Amiri turned the TV off and Shamsi asked if he would like something to eat or drink.

"No Khanum joon. I have just had dinner. I apologize for disturbing you at this hour, but I need to have a private word with doctor Amiri." He said politely, his apologetic eyes on Shamsi. Affronted by the request and distraught by the expression on the man's face, Shamsi took Yasmin's hand and pulling the girl behind her, walked to the kitchen from where listening was facile.

"Agha Azizi you have bad news for us?" Mohammad asked in a shaking voice.

"It is about Tirdad, Sir."

"They have taken him?"

"Yes Agha, yes." Azizi replied, shaking his head in remorse.

"I knew this would happen. I knew it. But he never listened to anyone." Mohammad whispered, tapping his rigid legs. Suffocating by sorrow, he closed his eyes to push back his tears.

"One of the men who took him, called Nary tonight. He is at Evin in a solitary cell. However, the man, unusually nice for a Pasdar, promised her, he would try to twist some rules so that he could receive visitors."

"Do you know what being in a solitary cell means?" Mohammad asked his moist eyes glowing with pain. "It means torture, and execution."

"Let us not conclude that yet Agha doctor. Let us pray for his release. You never know what happens tomorrow."

"Pray to whom my man?" Mohammad asked staring through him at the darkness in which his son was entombed. "If there was a God, he would have never allowed such barbarism to take place in his domain, and in his name!"

"Doctor joon there is a God and he will listen to your prayers. Tirdad is a good man and I cannot believe any harm will befall him." Whispered Azizi, his moist eyes fixed on Mohammad who was shaking his head in doubt.

"I must go now." He rose. "As soon as Nary hears anything new, either she or I will let you know."

"Thank you Agha Azizi." Mohammad said rising to escort him out. There was such sadness in his voice that would have dissolved the hardest block of ice. Mohammad put his unsteady arm around Azizi's shoulder and guiding him to the door whispered: "Thank you again. It was very considerate of you to come down and inform us. Thank you."

In the kitchen Shamsi stood in a state of shock. When she heard the closing of the front door, she turned to Yasmin munching at an apple and moaned: "They have taken Papa to Evin."

Yasmin swallowed her apple and asked: "Where is Evin, Shamsi joon?"

Suddenly wised up to her folly, she responded in as normal a tone as she could muster: "It is a village on the west of Teheran where there are hundreds of mulberry trees."

"Good. He loves mulberries. He will be able to eat them when they ripen. When would that be Shamsi joon?" Yasmin took another bite from her apple. It was sweet and juicy.

"It will be next summer."

"That long?" She replied with her mouth full.

"Yes azizam, but he will be back by then and we can all go to Evin village, sit in a cafe' and order as much mulberries as we desire." Yasmin discarded the stem of the apple in the nearby bin.

"That sounds good, Shamsi joon."

Shamsi sniffed. Yasmin saw the shine of tears in her eyes. Surprised, she asked: "Why are you crying Shamsi joon?"

"I just miss your father."

"But you have no cause to be worried about him."

"No you are right my love." Shamsi stood up. "Agha Azizi has gone – let's join grandpapa and watch our program – shall we love?" The little girl, her long curly hair waving in the air, ran to the sitting room and nestled besides her heaving, frowning grandfather whose colour had turned grey and his hand was pressing his chest's left side to subdue the sharp pains that were taking his breath away.

An hour later an ambulance took Mohammad and Agha Azizi to the nearby Mehr hospital. There, by the order of his good friend, Dr Mehran, he was rushed to the intensive care unit.

Ever since 1980, to punish the regime for taking the American hostages, the West had imposed various sanctions on Iran. Thus pharmaceutical companies could not deal with Iran. This created such a shortage of medicine that hospitalized patients had to procure their own medicine which meant someone had to go and purchase it from a pharmacy most of whose shelves were gathering dust. However, the street vendors at Topkhane Square had plenty. Iran had become the Western pharmaceutical companies' dumping ground for their products with expired due dates, sold to smugglers by their unscrupulous agents operating in Turkey. Thus the life and death of patients was indeed in the hands of the Almighty.

Mohammad having undergone a bypass returned home. This disappointed Nary. Had he died, his property would have gone to his sons.

In Paris Kobra celebrated Mohammad's recovery and almost guessed what had caused it. On the one occasion, before Tirdad's capture, that she had returned to Iran for her summer vacation she had met Nary and was repelled by her notorious aura and the extent she had influenced her brother in his behaviour towards her and their parents. He no longer pampered her the way he used to, nor did he visit his old and ailing parents as often as he ought. She noticed how disinterested he had become in his own daughter Yasmin and how his reluctance to parent her had affected the once twittering and smiling little girl. It was then that she decided to consult with Mohammad. She had to do it without her mother being around. So she waited until Mohammad invited her to accompany him to the nearby park where he took his afternoon walks.

It was five o'clock when they reached the expansive park with a huge well-trimmed lawn, paved walkways, tall trees and flowerbeds tastefully cultivated by annuals in full bloom. Mohammad took Kobra's arm and looking at her round and full face commented:

"I think there is something in your mind that is bothering you dear?"

"Yes. But how do you know that, Baba joon?" She asked amazed by his acute perception.

"If I didn't know my own daughter, who would I know?" He replied, gently squeezing her thick arm with fondness. Savouring his affection with delight, she smiled. The only person who had loved her unconditionally was this frail and kind man. She quickly stole a kiss from his pale, hollow cheek and tightened her grip of his arm. She took great joy in feeling his warmth. It injected life into her and nourished her self-confidence.

"Baba we have to get Yasmin out of here and to her mother. The poor child is withering away. She is victimized by her brainless senseless father, and, that bitch upstairs."

"I agree with you. But how on earth can we get a visa for her without her father's consent."

"We can go to the French embassy with you pretending to be her father. Now-a-days with having temporary wives legal, many men your age have young children."

140

"What if we are caught?"

"Then we tell them the truth."

Mohammad contemplated for a while and then said: "Why don't we tell them the truth right from the beginning?"

"French are adamant to bend rules. Let's try our plan and hope they are so busy that they won't dig too deep."

"OK. We stick with your plan."

"Has she got a valid passport?"

"Fortunately she has, but you must not utter a word to your mother until we return from the embassy."

They found an empty bench under an old mulberry tree facing the park's artificial lake on which a group of ducks were peacefully gliding. The afternoon air was cool, and the sun unusually benevolent. Ladies in their linen hejabs, solo or in groups were taking their crisp walks; children were excitedly mingling in their playground while their parents watched over them. At a corner, an ice-cream vendor was making a fortune. From afar two conspicuous, fat women in black chadors were monitoring the behaviour of the others. They belonged to a Government body called Khaharan-e-Zainab, (Zainab's Sisters) whose responsibility it was to control women, make sure they dressed in proper Hejab, wore no makeup and behaved in virtuous manner. Disobedience to Islamic mores merited prescribed punishments: fines, imprisonment, or one hundred lashes. One of the women saw them sit side by side. She hurried to their bench and asked: "Agha, who is this young woman with you?"

"She is my daughter."

"Tell her to pull her scarf down. Too much hair is showing."

"Chashm Khanum." Mohammad replied, in a subdued tone. In spite of his detestation of the intruder, he did not want to spoil the afternoon by getting into a verbal entanglement with her.

Grinning, Kobra pulled her scarf down.

The woman gave her a long cold glare, tightened her grip of the edge of her chador that was hiding half of her face, and wobbling her big bottom, returned to her partner who from a distance was watching her.

Early the next morning sitting around the kitchen table for breakfast Mohammad turned his scheming eyes to Kobra, "have you ever been to Golestan Palace?" Kobra reading his mind responded: "No Baba. But I would really love to visit this magnificent edifice." Mohammad smiled and turned to Yasmin. "Would you like to visit the palace in which your ancestors were borne my little princess?" "Yes Baba. Yes." Yasmin responded clapping her hands with enthusiasm.

Certain that she would refuse, Mohammad turned to Shamsi and asked: "Khanum would you come too?"

"No Agha. I have no love for my ancestors. They left us nothing but their diseases. I have no wish to remember any of them. You go and after your visit have lunch at the bazaar. There are several Kebab houses there. This will spare me preparing food for you." Mohammad smiled and winked at Kobra.

Within an hour a telephone taxi arrived and took the three to the French Embassy. During the drive Kobra took Yasmin's hand, squeezed it with care and said: "Yasmin joon, we are not going to the Palace. Instead we are going to the French Embassy to see if we can get you a visa so that I can take you to your mummy." At first Yasmin didn't understand the implication of the intention, and then suddenly she realised what it meant. Her eyes shining like a pair of aquamarines she wrapped her arms around Kobra's neck and took couple of hearty kisses from her cheeks.

Kobra patted her back and said: "You have to promise not utter a word to anyone except Shamsi. If Nary or Papa ever find out about our plan they will not allow you to leave the country." She untangled Yasmin's hands from around her neck and looked deep into her eyes: "So you must keep this a secret – can you?"

"Yes, yes aunty." Yasmin shouted nodding her head.

At the consulate, the consul attending to Yasmin's visa asked for Mohammad's birth certificate.

Lips tight, heart thumping, Mohammad gave it to him and scared of a betraying movement stood still. The consul opened the booklet, glanced at the photo on the first page, looked up at him, then at Yasmin and Kobra, both with a feigned smile glued on their rigid faces. Assuming that Kobra was Mohammad's wife he smiled at the old man's luck, returned his birth certificate without checking the other pages of the document and asked them to take a seat.

An hour later, Yasmin's visa was granted.

To celebrate the conquest Mohammad took them to a French restaurant, surprisingly enough still open. Most chic restaurants were either burnt down or closed and shuttered.

Back at home, Kobra telephoned Jill whose joy was beyond comprehension. Kobra could imagine from her trembling voice the tears of happiness rolling down her rosy plump cheeks. Yasmin talked to her Mammon and again was made to promise not utter a word to her father about her travel. The girl, extremely wise for her age of eight, kept her promise and continued to act as though nothing had changed in her life. However she made her visits to the upstairs apartment more frequent because in her heart she knew that these were the last days of her being with her father.

It was another Friday lunch at the senior Amiri's and the whole family had just had their meal and were taking tea and conversing in their usual scathing manner when Yasmin went to her room and returned with a photo of her Papa smiling at her Mammon and holding her in his arms. Handing the photo and a pen to him she requested: "Papa could you please sign this for me?"

Kobra's sharp eyes did not miss the envy that clouded Nary's countenance and the turn of her eyes to Ahmad who was devouring the biscuits one after another. He had become obese. Tirdad, surprised and flattered by Yasmin's request took the photo, put it on the table and wrote: 'For my lovely Yasmin with love.' He looked up at her and inattentive to the melancholy glow of her eyes smiled. "You make me feel like a celebrity cherie." He teased throwing the pen on the table.

"You will always be a celebrity for me, Papa – you are my father and I am very proud of you."

Her jealousy flared up, Nary tightened her thin brows, looked at Yasmin with hostile eyes and reproached: "Don't monopolise him Yasmin. He is also Ahmad's father."

Mohammad, nodded in negation, threw Nary a reprimanding glance and objected: "No Khanum, he is not Ahmad's father. He is his stepfather."

"Baba, Ahmad is also my son."

"Nary Khanum is a very lucky woman to have such devoted husband." Shamsi remarked, coming out of the kitchen from where she had heard everything.

"My brother is a very kind man. I never forget how, when I was a child, he pampered me and made me feel good. That is what he is doing now for Ahmad," Kobra remarked hoping to change the subject.

Suddenly Nary sat up in her chair, put her nose up in the air, fixed her disdainful eyes on Kobra and said: "My husband is an angel. He was kind to you out of pity – pity for an abandoned child and not out of love. He never loved you. In fact he always hated you. Only yesterday he told me that if we have a daughter, he is going to name her 'Kobra', so that everyone would know there are two Kobra's in this family: one who has Amiri blood running in her veins and one who hasn't."

A heavy, chilly hush fell in the room making everyone except Tirdad and his wife shiver.

Shamsi glared at Tirdad with enraged eyes: "Is this true?" She asked capable of cutting his head off there and then.

"Yes mother. Why not – Kobra is a nice, unusual name. Besides it was you who did not permit father to adopt her. If he had, she would have become an Amiri, with or without our blood running in her veins. And then she wouldn't have been filled with all the complexes she is harbouring and the resentments she is displacing on me and my wife."

"Shame on you man." Mohammad shouted rising to leave the room. He could not bear to look at that conniving bitch whose influence had turned his son into a despicable monster.

Kobra, as cold and as solid as ice turned to her mother: "Madar, please order these brutes to leave now and not return while I am still here."

"Do not worry, we won't return to this place while a shit like you defiles its space." Tirdad snapped, got hold of his wife's hand and pulling her up said: "Let's go Azizam?"

"You should be ashamed of yourself. Dirt is the woman you have married." Shamsi shouted, her eyes chasing them to the door.

Two days before Kobra and Yasmin were to depart, the girl caught measles. To everyone's distress Kobra had to leave without her. The girl's agony gave her a very high fever. Before leaving, Kobra sat on her bed, took her tiny hand, stroked it affectionately, consoled her with love and promised to return soon to take her to Paris. Yasmin just looked at her, too disillusioned to believe and too sick to care.

Days past without any news from Tirdad, then one day the phone rang.

Shamsi picked it up and whispered a weary 'hallo'.

"Mother, I want to come down and apologize to all of you for my misbehaviour."

"It is too late. The person from whom you should be begging forgiveness left ten days ago. What you said was heartless and totally unnecessary even if you choose to call your daughter 'Kobra.' I think you are going insane. Why cannot you tell your wife to shut up when she comes out with such outrageous statements? Have you no pride in your family?"

"Can I come down? We can talk there."

"Is she there?"

"Yes."

"That is why you do not dare to talk on the phone. Isn't that so?"

"I am coming down right now." Tirdad dropped the receiver on its cradle and ran down the stairs and entered through the door that had been opened for him. He saw his mother, frail and pale, in her house-dress hiding behind the door so that no outsider could see her void of hejab.

"Go, kneel by your father and ask his pardon. He is very upset with you."

"Why mother. You all have to learn to respect my wife too."

"Before expecting this from us, you teach her how to act like a lady."

"All mother-in-laws hate their daughter-in-laws. You hate Rose too."

"Rose is a lady. I disliked her because she took your brother away from his family."

"Have you ever asked yourself why my brother preferred to be in her family than ours?"

"Enough. Have you come to reconcile or start a new quarrel?"

"Why do you always twist the truth mother?" He asked tightening his brows. "The reality is that he found refuge in her family because they loved and respected him. If you do the same to my wife, she will be another daughter to you." He paused and challenged her with his taxing eyes.

"Respect is earned – it is not a privilege."

"Do not become a philosopher mother. You know nothing about human relationships. If you did, you would have never abandoned us."

She turned her back to him and walked into the sitting room where Mohammad, having heard everything, pretended to be immersed in his reading of the morning paper.

Tirdad followed her, offered his father a Salam and sat beside him.

"Baba I have come to apologize."

The old man let go of his paper. It fell on his lap and slipped down over his bent knees on to the floor with a hissing noise. He straightened up, fixed his solemn eyes on him and remained mute.

"Baba I said I have come to apologise."

"I heard you the first time. Why is that? You need money?"

Tirdad dropped his head like a naughty boy in need of redemption.

"If you want our forgiveness pick up the phone and apologize to your sister. You know how sensitive she is about her birth – and you know well that everyone in this family, including yourself, has always treated her as an equal. Why did you say what you said? Did you not think that your words would hurt her deeply?"

"I admit what I said was thoughtless. I am sorry – but she is also arrogant and cold towards my wife. By the way where is Yasmin?"

"Yasmin is sick in bed."

"What's wrong with her?"

"She has measles."

"Oh! Why did not you tell me?"

"Did you ever enquire about her wellbeing?"

In silence he rose and went to her room. "Papa" she exclaimed opening her arms. Leaning her head on his chest she said: "Papa I missed you. Why do you not come and see me? Do you not love me anymore? Have I done something wrong? Have I been naughty? If I have, please forgive me. I love you Papa joon."

Gently patting her back he replied:

"Hush love and do not say these things. Of course I love you. It is that I am so busy these days; sometimes I don't even have time to have lunch. You know that I have a lot of sensitive political responsibilities and one day you will be proud of me." She untangled herself from his fold, looked into his tired eyes with adoration and said: "Papa you are always important to me and I am very proud of you. I just wish you saw me more often. I miss you and Mammon so much Papa. Sometimes I feel I am worse than an orphan."

"Hush girl, you are not an orphan. In fact you have two mothers." He felt the shiver that ran down Yasmin's spine. "Darling, very soon, when these black cockroaches are sent to hell; I will have all the time in the world for you and the rest of my family."

"When will that be Papa?"

"Soon – very soon."

"I shall pray for that day Papa."

"That will be very kind of you Azizam. Now I must go."

Yasmin put her arms around his neck again and hugged him as tight as she could, as though if she let go of him, he would be lost to her forever.

And he was.

Suddenly Tirdad remembered why he had come to apologise. He kissed Yasmin, unfolded her grips, gave her his handkerchief to dry her eyes, tucked her in bed and returned to the sitting room.

"Baba joon, can I borrow two thousand from you?"

"If I lend you two thousand Shamsi and I will have to go hungry until the end of the month."

"We have nothing in our fridge." He said turning to his mother, his eyes pleading.

Shamsi, who would rather die than see him desperate, hurried to her bedroom, took out her purse from the wardrobe, extracted her last notes from its torn pocket, ran back and handed the rials to him. "This is all I have."

Tirdad grabbed the notes, pushed them into his pocket: "I must run to the grocery store and buy what Nary wants."

"Nary, Nary!" Mohammad exclaimed, shaking his head in disgust.

Three uneventful months past and then Tirdad was taken to Evin.

It was on a Tuesday evening, a week after Tirdad's imprisonment, when Nary having given up any hope of ever setting eyes on Ahmadi again, received a call from him telling her that he had managed to bend the rules so that her husband could see his family members on Wednesdays. Visitors had to present their birth certificates at the gate of the prison. Tomorrow, to make sure all went smoothly at the gate he would be waiting there for her, sharp at four pm. Since it was the first visit, it would be better if Amiri's parents did not accompany her.

Revived by hope of a bright future, Nary headed down the stairs, rang the bell and waited. A couple of minutes later, a convalescing Yasmin opened the door.

Startled by the girl's pallor and loss of weight, she asked: "Are you sick?"

"I am recovering from measles."

Nary pinched her round nose, distanced herself from her as though she was a leper and asked: "Where is Shamsi?"

"She is in the courtyard. Do you want me to go and get her for you?"

"No, not really, just tell her that Tirdad can have visitors on Wednesdays, starting from next week and not tomorrow. The first visit is only for the spouse of the inmate."

"Is my father in the hospital Nary joon?"

"No he is in jail. Didn't you know?"

"In jail?"

"Yes. In jail?"

"Why is he in jail?" Yasmin asked her eyes wide with apprehension.

"Ask him when you see him next. I have to go now. We have to thank God they have not executed him."

"What does that mean Nary joon?"

"It means they didn't shoot him."

Transfixed to the floor, the phrase 'shoot him' rang in Yasmin's ears, making her deaf and dizzy. Her frightened eyes followed Nary running up the stairs to her apartment. Suddenly something snapped in her head and she began to scream and scream.

"What is wrong Yasmin?" Mohammad called out, jumping off the sofa.

Screaming and screaming, she ran into the sitting room and collided with him coming to her. Without looking up at him she began hitting him with her clenched fists and shouting: "Why did you not tell me Papa is in jail, why? Why? "

Mohammad gently seized her hands and asked: "Who told you this?" He brought her hands down and let them go.

Yasmin dropped on the couch and fixed her desperate eyes on him. "Nary. Who else?" She moaned.

"That heartless bitch!" Mohammad shouted as though hoping she would hear and sat by the girl. He put his arms around her fragile frame, pressed her to his heart and whispered into her ears: "You are right, you are right my love; we should have told you. We did not, because you were convalescing and bad news slows recovery. Also we hoped he would be released soon. We are still hoping. Papa is a good man. But you know child, during revolutions even good men are taken for questioning. So let us pray for his early release. Shall we ma petite?"

Yasmin nodded, sat straight, joint her palms in prayer form, closed her wet eyes and began to whisper the catholic prayer her mother had taught her.

Shamsi carrying a basketful of mint, climbed up the stairs, entered the room and seeing Yasmin praying jokingly asked: "What are you requesting from God, now, my dear?"

"Yasmin was just told about her father."

"No." Shamsi exclaimed putting her basket on the nearby table. She sat by the girl and hugged her tight.

Mohammad waited for a few minutes and then, tapping his wife on the back suggested: "Khanum a piece of your orange cake would please Yasmin enormously."

Yasmin pulled herself away from Shamsi, smiled at her grandpapa and nodded her head. Suddenly she remembered the message she had to deliver. "Nary asked me to tell you that papa's visiting days are Wednesdays. But we cannot go tomorrow because the first visit is for the spouse of the prisoner."

Shamsi gently tidied the girl's curls and said: "This is good news, isn't it love? And by next week, you will be strong enough to accompany us."

Nary woke early that Wednesday morning. She took a long shower, washed her hair, epilated her legs, underarms and face. She ate little at lunch so that her stomach would not bulge out. At three in the afternoon, she put on her smartest Islamic coat, over which she had to wear the chador in order to be allowed inside the prison compound. She perfumed herself and moisturized her hands.

At three thirty she sat behind the wheel of her Paykan and drove to Evin. It was a cold afternoon and the drive was slow. Fifteen minutes past four she parked the car on the dirt road, away from the gate of the prison, in front of which was a long line of people waiting their turns to enter. She stepped out of the car and locked its door. Then she spread her chador over her head, pinching the two edges of the veil to hold it over her face. Sure that she was well covered, she walked with quick steps towards the gate. Ahmadi, in his khaki uniform saw her. He straightened his shoulders, and slowly and gracefully walked towards her.

From the tight slit of her chador she saw him. To reveal more of her visage, she loosened her grip on the ends of the fabric. "Salam Khanum. I thought you may not come at all today." He said in a firm tone that revealed his displeasure at her unpunctuality.

Disheartened by the man's cold reception she looked at him with innocent eyes and whispered: "I apologise for keeping you waiting, Agha. The traffic was awfully congested."

"One must respect time."

"Yes you are right, particularly when someone as important as you is waiting for such a wretched person as I."

Good. Now the whore knows where she stands. He thought his thick brows unfolding.

They ignored the queue and arrived at the busy gate. The gate guard saluted. The Commandant acknowledged his salutation with a quick nod and then turned to Nary: "Sister, give me your birth-certificate." She quickly unzipped, her black fake Chanel bag, extracted the document and in a subdued manner handed it to

147

her escort who was towering over her. His height accentuated his air of superiority making her feel humble. Unceremoniously he grabbed the document, showed it to the guard, "I will keep it myself. I know this Sister."

"As you wish, Brother Ahmadi." The guard replied, stepping aside to let them enter.

"How long do you think his sentence will be Brother?" Nary asked, looking up at him. He was so much taller than her.

"It depends on his charge. It might be a few months or several years. But knowing his rank it is more years than months."

"I do not know how I will manage without a breadwinner for that long?" She sighed and turned her eyes skyward, as though seeking God's assistance.

"If you allow me, I might be of help to you Khanum."

"Enshallah God grants you a long life. We need all the help we can get. My in-laws are awful to us; my parents have nothing and now my son and I will have to live on his government allowance given to us because his father was a martyr. Tirdad is my second husband."

"I know all about you Khanum. You were his secretary before you hooked him." He said in a deprecating tone. She blushed.

"Well, if you wish we can have dinner together tonight and discuss how I can help you. You will like my cooking." He smiled.

There was so much at stake that she couldn't afford pride. So she brushed the insult away and replied: "I will be honoured, but I do not know what to tell my parents who are living with me now. Where will I be going for dinner, a single woman without any friends? "

"I shall come to your door and order you to come to our Komiteh for questioning about your husband." (Komitehs were locations from which Pasdars operated)

She threw him an alluring glance and smiled her acceptance. He is not only powerful but scheming too! She thought satisfied with her find.

They arrived by the door of the building in which the prisoners met their relatives.

"Go to room number five. I leave you now and tonight I will come for you at eight. Your birth certificate will be returned to you at the gate. Just tell them your name. " He said as though addressing an inferior.

Awed by his superior air, which in a strange way installed in her a sense of security; she gently seized his arm, squeezed it lightly and murmured: "I very much look forward to tonight." A flicker of a smile passed over his set countenance. She let go of his arm and he stood there watching her enter the cold corridor, crowded by solemn looking men, unshaved young guards, rifles hanging from their shoulders and women in black chadors, seemingly lost in their miseries. She stopped by room number 5, grabbed the handle of its door, waited a few seconds before pushing it down. Prepared to face him without guilt, she entered. There he was, aged and bruised in the face, standing behind a glass partition. He smiled at her. She offered him her Salam. In his disillusioned eyes she saw anxiety, regret and longing. In hers, he saw nothing. He remembered her eyes were always cold, even when they were making love. He picked up the phone. So did she.

"How are you azizam?"

"How do you think I should be?"

"I am so sorry for what I have brought to you – you know that I love you more than anything and anyone in the world."

"If you did, you wouldn't have sacrificed our wellbeing for the sake of your damned ideology."

"A man without a conviction is not a man Nary joon."

"Conviction doesn't put bread and butter on the table."

"Are not my parents providing you with comfort?"

"You know better than to ask this silly question. No. All they do is pamper Yasmin. My parents have moved in with us."

"Good, thank them from me. Enshallah I will be back soon."

"Enshallah. What have they done to your face?"

"I fell down over a rock." He lied. He did not want to tell her about the tortures and the beatings that he was receiving for not divulging the names and locations of his comrades."

"Is there anything you want me to bring for you next week?"

"Yes, a change of clothes and a tube of antiseptic cream please." He paused, brushed his hand over his thick beard and said: "I hate this. But we are not allowed razors."

"It suits you azizam."

"Thank you for calling me azizam. I thought I would never hear that word coming from you gain."

She gave him one of her seductive smiles.

He locked her smiling image in his mind to visualize at nights when he lay sleepless, dreaming of her.

A bell rang – time was over.

He gave her a long tender look. The tenderness in his eyes aroused in her a deep sense of guilt which she quickly discarded.

"Next week your parents will come too." She heard herself say.

"How are they?"

"Very well."

"Please do not let them bring Yasmin. I do not want her to see me like this."

"I will tell them – but I do not know if they will listen to me. They will think I am lying to upset the girl."

The door opened and a head in a khaki cap protruded in: "Did you not hear the bell Sister?"

"Sorry Brother." She replied without turning to the door.

"I must go now."

"I love you Nary. Keep safe."

"I love you too." She said putting the receiver down. She adjusted her chador, threw him one last glance, turned and left the room. Outside she exhaled with relief. The hard task had been finally accomplished.

When she left, he lingered on inhaling her familiar aroma and staring at the door behind which she would be walking – walking away from him. How he loved her! How!

Watching other women's wet eyes Nary felt rather uncomfortable with herself. A strange pang in the pit of her heart disturbed her peace and made her think about her own life: she felt sorry for him, but that did not put bread and butter on her table. She was too poor to be sentimental, too poor to be proud and too poor to be unselfish. Therefore she had to act with prudence, if not for her own sake, for Ahmad's. Ahmadi was good looking and his appearance reeked of wealth – new or old did not matter anymore. The old wealth was changing hands – like Tirdad's pawned gold Rolex watch, the identical of which glittered on Ahmadi's wrist, who was probably an educated peasant boy. But it would take a long time before the wealthy thugs could learn how to live with their usurped wealth. They had to change their crude habits and adapt sophisticated ones before they could call themselves Agha. That would take years, perhaps generations. A smile bloomed on her face. It had happened to her and she had managed to become a lady in no time at all. Then, of course she was thrown into the bosom of an old and established family. Immersed in thoughts she found herself at the gate. She pushed her thoughts to the back of her mind, stepped close to the guard's kiosk, told him her name and asked for her birth certificate. From among a pile of booklets he found hers and politely handed it to her.

The earlier autumn breeze had turned into a gale at war with nature, its ferocity callously crackling the tree branches and spreading dead and dying leaves in the air somersaulting on their descent upon earth. On the ground dust and debris whirl-winded everywhere. A company of crows, disturbed by the storm's loud and rapid whistles, flapped their wings and flew away from the tree under which Nary's car was parked. She pulled away her chador, threw it on the back seat, sat behind the wheel and drove away.

At home, Shamsi was sitting by the kitchen window waiting for Nary to return. As soon as she saw her arrive, she ran to the door, opened it and hastily asked: "How was my son – how was he?"

"He looked fine and in good spirit. You will be visiting him next week. He sent his love and asked me to tell you not to take Yasmin to Evin."

"Why? The girl wants to see her father."

"He doesn't want her to see him in jail."

"Nary Khanum, you have already informed her of that fact, so it will not make any difference. One day Yasmin will grow up and understand why her father was imprisoned. My son is not a criminal. He is a political prisoner and that is nothing to be ashamed of."

"Please yourself Khanum. All I had to do was deliver his message." Nary replied, turned her back and ran up the stairs to her flat. Once inside she called out: "Is there anyone home?" The silence pleased her. She went to her room, threw her bag on the bed, shed off her covers and hung them in the closet. Humming a happy tune she walked to the kitchen and switched the kettle on. Then she headed for the bathroom to take a shower. She had to be clean and fragranced. She already knew what she was going to wear – a simple dress that complemented her curves. . Her parents had to be kept in the dark. If she dressed too provocatively they would immediately suspect that something was cooking up.

Refreshed by the cold shower she made herself a cup of tea and took it to her bedroom where she intended to dry and coiffeur her hair.

Sharp at 8 pm the Amiris and the Azizis heard the screeching sound of a car brake. Shamsi ran to the kitchen window from where she saw a tall young man in Khaki suit. He seemed familiar. Then she realized he was one of the men she had seen walking down the stairs with Tirdad. What did he want now? She mused, running to the door and quietly opening it enough to see better through its slit. The man rang the bell. Nary opened the door and she heard him say: "Khanum Amiri, I need you to come with me to the Komiteh; we need to ask you some questions about your husband." By now both Azizis were standing behind their daughter, anxiety etched on their worried faces.

"Wait please Agha." Nary said, in a convincingly alarmed tone and turned to her parents. "This Brother took Tirdad to Evin and now he wants me for questioning."

"My daughter is innocent Agha. She never knew what her husband was up to. She has nothing to tell you Brother." Mrs Azizi pleaded her eyes clouded by tears.

"Khanum, we only want her for questioning. Please do not worry. I shall bring her back myself."

They did not believe him. Zahra, their neighbour's daughter had been taken during one such evening and never returned. The wretched parents had searched and searched in vain and then they were told that she had been executed with four other Mujahids.

Visualizing the worst, the Azizis continued pleading.

The vision of her daughter's body pierced by bullets compelled Mrs Azizi to grab the Pasdar's arm and beg him not to take her away. Cool and calm, Ahmadi shook her hand off and staring at her with impatient eyes said: "Khanum, I told you I will deliver your daughter safe and sound myself tonight. It might be a little late but do not worry, she will be back."

Embarrassed by her mother's insistence, Nary ran to her bedroom clad herself again in layers of Islamic hejab, quickly sprayed some perfume on her wrists, grabbed her bag and pretending to be distressed, returned to the door. She turned to her devastated parents and said: "Brother Ahmadi is the gentleman who bent the rules so that I could visit Tirdad. I trust him. You should do too." Then she turned her attention to the Pasdar. "Brother I am ready."

Her parents followed her out, stood on the landing until she disappeared inside the van and the van from their sight.

Shamsi seeing Nary following the Pasdar and getting into the van wondered where he was taking her. Suddenly it dawned on her that he might be taking her to jail. A happy smile brightened her daunted face.' Let her taste hardship too – the ill-omened bitch!" She murmured heading to the sitting room to deliver the news to her husband.

Reza's flat was one of the two penthouses of a confiscated apartment building at the end of Avenue Kamranieh, one of the most prestigious areas of the city. On the landing there were two huge oak doors in front of which were several shoes. This indicated that his neighbour also belonged to the system. Reza chose the key to the flat from the gold key ring he was holding while kicking off his foot wear. Nary, behind him followed suit. As the door opened a welcoming waft of narcissus fragrance teased their nostrils. Reza switched on a huge chandelier that hung over the long and elegant mahogany dining table laid for two. The richness of the interior took Nary's breath away. Her eyes wondering around the open space with admiration, she handed her chador to Reza while taking her coat and scarf off. With all the heavy covers discarded she appeared very sexy. Her pink dress, tight at the waist, loosely hung over her protruding bottom. Its low neck revealed the soft texture of her skin and the largeness of her bosoms. She felt Reza's hands embrace her from behind. She released a moan of pleasure. He pressed himself to her while kissing the hollow of her neck. She moved to the rhythms of his body, teasing him with gentle swings of her buttocks. They each enjoyed the hissing sound of the other's breathing. Reza swung her around, grabbed her breasts, squeezed them hard and began kissing her. Within minutes they were peeling off each other's clothes like hungry beasts. Suddenly he lifted her up, ran to the four poster bed, dropped her down and climbed over her. Her sexual repertoire was undreamed of. They made love as though they had found each other in a desert island. After the third orgasm the two fell into an exhilarated state of exhaustion. It was around ten thirty that they came out of their stupor. Reza wanted more. Nary glanced at her watch, gave him a long kiss and then pushed him away. "I am already late. You do not want me to find my parents dead from worry, do you my Agha?"

He threw her a quick sceptical glance and rising up said: "I lied when I said I was a good cook. I ordered some Shami (meat patties) and Salad Olivier (Russian salad) from Moby Dick. They are in the fridge; I shall put them on the table. I am famished."

"Me too." She replied yawning and spreading her bare arms in the air like a ballerina. She lingered on enjoying the warmth of the bed and the musky odour of love making. Then she rose and headed for the en-suite bathroom into which he had already disappeared. She found him under the shower performing the compulsory wash ritual after a sexual act. She took the towel from its gold plated rail, waited until he stepped out and wrapped it around his torso. He kissed her forehead and began drying himself. She stepped into the bath tub, and careful not to wet her hair rinsed herself from the sins of the past hours.

By the time she was dressed he had put the food on the table.

"Who's flat was this Reza joon?"

"This belonged to an aristocrat, who was the Shah's pimp and for his services was rewarded handsomely by winning lucrative foreign contracts. He owned the whole building."

"It is indeed grand. Is the deed under your name or you are just occupying it?"

"It is mine as long as I remain in my present position."

"In daylight it must have a lovely view of the city from the south and the mountains from the north."

"Yes. Next time we meet, come during the day."

"Under what pretext am I going to leave home during daylight, azizam?"

"I am going to find you a 'nominal' part time job, say at a school from which you will be paid – let's say two thousand a month."

She gave him a coquettish smile, took his large hand, kissed it and said: "God has sent me a saviour."

"I wish to have you for myself Nary joon."

"You cannot while my husband is still alive."

"My dear, you never know what Khalkhali will decide for him and the like of him when he goes through their dossiers."

"Is it true what people say about him?"

"That he is 'a hanging judge?"

She nodded.

"Do not believe what people say."

She suddenly realized how stupid her question had been. Of course he would not tell her the truth. He was working for the like of Khalkhali.

The wall clock chimed twelve times. They both rose.

He delivered her home.

Her parents, each crumpled on a corner of the living room's sofa had fallen asleep waiting for her return. She didn't wake them up.

Chapter 6

Six months later

Tirdad, loyal to his cause and comrades, bore the pains of torture with tight lips and the solitude and darkness of his cell with the patience of Job. To keep track of time, with his nails, he scratched seven lines on the wall next to his bed. Every morning he rubbed his fingers on the dents and counted them. Thus he knew what day it was. For him the week started with Wednesday, the day in which he felt like a human being, not a caged animal. He was allowed a cold shower, the wearing of ordinary clothes and an escorted walk to the visitors' building during which he could inhale fresh air, enjoy the brushing of the breeze over his skin, take in the beauty of the surrounding hills, discern grass's different hues and wonder at the expansiveness of the blue sky. Ordinary stuff he had never before given a thought to. Freedom, the luxury he had taken for granted, now twinkled at him from a distance, beyond his reach. Regrets stabbed his mind and by the time he reached the visitor's sector he was ready to blow up something or somebody – often his parents. They always returned home with a lump in their throats. As for Nary, she didn't give a damn.

A dreadful year inched away, leaving behind a heap of bad memories for all involved in the drama. And, when the Tudeh threat turned into cold ash, Tirdad was tried in a court without a jury. He was given a ten-year sentence and moved to the main jail house with an option to learn a craft. He chose carpentry. Every week he turned a piece of wood into a beautiful figurine for Yasmin and one for Ahmad. Encircled by intelligent people, some Royalists and many from his own party, he began to recover his spirit and feel alive again. Now on Wednesdays his smile was bright especially for Ahmad and Yasmin who adored their statuettes and praised their craftsmanship. To him Ahmad appeared healthy and happy but not his daughter. He blamed her unhappiness on her mother's desertion.

At school, with her blue eyes and fair skin, Yasmin was a fish out of water. She was unfortunate enough to have an ignorant, almost illiterate teacher, the daughter of a scion of the Revolution, thus untouchable. The woman, assuming that Yasmin's mother was a foreigner and thus an infidel to hate, found faults where there were none and brutally abused her. One day she chided her over the way she wore her scarf, telling her it was pushed too far back letting her hair hang out provocatively. Another day she would take exception to her shoes, saying they were too fashionable for modesty. This went on until the day, Yasmin excelled in her math examination. The teacher called her to her podium. Thinking she was summoned to be praised she left her desk and hurried to where the teacher was standing. The woman glared at her with piercing eyes, dangled her exam paper in front of her nose, and, sneering at her, tore it apart and threw the pieces in the air. Her incredulous eyes on the floating papers, a loud offensive "why?" flew out of Yasmin's mouth, like the moan of an accused unjustly condemned to death. The teacher elongated her neck, faced the class and announced: "We all know Yasmin is a detestable infidel, but now she has proven to be a cheat as well by handing in an errorless mathematics' exam paper for which I am going to punish her so it can be a lesson to all those who might do the same." She turned to Yasmin pinched her ear and twisted it hard. 'Ouch', cried the girl, tears of embarrassment welling up in her confused eyes. "Not even Fatimeh, who is the best student amongst you all, has achieved this mark." Pulling at her ear harder she demanded: "Admit that you cheated otherwise I will have you expelled." A deep hush dawned and Fatimeh, who out of jealousy had lied to the teacher that she had seen Yasmin look at her paper, blushed with shame. Regretting her fib she felt awful.

Yasmin, with the courage of the innocent, looked the woman in the eyes: "Khanum Ashghari, I swear by the Koran that I looked at no one's papers. I just studied hard for my exam. That is the honest truth."

"Now you are a liar too. It is easy, when fibbing, to swear on a book that you do not believe is holy. For this alone I am going to extend your punishment. The days that foreigners mocked our religion have expired. We are in charge of running our country and penalize the wrongdoers in our own way. Go outside and stand by the tree on the left of the class room until the sun burns you. There you will taste what is awaiting you and the like of you in life after." Too proud to beg for clemency, Yasmin lowered her head and with steady steps walked out of the classroom and stood by the tree which lacked even one branch that could provide her with a semblance of a shade. There, in the empty courtyard, she let loose her tears. The school janitor, through the window of his room, saw her. He took out a bottle of water from his fridge, and took it to her. "Child, stop crying, drink this water. It is too hot here and you will dehydrate. That teacher of yours is an evil person. Do not take much notice of her stinging tongue. She is mean to everybody, including me."

Yasmin thanked the man, took the bottle and enjoying the chill of the glass took it to her mouth. "

"With the way she behaves, she won't last long – even though her father wears a turban."

Her thirst relinquished, she put down the bottle, threw the janitor a timid glance and in a throaty voice said: "Thank you again Agha Hamid. You are so very kind."

"Nothing at all child – now, if you don't want to break my heart, wipe your tears and give me a smile."

To please him Yasmin smiled and wiped her eyes with the heel of her hand.

When the final bell rang, Yasmin, as red as a lobster ran to her grandfather waiting for her at the gate and burst into tears. "What is it azizam?" He asked perplexed. "Papa you know that I worked very hard for my math, don't you?"

"Of course I know. Why, what happened?"

"When I got 20, Khanum Ashghari accused me of cheating, being a liar and an infidel. She tore my paper and sent me out to stand in the sun until now. She hates me Baba and I do not want to go back to her class ever again."

Yasmin stamped her feet couple of times repeating 'ever again'. Then she stopped, looked into his angry eyes and shaking her head said: "Baba I swear by the Koran, I did not cheat. I never cheat."

What insanity? Mohammad thought, before lifting her up. Gently he pressed her to his chest, kissed her face and whispered: "I know cherie. I know." Then he put her down and noticed she was without her satchel.

"Is your bag in the class-room?"

"Yes Baba." He gripped her hand and almost pulling her behind him, hurried to her class-room, where he intended to give the teacher a big piece of his mind. To his chagrin he found the room empty. His mind already made, he picked up Yasmin's bag from beside her chair, and together they walked out of the room and the school. Mohammad, to cheer her up, went to the nearest ice-cream kiosk where he treated her with three scoops of her favourite flavours.

"Baba, why do you think she hates me so much?"

"Because she is mean and ignorant and has a chip on her plump shoulders."

"No wonder Papa hates all the women in chador!"

"Some people are just nasty. It doesn't have anything to do with what they wear. It has to do with what they think and what they do. Now you just forget about Mrs. Ashghari and enjoy your ice cream. It is melting."

At home, Mohammad went straight to his room, changed into his pyjamas and dressing gown, sat on the edge of his bed, picked up the phone and called Kobra.

The next day he went to the office of Iran Air and bought a one-way ticket to Paris for Yasmin.

Kobra arrived with her air of arrogance intact. She had lost weight, tinted her hair and removed her facial hair. She looked nice. Her arrival brought life to their home and, with the exception of Nary, made them all happy. Her presence worried Nary and put her on guard. She knew Kobra hated her and would go out of her way to upset the established equilibrium of her routine. She had to neutralize her efforts by ingratiating herself to her. It cost nothing but lip service. To this end she planned.

Shamsi was in her kitchen when the phone rang. She dashed to the sitting room, picked it up and heard Nary say: "Shamsi joon Salam."

Stunned to hear her voice, she replied: "Salam Nary Khanum."

"May I speak to Kobra joon?"

Nary's voice for a change was sweet. She must want something. Shamsi assumed.

"Kobra is not home and I do not believe she would want to talk to you ever again."

"She has all the right in the world. I called to apologise to her and ask her forgiveness. Will you please tell her that?"

"I will, but do not count on her calling you back."

"I am sorry again Shamsi joon. Please mediate on my behalf. She will listen to you Shamsi joon."

"Ok, I will."

As Shamsi put the receiver down Kobra walked in, carrying a sack full of provisions she had bought from the supermarket. She put the sack on the table with a loud huff.

"I should have taken the car. This is terribly uncivilized to have to carry a heavy load. I wish we didn't have to eat."

"Guess who called for you?"

Kobra opened the fridge door.

"I've no idea!"

"Nary Khanum. She wants to apologise and beg your forgiveness."

"My forgiveness?" Kobra huffed, shoving the apple bag her mother handed her into the fridge's drawer.

"Over my dead body. I hope you didn't tell her to come down and apologise in person." She closed the fridge door and faced her mother.

"No. I told her not to count on you calling her back."

Folding the empty shopping bag, Kobra whispered: "Good." She drew out a drawer, fitted the sack into it, lifted her head up, and, smiling said: "Madar, you owe me twenty thousand Rials for the grocery and I need two hundred thousand to buy a pair of gold earrings I saw today."

"The twenty thousand I have, but for the rest you have to wait until the first of the month when I collect my pension. You be still here."

"Ok and thanks." Kobra smiled knowing that no extra money would be left to give to Tirdad.

After two days of silence, early in the morning, Nary, holding a huge bouquet of carnations rang the bell. Shamsi opened the door. Surprised to see her she greeted her curtly. "Shamsi joon I am sorry for bothering you this early. I hope Kobra joon has not left the house yet?"

"No. She is having breakfast in the kitchen."

"Wonderful." Nary exclaimed, stepping in and closing the door behind her. She followed Shamsi to the kitchen.

"Salam Kobra joon." Nary said, putting the bouquet down on the table. "I have come to apologize for my silliness and beg your forgiveness."

Kobra contrived a smile and turned her eyes to the flowers: "Thank you. They are beautiful. They must have cost you a fortune."

"Money counts naught in friendship, Kobra joon."

Of course if someone else is paying, Kobra thought puffing out a short breath. With her hand she pointed to a chair. "Please sit down and let us know how you are coping with life, without my brother."

Nary pulled out the chair and sat on it.

"Would you like a cup of tea Khanum?" Shamsi asked her nostrils pulsating. Nary looked up at her and replied: "No thank you Shamsi joon, I have just had my breakfast." Then she turned to Kobra.

"I do nothing much besides teaching part-time and counting my every rial."

"Yes, life is tough without a breadwinner."

"Indeed." Nary replied, glancing at her watch. She twirled her eyes between her two nemeses and said: "I must be off now; otherwise I will be late for my class." Then she focused on Kobra. "If you ever need anything, please don't hesitate to call me – after all, even with all my faults, I am family!" She rose and without waiting for Kobra's answer, waved a good bye and found her way out. She couldn't stand the waft of acrimony seeping out of the two.

Marvelling at her sudden friendliness, Shamsi and Kobra exchanged a long and questioning look and then burst into laughter. At that moment Mohammad entered with his basket of herbs. Surprised to hear laughter in his house, he raised a brow in wonderment. "Baba, you just missed the most cunning scenario of duplicity in your life." Pointing to the flowers, Kobra continued: "Nary brought these for me and apologized for her rudeness."

"She must want something from you my dear." Mohammad commented putting his basket on the table. A whiff of mint mixed with the smell of carnations removed the staleness in the air. Mohammad took a deep breath, smiled and left the room. He didn't want to engage in any kind of vicious backbiting. Outside the air was fresh, his herb patch irrigated and the courtyard washed cleaned. There he sat, rested his head on the cushioned back of his chair, closed his eyes and tried to visualize the happy moments of his life, particularly in Paris where the girls made him feel desirable, good and in demand.

From that day on, Nary became a regular visitor, mostly in the afternoons, presenting them with problems she had encountered at work – all lies to cover her deception and gain sympathy. Thus the unpleasant afternoons passed in mendacity on both sides. Amiris had to put up a show too. Yasmin was underage and to travel out of Iran needed the permission of her father. If Tirdad discovered their scheme, he could forbid her departure even from jail.

However, in spite of all apprehensions and worries what was meant to happen, happened. Nary's matinee rendezvous proved a blessing as no one was in her apartment to spy on the activities of the ground floor inhabitants when a telephone taxi arrived to take Yasmin and Kobra to the airport.

Both Shamsi and Mohammad knew in their hearts that they would never see this only grandchild ever again. But they were happy for her. She was flying to freedom and a life flavoured by love and an assurance of security. In the hallway they passed both travellers under the holy Koran, hugged them both, and read in their ears all the prayers they knew by heart. Shamsi could not stop kissing Yasmin and smelling her. "Khanum let the child go." Mohammad admonished in his usual soft voice. For once she obeyed him without an objection. Then Mohammad lifted Yasmin's case and handed it to the taxi driver waiting by the door. Kobra gave him her small suitcase too and then the two climbed into the cab. The driver fitted the luggage in the boot of his car, returned behind his wheel, started the engine and drove away. The old folks kept waving until the taxi made a right turn and disappeared from their sight. They returned inside, closed the door and went to their sitting room where each dropped on a seat and in spite of their sadness felt comforted. Finally they had been relieved from carrying a heavy load of responsibility. The flat was quiet without her babblings and running around; but the sacrifice was for her sake. Living with her mother, the girl would be much happier than with them. The thought gave them courage to face their son on their next visit.

At Orly airport, an excited Jill was pacing up and down the arrival hall, counting the minutes and eagerly perusing the incoming passengers when she felt two small hands grip her from behind. Shocked she turned around. It was her Yasmin. She let out a cry of joy, hugged her, lifted her up and began kissing her all over. The extent of their happiness infected Kobra with its purity and she began to smile too. Jill put Yasmin down and with hungry eyes, scrutinized her from top to toe. "You are so beautiful ma cherie." She exclaimed shaking her head in delight. Then she turned to Kobra and nimbly embraced her with all her might expressing her gratitude in gasps of whispers. A stranger to altruistic happiness Kobra felt its sweetness and smiled. A sense of pride invaded her mind and for the first time in her life, she liked herself. Instinctively she turned to Jill, "I want you to promise me to be both a mother and a father to her." She asked but didn't wait for an answer, "Don't keep your love a secret. Show it to her. That assurance will nourish her soul and give her self-confidence." She stopped and looked deep into Jill's understanding eyes.

"Kobra joon, she is God's gift to me. I love her and will do everything within my power to make her happy. That I promise you and I promise you that one day you will be a very proud aunty."

"Enshallah." Kobra replied, tickling Yasmin's head.

Too excited to keep still, Jill grabbed the trolley handle from Kobra. "Let me please? You must be very tired." Smiling at her joy, she let the handle go and tucked her hand under Yasmin's arm.

Together they sped to the Air France bus stand. On the long drive to their station, Kobra enlightened Jill with gossip she thought would amuse her without once mentioning Nary's name. Jill listened with interest and asked after friends she had lost touch with and at the end sighed over how changed life in Iran had become.

They disembarked at the Invalid bus stop, collected their luggage and pulled them to the metro station. They stopped by the descending escalator. Kobra gave both a warm hug and left to catch her train. If told, none would have believed that this would be their last encounter.

Jill was lodging at a small hotel nearby. Emotionally exhausted, mother and daughter had an early night. For the first time in years their sleep was not disturbed by nightmares, and when they opened their eyes their minds were devoid of anxiety. Jill looked out of the window and saw there were no clouds covering the sun. She smiled. Even the cosmos seemed to be celebrating her fortune. After a breakfast of coffee and croissant, hand in hand, they walked to Alexander III Bridge, crossed it, walked to avenue Champs-Elysees and turned into avenue Montaigne to window-shop. By the Alma Bridge, they caught a Bateau Mouche and sailed the Seine enjoying the grandeur of the buildings that passed them by. They talked, laughed and in their happiness celebrated life without fear – a marvel indeed. The tour finished, they disembarked, bought their lunch from Paul Patisserie and headed for the Bois de Boulogne, a long walk away, where, by the lake, under the shade of a tree, on a bench they sat and munched at their sandwiches, enjoying the taste of the smoked chicken bathed in mayonnaise. They remained there holding hands, feeling each other's warmth while admiring the magnificence of nature that lay in their view. Without any strictures they were free to enjoy life as it pleased them. Slowly Yasmin turned to her mother, kept her gaze on her tranquil profile for a while and then asked: "Mammon can you please tell me why you left Papa?"

Staring at a family of ducks that were indulging in their peaceful existence she replied: "Because I did not believe in his cause or its success in Iran. Freedom is the essence of life, as important as the air we breathe, the water we drink and sunlight. Autocracy devours individual freedom and confines human spirit within abstract dogmas. Man stripped of freedom is as good as dead and I didn't want to die young."

Yasmin removed her eyes from her profile and fixed them on the rippling trace of the ducks until it dissolved into nothingness. Then, to her horror she saw the sneering face of her teacher float on the water casting murk upon its translucency. To eliminate the horrible image she closed her eyes and thanked God for her release from bondage. Now she understood it all.

A huge black cloud slowly covered the sun and it became too chilly to remain immobile. They rose and holding hands walked around the lake. From a kiosk Jill bought a cup of coffee for herself and a can of Coca Cola for Yasmin. They kept walking and by sunset they were exhausted and hungry. On Avenue Victor Hugo they dined at Stella, famous for its seafood. For an aperitif, Jill ordered a glass of champagne. When the waiter placed it on the table, she poured a little into the water vessel in front of Yasmin, diluted it with water from the carafe on the table, and looking at her with glittering eyes raised her glass, "cherie let's drink to our luck?"

On the Wednesday following Yasmin's departure Mohammad and Shamsi, expecting an unpleasant encounter, braved a visit to their son.

There, when Tirdad didn't see his daughter, assuming she was ill, he asked: "Is Yasmin sick again?"

"No. She is healthier than ever." Shamsi volunteered with a bright smile.

"Then why isn't she here?"

"Because she is in Vienna." Mohammad replied, with a lifted chin, a raised brow and glow of achievement in his eyes.

"In Vienna?" He howled like a wolf.

"Yes in Vienna with her mother – where she belongs." Mohammad responded in a soft voice, with a firm tone.

Tirdad clenched his left fist and began to hit the glass partition, shouting obscenities. Patiently his parents waited for his fury to subside. Eventually it did. He dropped his head, unclenched his fist, banged his head on the glass and let it rest on it.

Mohammad put his palm on the spot where his head was, as though he could infuse in him his love and sympathy. But all he could feel was the chill of the partition. He removed his hand and attached his aching forehead to the same spot. The ache was so acute that he had to close his eyes. A deep silence engulfed them. The coldness of the glass reduced his headache and he was able to open his eyes. The phone still in his hand he whispered into it:

"Son, we did this because it was the best for her. You are to spend another eight years behind bars. She was lonely at home here and was so maltreated at school that she refused to attend it. What should have we done for her?" He raised his eyes to Tirdad, "What?"

Their eyes met. The bitterness shooting from Tirdad's stabbed Mohammad's heart so sharply that he shivered. Tirdad turned his sharp eyes to his mother's frightened face. She couldn't bear to look at them. Instinctively she grabbed her husband's arm for protection and hung to it. They both loved him so much. They shared his misery but could do nothing to help him. That notion was terribly hard to bear, particularly when their son was so hard-headed and distant from them. Suffering inside, neither could find any consoling words to offer, so they stood staring at him.

"Whose brilliant idea was this – ha?" Tirdad asked, his voice low but poisonous.

"Kobra's." Mohammad whispered.

"I should have guessed that." He said jerking his head back. Then he turned up his nose, sniggered and said: "I will kill her once I get my hands on the bitch."

"Son, Yasmin had no life here. Jill is a wise woman and has a good job. Vienna is a beautiful city and the Austrian standard of education is high. Yasmin will be happy there and that is what you should want for your child – her happiness. In fact, you should be thankful to Kobra."

"How on earth did you get her a French visa?"

"Kobra took her and me, to the French embassy. I guess we were lucky or they were too busy to notice that I was too old to be her father. Jill was told of the arrangement and she went to Paris and collected her. Now they call us every Sunday and Yasmin is very happy. If you really love her, you must be happy for her. In a way it is better for your marriage too."

"I suppose so." Tirdad murmured wistfully. Then he put the receiver down; picked up the wooden angel he had carved for Yasmin, turned and left the room. Mohammad tapped on Shamsi's hand still on his arm, and turning towards the door murmured: "At least this is out of the way."

The knowledge that each day brought him closer to his freedom gave Tirdad the peace of mind conducive to reflection. Days transpired peacefully giving him time to ponder on the course his life had taken and the decisions he had made. Like a film, the past rolled away on the screen of his mind and he clearly saw that he had never set one foot wrong. He had been a victim all his life: growing up in a broken home, having a brother who had stolen from him the love and respect of their father; a selfish woman conning him to marry her and then abandoning him when he needed her most, and finally being caught as the result of a traitor's defection. The only sunshine in his life was Nary. These other people were responsible for his misfortune and he would make them pay. He would. He knew knowledge was the sharpest weapon. Thus, within the confines of the compound, he began networking. He befriended all sorts of people, from members of the Mujahedin to Pahlavi cabinet ministers lucky enough to have escaped execution, common thieves, and murderers. Amongst them was a lout named Sed Ali, serving a one year sentence for having taken the virginity of a minor without consenting to marry her.

Sed Ali was a stout, happy young fellow of thirty or so, with tattoos all over his arms and chest and a constant tick on his left eye. Having taken a liking to Tirdad, one evening when they were sitting face to face, supping in the dining hall, he stretched his bulk over the table, tilted his head up, looked into Tirdad's amazed eyes and said: "Doctor joon I am not as noble as you, nor is the reason for my imprisonment as admirable as yours. But I have an interesting story to tell. Would you like to hear it?"

Flattered, Tirdad responded, "Sed Ali, I am no nobler than you because we are all children of the same God. Therefore as brothers I would like to know all about you."

Hearing this outrageous statement, Sed Ali stared into Tirdad's eyes with awe, stretched further, put his palms over his ears, and pulled him close enough to kiss both his cheeks. Sed Ali's out of character act not only surprised Tirdad but all those sitting along the long dining table. Suddenly sound of a loud applause echoed in the dining hall. Sed Ali, baffled and thrilled by the attention, rose, swept his proud eyes over every single inmate and then turned to Tirdad, pointed at him with his finger and proclaimed: "Friends, this noble, educated man, is the finest individual I have met in my life. Do you know why?" He paused to impress upon them the importance of his coming statement.

A mocking smile bloomed on the inmates' amused faces and expecting a good laugh they fixed their attention on Sed Ali and Tirdad. Sed Ali with his positive attitude, lively sense of humour and outrageous stories was their sole source of entertainment. And above all he was gifted with the capacity to laugh at himself – something rare amongst them all. Flattered by their attention he waved his head in wonder and continued: "Because this noble of the nobles, believes I, Sed Ali the Forger, am his equal! This, my dear fellows, is true brotherhood. Isn't it!" Heads nodded in agreement and the sound of laughter at Sed Ali's naivety brought the frowning supervisor in. Merriment turned into whispers of fear for Sed Ali's sanity. The man had gone mad. How could he believe that an intellectual snob thinks of himself as equal to an uneducated lout?

Unable to control his excitement Sed Ali bent over the table, cupped Tirdad's temples with his palms, again pulled him over and kissed his forehead. Then he dropped on his seat, lifted his water glass, gulped most of its content, banged the glass down and fixed his flashing eyes on Tirdad's flushed face seeking approval. Sed Ali's outburst had not only embarrassed Tirdad but frightened him. The ever-present gaoler could misinterpret the intention and report it as an insinuation to an uprising, or, worse, a homosexual relationship. Nevertheless Tirdad did not have the heart to refuse acknowledgement of such sincere sentiments. He gave him a broad smile and audibly said: "Sed Ali Khan you are too complimentary to me. I am just a fellow like all our friends here."

Sed Ali shook his head in negation and lowered his voice.

"No you are not the same. Doctor Joon, you are a very special person and I am honoured to be considered your brother. I believe there should never be any secrets between brothers. Therefore you must know all about me."

Tirdad moved closer to the edge of the table and staring at him muttered: "I am all ears my friend."

Sed Ali took a sip of his water, relaxed his posture and began:

"Doctor Joon, I was orphaned at the age of five. My uncle with an eye for my beautiful mother told her he would adopt me if she married him. We were poor. She had no choice but to accept the offer. In a way, we were both very lucky. Although he was as ugly as a monkey, he was kind and generous. He provided us with a secure and comfortable life. It all worked out well. My mother was happy because she had a breadwinner and a good and kind surrogate father for her son. I was happy to see my mother content and I found in him an excellent educator. God bless his soul, he taught me all the tricks of his business. Doctor I am the best forger in the whole of Iran."

Delighted by the information Tirdad interrupted him. "Can you forge signatures?"

"Of course I can."

"Will you teach me the art?"

"Of course I will."

"Great."

"Shall I go on with my story?"

"I am all ears."

"When I finished high school I became a clerk at bank Omran. It was there that I realized I was as good as my patron in forging signatures. And that was the beginning of a lucrative side-business particularly during and after the Revolution. It is diabolical that I am in here not because of fraud and forgery but for deflowering a virgin, who, believe me, was more willing than I. Well such is the way of life!" He sighed and shrugged his shoulders, as though offended by an insult. Tirdad lifted his water glass and pointed it at him, "I drink to your health, manhood and remarkable skill."

From the next day, educating Tirdad in the art of forgery became Sed Ali's main task. A keen learner there was no limit to the skills Tirdad acquired not only from Sed Ali but the other experts around him. Now in his repertoire of priorities, self-advancement replaced social betterment. Scheming and planning returned to him his lost self-confidence. Each morning he woke up with a smile, did his exercises in the court yard and paid attention to his appearance particularly on Wednesdays. This sudden attitude change surprised and disturbed his wife more than anyone else. She was counting on having a docile husband back at home so that she could continue with her affair without any interference. A man in charge of her life would spoil the pleasures she was enjoying. Thus to disturb his peace of mind and erode his regained self-confidence she arrived in tattered clothes, a half empty food basket and complaints about life, his parents and their handful of disloyal friends who had discarded her like their old clothes. Seeing her in such wretched condition not only did not corrode his confidence but made him more determined in creating a life for her that would compensate her endured hardships.

At home, after her visits, Nary would change, apply makeup and be the woman Reza expected her to be. In fact she had never been so happy in life. Her liaison was not only lucrative but enjoyable too.

He was now working for the country's Atomic Energy Centre with a hefty increase in salary. Before the revolution, the United States had given the Shah carte blanche to pursue his aim to make Iran a nuclear power. Now that the war with Iraq had finished the new government had decide to follow the project but albeit in secret.

Having an important position in the establishment, Reza's affairs were closely monitored by the spies of the Ministry of Information, which had replaced the Shah's secret service, SAVAK. Therefore Reza had to watch his every step and be very careful with his private life. This meant that he had to reduce his rendezvous with Nary. Besides the affair was losing its lustre and Nary was proving to be too demanding for his liking. This coincided with his parents finding him an appropriate virgin from a prominent clerical family who could become instrumental in his career advancements. A dinner was arranged during which the prospects met. The future bride, in her stylish Islamic coat and silk scarf was indeed beautiful, gentle, modest and soft spoken. Her large blue eyes shaded by long curled up lashes stole Reza's heart instantly. A week later together with his parents they went for Khasegari during which all the marriage terms and conditions were agreed upon. The wedding was to take place soon as Ramadan was approaching and they did not want to wait until its end.

This news he kept from Nary. A shrewd man, he had wised up to her true colour and knew she was not to be trusted. If he wanted his affair to end smoothly he had to find her a substitute for himself. Reza was not only a man with plenty of foresight, he was also sangfroid and ruthless; a man who would never allow any obstacle to impede his progress. He had to discard his whore in a very careful manner; otherwise she could cause a lot of unnecessary problems. In fact, once he had spotted her spying on him, outside his office, hidden in a black chador and fancy, fake Gucci sunglasses. He had recognized her from the sunglasses he had given her himself.

In his search for a proper substitute he chose Hashem, a university classmate, just divorced and very depressed. An affair would lift the man's spirit up. Hashem was shy and would appreciate a helping hand. If he liked Nary, he would remain his faithful friend and be indebted to him forever. One never knew when one needed whom! To this end he invited Hashem to have dinner with him at one of the outdoor restaurants at Darband, where the weather is pleasantly cool in summer and one can sit on carpeted benches, eat kebabs, smoke hookah and listen to the music of waterfalls rushing down their stony paths, spraying their surroundings with tear drops that, catching the light, sparkle like diamond studs.

He picked Hashem up from his flat and drove him up the mountain to where the road ended. There he parked. They got out and walked to Reza's chosen restaurant.

In his thirties, Hashem was a fairly pleasant looking man with happy eyes and a healthy bank account. He had bought his luxurious flat from the Foundation of the Emmam, for one third of its market value because he was a war veteran and had lost a toe in a battle. After the war, Hashem's mother had chosen for him a wife whose father was a rich carpet merchant. During the nuptial copulation he had realized that she was not a virgin. Deeply affronted, he had kicked her out of the bedroom and the next day had sent her back home. Her parents, to maintain face, particularly among the deeply traditional Bazaar community, had begged him to take her back, at least for a couple of months (for which they would pay him handsomely) and then divorce her under the pretext of being barren. The amount was worth a temporary reconciliation. His wife returned home, stayed for a year and when he got tired of her he divorced her. The solitude left him depressed.

Now, leaning on a heavy bolster, they were sitting on a carpeted large seat, eating their lamb kebab and chatting about his wretched state of mind when Reza, assumed an air of concern and said: "Hashem joon, you cannot live being miserable for the rest of your life. You feel bad because you are lonely. Why don't you look for a woman? There are plenty around."

The idea of having an illicit relationship had not occurred to Hashem's mind. He thought about it for a minute or two and found it appealing. Suddenly instead of feeling cold he began to enjoy the mountain breeze, the rustle of the leaves that had been irritating him and the tenderness of the lamb pieces he had found hard to chew. Smiling, he made himself more comfortable, crossed one leg over the other, put his fork on his plate, turned to Reza and said:

"My friend this is an excellent Idea." He paused and frowned. "But, Reza, I do not know anyone with whom I want to start a relationship."

"That is easy. You do not know anyone because you have not been looking. If you wish I can introduce you to some of the girls I know. One of them might make you happy."

"Oh, that would be great."

The waiter appeared with a tray of tea, dates and cane sugar. He put the tray between the two, collected the dirty dishes and vanished. Hashem's problem resolved, enjoying their tea, they turned their attention to the current events. After having discussed all the virtues and faults of President Khatami, the rial's constant devaluation, the rising value of gold and the vanished hope of reconciliation with the Great Satan (United States), they decided it was time to return home. Reza paid the bill and descending the slope towards their car, they each bought a cup of ice cream from one of the shops that would remain open till midnight.

Before reaching the car, Reza, discarded his ice cream cup in the gorge and turned to his friend.

"Are you free for lunch tomorrow?"

"Yes. Why?"

"I have a cousin who is a very good cook. Come and taste her cooking." Reza said in a tempting tone.

"Shall do with pleasure. I love good food." Hashem responded with a huge smile.

"I know you do. That is why I am inviting you. She is also gorgeous."

"That will make the meal even yummier."

"I am glad you think so." Reza unlocked the car doors; they climbed in and drove away.

Nary was rinsing her breakfast plate when the kitchen phone buzzed. Knowing it would be Reza, she hastily picked it up and murmured a sweet 'hallo'.

"Azizam can you come earlier to the flat and cook something delicious for me and a friend who is going to have lunch with us?"

"Of course, Reza joon."

"By the way, I have told my friend you are my cousin and because you are such an excellent cook, as a favour, I often ask you to cook for me."

"That is a compliment azizam. What would you like me to cook for you?"

"The choice is yours. Now I must go." The phone went dead. Nary put the receiver down her eyebrows tight. She had never cooked for him. On the occasions they had eaten lunch together, it had been kebab delivered from Yas restaurant. This was strange and she did not like it at all – nevertheless she had no choice in any matter that related to Reza. He was the Master and she, the Slave.

It was ten when she left her room and found her mother sitting on the sofa reading a magazine. "Mother I am leaving now. I have to go to the Ministry of Education before I go to school and today, I might come home a little later than usual. Please make the dinner yourself."

From behind the fold of her magazine Mrs Azizi replied:

"You always find some excuse to have me do your chores."

"You live under my roof, pay no rent, eat my food, so, you might as well do something to deserve my hospitality." Having stung her mother, she tied her scarf around her neck, put her coat on, picked up her bag and left the flat banging its door.

"I have given birth to a serpent and not a human being." Mrs Azizi murmured, returning her attention to the article she was reading. It was about how to come to terms with old age.

Nary let herself into the flat, put the grocery she had purchased on the kitchen top, returned to the corridor, took off her scarf and coat which she hung in the closet, returned to the kitchen, turned the radio on and commenced her preparations. Once all was finished she returned to the bedroom and perfumed herself so that she wouldn't stink of fried onion, the main ingredient of Persian cuisine. She went to the en suite bathroom, refreshed her rouge, and tied her scarf around her hair because of the guest. Satisfied with her image tilting on the mirror she returned to the sitting room, poured herself a glass of whisky and sat on the balcony chair looking at the ugly sprawling city Teheran had become. Gone were the beautiful private gardens dressed in roses and jasmines, weeping willows and persimmon trees. In their stead stood shining modern high rises competing in height with mount Alborz. She sat there calm, reflecting on the course her life had taken and wondering what lay ahead when she heard the rattle of a key in the lock. She turned and saw Reza enter followed by a handsome man.

A sunny smile on her face, she rose to welcome the two.

Reza sniffed the delightful aroma of food welcoming him and felt his mouth water. An unconscious smile opened up his serious face. He threw a quick glance at the dining table, to check if it was set properly. It was. Content he turned to Nary.

"Are we having rice with broad beans, dill and lamb shanks?"

"Yes Agha. From the smell of dill, it can be nothing else, can it?"

She turned to the stranger and politely greeted him with her Salam.

"Salam-alaikom Khanum." Hashem replied, unable to take his eyes from her. This was the most captivating creature he had ever set eyes upon. What joy it would be to spend the rest of one's life with this Aphrodite. He thought celebrating his luck.

"Nary, this is my friend Hashem Karimi. We went to university together. He is an electrical engineer working for the Ministry of Energy and a black belt Judo expert."

Lifting a brow in surprise, Nary exclaimed: "A black belt Judo expert! That indeed is something to be proud of, congratulations to you Agha."

Astounded and flattered by Aphrodite's obvious appreciate of his skill, Hashem fell in love with her there and then. Being a Black Belt was more important to him than being the Minister of Energy himself.

"Would you like to eat now?" She asked her eyes flitting between the two men.

"Yes Khanum." Reza replied in an imposing manner that surprised Hashem. He wasn't familiar with the other side of his friend's character.

Nary threw him a marred glance and left for the kitchen. There was something wrong in the air and she felt it. Once all was ready she called Reza to come and help her. He responded to her summon and soon food was on the table. Reza took the head chair allowing Nary to face Hashem who was so beside himself that he couldn't even hold his spoon properly. Reza noticed his raptness. It pleased him and put his conscience at ease. From under the table Nary felt Hashem's foot touching hers. The flirt pampered her vanity yet she quickly withdrew her leg and sat straight. He did it again. This second time made her uneasy. She rose, collected the dirty plates and carried them to the kitchen. The man's audacity had pinched a nerve in her vanity. What was going on? How dared the stranger flirt with her? The first time was just a complement or an accident, but the second innuendo was just an insult. She put the dishes on the kitchen top, picked up the tray on which the dessert and its bowls were laid and returned to the table. The two were laughing at a joke. As soon as they saw her they stopped and diverted their attention to her. She passed the plates around and put the mousse bowl in front of Hashem. "Please serve yourself and pass it to Reza."

"This looks yummy Khanum." Hashem praised digging the spoon into the thick mousse.

"Thank you Agha. I hope you will like its taste."

"I am sure I will. My friend here," he tossed his chin at Reza, "is lucky to have you cooking for him."

Reza smiled and took the bowl from Hashem.

They ate in silence. A second helping was offered and politely refused. As Nary moved to collect the plates she became conscious of Reza's eyes on her. She met his eyes with a gesture of question on her face. He smiled and broke the bad news. "Nary joon I have been posted to Pakistan. There is a professor there, they say he is the best in the field of nuclear science and I am to work with him for one year."

Nary froze.

"Congratulations Reza, this is wonderful and when you return you will be so important that you wouldn't even acknowledge our Salam."

"Do not be silly Hashem. It is just for a year and in Pakistan. I will die there. I hate humidity and their spicy cuisine."

"When do you leave?" Asked Nary staring at him with unblinking eyes: "Next Tuesday." He replied in a casual voice.

"That is the day after tomorrow."

"Yes Nary Aziz. But do not worry about a thing; Hashem, here will look after you." He turned to Hashem. "Won't you?"

"Of course I will and with pleasure." Hashem replied smiling at Nary whose colour had vanished.

"Nary's husband is at Evin and she lives with her parents and son. Give her your telephone number and get hers. It will be wonderful if you could help her in any way you can, Hashem Aziz."

Thrilled by this information Hashem took out his biro from the pocket of his white shirt, looked up at Nary and asked: "Khanum may I have a piece of paper please?" Nary went to the kitchen, tore a page out of the telephone note-pad, returned and offered it to him. He took the paper, tore it in two and wrote his number on one of the pieces and handed it to her. "This is my mobile number so that you can reach me at all hours."

"Thank you Agha."

"Nothing at all." Hashem responded pushing the other piece of paper towards her. "Could you please write yours for me?"

Hesitating she threw a questioning glance at Reza.

"Write it for him Nary. He is like my brother." Then he turned to Hashem,

"Call her early in the morning when her parents are still sleep. They are rather old fashioned and may object to their daughter receiving calls from a stranger."

Hashem turned to Nary and asked in a caring tone: "Won't I wake you up if I call at 7 am?"

Nary, picked up Hashem's biro, wrote her number, pushed the paper and the biro towards him and answered:

"I am up at six, doing my yoga exercises."

"Good, like me, you are interested in physical activities."

"Only Yoga." She replied curtly.

Reza consulted his gold Rolex watch, shook his head in regret and muttered:

"I must return to work now." He turned to Nary. "Khanum you leave the dishes for my cleaner. She will be here around five. Also leave the flat keys on the kitchen top. You won't be needing them anymore." Insulted by the innuendo in his manner of speaking to her Nary hurried to the kitchen, brought the keys and threw them on the table. Trying hard to stop from bursting into tears she returned to the kitchen where no one could witness her weakness. Exasperated by Reza's news and humiliated by his treatment of her in front of the stranger, she felt as though her life had reached its ebb.

Reza turned to Hashem and rising said: "excuse me won't you?" Hashem nodded with a raised brow and a meaningful smile. Yes she is his mistress and for some odd reason he is passing her to him. What an ass! The woman is gorgeous and being with her not only brings a man out of his doldrums but will send him to heaven.

In the kitchen, Reza hugged her from behind, kissed her head and whispered: "All good things come to an end Khanum joon."

"Will I see you when you return?" Nary asked, not turning to kiss him as she used to.

He ignored her question and added: "I have deposited a hundred thousand Rials into your account."

"Thank you." She whispered, wiggling to free herself. Suddenly his touch felt noxious. He sensed her discomfort and let her go. "We should leave the flat all together, now."

"OK, just let me go to the bathroom and collect my stuff."

"Hurry please." Reza ordered before returning to the dining area. His voice was cold, as though nothing had ever existed between them.

She ambled to the bedroom, picked up her bag, collected a few toiletry items she had in the en-suite, fitted them inside it; returned to the hallway where she lifted her coat from the peg and put it on. She seemed very calm. But inside she was fuming. She had been discarded like a stale piece of meat. What an end? She thought, her heart aching.

They were waiting for her by the open door. Her head up, she led the way, like a lady, but she knew she wasn't – at least in their eyes.

Down in the street, Reza addressed Hashem. "Would you please drop Nary home? I am already very late, and, you will learn where she lives."

Nary gave him a long icy stare, hating him with all her heart – the dirty dog. Then, it dawned on her that she was being passed over to someone else like a whore. Was she a whore? No she was not. She did what she had to do to survive till her husband was released. Women, who stay at home, slave for their husbands without loving them, just because they are good providers, are also whores – dignified whores – she kept reasoning while controlling her urge to strangle that hypocrite who was hiding behind a veneer of decency.

On Tuesday, Reza married his respectable virgin, deflowered her on the bed that still reeked of Nary's odour and did not feel an iota of remorse. Soon after, he left for Karachi with his wife. A few years later he became a scion of the Iranian Atomic Energy program and the mediator between Iran and the Pakistani professor who sold to Iran what he shouldn't have.

Soon, Nary found herself regularly visiting Hashem's flat where she was welcomed with open arms and respect. Hashem was very different from the bossy, selfish and boring Reza. He was talkative, funny, generous and genuinely caring. In him, she found not only a breadwinner but a friend as well. That brought a fresh sense of wellbeing into her life.

Happy with her man, she made herself scarce at the Amiri residence, in spite of the fact that they desperately needed her help. Mohammad was suffering from Angina and Shamsi was losing her mind. She had never been a capable and independent person and now that her husband was almost bedridden she could not run their lives without help. Six hard and miserable years had passed since their pensions were stopped being paid and their bank accounts closed because of their son. To survive, they had sold all their valuables including a carpet Rose had left with them. Fear and uncertainty had turned Shamsi into a neurotic paranoid. Sometimes they went without lunch because she had burnt the rice or whatever she had been cooking. In spite of his illness, Mohammad lumbered out each morning to buy what his money could procure for them to feed on. His little patch had become as sick as him. Only mint grew there. He was so dignified that he never asked for help from his friends or various nephews and nieces doing well under the new Regime. Kobra's visits had become rare and Datam could not return to Iran because of his high rank during the Pahlavi era. He was on their black list.

One morning Datam received a call from Golnar telling him that his parents could no longer manage without help. They were both sick and despondent.

When Rose returned from her jog around the park she found him withdrawn and sad.

"What is it darling? Are you feeling sick?"

He looked up at her and in a voice coming from the pit of a well replied: "Golnar called. My parents are unwell, there is no one to take care of them and I cannot do anything for them from here."

"What do you mean? What has happened to them? They live a floor below Nary. Isn't she taking care of them? They pay for her living expenses."

"I do not know what is going on there. Golnar told me Nary hardly ever visits them, especially since she works part time at a school. My father is almost bedridden and my mother cannot manage anything. At times they go hungry."

"That is awful." Rose hummed sitting next to her husband. A deep silence fell in the well lit room. The sun's rays, pouring in through the huge French window, were making the grains of the wooden floor shine like strings of agates.

Rose noticed the quivering of Datam's lips. She inched closer to him, bent and stole a quick kiss from his pale, hollow cheek. "Don't worry my love. I will go to Teheran and bring them here. I have no fear of the Regime. They have already confiscated everything I own, except the garden at Galandoak."

"It will be dangerous for you. You are my wife and bear my name."

"My passport is under my maiden name, so I certainly won't face any difficulties at the point of entry into Iran – unless someone dobs on me."

"There are plenty of informants around, Rose darling."

"The informants are not interested in me. They are after the enemies of the Regime and all my life I have been apolitical. I am not scared. Fear is worse than death. What has to happen will happen, so I am not going to let fear become a deterrent in my decision making." Rose stood up, went to her bathroom, took her shower, changed into jeans and a crisp white Armani shirt, drank her coffee and then headed for her study where she sat behind her mahogany desk, on which lay her address book. She picked it up, found the telephone number of her travel agent and dialled.

She booked a seat for 5th July.

Her airplane landed at six thirty in the morning of 6th July 1991. Ten years after the day she had left her country. As she stepped out of the airplane, a dry dusty air hit her face and she took great pleasure in its familiarity. For a few seconds she paused to sweep her eyes around the area she never thought she would see again. Then she followed the other passengers down the steps to a shuttle that took them to the arrival hall. The airport, once crowded by foreigners coming to visit or work in Iran was ruefully empty. Only one line led to the immigration posts. Passports had to be checked at four different stations. Rose presented her document with a good morning and a smile. Men of different ages respectfully examined and stamped her passport and each in his own way whispered a welcome that touched her deeply – she was once more amongst her own people, welcoming as ever – hospitable as ever. Her heart filled with an unprecedented joy that replaced her earlier anxiety. She murmured a 'Shokret' (Thank you God), found herself a trolley, and waited for her suitcase by the rolling belt. When it appeared she asked a young man standing by her to help her lift and put it on the trolley. The young man obliged. She thanked him profusely, grabbed the handle of the trolley and pushing it went through the green marked custom lane and out of the arrival hall towards the airport's taxi station. Gone were the days that her chauffeur driven Mercedes Benz was waiting for her. That was another era, in another life. She and Datam had gone through a Revolution that had claimed thousands of lives. Yet they were alive and had managed to keep their heads above water, what more could she expect of life? She whispered another "shokret", and stepped into an airport taxi.

The air drifting in through the car window was pleasantly cool and only a few cars were on the roads. Rose felt as though she had entered into a new city, so changed was Teheran. There were high rises and parks everywhere. The wall depictions of the Revolution era, debasing the enemies of the Islamic Republic were replaced by huge portraits of the war martyrs, or the respected clergies. No matter at which side of the highway she looked, a sombre face and or a horrific war scene caught her eyes, making her feel guilty for being alive. These men had given their lives for their country during a useless war that had served no purpose for either Iran or Iraq. It had just made the international arms industry and the middlemen richer. To break the monotony of the long drive Rose started a conversation with the driver. All Iranians are in the habit of chatting with the taxi drivers who are in fact more informed than the media's news-readers. She learnt about people's poverty, sanctions and the greediness of the Bazaar merchants who sat on their merchandize, causing an artificial shortage and a subsequent price hike.

Twenty-five minutes into their drive the taxi parked in front of the Amiri residence. The driver, impressed by Rose's unassuming nature, got out of his car, opened the door for her, unloaded her luggage and carried them to the door. He hardly ever did this for other passengers. He rang the bell. Rose joined him and waited for the door to open. It didn't. He rang again.

Worried in case something had happened to them, Rose ran up the stairs and pressed the bell button of Tirdad's flat. After a few minutes he opened the door. Surprised, the two stared at each other in awe.

"What joy to see you Tirdad?" Rose exclaimed in total surprise.

He smiled, "on good behaviour my sentence was reduced to six and half years."

"Wonderful. I am so glad for you and Nary. She must be thrilled to have you back home." Rose commented wondering why Golnar had not told them about his release.

"Of course she is. Nary has been such a faithful wife to me – any other woman would have divorced a prisoner husband. Sometimes I wonder how I can compensate the sufferings I have put her through."

"I am sure you will find a way." Rose turned her head to the road and saw the taxi driving looking up at them with impatient eyes, "Are your parents home?" she asked, her voice tinged with anxiety.

"They probably are both sleep. Wait, I will bring my key and let you in."

Tirdad ran inside and returned with a key, fitted his feet into his sandals left by the door, and ran down the stairs with Rose following him. The taxi driver was leaning on his car with a frown on his face. Rose apologised for keeping him waiting. She paid him his due plus a handsome tip.

Tirdad carried her case inside the dark corridor, switched on the light and then took the suitcase to the guest room.

"Tirdad is that you?" Asked Mohammad woken by the noise.

"Father, Rose has arrived."

The old man hurried out of bed, almost falling on his face.

"Shamsi get up. Rose is here. She has arrived." Mohammad yelled, shaking her curved back. At first she was disoriented and then she sat up, rubbed her eyes and asked: "what?"

"Rose is here. Get up and make her breakfast."

"She can make her own breakfast. I am not her servant."

"She is our guest and has come all the way to help us. Get up and act like a decent, hospitable hostess." Mohammad urged and putting on his old and tattered silk dressing gown hastened to the room in which Rose was unpacking.

Tirdad was in the kitchen brewing tea.

"Welcome my dear. I did turn the alarm clock on last night, but it is as old as me. Its mechanism must have rusted and become dysfunctional – like me." A smiling Rose opened her arms and hugged him tight. She heard his heart beat fast and felt his kiss on the nape of her neck. She kissed him too and then her eyes fell on Shamsi appearing at the door, staring at her with cold eyes. She let the old man go, took a step forward and offering her Salam, embraced and kissed her. Shamsi stood still, instead of kissing her, patted her back and whispered a curt 'welcome'. They moved into the sitting room where Tirdad had placed the tea tray and a plate of cake. Shamsi, still in her nightgown, resembled an asylum's inmate. Her grey, long hair was unkempt. Her deeply lined and elongated face colourless and her long nose, with its quivering nostrils, touched the tip of her upper lip. The malice that darted out of her eyes gave Rose the shivers. For an instant she regretted coming to her house. She should have gone to a hotel. But that would have offended her husband. She shook off the aversion and smiled. They sat around the stained and dusty coffee table. Tirdad placed the first cup in front of Rose and cut her a piece of the cake. She took her cup, threw him a compassionate glance and thanked him with a smile. For once he was acting amicably towards her. Probably imprisonment had put some sense into his stubborn head.

Mohammad was all absorbed in his favourite girl, she had put on a bit of weight. It made her look like a woman and not a porcelain doll anymore and her hair was now meshed and blond. He had preferred her black hair, but perhaps she had gone blonde to cover the grey which surely had invaded her head during the passing years. One could never escape aging, but, she seemed to know how to cope with it.

"How is Datam?" He asked his voice laced with love.

"He is fine, plays his tennis regularly, drinks his wine and lectures four days a week. His only concern is your welfare, and that is why I am here – to take you with me to London."

The news instantly evaporated Mohammad's incessant chest pain and tightened Shamsi's forever present frown.

"We cannot afford to come to London. Tirdad is unemployed, and we have to help him out."

"Shamsi joon, you will be our guests and I hope Tirdad, as educated as he is, will find a decent job, soon."

"I do not think an air trip will be good for Mohammad's heart." Shamsi snapped, avoiding her husband's eyes.

"It will be the best cure for my heart, woman. Stop introducing obstacles to the one good thing that has come our way in a decade."

"Mother, father is right. You should go with Rose and do not worry about us. God is great. We can live on your pension money, it will be ample – that is of course if you give me authority to draw it."

Mohammad was too excited to take in what Tirdad had requested. He rose, went to his bedroom and after a few minutes returned with their passports. Fortunately neither had expired but they belonged to the Pahlavi era and had to be changed. Tirdad accepted the responsibility to help them with that issue. Rose drank her tea and a piece of the stale cake, while Shamsi, nervously fidgeted in her chair, her nostrils quivering as thought an insect was tickling them from inside.

"Shamsi joon, you will have a lovely time in London, where your sister Farzaneh joon lives and perhaps Farideh joon will come to see you too. Paris is almost less than an hour's flight from London."

"I do not want to see either of them. Imagine, all these years that I have been living in misery, they have been enjoying their lives, in luxury and comfort, near their children without an iota of concern for me."

"It was people like their husbands who caused the revolution – Freemason traitors and, American spies." Tirdad added rising to leave.

"Do not talk about your family like this." Mohammad reproached him with a tight frown.

"Tirdad do you have a car?" Rose asked, changing the subject.

"Yes, I drive your old Fiat that Datam gave me before you left Iran."

"Is it possible for you to drive me to Galandoak one day?"

"Sure, and is Gholam Reza still looking after the villa?"

"Yes. We have been so lucky to have him."

"Shall we go tomorrow?"

"Excellent. Why don't you ask Nary to come with us? We can make a picnic-day out of the trip?"

"That sounds good. Now I must leave, otherwise my wife will worry about me. Every time I am late, she thinks I have been taken back to jail!"

He picked up the two passports from the table and ran out of the door without noticing the expression of reservation set on his parents' faces.

"I am coming too." " Mohammad exclaimed, raising his index finger and moving it to stress his intention. Then in a wistful tone he added: "I never forget the lunches we had there, by the river, and the cherries you used to bring for us. What a wonderful life we had without valuing it. Spit on man's ungratefulness." He began to shake his head in regret. Rose gave him a serene smile.

"Agha Doctor, fortunately the property is still ours and you can go there as often as you wish with or without me. You just have to make the effort."

"My dear it is not just the place; it is the company we had. They are all dead or displaced."

"But we are still alive and here, and because of that, we must use and enjoy it." Rose turned to Shamsi: "Would you like to come too?"

"No. There will be no room in the car for me." She replied, rising to return to her room.

Mohammad threw her a disdainful glance. He knew she did not want to come because she would be with her daughters-in-law. He often wondered why she was so unkind to them – Nary, he could understand, but Rose? Why her? As mentally astute as he still was, he couldn't fathom that one out.

Rose put the cups and the plates on the tray and walked to the kitchen. When she reached its threshold, shocked by its state she halted and exclaimed a quiet: "Oh my God!" The stained and rusted sink was filled with unwashed dishes, crumbs, wilted herb leaves and other dirt covered the floor. The cream tiles were murky, and a population of cockroaches, ants and flies seemed to be feasting on the grime. Her horrified eyes also spotted two tiny black round balls signifying presence of mice. A surge of sour bile rushed up her throat. With difficulty she swallowed it, entered, and fitted the tray on the crowded table. She started opening kitchen drawers in search of a pair of plastic gloves which she fortunately found crumpled under a heap of dirty dishcloths. In spite of her fatigue, she set to work. The noise brought Mohammad to the Kitchen.

"Khanum what are you doing here?"

"I am cleaning Agha Doctor. This is awfully unhygienic and bad for your health."

"I know, but we cannot afford a domestic, Shamsi has no sense of cleanliness and my hands shake. I wash the dishes as we need them."

"Well I am here now. You return to your room and I will join you when I have finished."

"Thank you Khanum." The old man mumbled in shame. How could all this have happened to them? Once they had a respectable and comfortable life, and now, they lived in squalor. The thought squeezed his heart. Rose smiled at him, tapped his hunched back and said: "You go now and read your morning paper, and don't worry about a thing." Lost for words, he dropped his head and lumbered out.

Two hours later, as Rose was discarding her tattered gloves into the full-to-the-brim garbage bin, Shamsi stepped in. Astonished she stood still. Rose turned to her with a smile. She narrowed her fearful eyes and fixed them on her face. The smile froze on Rose's lips.

"What have you done Khanum?"

"I have just cleaned your kitchen."

Shamsi kept sweeping her eyes around and then began hitting her head with both hands. "God! I won't be able to find anything anymore. What am I to do now that everything has been displaced? Oh God please help me."

"Please don't worry Shamsi joon. I have not touched the inside of the cabinets. I have just cleared the mess and washed the dishes and all the surfaces."

Shamsi sharpened the protest in her eyes and yelled: "This is not your kitchen. Why do you have to interfere with everything? Isn't it enough that you run my son's life; now you aim to run mine too?"

The unreasonable accusation punctured Rose's heart. Blushed, she ignored the pain and replied:

"Of course this is not my kitchen, and I am awfully sorry for not asking your permission. But while I am staying here, please allow me to clean and cook for you?"

Shamsi didn't blink, so absorbed was she in the intruder's invasion of her space.

Rose inched closer to her, opened her arms and hugging her whispered:

"If you allow me to help you, Shamsi joon, you can teach me all the skills you have and I lack. I am so lucky to have the best cook in Iran as my mother-in-law."

"I cannot even brew a decent tea anymore, let alone cook."

Rose patted her bony back and murmured: "I am so sorry to find you like this and even sorrier for offending you. I really am. I just wanted to help. That is all."

As the fog in Shamsi's head thawed out, she wiggled out of Rose's hold, "never mind dear," she murmured, "I get cranky sometimes, for no reasons whatsoever. I really think I am going crazy."

"No, you are not." Rose assured her, putting an arm around her waist, and together they headed for the sitting room.

"Why do you look so gloomy Khanum?" Mohammad asked, turning the TV off.

"I am so ashamed of myself. Rose, here, wants me to improve her cooking skills. With my memory gone, I cannot even boil an egg without setting the kitchen on fire."

"Shamsi joon, that doesn't merit your frown. You will remember everything once you see me making a mess of your recipes."

"Khanum, Rose is right. I vouch that when you set your mind to it, you still cook as well as ever." He stood up. "Now Ladies, it is getting close to noon and I am already famished." Rubbing his hands together he smiled at Rose and asked: "What shall we have for lunch Madame?"

"Omelettes. There are some eggs and a few tomatoes in the fridge. One thing I can cook well is omelettes," she looked at Shamsi with her smiling eyes, "that is what I fed your son when we were students, in the States. "

"Lucky Datam!" Mohammad exclaimed with a grin.

"He did not complain?" Shamsi asked sniffing her nose.

"Not at all, in fact he counted himself lucky. Most other wives fed their husbands MacDonald hamburger and salami sandwiches." Rose laughed, "And, after my siesta, I will go to your supermarket and buy what I need to show you that I am a moderately good cook." She asserted looking at Shamsi with smiling eyes.

"Wonderful my dear – wonderful!" Exclaimed Mohammad who couldn't remember when he had eaten a proper hot meal.

"Rose, do you have any rials?" He asked concerned.

"Yes, I do Agha doctor, and thank you for asking."

Mohammad beamed. For once, here was someone who did not need his financial assistance.

For dinner, Rose made them veal with spaghetti. It was so tasty that even Shamsi couldn't complain.

The next morning at 8.30, Tirdad and Nary let themselves in. They found Rose and Mohammad chatting, with a food hamper on the table in front of them. Tirdad was surprised by Rose's efficiency but said nothing. Nary in her crocked black scarf and navy coat hanging loosely over her trousers, portrayed the image of a poor man's wife. She greeted the two in her usual aloofness and asked: "Isn't Shamsi joon coming with us?"

"No. She doesn't feel well today." Mohammad replied in his usual brevity.

"What a shame. It is lovely outside and the trip would do her good."

"You are right Khanum. But she tells me she has no energy for socializing." Mohammad replied shrugging his shoulders

"Tirdad picked up the hamper and moving towards the door said: "Let's go before the roads become traffic-jammed." The three followed him, and in a jovial mood fitted themselves in the car with Mohammad not minding Nary occupying the front seat which, out of politeness, should have been offered to him. Tirdad put the hamper in the boot, sat behind the steering wheel and headed north. Soon they reached the foothills of the mountain range from where the road wiggled up and up to the top of a hill and then descended into a wide plain dotted by tall and healthy trees with glittering leaves dancing to the rhythm of the mountain breeze and shading a gorge with plenty of rushing water. Here was the village of Lashgarak. The path on the left of the village leads to the ski slopes of Shemshak and Dizin and the one on its right to Galandoak and Latian dam, constructed during the Pahlavi era, not only to supply water but also to act as a leisure centre for the inhabitants of dry and dusty Teheran, as well as for the Empress who loved water skiing. Now it lay deserted, serving no other purpose than irrigation. The dam was the belly button of Galandoak and the land around it had tripled in price and one day would become one of the most sought after residential suburbs of the Capital. But that was to come much later. Rose's estate lay by the Jajerude River that feeds the dam.

They arrived by the gate and Tirdad hooted. No one opened it. He got out of the car and rang the bell. After a few minutes, Gholam Reza slit the gate open, protruded his head out and when he saw Tirdad, smiling his greeting, he opened the gate wide and stepped out. Then he saw Rose coming out of the car. He ran to her; bowed deep and aimed to take and kiss her hand. She withdrew it, "no more of that Gholam Reza. You are my Brother now." She said looking at him with glowing eyes

"I will always remain your servant shahzadeh (princess) Khanum." She smiled at his loyalty, stepped in, and roved her hungry eyes around. Everything seemed to be in perfect order, as her mother would have wished it. Healthy trees brimmed with ample ripe fruit like, apples, apricots and more.

Yonder the river had turned into a ravine. That was usual in summer months. On the right of the gate, well away from the road, the villa, lamented the days of its past glory. Rose walked to its entrance, closed her eyes and went back in time. She saw her mother, coming out of the door, with a green gardening apron tied around her waist calling for Gholam Reza; and her bespectacled father, smart in his cream cotton trousers and white shirt, following her to the veranda where he would sit and watch her guide, order and yell at Gholam Reza. The sound of footsteps broke the spin of her memory. She opened her eyes and saw Gholam Reza leaving the food hamper by the door; turn and hurry towards his quarters calling for his wife to come and see who has arrived.

Behjat stepped out of her room and as her eyes fell on Rose, she let out a joyous cry. Rose turned and saw her running towards her. She spread out her arms and wrapped them around the breathless woman whom she had given up hope of ever beholding again. Behjat kissed her again and again. Rose did not have the heart to push her away. Besides, her familiar homely smell reminded her of good days – when they were all a large, happy family.

"Enough of that, Behjat Khanum." An impatient Mohammad scolded. His shirt soaked in sweat, he longed for a glass of ice water.

Concerned, Rose untangled herself from Behjat's hold and turned to him, "Agha doctor please go inside, I will join you after visiting my parents."

"We will all come with you." Mohammad replied without a flinch. So they all followed Rose and Behjat to the weeping willow, under which the Hands were buried. There, to her surprise, she found a square neat rose-bed, in the midst of which was a rectangular white marble with the Qajar insignia etched on it in gold. She knelt by the smallest rose bush and without sensing the sting of its thorns, passed her hand through its branches and placed it over the stone. Trying to capture her parents' energy she closed her eyes and began to pray. In her mind she saw them together, hand in hand greeting her with their everlasting smiles intact. The experience felt so real that she heard herself calling their names. Instead of their voice she heard the chirping of the birds. She opened her eyes to two beautiful yellow roses smiling at her. It was their energy that had fed these flowers and it was now capturing her soul and nourishing it with their love. Concluding that death is not the end she grinned at the enigma of life. How could one become extinct? The smallest iota of one's being is an atom which is made of energy. Energy never dies – does it? She withdrew her arm, stood up, inhaled a lung full of the fresh, rose-scented mountain air, smiled at her companions and together they headed for the villa.

She walked in and found the interior immaculately clean with all the memorabilia's collected in the past, still in their places. Nothing had changed within those walls. Time had stood still there. Rose ran to her room, took off and threw her cotton coat on her bed, and returned to the sitting room. A cheerful Gholam Reza entered with a tray of cold cherry drink.

"Doctor the sharbat (syrup) is made from our own cherries."

"I am sure Behjat has made some cherry jam too."

"Yes Agha and I will give you a large jar to take home."

"Excellent. I love cherry jam with yoghurt."

"Shahzadeh Khanum, this year I was able to sell some of our cherries and I have a buyer for the apricots too. The proceeds will pay for the manures and half of my salary."

"That is wonderful Gholam Reza, well done man and please do not call me shahzadeh anymore."

"And why not shahzadeh?" Gholam Reza asked, his wide eyes conveying rays of objection.

"Because these days, being a shahzadeh is considered a crime and they might take me to jail." Rose teased.

Gholam Reza straightened his stooping back, pushed his wide bony chest forward and declared:

"As long as I live, no one can take a single string of hair from your head my shahzadeh."

"Thank you for your chivalry Gholam Reza but please just call me Rose Khanum. I like that better."

"If that is your preference, this servant will obey."

"And you are not my servant. You are my brother."

Rose replied, patting him on the shoulders. He smiled and in his very polite manner asked: "Will you stay for lunch Khanum?"

"Yes, we have brought some sandwiches which we like to eat by the river. Can you spread a rug under the weeping willow and a sofreh (table cloth) on it please and of course ask Behjat to make us her very strong tea."

"Sandwich is no food for my Khanum. I am going to make you chicken kebab myself, the way I used to for the Prince – God bless his soul: marinated in lemon juice and saffron."

At the thought Mohammad's mouth watered and his eyes acquired a happy shine that illuminated Rose's heart, "that will be very nice. I have not had a good chicken Kebab for years now." She exclaimed with excitement.

Gholam Reza placed his tray on the dining table and dashed out to head for the village's poultry shop. It was only ten thirty and he had plenty of time.

"Please help yourselves." Rose invited, taking a glass and occupying her usual chair that faced the window. With her hand she indicated the arm chair to the doctor. Glass in hand he sat and praising the deep ruby colour of the sharbat took a sip. "This is divine!" He exclaimed before drinking the whole lot in one go. Life had taught him to take full joy of its gifts. He put the glass down and focused his eyes on the picturesque view showcased by the wall to wall window. Rose who didn't like sweet drinks took a sip and returned the glass to the table. As she looked up her eyes fell on Nary's brooding face on which wavered the green hue of envy.

She felt a twinge of pity for her, "The silly girl," she thought, "instead of enjoying the day, she is wasting it." She turned her eyes to Tirdad standing by the window, "Tirdad," she called out, "come and join us." He finished the last drop of his drink, walked to the dining table, left the glass on its tray and took the seat next to his wife. Behjat, who was observing everything with the perception of a concerned mother, collected the empty glasses, put them on the tray and hastened out of the room. A deep silence fell. Tirdad was calculating how much money his unworthy brother could make out of this property if he had the sense which, the lucky bastard probably didn't, by subdividing its land and selling the lots to developers. Nary, deep in thought was coveting Rose's prosperity; Mohammad was thinking of Datam and Rose was wondering why no one talked. She waited for a while, hoping someone would start a conversation. But no one did. The tediousness of the silence began to play on her nerves and when she couldn't stand it anymore she stood up and looked around. No one paid her any attention. She walked out of the room, took a deep breath and ambled to the weeping willow where Behjat was busy spreading the sofreh over the rug. "Let me help you Behjat?"

"You can put the plates and the cutlery on the sofreh while I go and burn some wild rue to take away the evil eye, which I am sure is hanging over you and this house. I didn't like the atmosphere of that room. It made me quiver."

"I didn't either Behjat. It is strange that nothing I do seems to please my husband's family – very strange. Or perhaps my hand doesn't have any salt."

"Rubbish Khanum. Your hand has plenty of salt, even now, after your long absence from their sight; those who tasted your generosity remember you and pray for your happiness. Sensible souls never forget people's kindness unless they are jealous, like your guests up in the villa."

Rose acquiesced with a nod and began to set the sofreh.

A few minutes later Behjat appeared with her sizzling rue burner, its curling fragrant vapour purifying the air from malice. Murmuring her prayer she swivelled the burner above Rose's head and then around the garden.

"Khanum can you hear the crackling sound of the seeds?"

"Yes. They are burning ferociously aren't they?"

"Yes. It is not just the seeds that are burning. It is their venom in the air."

Enshallah Rose murmured giving Behjat a serene smile. Then she turned and walked to the river shore. There, she took off her shoes, folded the edges of her pants up and stepped into the river bed. Like when she was a child, she tiptoed on the stones to reach the running water. It was cold and refreshing. She began to leap from one large stone to another. She heard Tirdad say: "Rose you are so lucky to still have this villa." She turned.

"Its doors are always open to my family, Tirdad joon. "

"Can we really use this place when you are not here?"

"Of course you can. Just call Gholam Reza and come. I will tell him to look after you as though you were Datam."

Tirdad moved closer to where she was standing. "Thank you so much Rose. You know, without any income, I cannot take my family on any holidays. This will do splendidly."

She started hopping back. "Tirdad dear, just treat this place as your own. It will make Datam very happy."

Tirdad's smile broadened.

Rose saw the steam of Gholam Reza's charcoal burner rising up, twirling upwards, and perfuming the air with mouth-watering aroma of the saffron-marinated chicken that was being barbequed. A perspiring Behjat was fanning the charcoals and Gholam Reza astutely turning the skewers for even cooking.

Tasting the kebabs in her mouth, Rose tiptoed out, dried the soles of her feet on the rug, put her shoes on and ran to the villa to call the others come to dine.

When the food was laid on the sofreh, Rose invited Gholam Reza and Behjat to join them. They refused. She kept insisting until they took off their shoes, sat on the grass and crossed their legs. No one except Mohammad noticed the flicker of objection pass over Nary's drawn face. "God knew the ass well. That is why he did not give it horns." Shaking his head in disgust Mohammad whispered, picked up a plate and served himself with the juicy chicken and tomato pieces that were soaking a layer of Lavash bread beneath them. Then he took a piece of bread from the sofreh, on which he placed two kebab pieces and a couple of basil leaves. Carefully he wrapped the flat bread around the ingredients and began eating his treat with utmost attentiveness, relishing the taste of every morsel. Having finished his wrap, Mohammad focused his eyes on the soaked bread.

Rose taking delight in his contentment stretched over the sofreh; and with her fingers lifted the largest slice and dropped it on Mohammad's plate. Then she began licking her fingers that tasted delicious. "You are spoiling me Khanum joon." He said digging his fork into the bread.

Behjat handed her a tissue. Rose took it with a smile and cleaned her hand.

"Rose, leave some for me and Tirdad." Nary demanded, pouting her mouth like a child.

"There is plenty more. Give me your plate please." Rose demanded.

Throwing her head back, "on second thought, I won't have any. It is too fattening," she said pinching her nose up.

Rose grinned and pushed the dish towards Tirdad. "I am sure you are not worried about your weight. In fact you need to put couple of kilos on."

"I do feed him well at home."

"I am sure you do Nary joon. But he seems to need more nourishment." Rose snapped without looking at her.

Tirdad entranced by the sumptuousness of his meal, pushed his empty plate away and pulled the kebab dish towards himself. Nary threw him a sour glance and puffed up.

The sun was sinking languidly. The horizon had turned copper colour and the air cold. They were having tea when a pensive Gholam Reza turned to Rose, "Khanum joon, you know that the price of land has tripled in the last two years and I have one leg in the grave. You are not here and sometimes I get nightmares as what will happen to this lovely house when I have gone. Why do you not subdivide the land, keep the villa and the area up to your weeping willow and sell the rest? Not a day passes without me getting a knock at the gate asking if the property is for sale."

Tirdad's eyes began to flash. Mohammad detected the wickedness in their glow and trembled.

Rose pondered for a minute or two and then replied: "Gholam Reza this is a brilliant idea but needs time and personnel. I cannot leave Agha alone in London and stay here for long. I wish I had someone to trust enough to give a power of attorney to supervise the plan, go to all the different institutions for the thousand permits required for the subdivision and transactions. There is a lot of office leg work involved in such a plan which is beyond me."

Gholam Reza, scratched his head full of white hair, swept his grey eyes around and settled them on Tirdad.

Suddenly a thought occurred to Rose. Here was a chance to off load the excess land and also financially help Tirdad. He had already told her that he needs a job badly and with the Tudeh stigma attached to his name and a jail record, he would never find one.

"Tirdad, are you willing to undertake the task?" She asked "I will pay you a regular salary, all the expenses and a commission on the sales."

Blood rushed to Mohammad's head, his jaw fell and a tight frown formed on his forehead. Tirdad's smile broadened and Rose noticed Nary's eyes shine with delight. It warmed her heart.

"Of course I will Rose – of course." Tirdad replied, his countenance as bright as a full moon.

Mohammad, pensive and sombre jumped up. "We must leave now. Otherwise Shamsi will worry about us."

Rose had never seen him so agitated before. It worried her.

"Yes. We better leave now." She said rising. Gholam Reza gave her a hand. "Thank you for the delicious lunch. I wish Agha was here too. Enshallah one day he will be able to return to Iran and taste your kebabs Gholam Reza."

"Enshallah Khanum joon. Enshallah."

"Agha Tirdad and Nary Khanum will be using this house in my absence. Please make their stay comfortable and pleasant."

"I shall Khanum joon. You do not have to worry about anything at all." Gholam Reza turned to Tirdad, "please let us know a day ahead so that we prepare the house for you."

"I shall Gholam Reza." Tirdad replied

Gholam Reza remembering something ran to his quarter.

Tirdad had started the engine when Gholam Reza appeared with a large jar of cherry jam. Through the open window, Mohammad grabbed it from him. "This will last me at least six months my good man." Suddenly he remembered the food hamper. "Behjat Khanum please bring our picnic basket."

"It is already in the boot of the car." Tirdad informed.

"Agha doctor, now that Agha Tirdad will be visiting us, you won't have to buy jam any more. Behjat makes good Jam and you shall have plenty."

Mohammad stretched his arm out of the window again, grabbed Gholam Reza's hand and shaking it in gratitude said: "That will be very nice of you my man."

The drive home was far more agreeable than the one from it. Nary and Tirdad, talked, cracked jokes and suggested various plans for the subdivision. Rose listened and responded but Mohammad remained silent and pensive.

At home they found Shamsi in bed. Mohammad took the hamper to the kitchen and emptied it. He chose what was to be eaten for dinner and the rest he put in the fridge. He returned the empty basket to its place over the fridge, hid his jam jar in a safe place and walked to Rose's room where she had already changed into her house dress. He sat on her bed and with his hand patted on the space next to him. Curious, she sat down.

"Rose I want to ask you a great favour."

"Anything you ask, I will do Agha doctor."

"Do not involve Tirdad in any financial affairs, please."

"Why, Agha doctor?"

"Do not ask why – just follow my advice – I beg you?"

"Agha doctor, he needs money and work. This will give him both. He has a family to feed and I need someone of my own, someone I can trust, to deal with the sale of the land."

"That is the point. I do not think you should trust Tirdad – he is not the same man he used to be."

"Why? Has he done anything to give rise to your suspicion?"

"Yes. He is stealing from us."

"I cannot believe it!"

"He lets himself in when he knows we are out and pinches whatever he can sell. I did not want to tell you, but a couple of the antique plates you left here are missing. It is his doing. When we enquire about the missing items, he raises his voice, tells us we are senile and to his knowledge we never owned such objects. He keeps his door closed to us. Whenever he asks for money, we give him. Nothing seems to be enough – it is entirely that woman's fault. She doesn't know how to economise. Besides, they both drink heavily – they drink whisky. Each bottle costs four hundred thousand Rials."

"Oh my God – this is awful!" Rose exclaimed shocked.

He took her hand and stroked it gently. She fell into a reflective silence, her conscience hard at work. She examined all the pros and cons of trusting Tirdad and then looked up at Mohammad and said: "Agha doctor, he must be desperate. Desperate men do worse things than steal. Let us give him a chance? Perhaps the dignity of being employed will direct him to the right path."

Mohammad looked into her eyes with great concerned apprehension. "If he steals from you, it will affect your relationship with your husband, and I will die of shame."

"More serious things have happened in my life without affecting my relationship with my husband Agha doctor. Do not worry about that. I was going to give him a total power of attorney to act on my behalf. I won't now. That I will give to you and to him I will give the power to act in dealing with government institutions without being allowed to sell or buy on my behalf. Then he won't be able to cheat me and you won't have to worry about anything."

"Still, I think you should not involve him in any of your financial affairs and please, before taking any steps talk to Datam and see what he will say."

"Ok, let's give him a call now."

Datam's response to her plan was the same as his father's: do not involve Tirdad in any of your affairs.

Believing in the magic of a second chance, Rose gave Tirdad the benefit of a doubt. She commissioned an architect to plan the subdivision and at Galandoak's Notary office she gave him and Mohammad the necessary powers to act on her behalf.

Chapter 7

London

Datam paced up and down the hall in an agitated state of mind. He could think of nothing but the worst. His father had already suffered two heart attacks. With all the usual hassles at the airport in Teheran, the one hour delay and the long flight, anything could happen to him. 'Oh, God please let me see him alive once more – please.'" He kept pleading until the landing announcement he was waiting for blasted out of the loud speaker. He rushed towards the crowded gate where several chauffeurs, clad in black coats, exposed name placards. Praying, he waited. As the passengers began to appear pushing their trolleys an animated commotion broke the earlier order and to his great joy and relief he spotted his father, a skeleton of a man, clad in his old, now too big, beige cashmere coat, manoeuvring a trolley. The task seemed too cumbersome for him. There was a smile on his tired face and an eagerness in his searching eyes. Shamsi, lumbered along. She appeared more dead than alive. Then his eyes fell on his wife's shining face, carefully guiding her trolley behind Shamsi. He exhaled a sigh of relief as though his saviour had arrived to deliver him from the loads that weighed on his shoulders. That had been the story of their lives. Right from the first moment when Rose had taken his hand and led him to the dance floor, his hand had remained within her hold, being pulled through life by her stamina and devotion. If ever anyone asked him what the greatest blessing of his life was, he would reply Rose. Excited, he began waving his hands until Mohammad caught his eyes. Their hearts dissolved in the warmth of ecstasy and the glow of happiness eroded the lines of fatigue from the old man's face. Datam ran to them and embraced the two at the same time, kissing and wooing them with all the love in his heart. Rose calmly waited her turn. When it came, it was as though Romeo had met Juliet for the first time. Mohammad took great satisfaction in watching them but not Shamsi. She kept coiling around herself like a disturbed snake.

Datam grabbed the handle of his father's trolley and chitchatting they walked towards the exit and the car park.

"Agha doctor you take the front seat please."

Mohammad threw her a tender and appreciative glance, and clutched the door handle.

The drive from Heathrow to Old Brompton Road past so agreeably that no one noticed the traffic jam, and the hour it took to reach home. Datam unloaded his passengers and their luggage in front of the entrance at Coleherne Court and went in search of a parking space which he found in the nearby Little Bolton. He locked his Mercedes and hurried home. There he found his parents standing by the sitting room's window, admiring the greenery that lay in their view. The manicured garden was two and half acres and private. It enchanted Mohammad.

He could take his morning walk without having to cross any roads. Cars here drove on the wrong side. That scared him. He could easily fail to look at the right direction and be hit by a car. Right now he wanted to live and enjoy the company of his two favourite people in this wide and crowded world.

Datam came close, put his arm around his parents' shoulders, "Our garden is very beautiful isn't it?" He asked kissing the crown of their heads.

"Indeed it is. Rose loves gardens and God loves Rose and always grants her wishes." Mohammad said looking at Rose with tenderness.

Shamsi sighed, turned to Datam and said: "Son I wish your brother was as lucky as you are."

The smile froze on Mohammad's face.

"Khanum Tirdad was never as wise as Datam. Please don't substitute wrong decisions with bad luck. He could have left Iran with Jill, worked in Austria and established a home for his family – perhaps even better than this. No, your righteous son had to stay, fight the system and bring disaster to his and our lives. You should be sorry for us and not him – my dear."

"Shamsi joon, do not worry about him so much. He is receiving a good monthly salary from me and enshallah he will earn a lot of commission from the sale proceeds of Galandoak. Then, he can buy a lovely flat in Teheran and put your mind at ease."

"Madar you are here to relax and enjoy yourself and not worry about anything at all. Rest assured, now that he is out, we will all do what we can for him. I think you should go to your room now, take a bath, change and let me take you to Hyde Park for a walk."

"Son, I am too tired for a walk. You all go. I stay here."

"Khanum, please come with us, and let us enjoy this lovely day together. The weather is so nice today. Tomorrow, it might rain, and you will be locked inside."

"Agha doctor, you and Datam go. I will stay with Shamsi joon and together we will prepare something for lunch." Rose suggested turning to her husband.

"Darling, I hope you have bought what I asked on the phone?"

"Yes, the fridge is full to the brim." Datam replied in a cutting tone that pleased Shamsi enormously. Thank God, at last, he has learnt how to treat her, she said to herself, a satisfied grin blooming on her hitherto pinched face. Rose noticed it but didn't care. After all these years she had gotten used to her malice and crow's cacklings.

Lately Datam had become very impatient, intolerant and egoistic. He detested being asked to do anything, even if it was for himself. To him all requests disturbed his routine. The little time left to him was to be spent on what pleased him and him alone – like a spoilt brat. His selfish conduct, at times abusive, wounded Rose deeply. But she said nothing. Her compassion was far greater than her pride and convenience. Often she put herself in his place and understood what went in his mind. If she was living with death as her shadow; a shadow that soon would catch up with her, she probably would be even more selfish than he had become since his illnesses. At times, when he was in a good mood, she would try to convince him that no one knows when his end will arrive; that she might go before he does; that life and death are in the hands of

God. He would smile at her reasoning and say: "If your time comes before mine, I will commit suicide." And she would smile back and warn: "If you do not want me to die, stop being selfish." Then they would embrace, kiss, laugh and forget about death and dying.

Now, in spite of being slighted, Rose said nothing. Retaliation would demean her own dignity and that she would never do especially in front of a snake.

Shamed by her tolerance and regretting his unnecessary grouchiness, Datam fixed his repenting eyes on her. Aware of them she raised an eyebrow. He blew her a kiss. It melted her resentment. He breathed with ease and then addressed his father:

"Baba, would you like to change before we go?"

"No son. I cannot be bothered. I can walk with these shoes. They are quite comfortable. Besides, if I take them off, my feet are so swollen that I cannot fit them into anything else."

Half an hour later, Datam parked the car at Rutland Gate, quite close to the path that leads to the Serpentine. Out of the car, Mohammad stretched his back, looked around him, "what a lovely day!" He exclaimed taking a deep breath. "Let's walk around the lake."

"Won't that be too tiring for you today?"

"No, I am not fatigued at all."

At the cross road, Datam gripped his bony arm and cautiously led him across and into the park that was animated by joggers, strollers, bicycle riders and little kids playing in the playground with their nannies or mothers monitoring their activities.

After fifteen minutes of promenade, Datam noticed signs of exhaustion on Mohammad's countenance.

"Would you like to sit down Baba joon?"

"Yes, for just a few moments though."

They found a bench under a chestnut tree, facing the lake. On it they sat side by side, so close that their shoulders met. It felt great. Once more they were together and able to delight in its intimacy. Neither had felt so light, well and happy in a decade now. Mohammad taking in nourishment from their proximity noticed his son's tranquil face was set with a heavy touch of weariness. There was plenty of greying at his temples, deep lines on his broad forehead and his eyes had lost their lustre. This premature ageing worried him but he said nothing. Later he would enquire about it from Rose. She always told the truth. He abandoned the worry to its nagging, patted Datam's thigh and said:

"Thank you for being such a wonderful son, and for giving me the opportunity to see you once more before I died."

Datam took his hand, kissed it and held it tight.

"Baba, I am so sorry for everything. I feel so ashamed for not being able to be there for you. Please forgive me?"

"What is there to forgive? We are responsible for our choices. Had your mother accepted your wise suggestion to leave Iran with you, our life would have been different. She wanted to be with Tirdad. She always thought he needed protection; from what only God knows!"

"Probably from himself." Datam whispered and sighed.

"Wisely put," murmured Mohammad wistfully.

They fell silent and let their eyes appreciate the stunning scenery that glittered around them. Above, the blue sky was patterned by different shapes and shades of clouds with which, the sun played hide and seek. A population of pigeons, organized in a semicircle glided over the lake, their shadows undulating on the water that shimmered like a sheet of polished silver. At a corner, an elderly couple, each holding a bag of bread fed the ducks and the geese that were competing for the crumbs. Near them a group of crows pecked at the morsels they were finding on the pavement. A cool breeze fluttered the leaves that caught the sun rays and glittered like emeralds. In this paradise Mohammad's heart opened to God and he whispered a "Khodaya Shokret.

"Father, I have made an appointment with a famous heart surgeon, at the Harley Street clinic. He is very good."

"Thank you. But you know I cannot afford Harley Street doctors."

"Baba joon, do not worry about money. We will pay for everything."

"Do you know that you have married a jewel of a woman?"

"Yes father. I am very fortunate to have a father like you and a wife like Rose."

"I cannot understand how two brothers can differ so much. I often blame myself for what has happened to Tirdad."

"Do not do that. He never listened to anyone, even when he was a kid. Enshallah jail has put some sense into his head. According to Rose, he has become tolerant of the world's inhabitants and if so, that is a miracle!"

"I am worried about Rose's decision to work with him. I hope nothing will go wrong."

"We both advised her not to. She, by herself, decided to go ahead, and I know if anything goes wrong, she won't blame either of us. Nonetheless enshallah he will do the right thing by her. Enshallah"

"Let's hope and pray so." Mohammad whispered.

"Has he done something new to earn your distrust?"

Mohammad just bit his lip.

A tennis ball landed by their feet. A black poodle ran to pick it up. A beautiful girl stood at a distance monitoring the dog.

The two smiled at her and patted the dog. The poodle looked at them with curious eyes, immersed the ball in his mouth and waggling his tail ran back to his owner.

"Once we had a black poodle called Blacky."

"I remember it. He was never allowed in."

"No, but before we left Rose gave him to a Dutch friend. He must be in Holland now!"

"Lucky dog!"

"Yes he was indeed lucky. Our neighbour had to put his dog to sleep before they left for France."

"Son, I need your advice. You know, I am old and ailing; I was thinking before I die, I should sell the duplex and buy two independent flats, one for Tirdad and one for you. Do you think that is a good idea?"

"Indeed it is. First it will make Tirdad and Nary independent from you and second it will boost Tirdad's ego and make him feel good. You know that I am on that bloody list, so I cannot own anything. You should buy the second flat under mother's name, so she feels secure too."

"I cannot give a child something and nothing to the other."

"Father, the chances of me coming to Iran again are remote. Besides we have enough. Neither Rose nor I will begrudge Tirdad, for becoming an owner of a home. We will be glad for him."

"It is because of your heart son, that God has been so kind to you."

Pensive Datam fell silent. He could not bring himself to tell him that his days were numbered and that no one should envy him.

"What is wrong son?"

Datam shook his head and in a voice tinged with remorse replied:

"Nothing is wrong with me Baba joon. In reality, nothing is ours forever – neither wealth nor health nor those we love. What we take to our grave is our body wrapped in a shroud. That is all – so why not be generous with what is in our custody!"

Surprised by the melancholy in his air, Mohammad asked: "Is there anything wrong son?"

"No Baba joon. I have not been as happy as I am now, sitting beside you, since the Revolution."

"Is there anything wrong with your health?"

"No, nothing Baba joon." He answered avoiding his father's concerned eyes for he couldn't look into them and lie.

The falsehood in his tone wasn't lost on a mind as perceptive as Mohammad's. Instinctively he clasped Datam's hand as though trying to save him from harm. He turned and smiled in sadness. They remained quiet until Mohammad pointed to the cafe on the other side of the lake, "I love to have a cafe au lait. Do they serve it here?"

"Yes, of course – it is just ordinary coffee with hot milk served in a long glass."

"Shall we go over there and have one each?"

"Why not Baba joon?"

Arm in arm they strolled towards the restaurant chatting and laughing at trivialities that had made moments happy.

After a few days of rest, Datam took his parents to the Harley Street Clinic for a complete check-up and once relieved that no one was about to die, they set to enjoy their time together. Weather permitting, they toured the parks, rowed on the Serpentine and picnicked on the lawn. During the evenings when they were not invited to friends, Datam took them to French restaurants for Mohammad to feast on entrecote and Shamsi chateaubriand. As bad luck would have it, her meat pieces were never tender enough to merit praise. On rainy days Rose drove them to the museums of their choice. Shopping they did very little. However, against her objections Shamsi became owner of a new wardrobe from Marks &Spencer at Oxford Street. Mohammad, the same size as Datam, chose what he wanted from his designer packed wardrobe accumulated by Rose whose taste was impeccable. She had always been very protective of her husband and his image. She believed most people judge by their eyes and never dig below the glitter that initially attracts their attention. Her husband was an introvert so hardly anyone was able to admire the decency, courage and wisdom hidden behind his serene smile and accommodating attitude. So they might as well recognize his elegance and boost his ego by their praise, that sweet booster of the soul. His happiness mattered to her a lot. For she believed happy men had a will to live and that will strengthened their immune system to defy defeat. Thus to this end she endeavoured hard. They had been married for three decades, gone through heaven and hell together without a word of blame – with a love that knew no boundary. In their love they were able to include the rest of humanity and thus live in peace.

As all good times come to an end, Mohammad and Shamsi's sojourn ended in tears and prayers for another reunion, which they all knew was improbable. Looking healthy, chic and a few kilos heavier they embarked into their plane and flew back home.

At the airport, Tirdad welcomed them without any warmth, appraised their appearance with envious eyes and remarked: "I am glad to see my millionaire brother has fed and clothed you well."

"Yes, Rose and Datam did. We had a lovely time and we all wished you were with us. " Mohammad responded ignoring the sarcasm in his tone.

"And he sent you a beautiful cashmere jumper." Shamsi added.

"How generous of him Madar," he said turning his eyes back to his father, "if he really had missed me, he could have invited and paid for me and my family's tickets to accompany you there."

Mohammad handed his trolley to him and smirked: "Without a passport you couldn't have travelled, could you?"

"No, but with his money, he could have bought me one?"

"Please don't be ridiculous."

"I am not being ridiculous. You and everyone else know that money resolves all problems."

"It might but not in your very special case."

Lost for words Tirdad pushed the trolley, purposely walking too fast to pain his parents' arthritic knees. By the car, grudgingly he fitted their luggage in its boot, banged its door shut, sat behind the wheel, waited until they got in and then drove like a maniac. By the time they reached home the old couple were on the verge of having heart attacks. He unlocked the entrance door, pushed their luggage inside and dashed out banging the door behind him. Overwhelmed by his enmity, they exchanged a glance and as they bent to pick up the cases to take to their room their eyes fell on the floor which had lost its Nain carpet.

"Well, he has taken that too!" Mohammad murmured pulling a case behind him. Shamsi followed suit. Half an hour later, changed into their pyjamas they lumbered to the kitchen to eat something. In the fridge they found some eggs, a bottle of milk and a small container of yoghurt – no bread, no fruit and no salad greens. Yet again he had not heeded to their simple request.

Mohammad rose early in the morning, took his shower, shaved and dressed up. Then pleased with himself, he sat by his unpacked suitcase and took out the packet of Quaker's Oat he had the good sense to bring with him.

"Khanum, I am making porridge. Would you like a bowl?" He yelled from the kitchen. To her curt 'no', he smiled happily. Once the concoction was ready he filled his bowl, sat down and with every mouthful he imagined he was in London, sitting in Rose's kitchen watching her extract vegetable juice for Datam. It was during one of those mornings that he had enquired about Datam's health. In a nonchalant way she had satisfied his curiosity by saying: "Please don't worry about him Agha doctor. He just suffers from Iron deficiency. That is why he is pale and at times lethargic." The information had set his mind at ease. Bless Rose, she never bears bad news. He had thought and given her a kiss on the forehead.

An hour later, in an excellent mood, smart in an Armani suit, like a man with a mission he left home to meet with the real estate agent who had found him his present property. There he told him he wanted to sell his duplex and buy a two and a three bedroom apartment, in the vicinity of Avenue Ghandi. From the agency he headed for Tirdad's flat encountering Nary on her way out. She offered a cold Salam, a brisk welcome and dashed off to meet Hashem. He had rented a small love nest nearby. In hiding her liaison she had proved to be more conniving than Machiavelli himself.

Mohammad entered the apartment, spotting some of their furnishing items the existence of which were denied by both Nary and Tirdad and the vanished Nain carpet, all tastefully displayed in the sitting room. He paled, yet thanked God that at least they had not been sold to a second hand dealer.

Tirdad, certain his father had come to check if their missing furniture was in his flat, offered a cold Salam and waited for his reproach.

Gasping from the climb, Mohammad dropped on the nearest armchair and asked for a glass of ice water. Tirdad grudgingly obliged and unceremoniously handed the glass to him.

Ignoring his effrontery, Mohammad thanked him, relinquished his thirst and placing the glass on the table pointed to the chair facing him. "Sit down son. I have to talk to you."

Finding his father's amicable tone strange, he sat down, totally confused as what to expect.

"As you know, with your release from jail the Government has removed the ban on our pensions and I am allowed to do as I wish with my properties. Hence I have put this building up for sale." Tirdad's heart sank. The bastard was going to make him homeless for the sake of an old withered carpet. He assumed feeling an excruciating pain invade his intestine. Tension always activated his spastic colitis and for days he suffered intermittent spasms. To divert his mind from the stomach-ache he began to crack his knuckles. Mohammad too involved in his plan didn't notice the pleats of pain wavering on Tirdad's face nor his tensed posture.

"I intend to buy a two-bedroom apartment for you and a three bedroom one for Shamsi. Separating from us will give you independence and will earn you more respect in the eyes of your in-laws. However, you must promise me on your honour, to never sell that flat and make yourself homeless. Will you do that?"

Unable to believe his ears Tirdad flinched. Anxiety subsided; he relaxed his shoulders and exhaled with relief. "This is extremely kind of you Baba." His eyes fell on the Nain carpet and blushed with shame. Mohammad noticed the rush of blood to his cheeks. At least he has enough conscience left in him to feel shame, he thought with satisfaction. Tirdad looked up at him and said: "Baba joon, of course I promise never to sell my flat. Every man's dream is to own a roof over his family's head and you are giving me that chance, for which I will be eternally grateful to you."

"No gratitude is necessary. I am doing what any father, who knows his days are numbered, would do. Why pay inheritance tax when it can be avoided?"

"When did you make this sound and generous decision Baba?"

"I discussed it with your brother and we made this decision together. It was he who told me to buy the flat under Shamsi's name and not his." A wave of resentment flared up the nasty side of Tirdad's nature and made him go green with envy.

"Baba, I hope you are not assuming that he made that suggestion because he is considerate. He has been his clever self again – being on that list prohibits him from owning anything – so why not be generous with what you cannot have anyway. That is my holy brother's way of thinking. Do not be fooled by his soft voice and phony good-intentions. He always gets what he wants, only just because people 'feel' for him – lucky bastard."

"Do not be unfair to your brother. I offered to buy it under Rose's name and yet he refused. She is not on that list."

"She has enough to last them for three generations. Good that they are childless. I guess if I outlive both of them I will inherit an enormous wealth. That will be absolutely wonderful. He is a sickly man and behind the wheel she drives that white Ferrari of hers like a lunatic."

"Who told you that she has a Ferrari?"

"A person who detests her arrogance."

Mohammad couldn't bear hearing one mean word about Rose. He narrowed his eyes and mocked: "You mean is jealous of her class, elegance and happiness?"

"What does she have that makes you so proud of her Baba?"

"All the things your wife doesn't. I cannot believe you say such things about someone who has been so kind to you. I really cannot." Mohammad shook his head in perplexity.

Tirdad frowned but remained silent. He didn't want to say anything disagreeable until the deed was done.

"Son, what she owns should not concern us. Datam, is my son and what I give you, I have to give to him too. That is being fair and I like my children to think of me as a fair father."

Suddenly something inside Tirdad's mind snapped and he gave vent to his pent up grudges. "Hah – you think by being fair with your wealth you can erase your unfairness toward me. You always preferred Datam to me. You never punished him for his misdeeds while I was beaten every day and when the time came you sent him to the States and me to France."

This was a new grievance that amazed Mohammad and made him wonder as to how his son's perverted mind had concluded that the French education was inferior to American.

He paused to overcome his irritation and then looked him straight in the eyes.

"Datam never misbehaved, you did. He applied and was accepted at the University of his choice, you applied and failed. Your next best option was France and you got in the same university as I went to, which is one of the best in Europe. What either of you did with that degree of yours was your own doing, not mine."

"Father, is it at all possible that for once, you stop defending Datam and understand me and feel for me?"

"Son, stop comparing yourself with your brother all the time. Jealousy, like a worm, eats the heart out. Cleanse your mind and heart from hatred; inhale the scent of love instead of the odour of hate and let it enhance your spirit and release it from its cage of envy. I beg you, Tirdad, believe in our love and respect for you and be the good son that you can be." Mohammad took out a handkerchief from his trousers' pocket, dried his perspiring forehead, tucked the kerchief back and took a deep breath. "My dear, remember each flower has its own beauty and scent. In my garden of passion, I have nurtured two flowers, each of which is unique in the joy it gives me. Let me enjoy you. Discard the dirt that is overwhelming your heart and mind and let the light of love illuminate your life. Please son, do this more for yourself than for us. Please!"

The old man stopped and wiped his eyes with the heel of his hand. He hated crying, which he thought was a sign of weakness in a man, especially in front of his sons who had to look up to him, obey and respect him, the way generations after generations had done in Iran. But, at that moment his heart was so tight that he had to cleanse it from the emotion that was chocking him.

Touched beyond his comprehension, Tirdad rose, took the old man's hand, kissed it and helped him to rise. They walked down the stairs and into the flat below. Before leaving his father, Tirdad said: "Baba, we had no floor covering, so I borrowed your carpet. It was hiding under the dining table and no one could really see it. I hope you don't mind."

"It would have been proper, if you had asked one of us first."

"Yes, you are right Baba. I will bring it back this evening."

"Well, let's say that is a gift from us to you."

"Thank you Baba and I am sorry again."

Two blocks away, Nary was taking a shower. Hashem, as bubbly as ever, entered the bathroom, cupped both her breasts within his large palms, squeezed them hard, stole a kiss from each nipple and whispered: "You are so delicious my love."

She gave him a tender glance and smiled. He turned from her and faced the vanity's slightly fogged mirror. A healthy looking guy stared back at him. Smiling he combed his jet black curly hair, rinsed his mouth, turned to Nary and said: "I forgot to tell you about my new job."

"What? I thought you liked your existing job."

"I did, but this one is much better. I have become a director of the Ministry of Information. Do you know what that means?"

She turned the shower off, grabbed her towel from its holder and before wrapping it around herself, looked at him with pleased eyes. "Yes. Now you can make Tirdad disappear without a trace."

He smiled, grabbed her arms, delved his head between her damp breasts and began licking her skin that tasted of soap. She gently tapped on his head. "Stop it. You have had enough of me today."

"I never have enough of you my love. Had I had my present job when Tirdad was in jail, he would be in his grave now and you entirely mine."

She giggled and pinched his cheek.

Hashem's new job made Nary feel untouchable, even if her liaison was discovered. Flying in the seven heavens she returned home carrying a bag full of her husband's favourite fruits and a bottle of Gin (given to her by Hashem) hidden in a rice sac. She found him in an exalted mood. That surprised her. She shed off her Islamic hejab, picked up her shopping and went to the kitchen where she deposited them on the dining table. A grin on his bright face, he followed her there humming a happy tune.

"Guess what I got you from George the Armenian?" She asked eyeing the rice bag.

"A bottle of arak."

"No, something better?"

"A bottle of Gin."

She pulled the bottle out and dangled it in front of his sparkling eyes. It had been so long since he had tasted the real stuff.

"How much did it cost?"

"Four hundred thousand."

"Four hundred thousand! Where did you get the money from?" He exclaimed with a whistle.

"Remember, yesterday was my birthday. Agha Azizi gave me five hundred thousand and because I love you so much, I decided to buy what pleases you most." She lied.

He opened his arms wide and wrapped them around her round shoulders. She moved to separate. "Not before a big kiss." Tirdad murmured, pulled her back and kissed her mouth. She gently pushed him away, turned her head so that he wouldn't notice her wiping her lips from his dribble. It tasted awful.

"I have news that will please you azizam."

"And what can that be Tirdad dear?"

"Baba is going to sell this building and buy two apartments, one for us and one for Shamsi."

"That is wonderful. We will finally have our own home and I won't have your mother spying on us from her kitchen window."

"Do not be unkind to her please. If you learn how to handle her diplomatically, you will find her a loving mother-in-law."

"That woman doesn't know what love is. Her heart is made of stone. Look at the way she treats your ailing father: as though he is her dog."

"Let us not talk about them. Today I went to the municipality in Galandoak and all the papers are signed and we are ready to sell. I shall make a lot of commission on that. Rose has been very generous to offer me 5%; the real estate agent's fees are only one to one and a half."

"You could make a lot more money if the land was yours."

"What do you mean – the land is not mine. It belongs to Rose?"

"You have a power of attorney from her – go to a friendly notary office and turn the deed of the estate under your own name. Dismiss Gholam Reza under some sort of pretext and as you sell the lots report to her that all the money is being deposited into her account. Once the lots are all sold we become millionaires and she cannot do a damn thing about it."

"I do not have a total power of attorney. She gave that to my father. Besides Gholam Reza will let her know."

"Did you not hear me? I told you to go to a 'friendly notary ' who can forge Rose's signature and prepare a total power of attorney for you with which you can turn the deeds under your name. And regarding Gholam Reza, you first tell him that Rose has changed residence and he shouldn't call the number he has and that you are waiting for her new telephone number which you will give him as soon as you know. He is such a simple man that he will believe you. And once you sack him, which number is he going to call?" She asked with a raised brow.

"My God, you are clever." He exclaimed and pinched her bottom.

"Khanum joon, with a total power of attorney I don't have to turn any deeds under my name before selling the land. I can just act on behalf of Rose. This is just a brilliant idea, why didn't I think of it myself?" Tirdad banged at his temple, remembering Sed Ali, with his everlasting smile and his tattooed arms. They were both released at the same time and he had his home's telephone number. Tirdad had acquired his skill but in this case he preferred Sed Ali's forged signature instead of his own, in case anything went wrong. He didn't want to leave anything to chance. That was the first lesson he had learnt from the thieves at Evin.

"Nary joon, I know the best forger in Iran. Soon, my love you be wearing mink coats and driving a Mercedes Benz."

"Enshallah azizam."

Three days later Tirdad became the possessor of a Sed Ali forged, total power of attorney from Rose. Sed Ali not only refused Tirdad's offer of a handsome payment but invited him to have lunch at Yas restaurant. Tirdad scared of being seen in such company refused. Sed Ali took offence. They parted – but not as brothers.

From then on, Tirdad doubled his efforts to sell the land lots. He also increased the frequency of his visits to the villa. Sometimes he took Nary with him to spend the weekends there – but never his parents. This surprised Gholam Reza and made him vigilant.

Unfamiliar with the dignity of old wealth, instead of trying to earn their loyalty by being kind and courteous Nary exercised haughtiness that provoked hostility and in the case of Gholam Reza suspicion. As shrewd as a fox he began to smell a rat. Every time Tirdad and a prospective client came to view the lots, he spied on them from within hearing distance. In spite of his slight deafness he manoeuvred his bearings in such a way that he was able to hear all that was being exchanged. What surprised him most was that the owner's name was never mentioned – it was all I, and I and never Ms Qajar. (All official documents of women in Iran are under their maiden names.) He also found it strange that doctor Amiri who had the total power of attorney from Rose, had not accompanied either of the two buyers, nor was his name ever mentioned. In fact, the gentleman had not come to the villa ever since the picnic day, nor thanked him for the jams he had sent him via Tirdad.

Curious and anxious beyond measures, Gholam Reza fretted about swearing at his own naivety for planting the idea of subdivision in his lady's head. Should anything go wrong how could he ever look into her eyes? About to have a heart attack he discussed the matter with Behjat, his trusted advisor. Considering all possibilities they decided, before conferring with doctor Amiri or Rose, Gholam Reza should go to the local Notary Office. Agha Nazari, the notary was an old and trusted friend of the family and as per Rose's instruction all transactions had to take place at his office. He would know what was going on. It was Wednesday evening and Tirdad had already called him to prepare the villa for them. So he had to wait till Saturday.

The next afternoon, the hooting of a car took Gholam Reza away from weeding the lawn to the gate. Thinking it was Tirdad, he opened it wide and was taken aback to find a four- wheel drive packed with teenagers, hopping to the tempo of a loud foreign music. He recognized Ahmad behind the wheel.

"Salam Gholam Reza."

Gholam Reza stood in the middle of the gate barring the entrance of the car and responded to the boy's greeting with a salute of his large sinewy hand.

"Protruding his head full of gelled hair out of the window, a boy called out: "Old man, if you don't want to die get out of the way." A roar of laughter wafted out of the open windows.

Gholam Reza, who had never been addressed in such a disparaging manner, threw him a fierce glance, ignored his remark, turned and addressed Ahmad:

"Son, I have no authorization to let anyone in, unless accompanied by Agha Tirdad or your mother."

Ahmad turned back, frowned at his friends and whispered a "be quiet please." Then returned to Gholam Reza, "I am sure one of my parents has told you we would be coming here tonight."

"No Ahmad Agha. I was only told that they, themselves would be coming tonight."

Swearing under his breath Ahmad switched off the car, opened the door, jumped out and said: "I want to call my mother?" Without moving, Gholam Reza gestured towards his room. "Go ahead Agha."

Familiar with the place, he ran to the domestic quarters and at its threshold collided with Behjat about to step out.

"Salam Agha Ahmad."

Ignoring her greeting, and without a word of apology, he walked in, grabbed the wall-phone and dialled his home number.

Surprised at the boy's strange behaviour, Behjat hurried to her husband.

Waiting, Ahmad shifted his heavy weight from one leg to the other, praying his mother to be home. And when he heard her 'hello' he blurted out:

"Mother, Gholam Reza won't let us in. This is very awkward in front of my friends. Did you not tell him we would be coming here?"

"No I forgot. Give him the phone." Ahmad let the phone hang, ran outside and shouted: "Gholam Reza, hurry, my mother wants to have a word with you."

Behjat was now standing by her husband, staring at the youths with hawkish eyes.

"You stay here until I return. Under no condition let them in." Gholam Reza mumbled before leaving.

Outraged by the disrespect shown her husband, Behjat spread her legs wide, rested her fat palms over her wide hips, and stared at the intruders challenging them with her wrathful eyes.

As Gholam Reza threw his sandals off, Ahmad grabbed the hanging receiver and offered it to him.

Gholam Reza snatched the phone, and pushed the boy away with his shoulder.

"Salam Khanum."

"How dare you stop my son from entering the house? Dr Amiri told you we would be spending the weekend there. Now we cannot and in our stead my son and his friends have come. Go apologise to him in front of his friends, let them in, and serve them well; that is if you want to save your job."

Her audacity infuriated him. He wanted to scream at her. But for the sake of Agha Datam he controlled his impulse.

"Khanum, first, neither you nor your husband can fire me. Second, I will not let in a bunch of wild teenagers without an adult supervisor and endanger the safety of the property which is entrusted to my care. The other day, the town's Komiteh sent their vigilantes to the neighbour's house, where loud music was being played. They took the youngsters to the Komiteh, lashed the boys fifty times each and jailed the girls for using Hashish and drinking whisky. Shahzadeh is not here, and I am not going to subject her villa to the intrusion of Komiteh louts."

"It is not for you to decide who enters the villa. My husband has power of attorney from Rose and can do as he wishes with the villa. Let the boys in or else Tirdad Khan will throw you out."

"They have to drive over my dead body, Khanum," exclaimed Gholam Reza, banging the receiver on its cradle. The veins of his temples throbbing hard, he turned to Ahmad and warned: "You heard what I said to your mother. Now be a sensible boy, leave without creating any further humiliation for yourself."

"We will go, but I promise, you won't have a roof over your head tomorrow."

"We shall see."

Ahmad hurried out, banged the door on Gholam Reza's face. It hit his nose and made it bleed. Gholam Reza sent him a curse, rushed to his kitchen sink, washed his face, pulled out a tissue, held it over his nose and dashed out. He saw Ahmad standing by his car. He sharpened his ears and heard him say:

"Guys we have to return to Teheran. After all, my parents have decided to come here for the weekend, which means there won't be room for all of us to sleep. Sorry about this – we will come next weekend."

Faces tensed in discontent and the audacious ones grimaced at Behjat whose determined gaze didn't waver. An insolent girl threw a handful of pistachio shells at her shouting: "You fat cow."

"Ignore them." Gholam Reza muttered closing the gate.

"What happened to your nose Gholam?" Behjat asked.

"The bastard shut the door on my face. It hit my nose."

"I hope God will punish him." Behjat cursed and as they turned to go they heard the screech of the car wheels over the uneven asphalt followed by the bang of a collision. They halted and looked at each other in awe. "I think God heard you Behjat Khanum." Gholam Reza said and opened the gate just enough to spy. Delighted, he saw that a coming car had hit the side of the four-wheel drive and the drivers were in the midst of a heated dispute. He noiselessly shut and locked the gate.

"Serves him right – the impertinent fat cow and his obnoxious mother, who thinks she owns the place." Golam Reza, whinged, in loathing.

"You better go to Agha Nazari, first thing on Saturday morning."

"Yes. They are up to something ungodly. I am going to call my lady right now."

"No. It is not right to accuse people before one has proof. Go to the notary, make enquiries and then call her with the correct information, if any." Behjat suggested and hurried to where the taps were. It was time to irrigate. She loved her flowers and couldn't bear to see them wilt under the heat. They were her friends. She talked to them, praised their beauty and cured their maladies with the spray Rose had bought her. Rose was always in her mind, particularly when she was attending the rose patch that was thriving.

Thursday met its end and Friday smiled at them warmly. The village became crowded with weekenders and Gholam Reza didn't even venture out to buy bread. Worry and doubt had robbed him of appetite, colour and strength. Nothing Behjat said put his mind at ease. Apprehensive that he might have a stroke she put into his hand their pruning shears and pushed him out of the door to take out his frustration on the plants. It was not time for pruning but she was sure he would only decapitate the dead branches.

That night he tossed and turned until dawn when he rose to pray. The neighbour's cock was serenading its call and through his living room's window he could see the river lumber on its stony path. Above, the blue sky was clear but not his conscience which for the first time in his life had become cloudy by doubts, suspicion and guilt.

Prayer finished, he raised his eyes and hands towards God, begging him to safeguard the villa for its rightful owner. He closed his eyes and meditated until karmic energy infused him with drive to act. He thanked his God, wrapped his prayer rug, stood up, placed the bundle on his mantelpiece and headed for the kitchen where Behjat was brewing tea. They had two wooden chairs and a small square table that had served them for forty years. He sat on his beloved chair that had offered him comfort for as long as he remembered, and enjoying its solidity waited for his tea. Behjat picked up the tea pot from the top of the samovar, poured some tea into his tea glass, topped it with hot water from the samovar's tap and placed it in front of him. She did the same for herself. Glass in hand she joined him at the table. Within that simple, cosy and harmonious atmosphere they partook of their breakfast of clotted cream, bread and honey. They did not talk much; both were too concerned for small talk. Gholam Reza finished first. He hurried out to turn the irrigation taps on. He enjoyed the dance of the jetting water whirling around like dancing dervishes. The whole garden's irrigation was mechanized so that he didn't have to work hard. Shahzadeh Khanum always thought of everything. She had inherited the sagacity, considerateness and integrity of her parents, God blesses their souls. They were always present in his mind, as though they were still alive and living in the villa. Perhaps it was the seed of goodness they had sowed on their land that had grown into a holy grill safeguarding it from being confiscated as an 'absentee-owner's property', like the other villas in the vicinity. Why should being absent from one's home be a crime or a sin? The notion had certainly not come from the holy book. It was his custom to go through the Koran during each Ramadan. He would start reading as soon as the crescent of the lunar moon was spotted and finish by Aid Fetre which celebrates the end of the holy month. At the beginning, he had read the holy book in Arabic until the Prince asked him if he understood what he was reading. To his response of 'no sire' the Prince had presented him with his own volume which was both in Arabic and Farsi. Now he could reason and outsmart any mullah in religious debates.

It was just five minutes before eight when Gholam Reza mounted his bicycle and peddled to the notary's office. There he parked and chained it to a tree. The door of the dilapidated building was open. He climbed a set of steps, turned right and found the office door open. He knocked gently and entered. To his delight he found himself the sole client. In reverence for the mullah, he put his arm on his chest and bowed his head: "Salam Agha Nazari." The mullah, who was reading something, looked up and recognizing him returned his salutation with a welcoming smile.

"Salam Gholam Reza Khan. Please sit down." Gholam Reza sat on a grey metal chair. It faced Nazari's desk on which a pile of dossiers was waiting for perusal.

"I have not seen you for a long time. I hope you are well, and in good health."

"God be thanked, I am in good health and still alive Agha."

"How is Behjat Khanum?"

"She is well and Da-a-go (praying for your health)."

"And the shahzadeh – how is she?"

"She is fine Agha. She and the doctor are in London."

"I know. Has the Municipality approved the plan for the subdivision?"

Gholam Reza's heart almost stopped. Beads of cold sweat bloomed on his forehead and a deep sigh escaped his lips.

"Two lots have already been sold. Didn't Agha doctor Amiri and Tirdad Khan bring the purchasers here for the transactions, as they were supposed to?"

Now it was the turn of the cleric to lose colour. He stared into Gholam Reza's wide and worried eyes and nodded his turbaned head up and down.

"No. No one has been here. I thought the delay was due to the usual obstacles created at the municipality to grease hands."

"No, things went well there – for once! I am very surprised that no one has been here though. I know shahzadeh specifically told them to do all the transactions at your office with doctor Amiri signing the deeds because, as you know, he is the only one with total power of attorney from her."

The cleric paused to contemplate. Then he brushed his hand over his long, well-trimmed peppery, beard, and said: "This is strange indeed. They know I charge less than others for what I do for the shahzadeh and am able to resolve Municipality problems, my oldest son being the Mayor. Then why would they not use my office?"

"I do not know sire. I haven't seen the senior doctor since shahzadeh left and Tirdad and his wife have been behaving strangely – in a way impudently, as though they own the property. I have a bad feeling about it all and I don't know what to do Agha Nazari. I do not want to accuse anyone of wrong doing before being sure."

"That is easy. Call the senior doctor; tell him you bumped into me on the street, told me that two lots have been sold and I became unhappy why my office was not used as per Rose Khanum's instructions. See what he has to say. He might have a logical explanation which will put your mind and mine at ease; and if anything wrong is going on, it will be his responsibility to deal with the matter and not yours my friend."

"The old man has had two heart attacks already. If, God forbid, he finds that his son is up to something sinful, he might have the third one. I do not want to have that on my conscience as well as the guilt of having recommended Tirdad."

Nazari flicked the end of his long and pointed mustachio a couple of times, licked his lower lip and staring at the gardener said:

"First, my son, life and death are in the hands of the Almighty, so never blame yourself for someone's demise. Second, you recommended Tirdad with all the good intentions in your heart and it was up to your lady to trust him or not. She did. Therefore, knowing her, she will stand by the consequences of her decision without blaming anyone but herself. Having said that, my man, your main responsibility is to do what is right by her and leave the rest to God. Otherwise you will be wasting your precious time on earth in worrying about things beyond your control and that won't please God."

Gholam Reza moved in his chair, and began rubbing his forehead with his long fingers as though trying to sooth its tension while searching for the right words to express his internal turmoil. He was not a man to leave the solution of any problems in the hands of God while still in sound mind. But the recent incidents had rubbed his mind from its functionality and he needed constructive guidance and not mere clerical sermons. After a minute or two he lodged his hand on his lap and looked up at the Notary, "Agha, as a man of God, you know his commands better than I. I shall call Agha doctor and deliver your message. But I hope God will forgive me for lying, and bestow upon your mind a solution for my lady's problem, should there be one."

"You will not be really lying. Changing a few words will not introduce sin into a good intention and the solution you are seeking has to come from the senior doctor and not me."

Gholam Reza rose, put his hand on his chest, bent his head, thanked him and hurried out. It was still cool and the road to the centre of the village blocked by cars. Many lived in Galandoak now and commuted to Teheran. Gholam Reza hated the crowd, the noise and the rising prices that accompany urbanization. He was born here, when it was just a stoney village in which one could hear the sound of rushing water in the streams, rustle of the leaves, whistle of the wind and bah bah of the sheep. Now all one heard was the noise of the traffic. Shaking his head in remorse and nostalgic for the peaceful bygone days, he got on his bicycle and peddled toward the town centre.

By the time he finished his shopping and reached home it was noon, and he thought it would be better to bother the old doctor after his siesta. He also needed rest himself. Behjat fed him with his favourite dish of rice with broad beans, dill and braised lamb ribs; gave him a glass of doogh (yoghurt drink mixed with mint) and put him to bed. She loved him dearly. An orphan with a cruel step mother, she had married him at the age of twelve. He turned out to be an ideal husband though fifteen years her senior. No spouse would have remained faithful to a barren wife like her. But her Gholam Reza was not an ordinary man. He was an angel. Now that they both were in the autumn of their lives, she prayed to die with him. Rose, the dear child that she was to her, aware of her fear of becoming a widow, had promised to take her to London to live with her. But she preferred to die in her own village and be buried under its earth, next to her Agha.

It was half past two in the afternoon. They were sitting in their sun-filled family room having their afternoon tea. Mohammad, unusually relaxed was listening to Shamsi criticising him for having sold their home and bought a flat in Avenue Ghandi, where she knew no one and was not within walking distance of Tirdad's new apartment.

In fact, Mohammad did not hear a word she was uttering. Long ago, he had learnt to switch off from hearing her never-ending complaints. The world, always owed her something. In the sixty odd years of their marriage, in spite of all his attempts, he had failed to fathom out the reason for her inability to enjoy life. However in the depth of his heart he blamed her mother for not nurturing this daughter with love. Why, only God knew. And when his turn came to show her love, she didn't recognize it for the elixir it was. As time passed, she fell deeper and deeper into depression and self-degradation. Because he loved her, he gave up the losing battle of changing her and instead, adopted the habit of switching off when she became cantankerous.

At that moment, when the future seemed so cloudy for Shamsi, Mohammad was in another world, with Datam walking by the Serpentine, listening to his soft and pleasant voice uttering kind words. How he missed him and Rose, that gift from God. When he thought of her, he felt light and blessed. He was smiling when the shrill sound of the phone broke his thread of thought and stopped her grumblings. He picked up the receiver.

"Salam Agha doctor, it is me Gholam Reza, your servant."

"Salam Agha Gholam. How are you, Behjat Khanum and the garden?"

"Agha, Allah be thanked, all is well except......"

"Except what Gholam Reza?" Mohammad asked in a panic.

"On Thursday, Agha Ahmad and a car full of teenagers came to spend the weekend here. I did not allow them entrance because no grown up accompanied them. He called his mother complaining about me and the lady talked to me in such a rude manner that shahzadeh would never use even with an ass. And then today, I met Agha Nazari, the notary you know. I told him about the land lots being sold by Agha Tirdad assuming he knew about them, because, as you know, my Khanum had instructed your Excellency and Agha Tirdad to do all the dealings at his office. The man is an old friend of the Prince, God bless his soul, and shahzadeh wanted him to benefit from the sale proceeds. Agha Nazari was surprised and deeply hurt that the sales had taken place elsewhere. He asked me to ask why you and Tirdad Khan have forsaken him."

Shamsi curious as why Mohammad had become so pale asked: "What is wrong Agha?"

Mohammad cupped the mouth-piece with his hand, turned his perplexed eyes to her and muttered: "Be quiet Khanum. I cannot hear anything when you talk."

Then he removed his hand and said:

"Gholam Reza I have to talk to Tirdad first and then I will call you. Say nothing to Agha Nazari or Rose until you hear from me."

"I will do as you wish, Agha doctor."

Gholam Reza put the receiver down, now certain that something crooked was going on; otherwise the doctor would not have been taken by surprise. He had to tell his Khanum. He looked at his watch. He had to wait another hour before calling London on the number he had had and not the one Tirdad had given him. This business of changing phone number must have been a trick; otherwise his Khanum would have given it to him herself. He knew Rose would be having her yoga class and he did not want to worry Agha Datam. He told his wife what the doctor had asked of him. Behjat agreed with the doctor. It was better to let him deal with the situation – he was a wise man and loved Rose. He, better than anyone, would be able to protect her interest.

Glued to his armchair, Mohammad's hand was shaking so hard that he couldn't fit the phone on its cradle. Impatient, he let it drop, turned to his wife and said: "That dastardly son of yours is stealing from Rose. He has been selling her land lots – how, I do not know." He lost his breath. A sharp pain shot through his heart. He put his hand on his chest and began to breathe heavily. Shamsi ran to the medicine cabinet in the bathroom and brought his pill with a glass of tap water. He took the pill, washed it down with a sip of water, rested his head on the back of the chair and closed his eyes. Drops of perspiration slid down the side of his undulating temples. Shamsi picked up the phone, called Tirdad whom she knew was home packing and asked him to run down immediately.

Ten minutes later he appeared in his dusty jeans and sweaty T-shirt; found his miserable looking parents sitting on their respective armchairs staring at him with baffled eyes. As insensible as ever, in an irate tone he asked: "What is it now?"

"You bastard – what have you been up to?" Mohammad shouted.

"What do you mean?"

"You have been selling Rose's land without any of us knowing. How did you manage that? Have you forged a total power of attorney? Have you son of Satan?"

For a second Tirdad lost his nerve. His complexion paled and his mind searched for an exonerating excuse. Not finding one he dropped on a chair, cupped his face with his hands and began to weep, like when he was a child – crying to gain sympathy. Shamsi rose from her seat, sat on the arm of his chair, and began to stroke his balding head, whispering endearing words.

Fuming with outrage Mohammad yelled: "How can you love a thief, woman – a thief you brought up. God, let me die so that I do not have to set eyes on the ugly face of this dog."

Shamsi threw him a contemptible glance and said nothing. Tirdad uncovered his face, looked him in the eyes and said: "Stealing from thieves is allowed. Rose was the daughter of a thief whose father was a bigger thief. All the Shahs were thieves. They stole from people and the people have the right to retrieve what belongs to them."

"Shut up you piece of shit. Right now you go and bring me that forged power of attorney you have, or I will call the police."

"How are you going to prove that my power of attorney is forged?" He asked with a sneer.

"Go and bring that piece of paper right now. You have two seconds before I pick up the phone." Mohammad glowered at him and when Tirdad did not move, he picked up the phone. Shamsi reading determination on his set face turned to Tirdad and pleaded: "Do as your father demands otherwise you have his death on your conscience. The man is on the verge of having another heart attack – cannot you see?"

Puzzled as to how his father had found out, Tirdad rose, went to his flat and returned with his power of attorney. He glared into his father's red eyes and asked: "Baba, do you not think I have the right to have as good a life as your spoilt brat?"

"Think hard before asking this question. You have neither the intelligence nor an iota of the decency your brother has. Besides, a comfortable life is earned and not stolen."

Scared, beaten and confused yet defiant, Tirdad threw the document on the dining table. "Here is my power of attorney and unless you are able to prove that it is forged I will continue to sell the land and pocket the money. Even if you tell her she won't be able to do anything at all until she comes here and revoke the power at the Notary office in which it was given. That she wouldn't be able to do as a forged document is not registered at any Notary office. You see Baba dear, none of you can stop me from getting rich by the grace of the stupidity of your darling Rose. Well, now I think you should love her more because she has made both your sons wealthy." He stopped and began to roar with laughter. His gaiety was out of desperation. He was caught again. Could he ever succeed in anything – anything at all? No, it seemed not. Suddenly he felt wretched and began to tremble. He sat on the nearest dining chair, cupped his head between his hands and began to swear at his fate.

Mohammad threw him a distasteful glance, rose and walked to his office. His steps were steady and his head up. There he pulled out a drawer and from it extracted a file; flipped through the papers inside it and drew out his total power of attorney. He threw the folder on the bureau, and returned to the dining table where he picked up Tirdad's document and placed it next to his own. He sat on a chair, drew out his reading glass from his pocket, fitted them on, and bent over the two documents, comparing them word by word. They were identical except the names and the signatures of the appointee. His heart's thumping accelerated and the veins in his temple hammered incessantly. He felt nauseated. He took a deep breath and forced his eyes meander over the documents again and again. Suddenly they rested on the digits of the dates. Bingo! They were different on the day and the month. Tirdad's was signed while Rose was in England. He let out a sigh of relief, took off his glasses, turned his head to Tirdad standing behind him now and asked: "How much did you sell the lands for?" Confident that his father had failed to find anything amiss, he smirked: "Three million rials for the two – good money hah?"

"Yah! Good money and congratulations for being such a good salesman." Mohammad replied in a neutral tone, as though nothing bad had happened at all.

Tirdad exhaled an easy breath. His muscles relaxed and his eyes began to twinkle. After all, his worries had been for naught.

Mohammad grinned.

"I am sure Rose will be grateful to you." Then he rose from his chair, picked up both documents, put one over the other and said: "Let's go to the bank and you transfer that sum into my account."

Tirdad's chin dropped. He turned his eyes to his mother.

She said nothing. Even for her, what he had done was beyond exoneration. Without any ally, he dropped his head and murmured:

"I cannot."

"What do you mean?" Asked Mohammad.

"I bought a Range Rover which Ahmad smashed and the rest went to pay my debts. On what do you think we have been living?"

Mohammad sucked all the saliva in his mouth and spat it on the man he realized, he detested with every fibre of his entity.

Then he went to the phone and picked up the receiver.

"Who are you calling?"

"I am calling the police to come and pick you up."

Tirdad rushed to him, grabbed the phone and pulled off its connecting wire from its socket. Images of prison raced in his vision and his body began to convulse.

"Look what you have done to my son." Shamsi screamed.

"Go and bring me the genuine power of attorney that Rose gave you."

"Why?"

Mohammad lifted his hand up and with all the power he could muster slapped him on both cheeks.

"Go and bring me that document."

Defeated and without a choice, his head bent, his shoulders hunched, he turned and lumbered home. For once he hated himself.

Mohammad stood by the window and watched the sky. It had become as cloudy as his mind.

Shamsi went to the kitchen to make herself a cup of camomile tea. She needed a relaxant.

Tirdad returned and threw the document on the dining table.

Mohammad left the window, went to the table, picked up all the papers.

"We are going to Galandoak."

"I am coming too." Shamsi shouted from the kitchen.

"No. You stay here and make my dinner."

Mohammad replied before picking up the receiver dialling Gholam Reza's number.

Behjat picked up the phone. "Salam Behjat Khanum. May I speak with Gholam Reza please?"

"Salam Agha doctor, please wait. He is in the garden. Would you like me to have him call you?"

"No. Go and get him please."

Behjat put the receiver down, ran out and shouted: "Gholam come. Agha doctor is on the phone for you – hurry."

Gholam Reza, trimming the hedges, switched off his electrical clipper, put it on the grass, ran in and picked up the phone and blew into it his Salam.

"Salam. Agha Gholam Reza, can you give me Agha Nazari's phone number please?"

"I am sorry, I don't have it."

"Then, could you please go to his office and ask him not to leave until we get there. We are coming to see him on an urgent matter right now."

"Yes doctor. I shall go to him straight away. Would you like me to wait for you there?"

"No, I won't need you there."

It was already three thirty in the afternoon and Nazari usually left at four thirty. Gholam Reza ran to his bicycle and pedalled hard and fast swearing at his own idiocy and negligence for not having the phone number.

"Where is your car?" demanded Mohammad.

"Nearby." Mumbled Tirdad like an android.

"Good. Let's go."

In the kitchen Shamsi heard the bang of the door. Numbed to what was happening she continued to sip her camomile tea staring at a void.

In the car, not one word was exchanged. As they approached the cross road where they had to turn to reach the villa, Tirdad reduced speed and changed gear. "Go straight, to Nazari's office." Mohammad commanded without looking at him.

"Why?"

"You should know why."

"You want to humiliate me in front of that pockmarked mullah don't you?"

"Do not flatter yourself. You have become irrelevant."

Tirdad changed gear, drove on and parked in front of the Notary's office. They got out of the car, entered the building, climbed up the stairs and stopped by the Notary's office door. "Be respectful of Agha Nazari and keep your mouth shut."

Tirdad did not reply. Mohammad knocked and then entered. The Notary was behind his desk writing something down. Mercifully no one else was in the room. As Nazari saw the doctor he rose in reverence, his usual smile missing. The men shook hands and then sat on the visitor's chairs. Nazari put his pen down, picked up the string of his prayer beads, coiled it around his palm and in a professional and not his usual intimate tone asked:

"What can I do for you gentlemen?"

"Agha Nazari, I received your message and have come in person to apologise for not using your office for the recent sales. Lately, I have been very ill and to be honest, couldn't face the long drive to here. So I used the notary office near my house. But rest assured that the rest of the deals will take place here."

"Agha doctor, there is no need for apologies. You are free to choose which office you prefer. It just surprised me when Gholam Reza told me about the sales. You are a respectable gentleman and I thank you for coming all the way here to visit me."

"Thank you Agha, I have also come here on another matter. Tirdad here, as I am sure you remember, has a limited power of attorney from Rose, but unfortunately cannot attend to her business affairs anymore. Since the power was given here, only here he can relinquish his responsibility." Mohammad paused, looked down on the documents he was holding, chose one and placed it in front of the mullah who was teasing his beard and trying to fathom out what had really happened to merit the old man's hurried visit to his office.

"Here is my 'power' from her. I can sign anything you require on her behalf." Nazari, stopped playing with his beard, bent over the document and read it. Then he pushed it away, picked up his prayer beads and smiling at Mohammad said:

"Agha you do not have to do anything. I need Agha Tirdad's signature. He has to write a note, surrendering his given 'power'. I will witness, sign and send it to the Ministry of Birth, Death and Transactions for its distribution to all the Notary offices in the country." The mullah paused, untangled his prayer beads and put them on the table. He didn't need any diversions to relax him anymore. Today's earning was as good as on the table. Smiling at the prospect, he leaned back and shouted: "Jafar, bring me a sheet of our official stationary."

The young clerk, in his ragged clothes, stinking of nicotine, walked in from an adjoining room carrying a piece of paper which with both hands he offered to his illustrious boss. Nazari, with his head pointed to Tirdad and in a stern tone ordered:

"Give it to the young doctor Amiri."

Jafar turned to the younger of the two clients.

Tirdad took the paper and curtly asked the mullah to dictate to him the content of the note he had to write and sign.

The clerk hurried out and a few minutes later reappeared with a tray of tea and a bowl of cubed sugars. Mohammad and Nazari took a glass each but Tirdad refused. The man, tray in hand, returned to his station. Tirdad pulled his chair close to the table and put the paper on it. The mullah commenced his dictating, occasionally pausing to sip his tea. Tirdad wrote and Mohammad drank in peace, his mind too tired to think any more.

Nazari finished. Tirdad signed the paper and handed it to him without a word. He took the stamp of his office, stabbed it over the blue ink paste and dabbed it over Tirdad's signature, thinking of Gholam Reza and his wish for a solution. Then he summoned Jafar. He came running.

"Take the doctor's letter, number and register its content on the registration folder; make three copies and bring me the copies.

A few minutes later Jafar returned with the three photocopies and a large envelope which upon his boss's order he politely offered to the senior doctor. Mohammad thanked him and fitting the papers into the envelope asked:

"How much do I owe you Agha Nazari?"

"Nothing at all."

"That is not right. Please you must allow me to pay for this service."

The mullah brushed his beard with his right hand, tossed his chin toward Jafar and said: "I won't take anything from you, but to please Allah, you can give him hundred thousand rials. He is getting married next week and needs help."

Jafar accustomed to his boss's ruses, fixed his shy eyes on the floor.

Mohammad's forehead tightened in surprise. A hundred thousand rials was a lot of money. He detested all clerics – Muslim or non-Muslim. Probably ten thousand would go to the future groom and the rest into his big pocket. Mohammad surmised with distaste.

Father and son rose, Mohammad extracted his wallet out, counted the notes and gave them to Jafar wishing him a happy union. Nazari walked them to the door, waited by the steps until they disappeared and when he returned to his desk the rials were sitting on it.

"Thank you for saving my face." Tirdad whispered opening the door for Mohammad.

He climbed in. "Next time you want to forge anything, pay special attention to its date. How could have Rose given you a power of attorney in Iran while being in London?"

"That fucking ignorant, Sed Ali!" Tirdad whispered.

"What did you say?"

"Nothing." Tirdad murmured banging his foot on the gas pedal, as though it was Sed Ali's spine. The car started with a jerk, its tyres skidding on the surface of the road. Mohammad's seatbelt saved him from a head on collusion with the front window. He waited for a second to overcome his shock and then keeping his eyes on the road said: "I am glad we are both relocating tomorrow. As long as I live, I do not want to see you again."

"I understand. But I am not sorry for what I did."

"I know. That is why."

At home Mohammad found Shamsi snoring. She had not left anything for him to warm up. He opened the fridge door, extracted an egg, and the yoghurt container. Then he took a mug from the crockery cabinet into which he broke the egg, discarding its shell into the odorous garbage bin lodged near the fridge. He spooned the yoghurt in his mug, added a dash of salt to it and with a spoon beat the melange until it became fluffy. The nourishing concussion was what he used to eat during his student days, when short of funds and very happy. He took a spoonful, closed his eyes and smiled. It was delicious. When finished, he washed the mug, put it on the kitchen top and headed for his bed, thinking how he could compensate Rose's loss. Suddenly he remembered the only valuable possessions still in his closet were two miniature paintings given to his great, great, great grandfather by Shah Abbass the Great himself. Rose would appreciate them very much. She loved antiques and they were truly valuable.

A week later, Rose received a parcel from Iran. Surprised she opened the thick envelope and in it found a letter and a slightly smaller envelope. She recognized doctor Amiri's hand writing. She put the letter aside and opened the second envelope. From it she extracted two beautifully gilded miniature paintings. She examined them with the eyes of a connoisseur and instantly appreciated their beauty, authenticity and value. Very carefully she laid them on the top of her bureau, picked up the letter, sat on her chair and began to read.

6th September, 2001.

"My dearest daughter and the most beautiful Rose in the garden of heaven,

My worst nightmare came true. The man you trusted and wanted to help proved unworthy. He forged a total power of attorney with which he sold two lots of land. As God always guards your interests, between Gholam Reza and Agha Nazari they suspected wrong doings and alerted me.

I confronted Tirdad, asking for the proceeds which he says he cannot remit because he has used them to pay off his debts. I annulled the power you had given him and have told the real estate agent at Galandoak to stop showing the land until you come yourself. I have no money to compensate for the theft. The enclosed two paintings were left to me by my father. They belonged to Shah Abbass the Great who gave them to my ancestor, his astrologer, as a gift for an auspicious prediction that had materialized. These two are the only worldly possessions I own worthy of you and I want you to accept them from me in lieu of Tirdad's theft. I want you to know that I have disowned him. Nevertheless, please forgive him as he is one of those who knows not what is right and what is wrong.

Rose Aziz, I beg you do not tell Datam of this. He will die of shame, as I will soon.

I love you Rose very much. Together with Datam you have been the light of my life. I thank you for that.

Your loving father,

Mohammad.

Rose, took the letter to her lips, kissed it with reverence and with her finger wiped her tear drop from its surface. She knew how hard it must have been for the old man to put pen to paper. To honour his request, she tore it and threw the tiny pieces in the waste paper basket under the desk.

She picked up her phone book, found their new number that she had not memorised as yet and dialled.

Mohammad picked up the phone.

"Agha doctor, it is Rose. I just received your beautiful gift and cannot find the right words to thank you with. They are just amazing."

"I am glad you liked them."

"Liked them? I love them, and also thank you for your kind words. Just forget the whole affair as I already have. Money comes and goes and you know it plays only a secondary role in my life."

"Thank you my daughter, thank you."

For the first time in days the old man felt light. He let out a sigh and whispered into the phone.

"Rose God bless you child. Rose ..."

Sharp pains began stabbing his heart, his breathing became heavy and then turned into heaves. He placed his hand on his chest pressing it hard to stop the stings while endeavouring to finish his sentence. Rose could hear his breathing struggles and then his last growl of pain.

Chapter 8

September 11 -2001

Her elbows on the desk, her chin cupped within her palms, Rose stared out of the window, too hurt to think. As she heard the rattle of Datam's key in the door lock, she jerked out of her haze, sat upright and turned towards the door. Her face was wet. She withdrew a tissue from its box and dried her eyes. Then she picked up the paintings, fitted them into the envelope; drew out the drawer of her bureau and put the envelope there. Later, much later, she would show them to Datam and tell him that she had bought them at an auction. She could never tell him the truth. That was a pity for under a different circumstance the possession of such precious patrimony would have made him proud.

He stepped inside the wide and well lit corridor.

"Rose, are you home darling?"

"Yes, I am in the study."

He smiled and closed the door behind him. Refreshed by his walk to and from Harrods, he hurried to their spotless, ultra-modern kitchen; put the bakery's bag on its black granite counter and then headed for the bedroom. There he dropped the key ring on the top of the dresser, took off his navy blue blazer and tie and hung them in his closet. He went to the bathroom and washed his hands with the antiseptic soap Rose had bought for him. The product was skin unfriendly, so she had left a bottle of hand cream on the sparkling white granite vanity top for him to moisturize his hands after each wash. Her worse fear for him was to catch an infection. With all those white blood cells so high, he even had to struggle hard to fight a common cold. Like a good boy, he obeyed all her instructions. Rubbing the cream on his skin, he walked to the study, where he found her staring at him with red eyes. Fear gripped his heart and glued him to the ground. She rose, took his hand and pulling him behind her led him to the TV room. "What is it Rose?" He asked anxiously.

"Let's sit down love."

He settled next to her on the sofa that faced the TV set.

She put his hand on her lap and patting it, lifted her eyes to his troubled ones and whispered: "We have lost Agha Doctor."

He let out a long and painful 'no', clutched her hand, and muttered: "When?"

"Only a few hours ago; I was talking to him on the phone and he sounded well. Then suddenly he heaved and hissed and fell silent. I waited for him to speak, instead I heard Shamsi scream. I held onto the phone hoping to hear him again until it went dead. I put the receiver down; waited a couple of minutes and tried to call back. The line was engaged. I tried again and again until Shamsi answered and told me that he was dead. She sounded awful."

A heart-rending expression of bereavement set on his face. He fixed his unblinking eyes on Rose and remained as still as a statue until his profound grief exploded in a wail. Rose hugged him as tightly as she could, so that he could cry on her shoulders and remember that she was there for him, sharing his grief.

Time crawled away in a woeful stillness until Datam gently freed himself from her hold. He pulled out a Kleenex from its box, dried his eyes and nose.

"We must go to Iran for his funeral. I must see him once more." His voice came from the bottom of a well.

"I agree. But you must know that it will be a long stay – as long as it takes for you to clear yourself from all those accusations and get yourself off that damned list – otherwise, you won't be allowed out."

"Yes, I know. I must do that sooner or later – getting off that list will be like breaking a noose from around my neck." He reclined on the sofa and closed his eyes, allowing memory to parade in his inner vision. "I love Iran though it is no more the country we knew it; but nevertheless, it is where our roots are and where we belong to."

"I am so proud of you Datam. You are not like all the cowards we meet every night, plotting against the regime from within the safety of their flats, not even daring to go to the Embassy to renew or change their Imperial passports into the Islamic ones." He opened his sad eyes, threw her a soft glance and murmured:

"You must not be harsh in your judgement my dear. Most of those we know are on the execution list."

Rose shrugged her shoulders, took the phone handset from its stand, and handed it to him. "Call your mother."

He sat up, sniffed and dialled.

In Teheran, Tirdad picked up the receiver and recognizing Datam's voice passed it to his mother. "It is Datam."

Shamsi took the phone and began to cry.

"Salam Madar joon. Please accept my condolences for our great loss." He swallowed the lump in his throat, "I am coming to Iran and want to see Baba once more. Please do not bury him until we arrive."

Surprised Shamsi pulled herself together and asked: "Are you really coming back?"

"Yes Madar, I am. I am going to book our tickets right now and will call again to let you know the date and the time of our arrival."

"Is Rose coming too?" She asked her tone as cold as clay, thinking how on earth the woman could be able to look Tirdad in the eyes. She, herself wouldn't certainly have been able to. Most probably coming here was another ploy to chain her husband to herself; or perhaps she was scared he might take a sigheh with whom he could sire a child. Then she heard Datam say:

"Madar, are you there?"

"Yes."

"Of course Rose is coming – she loved Baba."

"Ok. But she must not expect me to wait on her."

"Madar, Rose is my wife and she is coming to my parents' home as part of the family. Do not worry; she will not only be a burden, but a great help, which you need at this time."

"Enshallah." Shamsi exclaimed in a wistful tone and put the receiver down.

"As though I did not have enough on my plate – he is bringing that woman with him!" She said to Tirdad who was watching her like a bodyguard. With his father gone, he had found an accomplice in his hatred for Rose.

"He cannot breathe without her."

"I know and I hope she won't create any problems for us."

"If she does, I will deal with her and him, myself."

"Good. You do that son." Shamsi said, rising to go to the kitchen to make a cup of camomile tea. All of a sudden she had become pedantic about her health. Now that Mohammad had gone and Tirdad was pouring attention on her, she felt as though she had been released from a tight bondage. Finally life was making sense.

In London, Datam put the receiver down unable to look Rose in the face, so ashamed was he of the way his mother had talked. Rose had heard everything through the loud speaker. She huffed, tossed her head in wonder and picked up the TV monitor, and turned it on. On the wide screen she saw a plane dive into the breast of one of New York's Twin Towers and burst into flames.

At first she thought she was viewing a movie and then she read the running news-belt and the red flash of 'breaking news'. Her eyes widened and her chin dropped.

"Look, look what is happening in New York. Oh my God. Here goes the invulnerability of the United States – Ya Ali. (An expression used by Shia Muslims when frightened.) Look at what is happening there Datam, look. "

He directed his aching eyes to the screen and saw a second plane burst into flames. He exclaimed a loud 'Allah Akbar', and then fell silent. The two buildings were crumbling down, papers and corpses flying out of crushed windows and plumes of smoke, objects and dust floating, twirling and shooting towards the sky and then showering down on to earth.

For the next four hours, beside booking their tickets to Iran, the two, sat by the TV, watching the news on different channels to find out who was responsible for this most outrageous terrorist act of all time and when they found out that it was Osama Bin Laden, one of the CIA's most notorious affiliates of the past, responsible for this despicable attack, performed in the name of God and Jihad, they felt mortified. Almost in a state of shock, Rose thought it was the Crusades in reverse. The attacks to her heralded the vanguard of the caliphate-inspired dream of bloody confrontation envisioned by narrow-minded power-mongers in religious garbs. The fundamentalists not only had manipulated Islamic dogma to justify sectarianism within Islam itself, they were now using it to justify and rationalize Jihad against the West. She felt they were using Islam to justify acts of terror to pervert, manipulate, and exploit religion for their own political agenda. Their actions were not only antithetical to Islam, but specifically prohibited by it. Ashamed, she felt sure that within certain Muslim societies, the incident would be celebrated as a victory for Islam. The hijackers, by sacrificing their lives, had touched a nerve of Muslim pride. She was certain that those burning and collapsing towers represented to some, resurgent Muslim power; a Muslim payback for colonial exploitations and the domination of the West, and to others a combined political, cultural, and religious assertiveness. Unable to tame her protestation she burst out saying: "Now, the Westerners will look upon all Muslims as terrorists. The average Westerner will never understand that people like us, left their countries, because they did not share the dogmatic and twisted beliefs of their politicians." She halted, turned her wide bewildered eyes to her lamenting husband and asked: "Don't you think so, my love?"

Datam whose mind was elsewhere nodded his acquiescence, wishing she would stop. But she didn't. She had to unburden her heart, otherwise she would choke.

"You know, it will take the non-Muslims a long time before they can understand the fundamentals of our religion. Islam denounces inequality as the greatest form of injustice. It encourages its followers to combat oppression and tyranny. It enshrines piety as the sole criterion for judging human kind. It shuns race, colour, and gender as the basis of distinctions within society. During the Hajj ceremony princes and the paupers, all are equal in the eyes of their creator, walk side by side. Our religion is committed not only to tolerance and equality but to the principles of democracy. The Quran says that Islamic society is contingent on 'mutual advice through mutual discussions on an equal footing.' Islam condemns both cruelty and dictatorship. Crime of any nature is inconsistent with its principles. According to Islam, those who commit cruel acts sin against God's orders and thus merit punishment.

Islam is an open, pluralistic, and tolerant religion – a positive force in the lives of more than one billion people across this planet. It is a religion built upon the democratic principles of consultation (shura); building consensus (ijma); and leading to independent judgement (ijtihad). These are also the elements and processes of democratic institutions and democratic governance which these murderers do not understand nor respect. The damage these terrorists have inflicted, is not only limited to New York but affects the entire Muslim world."

She exhaled a heavy sigh, leaned back and sank deep into the sofa. Her outburst had somehow calmed her, as though through her words she had lashed at those responsible for her family's present predicament, dislocation and separations. She closed her eyes and murmured: "Oh! How I miss them all!"

Welcoming the silence that followed, Datam glanced at her with tired eyes and murmured: "Have you finally finished your oration?"

"Yes. Sorry love for giving you a headache. I think I am just about going mad."

"When you start, you do go on."

She sat up, looked at him with love. His face was as white as chalk. She put her arm around his neck and kissed his cold forehead.

"Darling you look terribly tired, why don't you lean back and try to have a nap?"

He tilted sideways and rested his head on the arm of the sofa. She placed a cushion under his head, took his shoes off and lifted his legs up and laid them on the settee. Her attention produced a serene smile on his drawn face. She kissed his smile and then turned the TV off.

Rose was right in believing that Muslims would be subjected to abusive treatment. For a long time, particularly in the States, mosques were burnt, Muslim shops vandalized and Islam thought to be a religion that fostered hatred and violence.

This did not bother either of them – the more security the better for all.

Their plane landed at dawn and to their delight and surprise, the passage through the immigration and customs was smooth and hassle free for Datam. Contrary to their expectations, his passport was not confiscated. This meant it might be taken from him on the way out of Iran which was worse. So he had to go to the passport office, surrender it and then test the justice system of the Islamic Republic. This worried Datam but not Rose. She believed, in Iran, one never gives up hope. Human relations count for much and she was sure he would find a person to help him.

Relieved to have crossed one of the dreaded bridges he had had nightmares about, Datam began looking around for his brother, who, he was sure would be there to welcome him. Rose guessed what was on his mind. It distressed her, because, she knew he would be disappointed. Acquainted with Tirdad's idiosyncrasies, she deduced, he most likely had planned to make his brother wait, worry, get angry and be embarrassed in front of his wife. How wrong he was! She exhaled. Even if Datam did get annoyed, he would never show it or allow it to give him cause to pick a quarrel. It was in Tirdad's nature to twist the intent within events, displace anger with himself on his victim and thus justify his reason to hate. Unfortunately the prison's hardships had changed the man for the worse and not for the best – a pity indeed. Had he been wise, he could have picked up the threads and begun a new life devoid of any grudges. She gave a discreet shake to her head, said nothing, waited alongside her anxiety-ridden husband and occupied her mind by admiring the grace with which the ladies carried their hejab. Some were very smart indeed. Suddenly she became self-conscious in her simple, loose white pants and long white cotton coat from Marks and Spencer. Her outfit looked more like pyjamas than a suit. This embarrassed her even more and she hid herself behind Datam. He was so much thinner that it made no difference. So she took hold of their trolley, "Darling, let me push this. You seem too tired." Surprised, Datam let her have the handle. She smiled and covered her ensemble behind the load on the trolley. Eventually, after walking the length and breadth of the hall several times, Datam relinquished hope. "Something must have detained him. Otherwise he would have been here for us."

"Never mind darling, we can get a taxi." Rose said guiding the trolley towards the exit.

Kobra opened the door to them. A deep sense of loss was evident from her drawn and pale face. She was still in her night dress and her hair was rumpled. She hugged Datam and began to cry. He kissed her head and patted her shoulders. Kobra let him go, looked up into his sad, tired eyes and murmured: "He was dearer to me than a father."

"He was so proud of you – so proud." Datam exclaimed.

"Was he really?" Kobra asked drying her eyes with her sleeve.

"Yes, he always praised your achievements and thought of you as the daughter he never had." Rose cut in expressing her own sorrow. They kissed and then Kobra lifted Rose's hand luggage and whispered: "Madar is still sleep. I have turned Baba's study into a bedroom for you."

In the bedroom, Rose, placed her case in a corner; discarded her foulard and coat and then followed her husband and Kobra to the kitchen where tea was brewing. They heard someone let himself in. "It is Tirdad. He always arrives at odd hours to spy on me." Kobra whispered, taking from the cupboard tea cups in which she poured tea. They each took a cup and sat around the table.

Tirdad, seeming at war with himself and the rest of the world, stepped in. Roving his hostile eyes over the three he offered a cold Salam to the room. Datam rose and embraced him warmly. With a twist he withdrew from his hold, pulled out a chair, sat on it and staring at Kobra ordered:

"Give me a cup of tea."

"The kettle is right behind you. Serve yourself."

"Fuck you." He said before standing up. Quickly he poured himself tea in a large glass and returned to the table; his eyes shooting shafts of detestation at Kobra. She met them with equal enmity. Rose noticed their mutual resentment and wondered what had happened between the two to create such deep hostility.

Datam who abhorred aggression eyed them with regret and sorrowful pity. Rose noticing his discomfort, and to break the irksome silence that was playing on her own nerves, turned to Tirdad and avoiding his eyes said: "I am so sorry for your loss. I hope it is your last. We all loved Agha doctor very much. He was such a wonderful gentleman and a fantastic father."

"Thank you shahzadeh Khanum." Tirdad replied in a derisive tone. She ignored his mockery for she had no intension of getting into any verbal entanglement with him. The guy's behaviour was awful and she couldn't bear him anymore. Besides, she blamed him for Mohammad's death – it was his misconduct that had caused his heart attack and nothing else.

Failing to get his desired response from Rose, Tirdad turned to Datam, lifted a brow and asked: "So finally you dared to return to your country, Mister Fugitive?"

"I wanted to see my father again." Datam replied avoiding his scorching eyes.

"You are a bigger liar than I thought you were."

"I am sorry you think that way."

Tirdad sniffed, grinned and began tapping on the table top with his nervous fingers. He wanted to pick a fight – but no one was willing to oblige. This inflamed his anger even more. Kobra reading his mind as clearly as a note on a pad narrowed her eyes and in a sharp and indignant voice commanded:

"Tirdad, in respect for the soul of our father, behave like a gentleman. That is, if you still remember how."

"You mean mine and Datam's father, Kobra Khanum Afati?"

"Yes. I mean your father and my mentor and dearest friend."

From under the table Rose patted Kobra's knee.

No one spoke. A trying silence engulfed them. Nervous, irritated and hot, they busied themselves drinking their lukewarm tea and intermittently exchanging meaningless words as though they were a bunch of frustrated strangers in a doctor's waiting room – not siblings sharing the same loss. Tirdad turned his attention to Rose and kept asking her silly questions. She satisfied his curiosity with utmost diplomacy. Twice he tried to talk about Galandoak and both times Rose changed the subject. He was counting on being rebuked. He kept darting hostile glances at her and his brother, wondering why neither was saying anything reproachful to him. He did not know that Datam knew nothing about his embezzlement. The tense atmosphere had become overwhelming, particularly for Datam whose fragile threshold for stress had ebbed. He turned to Tirdad and in an impatient tone demanded: "Could you please drive us to the Morgue before the traffic becomes too heavy?"

"Yes. I hope you don't mind driving in an old Peugeot and not a Mercedes Benz."

Datam just shook his head.

"When do you want to go Mister Fugitive?"

"Now please."

Kobra didn't budge.

"Won't you come with us for a last farewell?"

"No, thank you Rose, I prefer to remember him as he was – for me he is not dead."

Tirdad threw her a disdainful glance and grimaced.

Rose, already on her feet, gently rubbed Kobra's shoulder, "Oh, well, see you when we return." Wordless Kobra stood up to clear the table.

The drive was long and the passengers pensive. Datam, on the back seat, was wondering at his brother's cold and intimidating conduct. Behind the wheel, and fuming inside, Tirdad was impatient for his fight. Rose, next to him, just watched the portraits of the Martyrs, still on walls, running away from her sight. Unaccustomed to so much hostility she felt nauseated. Hastily she drew down the window; put her head out and inhaled several deep breaths. The outside air was not fresh but purer than what she had been sniffing – odour of hate and resentment, unsettled accounts and envy.

At the morgue the group was guided to a huge, empty, cold room that reeked of death. Their guide, in a white uniform, led them to a section that resembled a bank safe with rows and rows of large drawers with heavy levers. He gripped one of the handles and pulled out a stretcher on which Mohammad lay under a white sheet. Datam gently removed the corner of the cloth from over his head and saw that on his face dwelt an expression of peacefulness – as though happy to have left behind the burden of his unfulfilled life. He, and after him Rose, kissed his cold forehead, stroked his silver hair, whispered their prayers, kissed him again and then Rose looked up at Tirdad and with her eyes asked him to do the same. When he did not move, she covered Mohammad's face, took her husband's icy hand, thanked the guide, and walked towards the exit. From a side door a man in his forties, clad in a spotless, white overall stepped out. He greeted the group with a polite Salam, turned his sympathetic eyes to Datam and in a subdued tone asked: "You must be relatives of the late doctor Amiri?"

"Salam Agha, he was our father." Datam answered, surprised by the question.

"My name is Asghari. I am the Morgue's pathologist. I had the honour of being a student of your late father – a wonderful gentleman and so knowledgeable. Iran has lost a great scholar."

Pride pouring out of his eyes, Datam stretched his hand and shaking the doctor's said: "Thank you sir for your fond memories of my father. I am very proud to be his son."

"When all the other professors were pomp and pompous your father was gentle, kind and understanding. And, he was an excellent teacher."

"Would you like to come to his Khatm (wake) Doctor?"

"I'll be honoured."

"Can you please give me your telephone number so that I call you and confirm the date?"

"Of course Agha. Just wait a minute; I get my card for you."

As the doctor turned to go into his office, Rose pulled at her husband's sleeve and whispered: "Introduce Tirdad."

The doctor returned and offered his card to Datam who took it with thanks. Datam turned his face to Tirdad, "doctor, this is my younger brother Tirdad and the lady my wife Rose." The men shook hands and the doctor, without looking at Rose, acknowledged her presence with a head bow.

Rose smiled at his lowered eyes, turned to her husband and said: "Datam, may I have the doctor's card. It will be safer in my handbag than your pocket."

Datam gave her the card which she promptly dropped into her bag. Asghari, who so far had managed to abstain from looking at the lady, lost his control and stole a glance from her. He had never seen such a beautiful woman in his life. To stop himself from further sinning, he turned to Datam and mumbled: "Please excuse me. I have to dash off; an autopsy is waiting for me."

"It was good to meet you doctor and we hope to see you at the Khatm."

"Sure, just let me know when and where it is held." He said and dashed away.

"What a pleasant fellow!"

"Yes darling, and doing such an unpleasant job."

"Not everyone is as lucky as you – to do nothing and live in luxury." Tirdad remarked with an ugly grin.

"Tirdad, do not covet my life. One day you will regret it."

Aware of her husband's miserable state of mind she turned her angry eyes to Tirdad and for the first time attacked him: "Agha, luck is deserved not given. It is our deeds which bring us luck and nothing else. Just remember that. If you start trying, you might earn it too." She grasped her husband's arm and led him towards the exit. Neither heard Tirdad saying: "The bitch has taken charge again."

At home they found Shamsi stretched on the sofa, her head on Kobra's lap, gazing at the white ceiling and murmuring: "Now that he has gone, what is going to happen to me – what?" Gently stroking her peppery hair Kobra was pondering about what Mohammad had left her in his will. According to Islamic law she did not inherit anything from her stepfather unless bequeathed in his will. She had arrived the night before, and had not had time to search his bureau where she knew he kept his documents. In a corner Nary, comfortable on an armchair, was staring at Shamsi wondering how selfish a person could be. The woman was not mourning her husband of over sixty years but worried how to 'manage' without him – how heartless and detestable!

Datam offered his Salam to the room, walked to Nary and kissed her face. "Welcome back." She said in her monotonous voice. "Thank you Khanum." He replied, bending to kiss Shamsi's forehead. She opened her arms and hugged him tight. Patting her back he whispered: "Madar joon, do not worry about a thing. We are all here to organize your life and when Kobra and we leave, Tirdad and Nary Khanum will take care of you."

She let him go. He sat on the arm of the chair. "You are wrong son. Tirdad hardly ever visits me and Nary Khanum is always busy with her teaching. No one wants me No one!" Shamsi groaned and turned her eyes and hands to heaven: "Please God, grant me death and free me from the miserable, lonely life that lies ahead of me."

Rose came forward, kissed her and said: "Shamsi joon, I know how you feel. I have lost two of my loved ones too. It is hard. It really is. But you are lucky to have Tirdad and Nary here. They love you very much and will take good care of you."

Shamsi just shook her head in despair.

Rose kissed her again and stood up to go to her bedroom, when she heard Tirdad say: "Madar, I will come every day and you can come and visit us. We live two blocks away."

Kobra threw him a doubtful glance and huffed.

"Oh God! What will happen to me, now that he has gone?" Shamsi repeated pulling at her tousled hair.

Running out of patience Kobra took her mother's limp hand, patted it, "hush Madar. We are all here for you and you never will be left alone. Please stop this." Shamsi lowered her voice yet continued her growl. Kobra let her hand go and directed her flustered eyes to Datam who, shaking his head in lament, left for their bedroom. He found Rose lying on the bed, deep in thought. She was reflecting upon the scene Shamsi had choreographed with skill. Even dead, she was not charitable enough to mourn him, the man who had loved her so much, with dignity. The scenes were to divert attention from the tragedy of his loss to the void he had created in her life. What a farce? Datam noticing the trickles of tear sliding down the side of her face sat by her, stroked her hair and asked:

"Is there anything wrong?"

"No. I am just thinking."

"About what?"

"About Agha doctor, Shamsi and the rest of us."

Mentally and physically drained, Datam stretched besides her, took her hand in his, squeezed it with compassion, closed his eyes and went to sleep.

Since there was nothing in the fridge, lunch was delivered from the Kebab restaurant in Avenue Ghandi. It was consumed in the calm of bereavement and followed by disputes and disagreements over Mohammad's resting place, the major issue being the cost of the grave. Finally it was decided to bury him at

Behesht-Zahra and have his Khatm at home which was not fit to receive pigs, let alone people.

Rose was determined to arrange a reception deserving of Mohammad's social standing to which many people reading his death announcement would come. So she turned to taciturn Nary, "Khanum joon, can your cleaning lady come here this afternoon to help us clean up and prepare the flat for the reception?"

"No. I do not enjoy the luxury of having a maid."

Datam and Kobra exchanged a scathing glance.

"Then would you be kind enough to help Rose yourself?"

Datam asked in an affable tone.

Slighted by the request Nary furrowed her arched brows, turned to her husband and smirked.

"Nary has a bad back, she can only serve tea."

"Well, in that case you and I will do the cleaning up – Rose and Kobra will serve the Halva and the dates."

Rose smiled at life's wonders. She had never thought she would live to see her husband stand up for her against an Amiri sting.

Three days later, the burial at Behesht Zahra proceeded with the formality and dignity due to the respected Professor. Several of his old students attended the ceremony and were now present at the Khatm. The flat was full and the cleric had just finished reciting his verses of the Koran and the prayer for the dead. To Datam's delight Gholam Reza and Behjat had volunteered to come and help. Gholam Reza, in an old black suit of the Prince was serving tea and Turkish coffee. Behjat, a clean apron tied around her waist was washing up in the kitchen. Nary Khanum, clad in black, was warming her chair, and acting more like a guest than a lamenting daughter-in-law. Amongst those present were Doctors Asghari and Jafari. The latter was the, deputy to the Dadsetan Kol (Attorney General). A rather large, bearded man Jafari had written his thesis under the late doctor's supervision and had managed to receive a doctorate degree in physics from the University of Teheran. He had always remembered his professor with fondness and respect. The article by the editor of Keyhan Newspaper on the contributions of the late professor Amiri to the Colleges of Physics at Teheran, Karadj and Rezaieh Universities had boosted his ego and made him determined to show off his connection by attending both the funeral and the khatm.

Son of a butcher, mingling amongst the old, albeit poor, aristocracy, elevated his self-steam, particularly that he could boast about his special association with the late doctor, simultaneously exhibiting his pure jade prayer beads with which he very conspicuously played. The new rich didn't feel comfortable without showing off their wealth – and pure jade was very expensive. Elated by this rare opportunity, he eventually exhausted his targets and returned to Datam reiterating his condolences. Datam to reciprocate the man's cordiality engaged him in a light conversation which gradually led to more serious political issues ending up with him unjustly being on the black list that had robbed him of his liberties. Rather incensed by the revelation, Jafari frowned, affected an air of astonishment and said: "I find it unbelievable that the

217

name of a man of your calibre is on that list. I can almost vouch that there must have been a reckless mistake, made by one of those enthusiastic youths that ran things at the beginning of the Revolution. You know many of them were communists with grudges against established people, like yourself. They are finished now, and we are here to set right their mistakes by exercising justice and prudence." Smiling, he tapped Datam's back, "Agha, come to my office first thing tomorrow morning. There is nothing I wouldn't do for a man like you."

Datam smiled, took a plate of dates from the table and offering it to Jafari teased: "Let us sweeten our pallet in honour of justice that hopefully would prevail."

"Have no doubts doctor Aziz." Jafari stressed with a smile.

The overcrowded room was becoming uncomfortably hot and there was nothing more to discuss. Jafari took out his handkerchief and dabbing it over his sweaty forehead said: "I must go now. It was a real pleasure to have made your acquaintance doctor joon, and I hope to see a lot more of you." Jafari declared, putting his arms around Datam and kissing both his cheeks, not once, but twice.

At another corner, Rose noticed Asghari sitting by himself, looking lost. She picked up a dish of halva from the dining table that she had tastefully decorated with plates full of Khatm offerings like fresh dates, halva, ghaout (chick pea powder mixed with sugar and cardamom) and a large vase of white flowers that fragranced the stuffy air. Slowly she navigated her way to him. As his eyes fell on her, he blushed crimson. Immediately he moved to rise. Rose put her hand on his shoulder and gently pushed him down. The unexpected touch sent an electrical shock to his heart and for an instant numbed it. "Please do not get up Doctor." She said presenting him the halva dish from which he took a piece. "Thank you Khanum." He said in a low voice. She placed the plate on the nearby small table and occupied the empty chair next to him. He put the halva piece into his mouth, closed his eyes, sent a prayer for the deceased and began to chew it. It was soft, sweet and deliciously spiced by a melange of cardamom seeds and saffron powder. Rose noticed his coffee cup was empty. "Would you like another cup of coffee?"

"No, thank you Khanum, I have already had two."

Rose crossed her shapely legs draped in black silk pants, turned her bright eyes to Asghari's shy face and courteously asked: "May I ask what you specialize in doctor?"

"I started studying physics, took all Dr Amiri's courses and then decided there was more money to be made in becoming a cosmetic surgeon."

"I thought you were a forensic pathologist. What does a cosmetic surgeon do at the morgue?"

"That Khanum I cannot tell you. But my services are required and I am paid well."

"So if I want a facelift you do it for me free of charge?" Rose teased.

"You do not need a facelift Khanum. Nevertheless, I will be at your service whenever you wish."

"Thank you Doctor. Remember, I do have your card." She winked at him. There was something about her eyes that he adored. Near her, he felt a different person – somehow a livelier person without any inhibitions. Why? He knew not.

"At the morgue, I mostly do autopsy. I learnt it by watching my predecessor."

"Then you are not only charming but also a very bright and intelligent gentleman doctor Asghari."

"Khanum Amiri you are too kind.' He rose, "I must leave now. It was an honour to be present here and enshallah I will be able to meet you and your illustrious husband again and under happier circumstances."

"Enshallah doctor joon." Rose stood up and accompanied him to the door.

It was almost nine in the evening when the last person left. Exhausted they all slumped on chairs to relax. For an hour or two a sense of amity prevailed. Gholam Reza served more tea and Behjat began to clear the tables. Shamsi glutted in the glory of the occasion and for the first time in her life, felt proud of being Khanum Amiri.

"I never knew Baba was so popular amongst his students?" Tirdad exclaimed putting a piece of halva into his mouth.

"Stop eating that stuff. It is full of sugar," chided Nary with impatience. She couldn't wait to get out and away from them all. Spellbound by the long day's events Tirdad didn't even hear her.

Rose went to her bedroom, took a hundred thousand rials from her purse, returned to the kitchen and offered it to Gholam Reza.

"What is this for Khanum joon?"

"This is to thank you for saving the occasion for us. I don't know what we would have done without the two of you. Thank you again."

Gholam Reza ignored her stretched hand and shook his head, "Khanum joon you are shaming us with your generosity. It was our duty to be here and serve you. I cannot take money for what we both wanted to do for you and the late doctor." Knowing that arguing would be useless Rose said: "Ok, take this, buy a lamb, sacrifice it for the late doctor and distribute the meat amongst the poor."

"That, I will do with pleasure." Gholam Reza answered taking the notes.

"Now you better get ready to go. The taxi I reserved for you will be here in fifteen minutes. You better take my umbrella too. It is raining outside."

"No need Khanum joon. Behjat had the foresight to bring one."

"As wise as ever, your wife is!"

"Well it is autumn now and weather unpredictable."

"You know Gholam Reza we are very lucky to enjoy four seasons in Iran. In Europe it is mostly grey cold and rainy. And I hate that."

"Then why don't you come back for good Khanum joon?"

"Wish I could my man – I wish I could." Rose replied with a long, sad sigh.

It was a fine bright morning when two telephone taxis arrived at the front gate of Amiri's apartment block; one to take Datam to the office of the Dadsetan Kol in the heart of the city and one to take Rose across the snow smitten foothills of Elborz Mountains, to Galandoak.

Rose's taxi driver parked at the villa's gate and following her instruction bellowed his horn. A few minutes later, Gholam Reza opened the gate.

"Agha you wait here for me please." Rose demanded before getting out of the taxi.

Panting from running Behjat arrived to welcome her Khanum. They hugged and kissed like mother and daughter. Gholam Reza, his face twitching with the pain in his joints that intensified as soon as the sun relinquished its warming power, asked the driver if he wanted a cup of tea or a glass of water.

"No thank you Agha." Replied the driver surprised by the hospitality of the old man with the kindest eyes. "Pedar (father), how long do you think Khanum will stay here?"

Gholam Reza stared at him with cautious eyes, trying to judge if he could trust him with any information or not. Ever since the Revolution he had become suspicious of all strangers, particularly if they had an unshaved face, like this one. He shifted his weight from one leg to the other, contemplated for a second or two and then asked: "Why do you want to know son?"

"No offence is meant Agha. I just want to know if I have time to take a walk to the Dam and back. "

"I do not know exactly how long; but, not less than an hour – I am sure of that. It won't take you long to get to the Dam and back. Go son, and enjoy the crisp and clean mountain air that will cleanse your lungs from all the pollution in it." Gholam Reza leaned against the wall. "God bless my Master's soul for keeping my wife and I here otherwise we would have been dead from that awful air in Teheran."

The taxi driver smiled at the camaraderie of the old man and nodded his head in agreement.

Gholam Reza opened both gate doors and with his head, beckoned him in: "Son, park your car inside. There are so many car-thieves around nowadays."

"Much obliged Pedar." The driver said, getting into his car.

Rose and her entourage walked to the thriving rose patch. She knelt down, went through the same ritual. Closed her eyes connected with her parents, picked the loveliest rose, kissed it and placed it across the stone, in her heart appreciating Gholam Reza's sense for choosing roses that bloomed twice a year.

"I know they are in heaven." She said rising up.

"Of course they are – of course." Behjat declared putting her arm around her tiny waist. They walked to the building together. The chilly mountain breeze tapped at Rose's foulard. She took a deep breath of the fresh air and smiled. It felt scrumptious – just like a sip of spring water. By the entrance Behjat stopped. "You go in Khanum; I am going to bring you a cup of tea." She walked in, followed by Gholam Reza who left the door open for Behjat's return. Inside this old house where time had not ticked away, Rose felt a kind of pleasing nostalgia that lifted her spirits up. Everything had remained in its right place: the picture frames, the crystal fruit bowls and the ashtrays which were there for the guests. Here she could still inhale her parents' scent that came from the love that existed within their souls and gave them energy to go through life accepting their fate with grace. So different from the Amiri's: where even during a requiem she only could smell the odour of hate. It was because of their unforgiving nature that all of them had let hate enter their hearts and eat their morals like worms infesting leaves which eventually would shrivel and die an ugly death. Such a shame! Rose thought exhaling a deep sigh before sitting down. Behjat entered with a large tray on which was a bowl of fresh hazel nuts and three glasses through which the dark reddish hue of Darjeeling tea glowed like rubies. She placed the tray on the coffee table, picked a glass by its handle and put it in front of Rose. Gholam Reza picked up his and leaned on the wall. Behjat sat on the floor next to Rose's chair. Enjoying their drink they gossiped and reminisced without even throwing a glance at the window through which the new fences on the eastern side of the garden stood like sore thumbs. Suddenly an army of buzzing bees swarmed inside.

"Agha, go and close the window. Behjat said waving them away, "God be thanked, we collected much honey this year."

Gholam Reza limped to the window and shut it.

"His legs are killing him." Behjat whispered in a wistful tone.

"Has he listened to me and hired a helping hand?"

"No Khanum. He will never hire a helping hand. He even resents my help. I think he is jealous of anyone with the slightest intention to take his place here."

Rose fixed her caring eyes on the old man. He closed the window, limped back, sat on the floor and tried to bend and tuck one leg under the other when a wail of pain escaped his mouth.

"Gholam Reza, stretch your legs please."

"Not in front of you, Khanum."

"Then get up and sit on this chair next to me."

As obstinate as ever, he manoeuvred his limbs until he managed to sit in a crossed legs position. "Now this is better," he said with a satisfied smile.

Rose grinned at his obstinacy and asked: "Gholam Reza, who are our new neighbours?"

"Two Bazaar merchants, waiting to sell their land at a profit,"

"How much are they asking for?"

"Twice the amount they paid."

"OK. I will buy the land back from them."

"Do you really mean it my shahzadeh?" Gholam Reza asked, his face shining with delight.

"Of course, find their telephone numbers tell them you have a buyer and expect an agent's commission. Do not mention my name, because then they will triple the price."

"I have their numbers. They asked me to water their fruit trees for a monthly allowance. I did not think you would mind me treating my own plants, an hour a day, to keep them alive." The gardener confessed with a tinge of guilt in his voice.

"I am glad they have been useful to you. Now let's go and say hello to Agha Nazari."

"Khanum joon, Agha Nazari, passed away a month ago and now his youngest son has taken over the office and you would not want to do business with him. He doesn't have an honest bone in his body."

"These days who has, my dear?" Rose whispered, shaking her head in remorse.

"I really don't know Khanum joon. Perhaps I am too ignorant and too old to distinguish a good man from a bad one. All I know is that trust between people has diminished. What has happened to our world?" he shook his head, "perhaps we are approaching the end when corruption will devour decency, impelling Emmam Mehdi to return and save us from the fall."

"Gholam Reza, never lose hope. The power of goodness will always supersede that of evil. Things will change in their own good time. No evil persists forever; otherwise we would be fooling ourselves in believing in the Almighty. Now I want you to pray that Enshallah Agha's name will be removed from that awful list, and we can come and spend our summers here, with you."

"God be praised. I have been praying for that at every prayer, Khanum joon – five times a day." Behjat said, with her hand sweeping the last bee away from Rose's proximity.

A month later, after several lengthy negotiations, the fences were removed and in their place neat rows of apple trees planted.

To guard against evil eyes the news was kept from the rest of the Amiri family. Datam never found out about the fate of those two lots of land. Upon his visit to the villa, he was surprised to find so many young Apple trees where mature Cherry trees had stood. He turned to Gholam Reza and asked the reason. "Agha, some sort of fungi infected their roots and dried the poor plants." Gholam Reza replied hoping God would forgive him for his harmless fib.

"What a pity, but never mind, Enshallah next year we have plenty of apples."

"Enshallah doctor joon, not next year, perhaps the year after."

Datam smiled at his own gardening naivety and let Gholam Reza take him to the persimmon trees where their fruit were as large as tennis balls. It would take another few months before they turned red and soft.

Clock ticked away ceaselessly; dusk turned into dawn and nature progressed in its course. The trees shed their leaves, the birds migrated to warmer habitats, sky became overcast and the passive autumn languor spread over the sleeping pastures giving the air the sense of transiency that accompanies all life.

After the requiem, Rose and Datam moved to the Esteghlal Hotel, and Rose made herself a rare visitor at Fifth Avenue flat. She didn't want to participate in the ugly scenes Tirdad and Kobra were creating in front of their mother. Datam visited her daily but only for an hour or two. Shamsi blamed Rose for his short stays and Tirdad fanned the fire with his lies and gossips. Fed up, Kobra cut her leave of absence from office short and returned to Paris.

Datam continued going to the Dadsetani Kol (the office of the Attorney general), until eventually, he was received and questioned by the Attorney General himself, a prominent Ayatollah. The experience was awesome and demeaning, yet fruitful, all due to Brother Jafari's tireless endeavours. The ban on his exit from Iran was removed; however, all his confiscated properties remained confiscated. Nevertheless, from the date of the exoneration on, he could participate in financial transactions. So he became a free man albeit a very poor one. The next day Rose took him to Galandoak, where Gholam Reza sacrificed a lamb and distributed the meat amongst the local needy.

For the first time, in twenty years, they were going to stay the night, in a house filled with nostalgic memories, and sleep on a bed that had been waiting for them all these years. What an incredible joy, they each felt.

The long day over, wrapped in heavy coats they stood by Gholam Reza's charcoal burner on which he was turning the lamb kebab skewers for even barbequing, each arguing over which skew was theirs. Behjat, holding a large dish covered by Sangak bread was standing by her husband so that he could dispose of the ready kebabs on the dish for her to slide off the skewer and cover under the bread. When all was done they headed towards the well-lit rose patch where Behjat had laid a blanket over which she had improvised a sofreh setting. Gholam Reza following them placed the charcoal burner behind Datam and Rose so that they could enjoy its warmth. They could have dined inside. But Rose wanted to share her joy with her parents. At a short distance the river was alive again and on its surface the face of a full moon undulated. The peacefulness and harmony surrounding them was so beautiful that it hurt. Suddenly Datam felt a spark of envy grip his heart for he thought perhaps this could be his last visit to this beautiful place where he had felt so happy and so welcomed. Slowly he gripped Rose's hand, squeezed it with warmth, took it to his lips and kissed it several times.

For a few years Shamsi, Tirdad and Nary coexisted, sometimes amicably and often with enmity. Tirdad, in partnership with two friends, started a company involved with protection of the environment, which had become a hot issue in Iran. For a while, the company did well and prosperity increased Tirdad's craving for alcohol. Soon, he became alcoholic with all the characteristics that plague the addict. Early in the morning he was a good, kind and understanding husband, friend and colleague. As the day wore on, his moods changed and he became aggressive and paranoid. This affected his relationship with his partners to the extent that they offered to buy his share in the company. He sold but not before a physical fight. He went into other partnerships with the same ending until his reputation became so stained that no one wanted to have anything to do with him. He started to look for employment; but with his dossier, no one would hire him. Failure and frustration turned him into a beast with a foul mouth.

Nary began to feel the noose tightening around her neck. Her married life had become an unbearable farce. Her only solace was the few hours she spent with Hashem.

The Ministry of Information had its tentacles spread far, even beyond the country's borders, into everyone's life – friend or foe. It had become extremely sophisticated in its functioning and ruthless in locating and punishing the enemies of the Regime. Assassinations, murders and disappearances had become part of everyday life in Iran and abroad. Telephones were bugged, emails monitored, and the opposition ruthlessly annihilated. Hashem was a director of this infamous organization, which was in charge of the preservation of the country's security. But since he had a soft heart, and a shade of conscience, he did not abuse his power, nor was he as cruel as his colleagues in dealing with people who had 'diverted from the right path'. It was within Hashem's power to make Tirdad disappear without a trace, but all he wished for was his natural death. He desperately wanted to marry Nary and end their clandestine relationship. He knew adultery was a great sin and, if discovered, she would be stoned to death. He could stop that but his own name would be stained.

Sometimes at nights, his conscious flashed scenes of committed brutalities he thought he had buried in the depth of his mind. But the dreams were so horrific that he woke up exclaiming a loud 'astakhfar' which literally means 'God forbid'. Then to obliterate the guilt which lately had become overpowering, he would sigh and tell himself that he could do nothing but obey the orders that were blessed by men holier than him. He spent the evenings at home with his nagging mother who had introduced to him numerous respectable damsels – albeit to no avail. Seemingly he led such a celibate life that she began to suspect he was homosexual. How could a fifty year old man have no woman in his life, even a Sigheh? So she prayed for his salvation, night and day. When her friends wondered why she didn't have a daughter- in- law as yet, she smiled and teased: "With so many loose girls around, who wants to marry."

Hashem, to compensate the two hours he took off to be with Nary, went to work very early. He was behind his desk even before the janitors arrived. It was not just their gratifying sexual relationship that had glued him to her. It was his fascination for the woman herself, her aura, the softness of her voice and the twinkle in her eyes. By now, he was familiar with her virtues and little faults, her unreasonable demands and love of money. So, he flourished upon her what her husband was not capable of giving her – unconditional love, compliments and gifts – invisible gifts like huge deposits into a new bank account. Nary was wise enough to appreciate what he was doing for her and, in fact, had developed a peculiar kind of love for him. She certainly respected him for the purity of his devotion which she had never found in her own husband or that lout, Reza who was back from Pakistan. Lonely and without a friend she particularly valued the friendship that had developed between them. After making love, they often talked and tried to resolve each other's problems – mostly hers. He even tried to find a job for Tirdad but without success. As soon as his jail record was mentioned, doors slammed shut. Without any income, Tirdad put their apartment for sale. When his mother reminded him of his promise to his father, he told her they needed a bigger apartment like hers.

With the proceeds from the sale, he bought five year-bonds earning 18% which gave him a good income. They rented a larger flat and set to go through their income recklessly. Nary, to impress her peers, began to give lavish parties, take expensive holidays and do foolish things that not only did not impress anyone but devoured their savings like a hungry wolf. When the monthly interest proved inadequate, they began to liquidate the bonds at a loss because the five years had not expired. Hashem, cautioned her against extravagance while Tirdad indulged her whims. Consequently, her visits to the love nest decreased while Tirdad's share of her increased. In the meanwhile Shamsi suffered. She knew once the cash finished, they would be at her door.

It was a crisp and cold winter day. Weekend skiers had already gone to Dizin and other ski resorts near Teheran. A thick blanket of snow shimmered over the entire mountain range, roads and pavements. Tree branches were weighed down by their heavy loads. Drivers had to chain their tyres in order not to skid on the glassy roads. Windows were laced by ice and there were only few pedestrians garbed in heavy coats, woollen hats and long boots, hastening towards their destinations, leaving behind a chain of deep foot prints.

Shamsi had prepared a thick barley soup and lamb kebab with rice and cleaned the flat. The radiators were full on and the smell of food whiffing out of the kitchen mouth-watering. Content, she was relaxing on her corner of the couch, knitting a scarf. At intervals she checked her watch. They were already late by half an hour. It annoyed her. The entire week she waited for her Friday lunches, when her loneliness would break and she could exchange a few words with her son, hear his news and ultimately end the day with a quarrel – sometimes benign, often malignant. That didn't matter at all. She just needed to feel and see life around her.

The sound of Tirdad's key clicking in the lock filled her with joy. She set aside her knitting, and fixed her smiling eyes at the door. He stepped in swearing at the cold. Nary, red as lobster with Ahmad rubbing his hands for warmth followed him in. Mother and son, took off their coats and hats, shook the snow off and hung them on the peg of the coat hanger on the wall by the entrance door.

"Salam Madar." Tirdad said, heading for the kitchen to pour himself a glass of Arak from the bottle he kept in her fridge.

"Take off your wet coat first." Ordered Nary before bending to kiss Shamsi. Ahmad standing behind her took a deep sniff and smiled: "Shamsi, I smell Kebab?"

"Yes. Lamb kebab, just what you like, son."

"Shamsi joon, is there anything you want me to do?" Asked Nary.

Shamsi hugged and kissed the boy before looking up at her.

"No Khanum, just sit here beside me." She pointed to the sofa.

"Why there is no ice in the freezer compartment?" Tirdad screamed from the kitchen.

"Because the freezer compartment doesn't function. I told you that last week, and you promised to send someone to come and fix it. I guess you forgot." Shamsi replied, with a tinge of complaint in her voice.

"Grumble, grumble! Do you not realize that I have my own life to run, as well as yours?"

He is here to pick up a fight with me again. She surmised, shaking her head in despair. She put both hands on the coffee table to rise. Ahmad gripped her arm and helped her up.

"Thank you Ahmad joon. You look smart today with your gelled hair and nice white shirt."

"He always looks smart." Tirdad cut in, entering the sitting room, Arak glass in hand. He placed the glass on the table, took off his cashmere coat that had once been Datam's and then his father's. He shook the snow on its lapels over the carpet instead of the entrance tiles, hung it on the peg, lifted his glass and began drinking as though it was water.

"Why do you drink on an empty stomach Tirdad?" Asked an annoyed Nary.

"Because it makes me forget the miseries of my life."

"You should be grateful for your life. You are free, healthy and have a wonderful family." Shamsi called out from the kitchen.

225

"But I live in a rented apartment while you, a single woman, live in this huge flat."

"You had your own apartment. Why did you sell it – to spend the money on other people and arak?"

"Shut up you old bitch." Yelled Tirdad and kicked a dining chair which capsized and collapsed on the floor with a thump.

Nary lifted it up, threw him a disdainful glance and asked:

"Why are you so bloody rude to your mother?"

"She is selfish and inconsiderate. That is why." He replied before walking into the kitchen. He threw his mother a dirty glance and refilled his glass. Her earlier joy dead, Shamsi swallowed the lump in her throat and remained silent.

Ahmad rushed to the kitchen to console the old lady. "Shamsi joon, shall I take the soup to the table." He asked in the sweetest voice.

"Yes son and I will bring the kebab and the rice."

"One eats the starter first and then the main course." Tirdad remarked.

Ahmad, picked up the soup tureen, turned his frustrated eyes to him and commented: "We are in Iran and not Paris. Here we put everything on the table at the same time."

Tirdad grimaced at him and mocked: "All I need is an ignorant boy, to tell me where I am and what I should do!"

Ahmad ignored him, went to the dining table and put the tureen in front of his mother to serve. He pulled out a chair sat down, inhaled the aroma of Kebab and exclaimed 'delicious'.

Shamsi sat next to him and spread her napkin over her knees.

"Please, let's eat in peace." Nary begged, stretching her arms towards Tirdad for his soup bowl. "I don't want any soup" replied Tirdad, "I am not hungry at all."

Shamsi frowned in frustration. Nary fixed her sympathetic eyes on her and said: "Shamsi joon this barley soup looks delicious."

Lunch was consumed in a charged atmosphere and the brooding silence was broken only by the click clack of cutlery. Tirdad finished his second glass of arak, banged it on the table, turned his bloodshot eyes to his mother and ordered: "You must turn the deed of this apartment to my name so that once you are dead; I have a roof over my head." Surprised at the untimely, ugly-worded request, Nary stared at him with reproachful eyes. Ahmad stood up, collected the dishes and carried them to the kitchen. Tirdad's challenging eyes remained fixed on his mother's twitching countenance. Shamsi puckered her large nose, furrowed her brows, avoided his eyes and whispered: "I am going to turn the deed of the apartment to Kobra and Rose's name. Neither of them has inherited anything from your father and it is my responsibility to be fair to them."

"Neither Kobra nor Rose are my father's children."

"Kobra is mine and you owe Rose not only money but an apology too."

Tirdad stood up, pinched the edge of the table cloth and with all the might installed in him by rage pulled it off the table. Crockery and glass crashed on the floor. Horrified by the violence, the three stared at the mess on the floor awestricken. He turned his sadistic eyes to Nary and shouted, "let's leave this hell hole to its evil, degenerate, discriminating keeper."

Nary, pale and puzzled, left her chair, hugged Shamsi and into her ear whispered: "He is drunk again. Please do not take what he says to heart. He will regret it tomorrow."

Shaken to the bone, Shamsi stared at her in bewilderment.

Tirdad came closer and towered over them both. Nary kissed Shamsi's cheek, stroked her head and let her go.

He grabbed a handful of his mother's hair and pulling it asked: "did you hear what I said?"

In pain, Shamsi blinked her yes.

"Then, if you want to see us again, do something about it." He screamed letting her hair loose.

In mental and physical pain, her head hanging down Shamsi let her silence sting her son.

"Stop this madness at once." Nary shrieked, shaking with rage.

He turned to her and with his blood shot eyes threw her a murderous glance. Suddenly a surge of bile rushed out of his mouth and jetted out, just missing Nary's face and landing on the crumpled table cloth on the floor.

Ahmad pulled the napkin off Shamsi's lap and handed it to him. He grabbed it, wiped his mouth and chin, and then let the cloth drop on the floor. As though in a daze he stood still wondering what had happened. Then like a lunatic, he rushed to the hallway, pulled off his coat from the metal hanger tearing its silk lining. Swearing at the world he opened the door and trying to fit his hands in the coat's sleeves dashed out.

Ahmad and Nary cleaned the floor, took everything to the kitchen and threw the broken pieces into the garbage bin. Shamsi remained on her chair trembling. Nary washed the dishes and Ahmad dried them. Neither paid any attention to Tirdad's repeated calling yelps. To annoy him they took their time.

Finished, they kissed the bewildered woman and left her alone, in a confused state, not knowing why all that had happened. Emotionally exhausted and feeling cold she left her chair and managed to reach the sofa upon which she collapsed, closed her eyes and succumbed to oblivion. When she returned to the world, she found it dark. She sat up, looked around and remembered what had happened. She turned on the lamp by the sofa and to spare herself from going mad she telephoned Turan and invited her to come and eat the cake she had baked for dessert. Soon Turan arrived, accompanied by Homayon. One look at Shamsi's face told her the lunch had been a disaster. Over tea, Shamsi poured out her heart asking her for advice. Turan pondered a bit and then suggested: "Why do you not ask them to come live with you here. Then, he won't have to pay rent and you won't be lonely anymore?"

"I thought about this but where would Ahmad sleep?"

"He can sleep in Dr Amiri's, God bless his soul, study."

"No. That space is for Kobra. She will not like that at all."

"If you don't want to do that, pay half of their rent – that will reduce his load of expenditure?"

"No, it will not reduce his expenditure. It will increase his consumption of alcohol."

"Why doesn't Nary get a full time job? She is a capable woman. Before they married, she was his secretary wasn't she?"

"Yes. But now she is a Khanum and according to her, Khanums do not work full time. She tells people that her part time job is just to keep her busy and it isn't that she needs money."

"That is very stupid. Rose is a shahzadeh and she runs a business. Working is not demeaning. Asking for a handout is."

"You tell that to my son and see if he agrees with you."

"Shamsi joon, when will Kobra Khanum come back?" asked a keen Homayon.

"I think she will come in July."

"Good. I miss her very much. She is such a wise and beautiful lady."

Surprised, Turan wondered what was going on in his mind.

"Shamsi joon, she will be able to resolve all your problems. She knows where you keep all your documents and once when she was here, she gave me a few booklets to go and photocopy for her in Agha Khalil's shop. I noticed they were deeds to your land at Varamin and this apartment."

Turan bit her lips, and Shamsi marvelled why Kobra had done such a thing.

Disappointed at the silence that followed his revelation Homayon jumped up, collected the dirty crockery and took the tray to the kitchen. There he washed and dried everything with care. He returned to the sitting room, patted his mother's shoulder and said: "Let us go, I do not want to miss my serial."

Turan shrugged her shoulders, waved her head in self-pity and in a moaning tone complained:

"I do not even have the liberty to enjoy the company of my best friend just because this Agha wants to watch his soapy."

"Well, he is young and besides, in the absence of any better entertainment in these days, his only joy is watching films – why deprive him of it, Turan joon – why?"

"I never thought about it that way. You are right. What have these people left for us – particularly our youth? What?" Turan exhaled a heavy sigh and shaking her head in lamentation rose to leave.

"I will come and have tea with you tomorrow afternoon. You can see that plenty of this cake is left – I will bring it and we will finish it together."

"Come whenever you want – that is after four o'clock."

"Her ladyship" Homayon pointed his chin to his mother, "sleeps for two hours every afternoon Shamsi joon, which means I cannot make a single noise in case she wakes up."

"I too take a nap. At our age, nothing gives us more pleasure than sleep and pleasant dreams." Shamsi replied, accompanying her guests to the door.

That same afternoon, an inferno blasted at Tirdad's apartment that turned into ash the remnants of any affection Nary felt for her husband.

Upon arrival at their building, Tirdad parked the car in their underground parking lot, locked the doors and, pensive, loitered towards the lift, his wife and son, followed him. Ugly, destructive thoughts fought for dominance in his intoxicated mind.

"Mother, he is in one of those dangerous moods. Don't say anything to him please." Ahmad warned, concerned for both their safety.

"Frankly I have had enough of his disgraceful behaviour towards people. It embarrasses me to be called his wife." Nary whispered, squeezing the handle of her new bag Hashem had recently bought for her. Even the thought of him made her feel safe particularly now when her husband had turned into a monster.

"He used to be a kind man. I do not know what they did to him- in jail, to change him so much."

"It is just my luck son." Answered Nary in a wistful tone.

Head down they entered the elevator in which Tirdad, like an angry lion was waiting for them. He punched the button for the third floor. With a burp the door shut and the elevator commenced its ascent.

No one talked.

The elevator stopped and its door opened with a loud screech.

"Bastards, look at the way they maintain this decrepit lift."

No one responded.

As Nary stepped out of the lift Tirdad grabbed the tail of her scarf and forcefully pulled it back. A sharp pain shot through her neck and came out of her mouth in a loud cry.

"Answer me when I talk to you – bitch."

She threw her hands back, grabbed his torso and with all her might pushed him away. Unable to control his balance, he slid backward, letting go of the fabric and hitting his back on the wall of the lift. Ahmad hurriedly picked up his mother's hand bag dropped on the floor and handed it to her.

Nary hurried to the door of their apartment, and leaned on the wall waiting for him to arrive and unlock it.

Ahmad faced Tirdad, looked into his outraged eyes with loathing and said: "If you touch my mother like that again I will kill you."

Tirdad raised his hand and slapped him hard on both cheeks.

"Do not ever interfere in something that is none of your bloody business. I did not feed you to turn against me." He howled like a wolf, his eyes bulging out of their sockets.

Not expecting physical abuse, the boy ran down the stairs, and opened the door to get out. A gust of icy air slapped his sore cheeks. A flurry of pain exploded inside his head. For an instant he blacked out. It was still snowing and the pavement was hidden under mount of snow, at least a meter high. He regained his sight and realised it was impossible to walk to his friend's house, where he usually went to find solace. He never went to his grandparents, who now, after forty years of marriage, were in the middle of an ugly divorce. He hated his grandmother. He never forgave her for beating him when a child and swearing at his dead father for meeting an untimely death – as though it was his fault to be blown into pieces.

He closed the door and looked around him. The cold, empty corridor was deserted. He had nowhere to go but remain in this tomb. He sat on a stone step. It felt as cold as ice. He moved his bottom several times to warm the spot. Then he cupped his face with both hands and, mindless of what the incoming neighbours might think, gave vent to the sadness that was sizzling inside him. The emotional trembling warmed him a bit

Up in the apartment, Nary went to their bedroom to change. Tirdad followed her.

"Why did you support my mother when I was asking her to help us?" He asked in an accusative tone.

Without turning to look at him she replied: "I did not support either of you. I just don't think you should talk to her like that. We have stolen from her what we have wanted, and I am sure she knows. Not once has she confronted either of us. You have already forged her signature on her cheques. In fact you are dealing with what she has as though it already is yours – why then do you go out of your way, to insult and torment her? Why? She is your mother."

"If she knew what mothering is, she would not have left me." He replied banging his clenched fist on his chest and looking at her with tormented eyes, as though begging for her understanding.

"You turn into a beast when drunk." She retorted pulling her scarf off.

Not knowing whether it was his wife or his mother, he hated most; he grabbed her long hair from behind, coiled it around his fingers, pulled her head back and with his other hand began punching at her ribs, taking satisfaction in her screams. He threw her on the bed, turned her around, slapped her face, punched her on the mouth, and slapped her face again and again. Nary fought him like a tiger until there was no more strength in her. Then moaning she closed her eyes hoping to die. Panting and puffing, he gave her a final punch in the stomach, sent her a curse, walked out, slammed the door shut and like a criminal running away from the scene of his crime, dashed out of the apartment.

Stepping out of the elevator, he came eye to eye with Ahmad knees clutched, swinging back and forth to keep warm.

"Go upstairs and take care of your mother. I am not returning home tonight."

"I hope you never do." Ahmad murmured rising up.

Chapter 9

Hashem

On this lunar year, the birthday of the prophet Mohammad had fallen on Saturday and Muslims of the world were celebrating the event. To surprise and pamper Nary, Hashem had come to the flat at nine in the morning, intending to prepare a delicious lunch. He loved cooking. It relaxed him. The feast was to give Nary a break from the routine chores of being wife to two men; that is how he perceived of his relationship with her. The poor lady took care of him as well as that good for nothing husband of hers. He loved her so much that he wanted to see her smile all the time. Aware of her love of perfumes, he had brought her a bottle of Chanel No5, the fragrance of which he had smelt on an air hostess of the Emirate airline when returning from China. Politely, in his pidgin English, he had asked her for the brand name. Since he was travelling first class, the hostess had immediately presented him with a bottle from their duty free collection. Beside himself with gratitude, he had bought two bottles one for Nary and one for the obliging hostess.

To procure technologically advanced devices, he had to travel to Peking and Moscow frequently. During his first flight, he had hugged his travelling Koran, closed his eyes and silently chanted all the prayers he knew by heart, until he had hypnotized himself to oblivion – such had been his fear of flying. Now, accustomed to the experience, he enjoyed the comfort and luxury of travelling first class. However, as a high ranking official of the Islamic Republic of Iran, in public, he had to act like a good Muslim and good Muslims do not drink alcohol. Thus he begrudged those who could enjoy the frequently served French champagne for which he had developed a taste.

He was in the kitchen listening to the radio's news and wondering what tale Nary would fabricate to justify her absence on a holiday, when he heard the door click open.

"Nary joon, I am here, come and give me a kiss."

Nary murmured a Salam and went to the bedroom. This he found strange for she always came to kiss him before going to the bedroom to shed off her covers. Troubled, he wiped his hand with the kitchen towel, turned the radio off and hurried to the bedroom. There he found her stretched on the bed, staring at the ceiling, tears rolling down her bruised face.

"Oh my God! Who did this to you?"

"He did. Last night." She murmured.

"I am going to kill him."

"He was drunk. He has left home and I don't think will return, at least not soon."

"I hope never." Hashem bellowed, dropping on the bed and gently lifting her up and embracing her. She leaned her head on his broad chest, closed her eyes and let his love heal her pains, both mental and physical.

"God, curse him for ruining my life." She mumbled, more to herself than him.

He buried his face in the folds of her blond waves, kissed their softness, and felt the quick throbbing of her neck veins. Sharing her grief, he stroked her back, rocked her like a little child and murmured soothing words into her ears. She cuddled him tight, inhaled his familiar masculine odour, kissed his heaving chest and felt life regenerate inside her.

After a few moments of emotional succour, he unfolded his grip; looked deep into her dreamy eyes, kissed each one of them and then rose, walked to the dresser, picked up the box she had missed noticing and offered it to her with a smile. "I hope this will cheer you up my love."

"What is it Hashem joon?"

"Something that I am sure will please you."

Excited, she wiped her eyes with the edge of the bed cover and stared into his eyes. What she saw in them dissolved all her apprehensions. She stretched her arm and snatched the gift from him, took it to her lips and kissed it. Her gratitude touched him so much that he thought he would burst into tears. He bent, stole a quick kiss from her half open mouth and said:

"Open it love. I want to know if you like it."

"Of course I will, of course."

She opened the box and as her eyes fell on the bottle inside it, they glittered with delight. Hastily, she extracted the bottle out, lifted its black cap, pushed the spray button down. She sniffed the fragrance with half closed eyes and exhaled a long, sexy "ah". Laughing she sprayed it all over herself, the sheet and Hashem. Losing themselves in the cheerful moment, they hugged and kissed, made love and found solace in its purity. Exhausted, they fell into a state of peaceful contentment and eventual nap. Nary woke up first. She went to the bathroom to have a shower. The noise woke Hashem up. For a second or two he was disoriented until the scent of love brought him back to life. With delight he succoured a few more minutes of his comfort, then indolently climbed out of bed and headed for the bathroom.

Nary was in the kitchen tasting Hashem's cooking. It was delicious. The rice had plenty of saffron and the aubergine khoresht (stew) well spiced. She dished them out, put the dishes in the middle of the table and sat waiting for him. The flat was so peaceful that she could hear him sing under the shower. The sound of the water splashing on the tiles stopped and a few minutes later he appeared in his blue jeans, brown polo neck lamb's wool sweater and a cream coloured cashmere cardigan. Only recently, every time she glanced at him, her heart beats accelerated. She enjoyed this new and strange sensation. Was it real love? She pondered with amazement. Her heart had hammered for Tirdad but not like this. He noticed the change of her colour. "Is there anything wrong my beauty?"

Smiling she shook her head in negation. He bent, stole a quick kiss from her damp hair and took the chair facing her.

Nary, never so happy, began serving him.

Spreading his napkin over his lap Hashem, (a habit he had picked up from foreigners) looked at her with teasing eyes and asked: "Tell me if you honestly like my cooking?"

Nary put his plate in front of him: served herself, took a spoon full of rice moistened by the Kohresht, chewed it slowly and then swallowed it with a delightful expression of praise on her luminous face.

"You liked it?" Hashem asked sounding like a child whose hope for praise had been fulfilled.

"It is yummy," she said and then teased, "you should leave your job and open up a restaurant. Then I wouldn't be worried about something bad happening to you."

"Do you really worry about me?"

"Yes. I do all the time."

"I love you Nary."

"Good I am glad." She replied with a broad grin.

Outside the snow had stopped its dance; the sky had cleared and a pale sun was showing off its presence. Down below, the ground shimmered like a spread of pearls from the South Seas. In spite of the dangerous condition of the roads and icy weather, they decided to go for a drive. It would be fun to navigate through the empty city and view the trees, shrubs and evergreens dressed in a white that glittered in thousand hues. To this end, they wrapped themselves in their thick, warm gears and ran to the lift that took them to the underground car park where Hashem's Mercedes Benz was parked. The rumours had it that the Government of Germany had owed the late Shah certain amount of money which was paid to the Islamic Republic by two hundred Mercedes, which were allocated to the Ministry of Information to be used by its important officials. They were all black with Government number plates which gave the drivers immunity against traffic violations.

Hashem sat behind the steering wheel and Nary next to him, her hand on his lap. She felt so insecure that clinging to him gave her peace of mind. She hooked her gaze on his handsome hairy profile and murmured: "I hope he will never return home."

"That will not resolve our problem Azizam. I want to marry you, and as long as he lives, I cannot."

His determined tone sent a shiver down Nary's spine. She coiled around herself, bit her lower lip and said: "Azizam, he is an alcoholic. He suffers from spastic colitis and he has liver problems. I think, soon, very soon, he will die. We just have to be patient."

"My patience is running out Khanum." He retorted giving her a dry look.

The thought of what he might do sank her heart. Unconsciously she inched away from him. As yet, she had not reached that level of inhumanity to think of murder.

He sensed her aversion and threw her a sideways glance. She had paled. He fixed his eyes on the road and tamed his tone. "I have made a lot of money Nary, and, to be honest, I am not comfortable with my work anymore. People at the top, the decision makers, have changed and some are real brutes without any conscience whatsoever. All they think about is how to amass fortune by pulling their power's strings." He shook his head in despair, "and those who dare to stand on their way disappear without a trace. We are trained to annihilate the enemy, not our own brothers. What some of these people do is really sickening." He turned his head and looked into Nary's eyes. They were pensive. "Don't look so serious azizam." He patted her lap and diverted his eyes to the road. "I have been going to China, Russia and Australia. Life in these countries, particularly Australia, is far better than here. Sydney is a beautiful city and Australia has a very good relationship with Iran. I know a few high ranking Australians in the embassy here and can, with their help, get us emigrant visas." He turned to gage her reaction. Her face had remained as cloudy as a winter sky. To get her out of the dire mood he added: "you will love that city." He returned his attention to the road. "It has the bluest of the skies, cleanest of the airs, a beautiful harbour, a huge bridge across the ocean and a gigantic Opera House. And, the people seem very friendly. Best of all, they speak English. We will take Ahmad with us. He can go to university there. Their standard of education is high and perhaps he can become a medical doctor – that is what you told me he wants, right?" He faced her with a broad smile. Their eyes met. His were triumphant hers begging. She put her hand on his that was gripping the steering wheel and squeezing it with warmth pleaded:

"Hashem joon, please do not plan so far ahead. You are giving me stuff to dream about and that makes my miserable life harder to bear. Let us be realistic, and pray he dies soon and from a natural cause."

Her devotion to that alcoholic beast always surprised and touched him. He bent and stole a quick kiss from her forehead.

"Nary, I love you so very much."

"I love you too. You are God's gift to me. Please promise you will not do anything that you might regret for the rest of your life."

A thought went through his mind and settled as a smile on his face. Instead of obliging her request he said:

"I know what I am going to do next Thursday."

"What?" She asked frightened.

"I am going to take you to Mashhad. We will go to the shrine and ask Emmam Reza, to forgive Tirdad's sins and take him to heaven. He has committed several ungodly offences – I know he has – when he was the leader of the Tudeh – so, if we ask for his death, we would not be making an unethical request. In fact, we will be following the right path by praying for the demise of a 'Corrupter on Earth'."

Suddenly she burst into a nervous laughter.

"Did I say something that was funny?" He asked taken back.

"Yes, something incredibly funny."

"Oh – yes?"

"Yes my love. Do you think any deity will listen to the prayers of people who have been living in sin for so many years?"

To answer this question, Hashem had to tickle his brain to find some sort of justification. It took him only a minute.

"True we have lived in sin, but without a sinful intention and once we marry and lead a pious life God in his magnanimity will forgive us." He replied with a smile of certainty on his face.

Nary puckered her face, and shaking her head in denial said:

"I do not believe in God or the Emmams. If there was a God, he would be a just one. Look at my life," she beat at her chest and stared at his set profile, "what have I done to deserve all the sorrows I have suffered: first to lose my first husband in a bomb blast, and then, have to put up with this alcoholic and become involved with the love of my life in an illicit relationship?"

He gave her a frightened glance and said: "Please, send an astakhfar (ask for forgiveness) before something awful happens to us in this car."

"If there is a God, he wouldn't be so vengeful as to punish me for complaining. And if anything happens, it will be to me and not to you," she maintained her stare on his twitching profile and tapped his lap, "now would a just God punish a true believer named Hashem Karimi for the sins of a wretched woman like me?" She asked with a tinge of tease in her soft voice.

"Nary please do not make me angry."

Nary removed her hand and turned her head away in a sulk.

After a few minutes of silence, unable to see her brooding, Hashem took her hand, and kissing it whispered: "Nary joon, why cannot you believe the fact that I love you so much, is a gift from God?"

She was too confused to answer him.

From the side of his eye he glanced at her, changed gear and reasoned:

"Azizam, look at it this way: the path you travelled through life led you to me. God works in strange ways. You must believe in him or he will turn his grace from you."

Nary contemplated for a second or two, then she inched closer and stole a quick kiss from the loop of his ear. He turned his head and their lips brushed against each other. She leaned back, turned the radio on and let the sound of Maestro Marofi's piano enchant them both.

Determined to go to Australia, Hashem began an intensive course in English. It was paid by the Government's special budget dedicated to the education of high ranking officials.

Life took its course. Tirdad lived with his mother and tormented her with unreasonable demands. Not a day passed without Turan hearing him shouting and swearing at her. Shamsi, content to have him under her roof, suffered the indignities with incredible patience and waited for the summer vacations, when Kobra would come and illuminate her life. Even then, the chance of finding peace, with the siblings verbally tearing each other apart was slight. One bright spot in her life was Golnar's regular visits and talks about the great wealth that could come to them once their problems were resolved. The price of land was hitting the roof in Teheran's periphery and Golnar had managed to sell a small part of their estate and distribute the proceeds amongst the owners. Tirdad had immediately transferred the amount into his own account without telling anyone. He was working towards usurping everything his mother owned. So far, the only deed not in his mother's closet was the one held by Golnar. She had ignored his insistent demands and refused to hand it to him. Fed up with his persistence, she had informed Kobra and Datam of her mistrust of his intention. Datam, unable to believe Tirdad capable of depravity, had doubted the validity of her supposition. Rose faithful to Agha Doctor's plea, expressed no opinion at all. She remained reticent, albeit with resentment. But Kobra was alert, and on guard. That was why she had had Homayon take photocopies of all the deeds. She had also taken the actual deed of the Fifth Avenue flat which Shamsi, without Tirdad's knowledge, had turned over to Rose and her names soon after that infamous Friday lunch. Since Kobra was never told about Tirdad's sale of Rose's land, she did not know that he could forge signatures. Nevertheless from the way he had been acting and keeping secrets from her, she had suspected that he was up to something – but what? So on her return to Iran she became even more vigilant.

On the first day of her stay, she called her mother's bank and pretending to be her, asked for her account balance. Not much was there. The next day she waited for the daily domestic Datam had employed for Shamsi and when the woman did not turn up she decided to confront her brother.

They had just finished lunch when Kobra casually asked Tirdad if he knew why Mehri Khanum hadn't come today.

"I sacked her. She was a thief."

"Oh I see." Kobra exclaimed with a raised brow.

"Have you told Datam about what you have done?"

"And why should I inform Datam about what I decide to do?"

"Because he employed her and he arranged an automatic bank transfer to your account for her wage. He has the right to know and cancel that transfer. Besides, I cannot believe that she was a thief. She had worked for Golnar's friend for ten years."

"Since when have you become a fan of your older step-brother?" He scoffed, peering at her with narrowed eyes.

"Since I lost respect for you."

"Fuck you, bitch." He swore controlling his impulse to punch her mouth.

Kobra puffed at his insult as though he was a dog, rose and left the room. She patiently waited until she heard him leave and bang the door. She returned to the sitting room and phoned Datam. He answered surprised to hear from her. She hardly ever phoned him and when she did it was bad news.

"Salam Kobra joon and how are you Khanum." He said in a brotherly tone

"I am fine. I am in Teheran and not happy with what is going on here. Tirdad has sacked Mehri Khanum and now there is no one to take care of Madar. The flat is filthy and he is stealing from her and you."

"How do you know he is stealing from us?"

"I checked Madar's account and only fifty thousand was there instead of three million. He sacked Mehri Khanum without telling either of us because he is pocketing her salary."

"Kobra I am not going to cancel the transfer. He must be in need and even if he is stealing from Madar, he is looking after her while me and you are away. Just turn a blind eye and let him be. He has no job and a family to feed – a desperate man indeed." Kobra heard him sigh. She gritted her teeth and nervously clenched her hand as though intending to hit him on his thick head.

She took a deep breath and burst out: "It is well for you to overlook his theft. You don't need money but I do. I have had to work for every penny I own while all your life, you have been spoon fed by that filthy rich wife of yours – you lucky bastard." She banged the receiver down, "the bloody asshole! I have never known anyone so stupid in my life!" She groused with a throbbing pain in her head.

In London, Datam calmly put the receiver down, pulled a Kleenex from its box and dried the beads of sweat from his forehead.

Shamsi was still in her room. Her siesta's were becoming longer and longer. Kobra ran to her own chamber; fell on her sun-flushed bed. The light hurt her eyes. She closed them. She needed to think and think hard. Intent on possible options plans shaped and unshaped in her head until her lips bloomed into a smile. She opened her eyes. The sunlight pouring inside the room didn't bother them anymore. Soon all this ugliness would be over and she could lead a normal life without a worry in the world. With that in mind she decided to ignore Tirdad's usual stings and try to enjoy the rest of her vacation.

Two weeks later she left for Paris.

As time passed, alcohol eroded most of Tirdad's brain cells and turned him into an unbearably obnoxious individual. Friends discarded him and his wife hardly ever called or came to visit. Once a month he went home, gave her money and took his pleasure from her reluctant body without noticing the love marks on her neck.

Poverty and despondency were increasing his detestation of his siblings who did not lift a finger to help him. At times he even begrudged his mother's clinging to life. He often left her alone, hoping for an accident. And when he returned and, found her alive and expecting service, he hated her even more. He enjoyed ignoring her demands for food or even a glass of water. Often the poor woman had to cry for a piece of bread, or a cup of tea. Aggravated by her persistent moans, he would lose patience, go to the kitchen and fetch her something to shut her up.

Gradually, malnutrition and his verbal and physical abuses began to deplete Shamsi's fragile health. She lost her appetite and her memory became selective. Melancholia took over and made her almost mute – only at times her lips moved as though she was talking to herself. From her facial expressions Tirdad could often guess whether she was in heaven or hell. Then it dawned on him that once she dies, this flat that had become his place of refuge, would go to Rose and Kobra and he would be left with nothing at all. Shamsi had kept the name change from him but Kobra, to spite him, had shown him the copy of the deed she always brought to Iran with her, and sneered at his twitching face. The Varamin land and the rented house would be divided between the three of them which they had to sell. He was sure that neither Rose nor Kobra would allow him to live in this flat rent free. Rose might – she had already proved her 'nobility' but not Kobra, that half cast of a sister, was as low as a worm and as conniving as a fox. So, this time instead of forging a signature he went in search of a notary who would sell his soul for money. They were plenty now-a-days. One day under the pretext of taking her to a new doctor he took Shamsi to the notary office and the dishonest official, knowing that the lady was senile and her signature under the law unacceptable turned the deed of the rented house to Tirdad's name. Now he became the owner of a roof over his head, and when his mother died, hopefully soon, he would take his family to their own home. At the moment, it was wise to let the property remain rented. He was collecting the rent anyway.

Summer spread its dusty dry heat over Teheran and Kobra returned for only a two -week holiday. Now she was a director and could not take long vacations. She found her brother's attitude spiteful and more aggressive than ever. That did not bother her until one day when Shamsi was talking to herself she kept repeating, "I did not like... new doctor – he ... in a robe. Ah – awful with – ugly beard – awful."

Kobra's sharp antenna began to sense foul play. She moved close to her mother, took her bony hand, gently patted it and pronouncing each word clearly asked: "Madar, your doctor always comes here doesn't he?" Shamsi looked at her with perplexed eyes, trying to comprehend her question.

"Madar, who took you to the doctor?"

"Datam. I think it was him – I cannot really remember Golnar joon." Shamsi stuttered with difficulty.

"Madar, I am Kobra. Never mind, I will ask Tirdad." Suddenly Shamsi's eyes widened and fear clouded her twitching countenance. She began to pull at her hair and mumble: "No, no please – no – ask Tirdad. He – beat me again. No."

Astonished, Kobra asked: "He beats you Madar joon?" Shamsi's eyes turned in their sockets like a lunatic. She stopped pulling at her hair and focused at Kobra with confused eyes. "Did I say that?"

"Yes you did."

"No – no. Please – no – say anything to him." She begged, tears soaking the pleats of her cheek.

Kobra hugged her tight and tried to calm her down. The door opened and Tirdad stepped in without a Salam.

"Is lunch ready?" He asked as though talking to his cook.

Kobra carefully laid Shamsi on the sofa and then turned to him.

"I have left a piece of take away kebab for you in the oven."

"So you have already eaten?"

"Yes. It is practically two in the afternoon."

"I am the master of this house. You should have waited for me."

"The master of this house is in his grave and the mistress of this house eats at one. You know this very well and should make a note of it for when I am not around."

"My dear, here, life runs far more smoothly without you than with you around." He snapped and headed for the kitchen from where he yelled: "Tell Madar I am going home to visit my family tomorrow so that she won't worry why I haven't turned up."

Shamsi kept her imploring eyes on Kobra who was smiling now. Instinctively she was sensing some sort of catastrophe. Tirdad's regular brutal behaviour had inflicted so much pain on her that she had become terrified of him. When he disappeared in the kitchen she exhaled a sigh of relief and closed her eyes.

That afternoon, Kobra did not ask any questions or do anything to aggravate him. The next morning when he went to the bank to draw some cash she headed for the drawer in which she knew all the documents were. There she found the deed of the house changed under his name. She picked up the phone and dialled Turan's number. Homayon answered.

"Homayon joon, it is me, your Kobra."

"Oh Azizam." Homayon whispered delighted to hear her voice.

"I need you to come here right now. Can you please?"

"Of course I can."

He put the receiver down, smoothed his hair with his palm, dashed to the bathroom where he splashed some Old Spice over his face and without telling his mother where he was going, tiptoed out of the flat. Kobra was waiting for him behind the open door. He entered. She gave him a huge hug and a kiss on his lips. He held her tight. She tried to separate but he wouldn't let go. She put her hands on his chest, gently pushed him back, looked into his surprised eyes and said: "Cheri, you have to do something for me right now." She paused, patted his face gently, tickled his lips with the tip of her long manicured nail, which she took to her own lips and kissed; then in a seductive voice murmured: "If Tirdad stays at his wife's flat tonight, I will call you after Shamsi goes to sleep – we can have our usual fun!"

"I cannot wait until the evening." He whispered his eyes on her breasts protruding out from the slit of her low neck T-shirt.

She smiled at him, pinched his cheek, picked up the deed she had put in an envelope from the table top and handed it to him. "I need two photocopies of this document. Please hurry."

Ready to climb mountains for her, he grabbed the envelope, stole a quick kiss from her lips and left the apartment. Like a man with a mission, he ran down the stairs and into the street.

Kobra closed the door behind him, went to her room, picked up the phone and dialled Datam's number. She heard Rose's Portuguese house-keeper say: "Amiri residence, may I help you?" Turning green with envy she grimaced.

"I would like to talk to doctor Amiri please."

"The doctor is not available but the Princess is. Would you like to talk to her highness?"

"Yes please."

"Who may I say is calling?"

"Doctor Amiri's sister."

"Good morning Madame. Please wait."

A few minutes passed before Rose, coming out of the shower room, her towel wrapped around her breasts, picked up the phone in her boudoir.

"Salam Kobra joon."

"Salam Rose. I have bad news for you. Somehow Tirdad has turned the deed of my Madar's rented house to his name. Please tell Datam we should take a lawyer against him. Otherwise he will do the same with everything else."

Rose listened without any surprise.

"I shall deliver your message but I do not think Datam will agree to take a lawyer against his brother."

"He should – for my sake. Datam is lucky to have a wealthy wife. I do not enjoy that luxury – so he has to help me to preserve what is ours."

"Kobra, your brother is seriously ill. I am not going to disturb his peace of mind with your news. Let me see what I can do to resolve this problem."

"What is wrong with him?"

Regretting her slip of the tongue, Rose replied:

"He is suffering from a serious infection."

"Oh – I see! Rose Khanum, you must understand that he is my brother, and I have the right to talk to him about our financial problems – which obviously does not concern nor alarm you, being so rich."

"Kobra Khanum, my wealth is irrelevant to this discussion and I will not give you the right to disturb my husband's peace of mind over money, particularly that he cannot do anything effective from this far away. If you want to take a lawyer against your brother, you do so; but please, spare us this new hassle. Tirdad is a desperate man with a family to feed. I am sure Datam is not going to begrudge what he needs to survive even though he is obtaining it in a dishonest way. You do as you deem necessary, but please do not involve us in it. I am prepared to do what it takes to preserve your share of your mother's inheritance. I will ask Datam to make Tirdad agree that they divide her inheritance equally between the three of you, instead of giving you half the amount of each of their share as prescribed in the Sharia law. "

"I do not need hand-outs, especially if it is instigated by you, shahzadeh khanum." The malice in her tone grated Rose's ear. She distant the phone from her face, as though it had turned into poison ivy.

Kobra banged the receiver on its base and puffed a heavy sigh. Shaking her head in frustration, she ambled to the kitchen, made herself a cup of camomile tea and took it to the sitting room where her mother was. She hadn't sat yet when she heard the doorbell. Knowing it would be Homayon; she put her cup on the table, and with quick steps hurried to the door and opened it with a smile. "Here you are my pussy." Homayon said handing her the copies and the original document.

"Thank you azizam, and how much do I owe you?"

"A big, big kiss." He brought his face forward. She pulled hers back.

"You have that tonight. I will call you as soon as I know what Tirdad will be doing."

"Enshallah he stays with his wife for the entire duration of your stay here."

"Enshallah." Kobra whispered closing the door and heading for Tirdad's room. There, she returned the original deed to its place and then went to her bedroom again, hid the photocopies under her mattress, sat on her bed, picked up the phone on her bed-side table and called Mina Mostofi's direct office number. She was her best friend and privy to a lot of her secrets.

Mina picked up the phone.

"Mina joon, I am sorry for disturbing you but I am in desperate need of your advice."

"I am all ears. But be quick as I have an appointment in ten minutes."

"Somehow Tirdad has turned the deed of Madar's rental property to his name."

"Look at the date on the deed. If it is this year's then I can take him to court and if it is before your mother was medically recognized as senile then it is valid and unfortunately you can do nothing."

"Let me check please." Kobra said putting the phone on the table. She bent, pulled out the envelope from under the mattress, extracted one of the copies out and roamed her eyes over the top where the date was. The clever notary had put the date five years back, when Shamsi was in full control of her faculties. "Merde!" she exclaimed before picking up the phone.

"He is a rat. The date is five years back. What am I to do now?"

"Do not let him have access to any other legal documents. He must be working with a conniving, crook of a notary. I am so sorry for you Kobra. This is really nasty."

"Yah, very."

"Shall we have lunch tomorrow at Yas."

"OK, I meet you there at half past twelve."

"Fine."

Kobra returned the receiver to its base, fitted the paper back into its envelope and returned it to its hiding place; then she fell on her back, crossed her arms under her head, closed her eyes trying to figure out how her brother whom she had once loved and trusted so much, could have turned into a ruthless criminal. All his misbehaviour had started from the day he had married that slut. It was all her fault. She had corrupted his mind, milked him dry and then sent a desperate man back to the bosoms of his family to steal from them for her. She had to stop him. How? She pondered and pondered without finding a better alternative to her original plan that she had abandoned in hope of being proven wrong in her suspicions of him. The thought made her shiver but he had left her with no other choice. She opened her eyes, took a deep breath, sat upright, picked up the phone again and dialled Nary's number. To her delight the woman herself took the call.

"Salam Nary."

Surprised, Nary paused for a second before responding. Kobra had never called her before. What did she want? The girl was devious and Nary had always feared her and now more than ever.

"Salam Kobra joon. I hope you are well and enjoying Iran."

"Yes, I am well and happy to be with Madar. I called to see if Tirdad was staying the night there or would be coming home, so that I prepare dinner for him?"

"It is very thoughtful of you. However, for a change, he has decided to spend the night here with us. Would you like to join us? "

"Thank you for asking, but I cannot leave Madar alone."

"I understand Kobra."

"Thank you."

"Good night my dear and I hope we see each other before you leave for Paris."

"Enshallah." Kobra replied putting the receiver down.

The call bothered Nary. She began wondering what new plan the bitch was concocting now.

That evening, before serving Shamsi's dinner, Kobra dissolved one of her strong sleeping pills in her Coca Cola and handed it to her. Shamsi loved the drink. Without waiting for her dinner she went through the whole glass. She was so happy to have her darling with her that she had regained some of her appetite. Her body didn't ache anymore and she could open her eyes without any giddiness. It was a real blessing to be able to see clearly. Wobbling images made her nauseous. She could move too. At times she felt alive and aware, particularly when alone with Kobra.

She was watching the TV and yawning when Kobra arrived with her dinner tray. Smiling at her, she took the tray and thanked her with her eyes. By the time she got to her peeled apple she felt so drowsy that she pushed the plate away, put the tray on the table and mumbled: "I don't know why I am so sleepy. Can you please help me to rise – I want to go to bed."

Kobra took her hand and gently pulled her up. Arm in arm they walked to the bedroom. There Kobra helped her to wear her nightgown and then led her to the bathroom. When ready she led her back, tucked her in bed and asked: "Madar would you like me to stay and chat with you?"

"No dear. You go and watch TV. Tonight I am very sleepy." Shamsi yawned, turned her back to Kobra, rested her face on her arm and closed her eyes.

Quietly Kobra left the room, shut the door and locked it.

Ten minutes later, nude and whisky glass in hand she heard the ding dong of the bell. She left her room and hiding behind the door, opened it. Homayon entered. She closed the door and locked it. As Homayon's eyes fell on her voluptuous form, a loud whistle escaped his mouth. She grabbed his hand and pulled him to the bedroom where a full glass of whisky on ice was waiting for him. On her previous visits she had introduced him to whisky which she bravely enough, had smuggled in. To have sex with him was an enjoyable biological need satisfaction. But for Homayon, it was a visit to paradise. He was much younger, and his libido insatiable. The poor fellow, a prisoner of his mother's protectiveness, had never had the chance to bed another female. Kobra was his first and he was crazy about her. He often, with delight, remembered the first time, when she had robbed him of his innocence: she had taken his hand, led him to her bedroom, unzipped his trousers, delved her soft hand inside his under-pants and grabbed his genital, teasing it gently. The sensation had spread through him like warm honey, the delightful taste of which had sent him into an unknown realm where there was nothing but pleasure. Looking into his eyes and breathing on his face, she had withdrawn her hand, undressed him and herself, pushed him on her bed, squatted on the bed with him between her thighs. She had kissed him on the mouth, nipples and belly button. Then she had lifted her soft bottom up and with her hand guided him inside the heaven's gate. Other delicious things had happened too. The thought of them at times gave him erections.

In the bedroom, he put one arm around her round hip and squeezed it hard. The softness and the warmth of her flesh intoxicated his senses and he imbibed her moan of pleasure with joy. He buried his head in the folds of her wavy hair, sniffed its aroma and inhaled it with hunger.

"Have your whisky love."

"Do I need it azizam?"

"It will wash away all your inhibitions." She said in an alluring voice.

"Oh. That!"

"Yes. That." She half moaned. He turned to the table, picked up his glass and gulped half of it. The alcohol burnt his throat. He grimaced and put the glass down. With the back of his hand he wiped off his moist lips and then he swung around, grabbed her torso, lifted her up and threw her on the bed. Mad with desire, he peeled off his own clothes and then ravaged her body: kissing, touching, biting, licking, doing 'that' until she could take no more. Exhilarated and exhausted, she gently pushed him away. He objected, she insisted. Then, sulking like a child, he left the bed, dressed and tiptoed out of the room. She followed him to the door and locked it behind him. She went to her mother's bedroom, unlocked the door, checked on her and then retired to bed. Her sleep was deep and dreamless.

Three days later she returned to Paris.

On her first day in her office, Kobra spent three hours at her laboratory.

In Teheran, Tirdad loitering between sobriety and intoxication liquidated the last of the five-year bonds and spent the proceeds on foolish whims which neither pleased his wife nor brought his friends back. Left to rely on his parents' pension to subsist on, he could no longer afford to buy arak from the Armenian merchant. Instead, he resorted to purchasing white alcohol from an obliging chemist. To make the liquid palatable, he mixed it with a concoction of lemon juice and sugar – just as if he was making vodka lime. Rotting in loneliness he started drinking in the mornings. Insobriety was his means of escape from the reality of a life he could no longer bear . When drunk, life became rosy again. He saw himself as the flag bearer of a just society in which he was highly respected; not only because he was the Leader, but because he had been instrumental in bringing it about. There, in the midst of his Utopia, he saw the effigies of his infamous family members burning and turning into ash and, if he listened hard enough, he could hear Kobra's cry for help, and the howling of the man who had taken his mother away from him and then, sent her back, pregnant. How awful – how awful everything had turned out. Suddenly hideous thoughts would whirl and whirl in his head and then turn into a savage rage which he often directed at his mother. The woman would shake and shake, cry and cry until overwhelmed by exhaustion, faint.

The extent of his alcohol intake swiftly deteriorated his fragile health, particularly his colitis which, untreated, led to chronic diarrhoea. He lost ten kilos in one month. Sick and despondent, he sat on a sofa staring at his mother; blaming her for all the wrong decisions he had made in life and wishing her dead. Yet he continued to take care of her. He did not know why, but he did it. She had always been part of his life and now more than ever. Even in his drunken stupors, he knew that in this world, it was only he and she and no one else. Before his health deteriorated, he used to bathe her, pluck her eyebrows, and do her nails. At times he took joy in pampering her but when the devil inside him came to life, he purposely cut into her skin, or pinched it with the tweezers, or let hot water burn her skin. Her cry of pain gave him pleasure, for she would be feeling what he had felt, when she had left him to bed a stranger. And in jail: the tortures he had undergone. He never forgot the hours of pain he had to endure. They used to feed him laxative, knowing he suffered from spastic colitis. He had to suffer the excruciating spasms without being allowed to go to the lavatory. Unable to control the attacks, he would soil himself and live with the shit and its stench, until it became too offensive for his gaolers. Then, he would be given a shower and a pair of clean pants – but the rash, caused by putrefied faeces, would infect and become pussy. The puss would go into his blood stream and induce high fever. It made him tremble for hours and hours. The bastards enjoyed watching him tremble and laughed at him. Oh God, their sneers – how degrading they were – the humiliation hurt more than the malady.

Thus, he believed, he had already experienced hell; therefore, he had carte blanche to do as he wished. It was never 'written' that a human being would experience hell twice. Hence, all his wrong doings had already been paid for and he could die redeemed from all sins. Perhaps, there was life after death – and if there was any justice – he might enjoy it then.

Kobra knew of her brother's spastic colitis and she knew what combination of chemicals could turn it into sever dysentery which, if not treated promptly (which it wouldn't be) would dehydrate him, cause intestinal bleeding and kill him. So, just before returning to Iran again, she revisited her lab, mixed all the ready ingredients and injected the powdery blend into a little labelled jar with a tight lid. The powder was odourless and insipid, so it could be mixed into any meal without being detected. However, if it was exposed to air for a long period of time, it would emit a horrid odour, like a constipated fart.

In Iran, Hashem had already made up his mind. He was going to send a sinner to hell. He knew that two of the keys on Nary's key ring belonged to her mother-in-law's flat. One afternoon when she was showering, he went to her handbag, extracted the keys and with the paste he had brought from his office took an impression of them. Then he wiped the keys clean and returned them to her bag. The next morning he had duplicates of all her keys. He knew that the mother and son took long naps in the afternoon and usually the corridor was empty. After lunch, pretending he had an emergency meeting at the Ministry, he dropped Nary home and headed for his destination. He parked his car in Avenue Ghandi and walked the distance to the apartment block. At the entrance, he tried the keys until the right one fitted. He let himself in the entrance hall without being seen. He extracted a Magic pen from his coat pocket and put a cross on the key.

Knowing that the elevator was not reliable, he climbed the stairs, two at a time. He met no one on the way up. In the corridor, he faced south to make sure of his direction. He knew Turan and Homayon occupied the left side apartment. Very gently he tried the keys until one clicked open. He twisted the key back, locked the door again, extracted it from the lock, marked it with his pen, shoved the keys into his trousers pocket and was about to descend when the neighbour's door slit open and Turan's head protruded out.

"Who are you after son?" She asked politely.

"I have just delivered Pizza to one of the occupants of the sixth floor Khanum and am heading out."

"God be with you son. I thought you might have come for someone I know."

"No Khanum. I am just a courier."

"God be thanked son that you are just a courier and not member of that dreadful Ministry."

He felt the rush of blood to his head. With downcast eyes he responded:

"No Khanum I don't belong to any Ministry." and dashed down the stairs. Outside he bumped into a beggar, without a leg, leaning on his crutch, his palm open for a donation. His young and disillusioned face seemed familiar. He extracted a note from his pocket and placed it on the man's palm. The beggar looked at the money and clenched it within his long, thin fingers. Then he looked up. Their eyes met and a flash of recognition passed through each of their minds. The crippled stiffened, but he did not remove his penetrating eyes from Hashem's set face. With a sarcastic smile tilting on his lips, he stretched his arm towards Hashem and similar to a rose that gradually opens its petals untied his fingers and let the note fly away, like the soul of a dead man. At that moment Hashem wanted the earth to open up and gulp him down – so ashamed he felt. The memory of that torture and amputation had stayed with him for years and years. The prisoner had been the son of a Mojahid in hiding and only twelve years of age. His cry of: "Agha, I swear by the Koran that I don't know where my father is. Please have mercy on me. Please ..." still echoed in his ears He dropped his head, turned and hastened away. He didn't hear the whisper of: "curse of God be upon you – murderer."

June 8th was a pleasant summer morning. The air was fresh, the sky blue and the sun benign. It was too early for traffic to jam and the drive from the airport was swift. Kobra paid the driver. Lifted her light suitcase up, climbed the two steps to the entrance door, extracted her keys from her bag and unlocked the door. No one was in the corridor. She took the lift which fortunately worked and very quietly she let herself in the flat and heard them snoring. On tiptoe she pulled her case to her bedroom, shed off her Islamic layers, hung them in her wardrobe and flung herself over her bed. She was tired and restless. Half of her was committed to her plan and the other half apprehensive of its unforeseen consequences. She knew she had to do it otherwise she would go through old age living on her meagre pension. The French were very punitive with their pension system.

She was staying for only one week and had to be out of the country before the deed was done. She knew Tirdad was not on speaking terms with Nary, so even if he called her for help, she wouldn't come. And she was sure Homayon would follow her instructions step by step. The poor boy, she felt sorry for him – but she had given him enough pleasure to expect this little favour. She had no qualms about him. No one would ever connect him to anything malicious.

Thoughts raced in her head till she fell asleep.

The morning light penetrating through the open window woke Tirdad up. He opened his eyes with the usual excruciating headache which is the concomitant of alcohol intoxication. Cursing white alcohol, he got out of bed and headed for the kitchen when through the open door he saw Kobra sleeping.

'The bitch is back again', he thought turning left to his mother's room. She heard the creak of the door and opened her eyes.

"She has arrived."

"Who – arrived?"

"Kobra – your darling brat."

Kobra's name filled Shamsi with energy. She tried to rise but without success.

"Son, give me a hand, please."

Tirdad ignored her request and headed for the entrance door. He picked up his newspaper and with it went to the kitchen. There he threw the paper on the table; lit the cooker's gas, filled the kettle with water, put it on the stove and began to tidy his left-over mess from the night before. He never washed the dishes after dinner. In his state of wooziness, he had broken enough crockery to give the chore up in the evenings. His decision had made the cockroaches and the rats extremely happy. Their size and numbers were multiplying fast.

He made himself a strong cup of tea. From the fridge he extracted the bread basket, butter dish, and honey jar and settled to enjoy his breakfast. Shamsi called his name several times. He paid no attention. Let the bitch wake up and take over the chore of mother-sitting for a while. I am going to take a rest. He told himself with a sardonic smile on his unshaved puffy face. Alcohol was playing havoc with his flesh and organs. He picked up his paper and began to read it.

Shamsi's last shriek woke Kobra. Panicked, she rose and ran to her mother's room. The sight of her lit Shamsi's countenance like a flash light suddenly turned on. She opened her sagging, bony arms into which Kobra delved. She was everything to her – absolutely everything. Shamsi saw herself in her. That was why she adored her – narcissists even worship their own shadows let alone mirror images of themselves. But Kobra was not a mirror image of Shamsi – she was Satan incarnate.

She helped her mother out of bed, took her hand and together they trudged to the kitchen.

"Salam Dadda (brother)."

"Salam," responded Tirdad, his face hidden behind the spread of the morning paper. "Madar, I am returning home, now that you have your darling with you."

Kobra went cold. If he lived at his own home, her plan would fail and all her endeavours would be for naught.

"That is fine son." Shamsi responded, her eyes admiring Kobra's new hair style. She had had her hair straightened. It made her look better than when it was curly.

"Dada, please remember, I am here only for one week."

"I will return the night before you leave for Paris."

"Would you like me to cook you anything special for dinner that night?" Kobra asked her voice unusually tender.

He lowered the pages and glared at her with mocking eyes.

"And since when have you become domesticated, doctor Afati?"

"Since I have had to live by myself – that is twenty years now."

246

"If that pleases you, some sort of Khoresht (stew) will do. My wife will be spoiling me with her excellent cooking. She is better than any French chef."

"Everything she knows, she learnt from Madar."

Shamsi smiled and shook her head in affirmation. In the midst of the haze overcasting her mind the memory of her cooking classes flashed out. She sighed, closed her eyes and saw herself mixing something in a bowl that looked dark and shining. "Chocolate Mousse," she exclaimed and opened her eyes with a smile. Yes, she could make Chocolate Mouse and must make it for Kobra. The thought excited her so much that she didn't hear Tirdad say:

"You have always been jealous of her, have you not?"

Kobra huffed and threw him a contemptuous look.

"You are jealous of her because with her creamy complexion and blond hair she is much prettier than you nigger."

"I am glad you think so. She is your wife and I am only your sister, nigger or not."

"Half-sister." He remarked throwing his paper on the table.

"I wish I wasn't even your half sister." Kobra answered picking up the papers to read.

Nary was about to leave for her love – nest when the phone rang. She picked it up and murmured a quiet "Hallo"

"It is me Nary joon."

In her ears, his voice rang like cry of a hyena. She paused to control her fear and repulsion.

"Salam Tirdad. It is good that you have remembered you still have a wife."

"I never forget that I have a wife, I also have a sick mother. Now that Kobra is here, I can come and stay at home, with you my love for the duration of her stay."

Nary's heart sank and excruciating bells began to ring in her ears. She paused again and then asked: "When will you arrive, and what would you like me to cook for you?"

"Nothing. Tonight the three of us will go out. Madar's pension was deposited into her account yesterday and I withdrew most of it to spend on you."

"Thank you. I will be waiting for you."

"Bye my love."

"Bye." Nary whispered, put the receiver down, collapsed on the chair next to the telephone table, cupped her face with her hands and began to cry. She was just tired of him and her own duplicity – tired.

Tirdad was beside himself with joy. How he loved the tone of her voice, the softness of her skin and the natural odour of her body. Alive again the dark thoughts and the pain in his stomach disappeared, as though they had never existed. He became his old self: vibrant, loving and domineering. Whistling a happy tune, he returned to the kitchen. In his presence, the other two, in anticipation of further malice stiffened like hard rocks. He smiled. They exchanged a curious glance. He extracted a large bottle of white alcohol from the fridge and put it on the table. Instinctively, the two inched away from him. He picked up a sheet of the morning paper, wrapped it around his bottle and took it to his bedroom. There he laid it on his bed. From his wardrobe he collected some essentials. From above his wardrobe he pulled down his shabby travelling bag and put it on the table. Neatly he folded and fitted his stuff into the bag, secured the bottle up right in it and fastened the zipper with the neck of the bottle protruding out, like the head of a duck. He walked to the bathroom, showered and shaved; returned to his room, dressed neatly, appraised his image in the looking glass; satisfied, he picked up his bag and without a good bye, left the house. Outside, the morning air was still fresh and the sun bright but not as bright as the love inside him. He felt light and in unity with the rest of the world. He took couple of deep breaths, looked up at the spotless blue sky and sent a silent thanks to the Almighty he had forgotten for a long while now. He was so impatient to hold her again that he found himself almost running. A neighbour coming down the road threw him a suspicious glance, passed him without a greeting, wondering if he was escaping from authorities. His history was known to all and no one had any sympathy for him. In fact most of them tried to avoid him.

On Avenue Vali-e-Assr, he spotted a large florist. As he passed its entrance the smell of flowers whiffing out lured him in. The shop was crowded by beautiful baskets of exotic flowers costing a fortune. All his money could buy was a bunch of red roses.

On the other side of the city, at his office, Hashem put the receiver down and with his fist punched the top of his mahogany desk. Exploding from jealousy and angered by his helplessness he cupped his face with both hands and burst into tears – something he had not done since the last beating he had received from his father forty odd years ago. The thought of that creep touching her was driving him crazy. She belonged to him and only him.

Half an hour after Tirdad's departure, Kobra called Homayon and invited him to the flat. She had already fed her mother with a sleeping pill and the old lady, stretched on the sofa, was snoring heavily.

Homayon arrived with a bunch of flowers. She gave him a smile, took the flowers and asked: "Does your mother know where you are?"

"No. I told her I am going to visit a friend. She saw me out. I went downstairs and out, bought the flowers, returned and took the steps up. I did not take the lift in case she heard its door screech open and poke around. The awful machine still makes so much noise."

"Good. Let's sit in the kitchen so that we won't wake my mother up."

"Why not go to the bedroom."

"We do that later. I need you to do something for me and I need you to promise not to say a word to anyone about it."

"You know I do anything for you cherie."

"Is cherie the new word you have learnt?" Kobra asked fascinated by his correct use of the word.

"It was the first word I learnt, ma cherie, cherie."

Smiling Kobra pinched his shapely nose.

"Homayon joon, I am going to ask you to help my brother. You know he is an alcoholic and drinks white alcohol instead of arak which he cannot afford to buy. This will soon kill him. I have advised him several times to go to a hospital and get rid of the addiction, but he won't listen. Now, there is a new medicine in

Europe that helps alcoholics rehabilitate. It is a powder and they have to take it only once." She picked up her small jar from the table and showed it to him. "This new medicine is in this jar. The day after I leave for Paris, when your mother is having her afternoon nap, I want you to go to Agha Reza's take-away restaurant, buy a portion of rice and whatever Khorshet he has and bring it home and hide it from her. Then, when she is engaged in her evening prayer, heat the container in your microwave oven for just two minutes, lift the lid, spray the contents of the jar over the food, secure the top of the container and then bring it here and give it to Tirdad as a Nazri (religious donation) from a friend of yours and not your mother. Please remember that. If you say it is from your mother, he might see her in the corridor and thank her for it and you don't want that to happen – not at all."

To please her, Homayon nodded his incomprehension.

"It will take a few days for the medication to work and for saving a life you will be rewarded in both worlds." She patted his hand and pierced into his puzzled eyes.

"I am in heaven right now and want my reward immediately cherie." He moaned taking the jar and putting it into his trousers' pocket.

"Be careful with handling the jar. We do not want it broken do we?"

"Do not worry Kobra joon. It is in good hands." Then she rose and led him to the bedroom.

Panting from exhaustion of the long walk Tirdad let himself in and called out: "Azizam I am here." His voice pierced her heart and made her tremble in pain. She waited for a few seconds before walking out of the bedroom. They met in the hall. She offered him an insipid Salam. Without any makeup she looked more like a cleaner than a wife welcoming her husband. All smiles he offered her the Roses saying: "Flowers for a flower." Praying for strength to endure his presence, she took the bouquet and turned towards the kitchen. He followed her waiting for a welcoming word. From a cabinet she extracted a vase, filled it with water from the tap and delved in the bunch. "They are beautiful." She muttered with reluctance, picking up the vase and putting it in the middle of the kitchen table. He let go of his bag, surrounded her with his arms, pulled her to him and kissed her lips. Nauseated by his taste, she twisted out of his hold and said: "I have just brewed tea; would you like a cup?" He pulled out a chair, sat on it, and replied: "I would love one if you make me a cup like the one you used to at my office."

"With a touch of cardamom?" She asked without any emotions.

His twinkling eyes on her he replied: "Yes – with a touch of cardamom."

She made two cups, put them on the table and sat in front of him.

He picked the cup and took it to his nostrils, sniffed its aroma, closed his eyes and smiled.

"How long is your sister going to stay this time?"

"She said only a week. The bitch looks healthier than ever. Someone must be poking her well!"

"I hope whoever is, will marry her and take her away from our lives – forever."

"Enshallah Nary joon – Enshallah."

"Then perhaps she can take your mother with her and let you be a husband again?" At that moment he was so happy that he did not want to engage in any stressful disputes. So he turned a deaf ear to her sneer, sipped at his tea longing for the warmth of her body and a good night's sleep in he r arms without the crescendo of his mother's snores disturbing his rest.

Together again Nary found herself remembering the initial happy days of their married life. They were just marvellous but unfortunately transient. Then Ahmad returned from school and was delightfully surprised to find his father sitting next to his mother like they used to – in peace.

Tirdad went to their bedroom, unpacked his bag without putting his bottle in the fridge. After lunch he made love to his wife. They had a short siesta after which they all walked up to Tajrish which took an hour. They window shopped at the modern mall that had robbed the old bazaar of its charm and had pizza and ice cream at a busy pizzeria.

Two days passed in total contentment. Then their talks changed hue. Tirdad put his bottle in the fridge and Nary began comparing her life with women whose husbands' were successful. To Tirdad her stings felt sharper than those of an asp. Thus disillusioned he took refuge in his alcohol and then one morning, over a trivial matter, hell broke loose. He returned to his mother's home with scratch marks all over his face. Shamsi did not notice them and Kobra asked no questions.

On the 14th of June Kobra returned to Paris.

On the 15th of June, to his mother's surprise Homayon rose earlier than usual, had a long shower, shaved and splashed his face with plenty of Armani eau de cologne given to him by Kobra. He examined his reflexion on the looking glass and it pleased him to see a man about to perform a praiseworthy deed. Too impatient to remain home, while his mother was busy in the kitchen he slipped out and took a long walk, up Avenue Ghandi, turned left to Vanak square where he bought himself a glass of fresh carrot juice from a busy kiosk and leaning against a tree trunk sipped it while eyeing the beauties that paraded in his view. He enjoyed the flirting glances they threw at him and wondered why they all had the same nose-shape.

Homayon returned home with fresh sangak bread for his mother. Turan, worried to death about where he had disappeared to without a word to her was sitting on the sofa, her eyes on the door. When she heard the key turn in the lock she straightened her back, ready to voice her objection. As he stepped in, her eyes fell on the newspaper wrapped loaf under his arm. She forgot her complaint and smiled with joy. She loved Sangak and it was a treat to have warm bread with lunch. It had been such a long time since she had had sangak just out of the baker's oven that her mouth watered. Nowadays no one had time for a daily bakery visit which entailed a long wait in a queue. Usually a week's supply would be bought, loaves cut into small portions to be frozen. Depending on need, pieces would be taken out and toasted. This new habit was an off-spring of the Revolution which Turan abhorred but could do nothing save close her eyes to it and pretend life had remained unchanged.

Today Homayon's simple treat brought her spirit out of its doldrums and made it waltz in happiness. Her bright smile and the delight in her eyes pleased

Homayon enormously. Within the limited scope of his mind, he was conscious of the emptiness of his mother's life particularly now that Shamsi had fallen ill. At least then she had had someone to talk to and pass the time over a sip of a tea and taste of a cake. Now she only watched the TV and sometimes talked to herself. His father had died thirty years back, when she was only forty five. How could she have gone through all those years without sex? He kept wondering, and feeling sorry for her.

Mother and son headed for the kitchen where the table was already set. Homayon took out a scissors from the cutlery drawer, cut the bread into small pieces and then wrapped them in the napkin his mother handed him. Turan dished out the meal and they sat face to face enjoying their lunch. She was so busy munching at her sangak sandwich of feta cheese and fresh coriander that she didn't seem conscious of time. But Homayon was. It was already one thirty and if she didn't retire soon Agha Reza would finish all his food and he couldn't buy anything from him. Nervous he rose to take the dishes to the sink. "What is the hurry son?" She asked looking up at him in disappointment.

Homayon faked a yawn and replied: "you fed me too well mother. I want to take a nap."

Reluctantly Turan rose and picked up her plate. Homayon grabbed it from her and said: "You go to bed I will do the washing up."

Turan thanked him warmly and limped to her room wondering what had come over her son. He was not his usual self today.

Homayon washed the dishes, gave her a further few minutes to fall sleep before he threw the dish cloth on the table, tiptoed out of the flat closing the door, as noiselessly as possible. He ran down the stairs and the length of the Fifth Avenue to reach Agha Reza's joint in Avenue Ghandi, praying he had not run out of food. He arrived in time to buy the last portion of rice and aubergine khoresht. Too nervous to remember Kobra's exact instructions, at a secluded corner, facing a wall, he squatted on the pavement, put the container down; took the jar from his pocket, twisted its top off, shook the powder over the food and in a hurry not to attract any attention closed the lid with the jar inside the container. Satisfied that all was done to perfection he rose, returned home and hid the container under his bed. He opened his window so that the food odour would not make his room stuffy and God forbid, augment suspicion in his mother's mind. A breeze began to drift in. It dispersed the smell and cleansed the air. He took a deep breath, kicked his shoes off and laid on his bed for a nap. The sound of the doorbell woke him up. He heard his mother talk to one of the neighbours. He glanced at his watch. It was only four in the afternoon. He picked up last night's newspaper from the floor beside his bed and began to read it. All bad news and awesome pictures of streets jammed with Basiji's, the Government's dedicated paramilitary force, guarding against further Green demonstrations. There had been more arrests of those objecting to the validity of the electoral procedures that had recognized Ahmadi Nejad as the President elect. Only God knew what had happened to the Green votes, thought Homayon throwing the paper down. He had not voted at all but he sympathised with the greenies as he called them who must have stood for the preservation of nature. He rose, put his shoes on and went to the kitchen to join his mother for tea.

Eventually, the sun drifted into oblivion, leaving the sky to the glitter of the stars. From the nearby mosque the Muezzin's song called the faithful to prayer. Spread on the sofa watching the TV he saw his mother come out of the kitchen where she had finished preparing dinner. She limped to the bathroom, turned the tap on and performed her ablution necessary for prayer. Then she went to her bedroom, spread her prayer mat on the carpet; hung her chador over her head, tied its edges under her chin and facing Mecca commenced reciting the obligatory verses from the Koran.

Homayon sneaked across the corridor and peeped through the open door; sure that she was fully engrossed in prayer he hurried to his room brought out the container from its hiding place, rushed to the kitchen and did precisely as told. Then he tiptoed out, without closing the door behind him. He pressed the neighbour's bell button. It made no sound. He remembered it was out of order. With his knuckle he tapped at the door couple of times before he heard Tirdad ask: "Who is it?" From the slur in his voice Homayon guessed he was already tipsy.

"It is me Tirdad joon, Homayon."

The door opened and Tirdad's head protruded out. With unkempt hair and unshaved face he resembled a derelict stinking of alcohol and sweat.

Repulsed, Homayon took a step back.

"What do you want?" Tirdad asked wobbling on his feet.

"Agha Tirdad. I have brought you a Nazri meal, donated by a friend of mine.

Tirdad took the pack, lifted its top up and sniffed its odour. The smell was strange but the khoresht looked appetising.

Then his eyes fell on the empty jar. With his free hand, he picked it up and showing it to Homayon asked: "What is this?"

Homayon paled and without uttering a word he grabbed the jar, dashed to the kitchen and threw it into the garbage bin. Tirdad, too drunk to notice any irregularity, holding tight to the container, turned towards the kitchen.

"I haven't had anything all day and am famished. Thank you boy." He drawled, stumbled forward and wobbled back. "For whom shall I be praying when eating this feast?" His voice slurred and he began to hiccup. Lurching, he took couple of unsteady steps, belched and fixed his drowsy eyes on Homayon.

"Ali Khan." Homayon replied and then added: "Agha Tirdad, please do not drink alcohol when eating a Nazri."

"Of course I won't drink arak with Nazri food. That is haram (forbidden) isn't it?" Tirdad responded a mocking smile lurking on his, dry, cracked lips.

"Indeed, and I hope soon you be rid of your love for arak."

"Who told you I love arak?"

"Your breath." Homayon murmured, passing him by and stepping out.

"All I need is for a simple-minded asshole to advise me!" Tirdad mumbled banging the door behind him.

Shaking his head in pity, Homayon whispered to himself: "God give my angel Kobra a long life for making me do this. Enshallah the poor fellow be cured soon. Enshallah."

Careful not to fall, Tirdad took the meal to the dining table, put the container down, returned to the kitchen, picked up a spoon, made himself another glass of 'vodka lime a-la-Tirdad', and spilling part of the liquid on the floor returned to the dining room. He sat down and with the appetite of a wolf, devoured the Nazri. His hunger satiated he remembered he had to send a prayer for Ali Khan. He lifted his hip up, let out a loud smelly fart and said: "This is for Ali Khan and his Nazr (wish)." Then he burst into a loud laughter.

"What is happening Tirdad?" called out Shamsi from her room.

He suddenly remembered he had to feed her. He prowled back to the kitchen, opened the fridge door took out a container of yoghurt and a piece of stale bread, put them on a plate. Picked up a dirty spoon from the sink, shoved it into the container and was about to lift the plate when a dreadful spasm stabbed his inside. He pressed a palm on his stomach hoping the pressure would stop the pain. It did. He took the plate and loitering carried it to his mother's bedroom. As soon as she saw him enter, struggling, she sat up, smiled and took the plate from him. "Thank you son."

Another spasm attacked. Groaning he dashed to the toilet and was there for quite a while, putting pressure on his abdomen hoping the release of further loose defecation would relieve him from the pain. Eventually the pain subsided and he returned to take her plate away.

She gave him a shy smile and asked for a glass of water. Taking the plate, he threw her a resentful glance, left the room and returned with a glass half empty. His hand couldn't hold anything steady.

"Do you want to go to the toilet now?" He asked hoping for a no answer. He was feeling dizzy and wanted to go to bed.

"Yes son."

He helped her out of bed; using her as a crutch, led her to the toilet. With unsteady hands, he cleaned her and tried to pull up her under-pants. He couldn't. She did. Then he tried to spread tooth paste on her tooth brush and let her clean her teeth. He couldn't. So he handed her the brush with a shade of paste on it. She cleaned her teeth, and then splashed some water on her face. He pulled her towel from its holder. It fell off his hand. Bending to pick it up, he hit his forehead on the edge of the vanity with a bang. He howled in pain. Panicked she screamed. "Shut up woman." He moaned picking up the towel. His bruised forehead furrowed in pain he handed it to her. She dried her face, dropped the towel on the sink and gave him her hand. Lurching and stumbling he managed to get her to bed. He turned her light off and retired to his own bedroom feeling awful. It seemed as though there was fire inside his intestines. It burnt and burnt. He collapsed on the bed feeling the tinge of cold sweat sliding down his temples. He kept tossing and turning until eventually sleep overtook.

Shamsi woke up early in the morning. Slowly she managed to sit up and waiting for her breakfast tray she picked up her dentures and fitted them in her mouth. Since becoming bedridden she had lost the concept of time and had become a slave of her biological clock. Minutes ticked away. She dozed off for a while and then the hunger contractions woke her up. She called: "Tirdad, breakfast?"

He didn't answer.

Frightened she screamed: "Tirdad ..... where you?"

The silence was deadly.

She screamed and screamed until he woke up and opened his eyes and shut them instantly. The load of pain in his head weighed heavily on his eye lids.

"Mother I need a doctor. Please call Nary?" He moaned.

She heard his plea, made a hasty move to rise but couldn't adjust her balance so she fell back. Desperate, she began to cry. His continuous moans tore her heart apart. She looked around like a lost child searching for a parent. They were all dead. It was only her and him. She moved again. This time the urge to help him forced her to slide her legs down the bed until her bottom hit the solid floor. She took a long breath and tried to stand up. No, she couldn't. Then instinctively she went on her knees and hands. Her hands and left knee inched ahead but not her right leg. It was entangled amongst the crinkles of the sheet. Twisting, kicking and turning she managed to free it. Worn out she collapsed on her face. She heard him again. She lifted her chest up, took several deep breaths and then crawled, paused and crawled until she reached the sofa. Breathless she rested her head on its edge. The moan came again. This time it was of a dying man. The determination to save him invigorated her with an extraordinary energy. She put her hands on the seat and, pushing it down, pulled her torso up and let it fall on the sofa. With further manoeuvring she managed to sit up. The moans had stopped and the only noise she heard was the clink- clanking of her dislodged dentures. She could not bear the discomfort. Unconsciously she opened her mouth and spat them out. They dropped on her lap, their moisture wetting her gown and irritating her skin. With her hand she brushed them away. They fell on the carpet. Suddenly she remembered what she had to do. Her trembling hand picked up the phone and her fingers dialled the correct numbers. She heard Ahmad's "Hallo."

"Salam ... how ... you?" She whispered almost incoherently.

Ahmad accustomed to deciphering her utterances replied: "I am fine Shamsi joon. It is lovely to hear your voice, after so long."

"Nary home?"

"No Shamsi joon. She will be back around four in the afternoon. Shall I ask her to call you?"

"No home?"

"She has gone shopping."

"Tirdad very sick, needs doctor."

"What is wrong with him?"

"Help – please... help," she begged before the receiver fell off her shaking hand.

"What do you want me to do Shamsi joon?" Ahmad asked waiting for a response and when he heard nothing but a hissing sound of nervous breathing, he assumed the scenario was a Tirdad concocted plan to get his mother there for reconciliation. Thus he did not take the demand serious and hung up.

His mother had not gone shopping. She was at her love nest. They had already made love and were having tea when Hashem picked up a large envelope from the coffee table and from it extracted three passports.

"Look at these my love and guess what they are?"

"They are passports."

"One for you, one for Ahmad, and one for the father of the family." Nary snatched them from him, browsed through the pages, threw them on the table, turned to him and asked: "How on earth did you manage make me your wife and Ahmad your son?"

Lifting an eyebrow he shook his head and meeting her curious eyes exclaimed: "I am astonished that you ask this question of me – 'me' the Director of one of the most important institutions in Iran." There was an edge to his voice that somehow frightened her.

She dropped her eyes and murmured an apology.

Hashem, picked up one of the passports, flicked through the pages until he found the Australian immigrant visa. Showing it to her he said: "Look, here is a valid Australian visa – one for each of us."

Nary fell into a pensive silence. His words, like a heavy chain around her neck were strangling her. She couldn't utter a word so tight was her throat.

He threw the passport on the table. "I have booked three business class seats on Emirate airline for 20th September which incidentally is the date I have to go to Sydney for an important work mission. So my fare is paid by the Government."

Her lack of enthusiasm disappointed him.

"Nary, are you not happy at what I have done for us?" He asked, lifting her dropped chin up with his index finger. Their eyes locked into a terrifying, unresolved dilemma. The silence was so deep that each could hear the other's crazy heart beats. Nary took Hashem's finger away from her chin, kissed it, and shaking her head in despair said:

"My dear Hashem, I do not know if I can be happy, living in an illicit relationship for the rest of my life. Men can have as many wives as they wish but for us women, there is only one husband – and I am already married to one."

Hashem's face turned as white as chalk and the veins in his neck began to throb frantically. It took him a minute or two before he overcame his rage. He narrowed his eyes, fixed them on her face and in an admonishing tone asked:

"You have been having an illicit relationship with me for years now. Do you want to tell me it has been for any other reason than love?"

"I love you Hashem. You have been my rock but I cannot desert Tirdad; he is a lost soul – in spite of all his faults, I know he loves me dearly and I feel I am the sole reason for his struggles, thefts and frustrations. He feels abandoned by all except me, and if he loses me forever, he will do something terrible either to his mother or to himself – and that will not please your God. Will it?"

He couldn't answer her, so he rose from his seat, knelt by her chair, grabbed her knees, put his head on them and began to weep. She kept stroking his thick curly hair and rocking back and forth. Thinking and not thinking. Wanting and not wanting. Being and not being. Living and wishing to die. Unconsciously she teased his head with her lips. He looked up at her wet face, "Nary, I promise, you will become my legal wife sooner than you think – where there is a will, there is a way."

"How my love – how?" She asked, nodding her head in despair.

"Never mind that – just trust me."

In Paris, Kobra had just stepped into her flat when her phone rang. She threw her briefcase on the table, and picked up the receiver. It was Homayon.

She sat on the arm of the sofa and asked:

"Azizam, are you bearer of good news?"

"Of course I am. God willing, he be off it soon and grateful to you forever."

"Thank you Homayon. You did get rid of the jar, did you not?"

"I followed all your instructions, letter by letter."

"Fantastic and bravo cheri."

"When are you returning?"

"Next summer, I have no more holidays to take."

"I will be waiting my pussy."

"Hush up; someone might hear you."

"I am calling from a phone booth – as per your instruction."

"OK – I must go now – love you." She put the receiver down, took a deep triumphant breath, closed her eyes and relaxed for a minute as though a heavy burden had been lifted off her shoulders. Then, feeling as light as a feather, she rose, took off her raincoat, hung it on the peg in the corridor and headed for the fridge from which she extracted the bottle of Champagne she had been chilling for this occasion. She opened the bottle, took a flute out of the cabinet, filled it to the brim and together with the bottle returned to the table.

A week passed with Tirdad so ill that he could barely feed his mother. He himself had no appetite and to relieve his pain he drank alcohol sec. It was lucky that he had stored so many bottles. In the absence of any domestic help, the flat had turned into a pig sty. No one had been inside since Homayon had delivered the Nazri. His diarrhoea had become bloody and he was losing the control of his bowl movements. Sometimes it just rushed out and he had to run to the bathroom to change his pyjama pants. The bathroom stank and he had no more pyjamas. One day when the pain had temporarily subsided he threw the dirty clothes into the bath tub, opened the tap and let water soak them. Then he climbed in and kept stepping on to them and splashing the water all over the floor. It felt good. He was stepping on all those who were responsible for his sufferings. The joy ended with the thud of his head on the edge of the bath tab. He swore at his luck, rose and stepped out. He undressed, threw the wet clothes into the tab, dried himself with a towel, let the tap water empty and left the clothes to dry by themselves. They did. It was summer and the old air-conditioner had already died.

Two nights later, when asleep, he soiled his bed without realizing it. Early in the morning, the stench woke him. He pushed his cover away and what he saw made him scream. He summoned all his strength and rose. He lumbered to the bathroom, washed and changed into a pair of pyjamas that were in the bath tub. Then he pulled his mother out of her bed and dragged her to the sofa in the sitting room where she could wait for Nary's call. Why had she not come? Why? Torn apart, he kept asking himself. There was no more alcohol left in the house. Somehow he didn't want it anymore. He had no appetite for anything at all and was so week that slightest light bothered his eyes. Besides in his state night or day made no difference, hence he drew all the curtains and decided to live in darkness. He found himself drinking plenty of water which seemed to clear his mind from the fog that had clouded it for so long. Sober again he began to miss her much. In fact he yearned to touch her soft milky skin, inhale her familiar scent and look into her soft eyes. Where was his jewel, the light of his life and the nourishment of his soul? Where? "Oh God – what have I done to her – to myself and to the love that once had illuminated my life?" He whispered to the darkness that surrounded him. Then a voice inside him murmured: repent. Open your heart to her and let her rejoice in the warmth of the love you bear her. Only the purity of your love can cure her wounded heart and return her to you. Do it now. Now before it is too late. So he ambled to his room, from his drawer took a writing pad, a pen and Rumi's book of verses which he loved. There was a poem there that fitted his feeling for his beloved. He sat behind his desk, turned the reading lamp on, and flicked through the pages of the book until he found the poem. He read it with moist eyes. Then he began to write. When finished he realised he was too weak to go out and post it. He returned everything including the letter to the drawer and turned the lamp off. Mentally and physically exhausted he walked to his mother's room and collapsed on her bed like a corpse.

Shamsi lay on the sofa, her eyes fixed to the ceiling, waiting for a miracle. Her numbed mind couldn't think of a solution. She was so agitated that she did not realize help was a door away. A call or crawl to the door and loud screams could reach Turan or Homayon's ears. But hunger, thirst, fear and desperation had stolen her power of rationality and the will to live.

Morning turned into noon. Tirdad kept moaning, its sound not reaching her ears any more. Semi-conscious, she felt giddy from hunger and thirst. At times she tried to rise but without success. Then she saw Tirdad crouching and holding his stomach, limp towards the kitchen.

"Son – I ... hungry."

She saw him shrug his shoulders and disappear into the kitchen. She heard the tap run and something shatter. It was the water glass Tirdad had not been able to hold. He put his head below the running water and drank and drank until he threw up in the sink. His head bent he remained still. Then he drank again – just a bit to wash the taste of acid away. He held his head up, dried his face with the kitchen towel, straightened his back and as he passed the dining table his eyes fell on the Nazri leftover. Slowly stepping one foot at a time, he reached Shamsi, gave his hand to her and helped her up. They both limped to the dining table where they sat, and using the dirty spoons partook of the leftover which by now tasted and smelled awful. But they were hungry and there was very little else left to eat. There was plenty of rice and lentils but they needed cooking. Tirdad, holding his aching stomach slumbered back to bed.

Thirst and hunger impelled Shamsi to rise and leaning on the wall slither into the kitchen. One hand gripping the top of the kitchen chair for support, after several tries she managed to open the fridge door. A cold foul smell offended her nostrils. She pinched her nose and sharpened her eyes. There was a rotted potato with roots shooting out of its shrivelled, mouldy skin, half a decomposing cucumber resembling a layer of disintegrating green jelly covered by icing powder, and a large red apple, with a patch of brown mould on its skin. Smiling she took the apple, dropped on one of the chairs. Her hand trembling, she picked up the knife on the table and with it tried to peel the apple, almost cutting into her own skin. She managed to dissect the fruit, discard the decayed segments and toothless munch at the remaining soft pieces. She stretched towards the fridge and opened its door again. From it she extracted a bottle of water. She put it on the table and tried to rise. She did not have enough strength. She yelled for Tirdad to come and help her. He was in so much pain that he couldn't move. She sat there not knowing what to do. An hour passed. Her muscles stiffened and she felt cold – very cold. Instinctively she knew if she remained in that position she would die. Concentrating hard she gripped the edges of her seat, slowly stretched her legs and slid down the chair until her bottom thumped on the floor sending her arms in the air. The released chair capsized backward with a bang. Frightened by the noise, she remained still, her ears pricked up. No more noise. Nothing but silence engulfed her. She took a deep breath and called Tirdad.

He didn't hear her.

She called again.

No response.

She went on all fours and creeping and crawling at a snake's pace reached the sofa. Panting she rested her head on the seat cushion, closed her eyes and blacked out.

Three hours later she woke to find herself slumped on the floor in dreadful pain. She moved, coiled, pulled and pushed until she lodged herself on the sofa. She closed her eyes and exhaled a sigh of relief as though she had conquered the world. Few peaceful moments passed until she heard Tirdad give out a long, loud fart followed by a whine of pain.

"Tirdad." She called out, her voice loud and desperate.

"Shut up. Let me alone woman. Can't you understand that I am dying?"

She fell silent, her fingers scratching her arms. Her nails long and sharp, left red trails on her pale, sagging, parched skin, but she felt no pain, in fact nothing at all. She leaned her head back on the arm of the sofa and closed her eyes. The world whirled around inside her head. She felt giddy; her stomach churned, bloated, filled with gas. She moaned. Suddenly bitter bile rushed into her mouth, she bent over the carpet and spewed the poison out of her system. "God, help me. I am dying." She heard herself murmur before oblivion saved her from further hurt.

Tirdad rose, lurched to the toilet where he relieved himself with awful spasmodic rushes of mucus- like liquid mixed with blood. Then he opened the medicine cabinet and found a packet of charcoal tablets. He consumed two and washed it down with a handful of water from the tap. The exertion exhausted him. Still thirsty he relinquished the task, leaned against the wall and slithered against it until he reached his mother's room and fell on the bed.

It was Thursday when Hashem took Nary to Mashahd. In the shrine, each in their allocated section (men and women were segregated) held the golden grill surrounding the tomb of the Emmam, and pleaded for absolution and Tirdad's natural death. Then feeling consecrated by the holy spirit of the Emmam they walked to the bazaar which is by the grounds of the Shrine. Hashem bought Nary a huge gold broach on which Allah was etched and studded in large turquoises. They had lunch at a restaurant nearby, shopped more, bought several boxes of saffron and then caught a taxi for the airport.

The next day, Hashem called his most trusted lackey, a young ambitious fellow named Kazem to his office and showing him a picture of Tirdad ordered him to survey the building at Fifth Street for the Communist's movements. He gave him instructions as what to do, where to go, what to wear and shave when on this duty. Once Hashem became sure that Kazem understood what was expected of him, he handed him a key ring holding two keys and Tirdad's photo.

"Anything to be done to this corrupter on earth, Brother Karimi?"

"Not yet. Just let me know of his movements out and into the building and if there was a pattern to his behaviour."

For five days, smart in T-shirt and jeans Kazem, shaved and hair gelled in spiky fashion and a cigarette dangling out of the corner of his thick lips, discretely monitored the entrance of the block without seeing the man on the photo. Then one day carrying a parcel, he let himself in and knocked at Turan's door.

"Who is it?" asked Turan surprised at the knock. She was not expecting anyone. Nothing needed repairing nor had she asked for any deliveries.

"I am a courier and have to deliver this parcel to your neighbour but no one opens the door. Do you know where they are?"

From behind her closed door Turan replied: "They must be asleep son or out. I do not keep watch over my neighbour's activities. However, if you have something for them you can give it to me. I am bound to see one of them soon."

"Thank you Khanum, but I need a signature." Kasem said before dashing down the stairs.

'What on earth has come for Shamsi which needs a signature?' Turan wondered returning to watch her TV serial.

"I think he stays inside the apartment at all times or has taken a trip." Kazem reported to his superior with the confidence of a professional spy.

"Ok, thank you Kazem. Now give me back the picture and the keys."

Kazem first dug into his pocket and took out the keys. He put them on the table, in front of his boss. Then he pulled out his wallet from his coat pocket, extracted Tirdad's creased photo from it, looked at it for the last time and with both hands offered it to Hashem.

It was way past midnight. The streets were almost empty. There were only a few speeding cars belonging to teenagers, heading home from their night out. Hashem parked his car two blocks away, opened his dashboard, took out his little Koran that he kept there for safekeeping, kissed it, whispered a pray and fitted it into his coat pocket. Then he took out his electrical baton, and checked its battery which to his delight was full. He fitted it inside its case already attached to his belt, got out of the car, checked his pocket for his torch, locked the car door and calmly walked away. His face was expressionless, his posture erect, his mind set and his steps quick and soundless.

Whispering verses of the Koran, he let himself into the entrance hall and then the flat without anyone seeing him. An auspicious feeling warmed him. Not encountering anyone on his way was a sign that his mission was approved by the Almighty. This strengthened his resolve to terminate the vermin.

As he opened the door a foul smell hit him hard. He remained rooted to the spot, his palm over his nose and his eyes roaming around without seeing anything. His right hand slid into his pocket and extracted a small torch which he switched on. Hashem heard himself murmur, Ya Allaha (Oh my God). For a minute the deplorable state in his view weakened his resolve and made him pause. On a sofa lay a creature resembling a skeleton. He focused on the figure. It was of a woman, skin and bone, shrivelled, hollowed eyes and a round chin covered in a peppery beard. 'Surely it couldn't be Shamsi Khanum, the graceful lady of whom Nary had spoken often?"

He shook his head in denial and swung the light away from her.

He knew Tirdad's bedroom was on the left of the corridor. He transferred the torch to his left hand and with his right pulled out his baton; he pressed its ignition button. A bright blue spot began to flicker. Directing the torch towards the corridor, he tiptoed inside. He turned left and before entering Tirdad's bedroom switched off the torch. The glimmer of his baton light was enough for him to see. Soundlessly he crept inside, approached the bed, raised his arm and began striking at the protrusion until the bed disintegrated with a crunch and feathers flew out of the tattered quilt cover and scattered around, on the bed and a few on the carpet. Only then did he realize he had been striking at a crumbled eiderdown. He cursed himself for making such a mistake. Mistake, he had never made mistakes in his assaults.

"Who is there?" A whine waved out of somewhere.

Hashem crept behind the door. He heard it again. The cracking of the bed must have woken the bastard up. He twisted his lips and shook his head in disgust at himself when he detected the din of slow sluggish footsteps. He cautiously protruded his head out from behind the door and looked towards the noise. He saw Tirdad, barefooted, wobbling and lurching towards the sitting room. Slowly, he stepped out, and following him raised his baton to strike at his head when Tirdad lost control, fell forward, hit something and screamed.

Hashem brought his arm down, and lit the torch in his left hand. He saw Tirdad sprawled face down on the floor, by a coffee table, blood rushing out from under his head, spreading on the carpet like cancer cells. He knelt down, put the baton and the torch on the floor and gently lifted Tirdad's head up and stared at him. His forehead was deeply cut. He dragged him towards the wall and leaned him against it. He took his pulse and listened. No beat. To be sure he put his fingers against his nose. No breath. He turned his head to the woman. She must be dead, he assumed. For a minute or two he contemplated and then smiled. He had done the right thing to lean the corpse against the wall before it hardened. In that position, no one would ever suspect any foul play – not that any had taken place – but one had to be sure. It was obvious that in the dark, being drunk, he had lost his balance, fallen and hit his head against the sharp edge of the glass table. Bleeding hard he had dragged himself to the wall, against which he had leaned waiting for help.

Hashem didn't leave the apartment immediately. He squatted in front of Tirdad, the subject of his envy and sleepless nights. His eyes wide with concentration, he began to scrutinize his features, comparing them with his own. What he saw was very different from the pictures he had seen. Here was a bloated, balding, bitten, pathetic individual with signs of wretchedness painted all over him. A sharp feeling of shame shot through him. He bit his lips hard and felt his eyes moisten. For an instant he hated himself. In that bewildering state of mind when his conscious was trying to awaken from a long slumber, he asked himself what could turn a decent, respectable human being to this wreck, whose only solace was alcohol? Deep down, he knew the answer but didn't dare to admit it. That iota of consciousness that had dared to resurface whispered, "men like you." A shiver took hold of him. He closed his eyes and saw the crippled beggar from whose palm had flown away his half-hearted charity, mocking him with his grin. He opened his eyes wide, scared of blinking, in case there was another flash of memory. A fierce fear chained around his thick neck, making breathing hard. He shook his head to unchain his neck and breathe – but to no avail. The power of guilt was suffocating him. He couldn't remain in the room any more. He picked up his baton and torch, shoved them into his pocket, jumped up, took two long steps to the sofa, put his hand near the large nose of the old woman and felt a tinge of warm breath. She was alive. He exhaled a long flow of air. God be praised for that. He murmured looking at the blood on his hands. He returned to the corridor, found the bathroom and washed his hands, avoiding looking at his own image in the mirror. He was scared to face the monster that would be staring back at him. Like a zombie he sauntered to the door, opened it, got out, closed it noiselessly, and quickly locked it so that the ghost of the dead man couldn't follow him out.

Back at home, he took a long shower, performed his ablution and set to pray. When finished, he raised his hands skyward and whispered:

"Ya Allah I beg you to forgive me for all the sins I have committed. I know I have done some wrong things but they all have been to preserve the principles with which I grew up. My Creator, you are the source of forgiveness. It was by your inspiration that Mohammad, upon conquering Mecca, forgave Hend who had eaten the heart of his cousin Hamzeh in a battle field. He also forgave Abu-Sofian, her husband, his own uncle and his staunchest enemy. Almighty, you are the source of all the goodness that exists in this universe. Koran teaches us, if we repent and return to the right path you will forgive us. Therefore I, your misguided, undeserving creature beg for your mercy, forgiveness and guidance. My compassionate Allah, give me the wisdom to become a deserving soul so that I can make up for all my wrong doings. Then if you still find me undeserving let me face my punishment in both worlds. My Allah, I pledge to leave my job and never engage in anything which might hurt another human soul. If I fail this vow, bestow upon me the most hurtful death." He, rested his hands on his thigh, remained on his folded legs listening to the noise of the night.

Chapter 10

From 30th June until the end

Ahmad dried his running nose with a crumpled tissue he had been squeezing within his clenched palm. In his ears echoed Shamsi's cry for help. His chest about to burst by flow of guilt, he looked into his mother's lacklustre eyes and said: "Mother, I have a confession to make."

A frown pecked on Nary's forehead. She threw him a suspicious glance and asked: "Have you been light fingered again?" He shook his head indolently and remained silent. "Then what have you done?" He kept shaking his head and biting his lips. His silence irked her. "Don't make me angry now. I have had enough of drama for one day."

"Sometimes ago, Shamsi joon called. You were out. She told me Baba Tirdad was sick, needed a doctor. In my utter stupidity, I thought he had made her fib to lure you there for reconciliation. So, I thought nothing of it. It seems he really needed help, and had I told you, he might not have died this way. I hope God will forgive me, for I am to blame for his death." He cupped his face with his quivering palms and let his grief pour out in tears. The crumpled tissue escaped his hold and landed on the floor. The frown disappeared from Nary's forehead and in its place appeared an expression of wonder at the insouciance of destiny. She wrapped her arms around his tense shoulders and pulled him to herself. He rested his head on her breast and found her warmth soothing. She kissed the crown of his head, patted his back, "don't cry son. He died of a fall, and not illness. You must not blame yourself at all. It was meant for him to die this way." With her finger she lifted his chin up and gave him a big smile. Surprised at her lack of emotions he wondered if she ever cared for his Baba or in fact for anyone else but herself. He took a step back and looked deep into her eyes. They were as cold as ice. A shiver went through him. "Mother, are you not sorry for losing a man who loved you so much?" He asked in a sour tone.

Without hesitation, she shook her head and whispered a 'no'.

"No?" He asked, staring at her with unbelieving eyes.

She raised her brows and replied: "You saw the way he treated us. He only loved himself, the rest of us were pawns in his game." She paused to gauge his reaction. All she received was a bitter glare. "In a way, I am glad he has left us – his death is our liberation. Perhaps now, I can find a good man to marry, and settle into a normal married life – with you at my side."

Appalled by her insensitivity, a surge of disgust attacked his gut. To avoid looking at her cold, expressionless face, he turned his eyes to the stone floor which seemed warmer. "How can you think this way – he is not yet in his grave?" He asked avoiding her eyes.

"Son, we need a breadwinner, do we not – or do you wish me to sell myself?"

"Still, you shouldn't jump at the thought – so soon. Besides, you can work full time and earn an honest living. You did before, didn't you?"

Piqued by his fidelity, she grabbed his hand and turned towards the stairs.

"Let's go now. At this moment I cannot think straight."

He pulled his hand away and pointed it at the door. "What about the lock?"

"This flat doesn't belong to us. Let the owners take care of the Lock."

"This is not right."

"'RIGHT is what puts bread on our table. Come give me your hand and let's go. This life is behind us."

To avoid her touch, he took another step backwards. She tilted towards him, tucked her hand in the crook of his resisting arm, and, pulling him, descended the stairs. The repetitive bang of their heavy steps echoed in the cold passage-way and gave Ahmad an excruciating headache. They reached the hallway without encountering a single soul. As Nary opened the entrance door a whiff of fresh air kissed her sombre face. She took a deep breath and smiled. Silent, they walked to Avenue Ghandi where they caught a taxi for home. Inside the cab, drowned in thoughts, neither uttered a word. Ahmad was wondering how they could survive without a breadwinner. While Tirdad was alive, he led a comfortable life and now what? Perhaps he had to quit school and work. The thought was not appealing at all. His throat tightened again and he felt tears blurring his vision. He took a deep breath and sighed through his nose.

Gazing out of the window, Nary was blind to the scenery passing her sight. She was in another realm, imagining the comfortable life waiting for them in Sydney – far away from all the ugliness she had experienced in life.

At home, Ahmad went to the bathroom, washed his face with cold water. Then to quell his excruciating headache took an aspirin from the medicine cabinet, swallowed it with a drink of water and went straight to his room to study for the coming exam. He read and read but nothing could enter into his head. It was totally blocked. He closed the biology book and dropped on his bed hoping sleep would obliterate that awful image of the man who had once been his father.

In her bedroom Nary hastily changed into her house dress and then went to the kitchen where she could call Hashem without having to whisper.

Hashem, as was his habit, had risen at dawn, performed his morning prayer, done his fifty bar pull-ups, showered and headed for his office where he would be served his breakfast of bread, butter and honey. His staff liked and respected him very much. Unlike the other directors who had forgotten their humble backgrounds, he had remained the down-to-earth son of a baker (come rich grace of the revolution) that he was. They knew his likes and dislikes and served him with unprecedented loyalty. He was a disciplined operator and worked hard. A sincere believer of equality, instead of having his lunch served at his office, he went to the cafeteria, ate with the lesser souls, shared in their jokes and listened attentively to their gossips. In his job information was of paramount importance

When his liaison with Nary intensified, that egalitarian interaction dwindled for a while and then stopped. Upon being asked the reason for his absences, he created the myth of having to feed his bedridden mother. This increased his respect in the eyes of his colleagues, secretary and the elderly female employees dreaming of a son like him.

Ali Agha, his secretary, was a tall, handsome young man with a tidy beard and not a week's stubble like the other fellows. His skin was olive and his sharp eyes green. Proud of his important position, he dressed accordingly: suit, white shirt and no ties. His first chore of the day was to fetch the Director's breakfast from the canteen and this morning, he arrived smiling his greeting. He put the tray on the table, turned his eyes to Hashem's tired face and in a concerned manner asked: "Are you ill Brother?"

"No. Why?"

"You look pale and tired."

"I am overworked Ali." He pointed to the pile of files on his desk, "please cancel all appointments," I have to go through all these today.

"I shall do so Brother." Ali replied with an understanding glow in his eyes.

Tension was playing havoc on Hashem's nerves. He had no appetite and his mouth was as dry as sand. To relax he went through the entire content of the tea pot without feeling any calmer. He kept glancing at the pile on his desk and sighing. The files contained information he wanted to turn into ash before starting a new life. But could he bury the memory of the deeds done? He knew he couldn't and that thought was eating him up. His body was wet with sweat – cold sweat. After a few minutes of aimless fidgeting he picked up his briefcase from the floor and put it on the table. His heart was hammering so hard that it made him nauseous. He took a deep breath, swallowed the saliva gathered in his mouth and stared at the files with mortified eyes. There were names on those folders that he didn't want to see – names etched on grave stones at Behesht Zahra's cemetery. His hands began to work as though they had a will of their own. With swift movements they picked up the files and shoved them inside the briefcase which became so full that its lock refused to clink closed. Further manoeuvring succeeded in burying the reports in their temporary tomb. He placed the bag by his chair and exhaled a heavy sigh and began to play with his fingers, making shapes he had learnt from his father when a child. As time ticked away, the churning in his stomach intensified. In fact, this morning, he had nothing to do except examine the contents of all daily newspapers not on his desk as yet. Even that wouldn't be mind-absorbing. The Green Movement was already crushed, and the foreign journalists' forced out of Iran. Agitated and restless he left his desk and began to pace up and down his large office. The room was cool and the air-conditioning worked at full force. Yet he felt boiling hot. He went to the window that was overlooking a private garden, opened it and inhaled a lungful of air. Against the rules he left the window open. The light coming through was pleasant. He hated the opaque glass of their offices. They made him feel as though imprisoned. It was good to be able to see the sky, the milky clouds and below, the top of the trees. Suddenly he remembered a few names he had deprived of these little pleasures and trembled with regret.

A knock at his door broke the chain of his thought. It could only be Ali.

"Come in."

The door opened softly and Ali stepped in carrying his newspaper bundle which he politely put on his boss's empty desk. Hashem murmured his thanks. Ali smiled, turned and left the room as quietly as he had entered it. He returned to his desk and wondered how in such a short time Hashem could have gone through that pile. Today he wasn't his old self. Why? Ali shook his head and made a note to ask around. Perhaps he was being demoted or sacked. That would be bad news for him. He liked Hashem and enjoyed working for him. He made a mental note to pray for his safe-keep at noon, when they would all go to the prayer room for the mid-day prayer.

The phone buzzed and he picked it up.

Hashem had to read every page of the stack through the eye of a needle, searching for articles that smelled of criticism of the regime. If such a script was found, he had to order a raid on the publishing House or confiscate the publisher's licence, or fine him. Extent of the punishment met the measure of the criticism.

He started with Omid Iran published by Ayatollah Kahroobi and then moved to Hamshari and by the time he got to Keyhan he couldn't concentrate at all. Time was dragging on and the wait was unnerving him. At that moment, no news was more important than the one he was waiting to hear.

The thought that was weighing on him most heavily was whether he had missed hearing Tirdad's pulse beat – he had listened to it carefully yet under that special circumstance he might have been too hasty in his conclusion. The man might be in a coma and not dead – what then? The more he thought about it the harder he felt the throbbing in his head. He was about to choke with guilt when his mobile's cock began to crow. He took the call and whispered a hasty 'hello.'

"Salam azizam – you may not believe what I have to tell you – Emmam Reza heard our prayers and has granted me freedom."

He closed his eyes and thanked God in his heart. Relieved from misgivings he became his controlled self again. Pretending ignorance, in an excited voice he asked:

"How – tell me?"

"Tirdad is dead and his corpse is at the city's morgue. I will tell you all about it when I see you this afternoon. I cannot have lunch with you today. Ahmad was with me when we found him, and he has taken it hard. I am going to take him to a Kebab restaurant. I will be in the flat around five."

"Ok my love. By the way was the police involved in the incident?"

"Yes, an officer by the name of Amir-Hussaini – a decent fellow. Why?"

"Ordinarily, it takes five weeks for the morgue to release a post-mortem report. We not have that much time left. I am going to see if I can expedite matters. See you at five."

Hashem clicked the mobile off, picked up the phone, called Ali and asked him to get doctor Asghari at the city's morgue.

When the doctor came on line, knowing with whom he was speaking, he curtly asked: "Who is it this time?"

"A man by the name of Tirdad Amiri; I do not want you to do anything to the body. He has died apparently of a fall; so an autopsy is not necessary. Send your report of 'accidental death' to his widow as quickly as possible – and a copy to me."

"You get it by tomorrow afternoon."

"Fantastic – I owe you one."

Asghari put the receiver down; hastened to where newcomers were kept and asked his assistant to lead him to Tirdad Amiri.

"He is in number five." The assistant said leading the way. He stopped by drawer number five, grasped its handle and pulled it out.

"Oh my God!" Asghari exclaimed, horrified by the sight in his view. He turned to his assistant and asked: "By whose orders was he sent here?"

"Officer Amir-Hussaini, Doctor."

"And this officer claims his death is caused by an accident?"

"Yes Sir."

"Ignorant bastard – look at the colour of his lips and the swelling of his face and limbs. This doesn't match an 'accidental fall' or whatever claimed by our competent officer Amir-Hussaini." Asghari proclaimed his voice uncharacteristically harsh.

He considered the pros and the cons of disobeying Hashem. Then he turned his gaze to his assistant and ordered: "Prepare him for an autopsy right now. I know this man – his father was my most respected professor and this man did not die of an 'accidental fall'. Bullshit. He died of poison."

Hashem was already in the flat when Nary, dressed in the black of a widow, arrived. He glimpsed at her fake mourner's air, opened his arms and laughing they embraced. Hashem whispered into her ear: "I hope you are not going to think of him anymore."

"No. But the sight in that room was awful – really awful." Frowning she twisted out of his embrace. "His shaggy face covered in blood was so swollen that he looked more like an injured ape than a human being. I felt sick looking at him." She shook her head side to side. "I am surprised at my own lack of sympathy for him." She walked to the sofa and settled on it, "I think, it was good that he died – with the amount of white alcohol he consumed, he could have eventually harmed someone. Drunk, he was a beast – savage and brutal. Now, perhaps he will find the peace he never felt while alive."

"Enshallah." Hashem consoled sitting by her. He took her cold hand to his lips, kissed it several times, looked deep into her eyes and whispered: "Azizam, take off your coat, relax and let us celebrate the fulfilment of our wish." She gave him a tender glance and smiled

Whistling a happy tune, he went to the kitchen and returned with a tray on which sat a bottle of Champaign and two crystal flutes. He put the tray on the coffee table and settled by her. She leaned towards him. He kissed her lips. Then he picked up the bottle, uncorked it with an explosion that sent the cork to the air, and the bubells over him, her and the table. Their loud laughter invaded the air.

They would have laughed at anything at that moment – so exhilarated they felt.

"Hashem joon, why is this Champagne pink?"

"I have no idea. Yesterday Abraham brought a dozen, charged me equivalent to Ali's monthly salary, and told me pink is better than white."

"And you believed him?"

"He is the connoisseur, and not I."

Her eyes brimming with joy, she gave a sexy swing to her curls, grinned and asked:

"By the way who is Ali?"

"My secretary, a nice fellow – I like him very much."

He poured the Champagne into the flutes, this time paying attention not to make more mess. Amorously looking into each other's eyes, they raised, touched glasses and drank to felicity.

Reclining on the settee, she began to tell Hashem about her day when he pointed his index finger at his nose, "hush my love. He is gone and I do not want to hear his name ever again."

She tensed up, gave him a firm look and said: "Ok, but we must tell everything to Ahmad. It is necessary for him to accept and respect you – otherwise we will have a lot of difficulties with him. He is surprisingly loyal to Tirdad's memory and a very stubborn youngster."

Understanding her concern he took her hand, squeezed it tenderly, "Please, my love, don't be afraid of the future. I promise I will do my best to earn Ahmad's love and respect."

His words made her bathe in confidence. Her lifeless eyes gained some verve and she felt as hopeful as a youth with sweet dreams. Here was a man who would care for her and her son with genuine affection, respect and consideration. She inhaled a lung full of air and exhaled her bliss with a shining smile for the source of her happiness. He pulled her to himself, kissed her earlobe and whispered: "Now, let's celebrate and be happy azizam." She gently pulled away and murmured:

"I am happy – very happy. But I cannot celebrate anything until I know my son is happy too." Once the words were out regret set in. Had she thrown ash over a delicious fire? What a fool I am? She told herself biting her lip hard. She stared into his eyes so that she could reach his soul and apologize. But, lost to the present, he was far away; sailing on the moon with his bride.

He returned to the world of the living when her lips touched his and he breathed her familiar scent. He hugged her tight as though he would never let her go. They stayed like that until the phone rang. She moved out of his grip so that he could go and take it.

"Let it ring." He pulled her back to himself. She kissed his neck and rested her head on his shoulder feeling secure and relaxed. Stroking her hair he whispered:

"I promise I be a good father to your son. Bring him here tomorrow and let's talk to him," he paused and then smiled, "no, bring him the day after tomorrow – when we are already married. I am going to call my notary and ask him to come to the flat early tomorrow morning and marry us. Then you will be bringing your son to introduce to your husband – he would not be able to object to anything – would he – even though he may do it in his mind?"

Nary smiled at the thought and tightened her grip of him.

The next morning, just before nine, Hashem married Nary. He paid the notary handsomely and ushered him to the door, with all the respects due to a clergy. Then he returned to the sitting room, kissed his wife and was about to depart for his meeting at Pasdaran's Headquarters when the crow of his mobile's cock stopped him. He took it to his ears and pushed the button.

"Hashem Salam."

"Salam doctor?" Hashem whispered. He did not want Nary to know about his contact with the morgue doctor.

"I am fine; just to let you know, for my own sake, I had to do an autopsy on Amiri. I found some sort of strange substance inside his intestine and stomach. The lab test proved it to be a toxic laxative. I also found the victim had been suffering from spastic colitis. Whoever fed him the drug, must have known of his condition. This substance causes heavy diarrhoea and internal bleeding that leads to a gradual, painful death. Those with spastic colitis die quicker than others. Amiri must have died and then collapsed and hit his head on the edge of the table top as described by Officer Amir-Hussaini. I would call this a cold blooded murder and not an Accidental Death. Now, what would you want me to put on the report?"

Perplexed, Hashem put his free hand on his forehead rubbing it, contemplated for a minute or two, removed his hand and asked: "What personal reason did you have for performing an autopsy against my orders?"

"Professional curiosity my friend: his dry chipped lips were purple, his extremities, abdomen and face swollen, the white of his eyes murky and his nails almost blue. These deformities don't emerge just because of a fall."

"The guy was an alcoholic."

"I did not know that. Besides, signs of alcohol poisoning are different. It usually causes swelling and flushing of the face, giddiness and nausea. It doesn't induce gradual intestinal bleeding or severe diarrhoea. Alcohol mostly affects the liver and not so much the intestine. Amiri's whole body was swollen and his skin as dry as desert sand which indicates severe dehydration. His intestines were on the verge of dissolution. The morsels of faeces' found on his rectum were blood saturated. He died of poisoning. And the murderer knew what he or she was doing."

This finding introduced a new dimension to the whole affair which disturbed Hashem's curious mind. As he could not get involved, he turned his anger towards Asghari's disobedience and in an irate voice ordered:

"You, just confirm Accidental Death and don't worry I will find the murderer for you."

"I will obey your orders only if you give me your word of honour to punish the murderer when found."

"I will, and thanks for disobeying my orders to satisfy 'your' curiosity."

"I owed it to his late father – one of the most decent men I knew." The doctor said, putting the receiver down and swearing at the arrogance of the ruffians in power.

Asghari was an intelligent fellow. Two issues began to bother him. First: why Hashem should be interested in Tirdad Amiri's death report; and second, now that he was involved, he could not reveal the truth to Datam and Rose with whom he had been in touch by email. He was sure they would either be in Iran or come soon for the funeral.

Hashem's interference in his work always involved political prisoners' murders, either in jail or out in the streets – their corpses had to be meddled with so that the reason for death appeared natural. Heart attack, stroke, suicide and car accidents were the most common causes presented to the next of kin who were in fact fortunate enough to be informed of the demise of their beloved and did not have to fritter away in uncertainty. Asghari felt terribly guilty about having to keep Tirdad's murder from his relatives. But, considering the involvement of the most notorious organization in Iran, what could he, a little pawn in their dirty games, do? What and that 'what' kept him awake at nights, until he received a call.

Datam, after walking the streets like an amnesiac, arrived at the hotel, soaked in perspiration. He passed through the entrance hall, and politely acknowledged the various porters' greetings with a smile, or a head gesture. He stopped at the threshold of the cafeteria and looked for Rose who he knew would be there, waiting for him. He spotted her in a secluded corner by the wall to wall window, perusing a newspaper. The hall was crowded by foreign entrepreneurs, mostly from the Far East and Africa, seemingly engaged in serious conversation with their Iranian counterparts.

A piano player entertained them with his melodious music.

"Rose." Datam called in a soft melancholic voice.

She looked up at him with a smile. The pallor of his skin, the pearls of sweat on his forehead, removed gaiety from her heart. Without taking her anxious eyes from his daunted face, she folded the paper, put it on the table and in a low and deeply troubled voice asked:

"What is wrong darling? Why do you look so miserable?"

"I was just kicked out of my brother's home."

"No!" she exclaimed, her horrified eyes glowing with surprise.

He looked frail and ill.

"Sit here darling." Rose pointed to the chair facing her, "and tell me why."

He settled down shaking his head in remorse.

"What happened darling?" She asked leaning forward.

He leaned back, exhaled and glued his weary eyes on hers.

"Get it out Datam." She commanded impatiently.

"They have already buried him – she showed me the official post-mortem report from the morgue doctor. There had been no foul play. Apparently he had died of a fall. And when I asked her why she did not wait for us to be present at his funeral, she reproached me for not having helped them while in financial need. The whole affair seems so bizarre. I do not know what we should have done and why everything, particularly the burial happened so fast. It usually takes a month before the morgue's report is delivered – and, a decent wife would have waited for the rest of the family to arrive for the funeral. When I voiced my objection she ordered me out of her home and her life." He put his hand on his aching forehead and began to rub it. "All seems so strange – so strange!"

Rose summoned a passing waiter. He came forward and stood in attention.

Turning her eyes to Datam she asked: "Would you like tea or coffee darling?

"A cup of poison."

"Nonsense, a cup of camomile or verbena infusion will do you good."

Datam looked up at the waiter and ordered. "I will take verbena please."

The waiter asked for their room number and when told he registered it on the order pad he was holding. Quickly he turned, walked to the tea bar where a huge electrical samovar was boiling water, and delivered the order to his colleague. Datam's beverage arrived. He signed the invoice presented to him, searched his pocket for a note to add to the 15% service charge included in the bill. Finding nothing, he looked up at the waiter and expressed his apology. The man threw him a disappointed glance, turned and walked away.

"Do not worry. We shouldn't be really tipping when charged 15%"

"Yes but they do expect it."

"They expect it because they think since we live overseas we must be loaded."

"Compared to them we are loaded."

She smiled at his logic and said:

"Darling, Tirdad is gone and his wife probably doesn't want to have anything to do with his family anymore – in a way, one cannot blame her. None of you ever loved her. You must remember, like all of us, she is a human being with pride. So, do not begrudge her impudence or perhaps revenge. The poor lady, she has lost two husbands and in these days and age, has to take care of an adolescent son – with what, only God knows."

"I never was unkind to her."

"No. But you were the subject of her husband's hatred and you led a life envied by both of them."

Datam nodded his consensus and sipped his tea. It tasted awful; nevertheless he finished it, put the cup down and looked up at his wife. "You know Rose, I am very surprised she received the morgue's letter so soon, and cannot understand why they did not perform an autopsy on him. With all the excrement and blood all over the flat, he could have been poisoned by someone with a grudge: his wife, or one of those from whom he had borrowed money and hadn't paid back."

"What faeces and blood?"

"Just before we left London, I called Golnar and she warned me that the flat is filthy and foul-smelling. There are patches of defecation and blood on the floor covered under heaps of dead insects."

Rose frowned and said: "Then Tirdad must have suffered from severe diarrhoea. That is terrible. With his spastic colitis, the poor fellow must have felt awful."

She paused, narrowed her eyes, furrowed her forehead, reflected for a second or two and then asked more of herself than Datam: "Why didn't he call a doctor or his wife, even if they were not on speaking terms?"

"He might have called her and she refused him her help. Perhaps she wanted him to die. Today she didn't seem like a widow in mourning."

"Then Tirdad could have called Dr Mehran or Golnar."

"Yes. But why didn't he?" He paused, stared into Rose's pensive eyes, waved his index finger in the air and emphasized: "Because he was murdered – my brother was murdered."

"Datam, do not start imagining melodramas. Nary had ample reason to divorce him, and she did not. Why would she want to kill him; and people do not murder for unpaid debts – they take a lawyer. Even if foul play was involved, you cannot prove anything – the man is already buried and Islamic law forbids exhumation of a corpse. Regarding the morgue's letter, since they have had to deal with so many cadavers dumped on them recently, they must have printed a standard form to complete and send out."

The statement was so outrageous that they both burst into a hysterical laughter. Suddenly, several heads turned to the couple, their eyes condemning their misconduct. It was an offence to break sobriety in public. Embarrassed, they cast their heads down and began biting their lips as a sign of regret. Their apologetic gesture worked its magic – furrows opened up, heads turned back and restraint returned to the dignified ambiance. The piano player paused for repose and Rose turned her eyes to Datam and whispered:

"How was your mother darling?"

"She is breathing. I hope she can talk soon. She will be able to tell us what happened."

"Let's hope she can. But now that Tirdad has gone, she cannot live by herself. You must find and enrol her in one of these homes that have mushroomed up all over Teheran. With so many families dispersed all over the world, they are blessings for the aged and immobile."

"Yes. But I have to talk to Kobra about it. I think we should all meet at Golnar's and decide what to do with Madar once she is out of the hospital."

"That is a good idea. Give Golnar a call and set a time for tomorrow."

Datam nodded his acquisition and picked up the paper to peruse it. Finding concentration hard, he threw it back, leaned against the back of his comfortable chair and closed his eyes.

The piano player stood up, Rose began to clap for him. The others followed suit. Delighted by the ovation he swept his enchanted eyes over his audience and then put his hand across his chest and made a low bow. As he passed Rose's table she smiled at him and said: "Bravo Agha!"

"Thank you Khanum." He whispered blushing. This was the first flattering remark he had received since the start of his career, two years back and coming from such beautiful and dignified lady. That was indeed auspicious. He made a mental note to ask her, next time he saw her, what she would want him to play for her.

For Datam, at that moment, the lobby sounds, the muted noise of conversation around him, the rattle of crockery, the thud of waiters' steps on the marble floor, all blended into a confused and irritating roar, giving him a dreadful headache. Rose read the signs of discomfort on his scrunched up face. She gently tapped at his arm.

"I think we should retire to our room for a short siesta. You look exhausted my love."

Without an answer, he stood up, tucked the paper under his arm and followed her to where the lift was.

The next morning, they went to the flat which now was locked. Datam called Kobra on his mobile and was told a key was with Turan Khanum. He rang Turan's bell. "Who is it?" Homayon asked. "It is me, Datam Amiri. Kobra told me Turan Khanum holds my mother's flat keys. I have come to collect them."

Homayon opened the door. "Salam Agha Datam, Salam Rose Khanum. Please accept my condolences."

"Thank you Agha Homayon." They both responded unanimously.

"Agha Datam, my mother is not home. But I know where she keeps the keys. If you wait, I will get them for you."

"Thank you Homayon joon and I am sorry for bothering you."

"I will do anything for Kobra joon and her relatives."

The intimacy in the man's tone shocked Rose. Datam took it for neighbourly partiality.

Homayon reappeared with the keys and headed towards the locked door.

The two followed him. Before opening the door, he looked up at Rose and Datam and warned: "You better take out your handkerchiefs and cover your noses. The flat stinks."

"Didn't Kobra get someone to clean it?" Datam asked quite surprised.

"Not that I am aware of. Kobra joon tells me everything – we have a very special relationship. I often do things for her – especially her photocopying."

"What have you been photocopying for her Agha Homayon?" Rose asked, in an off handed manner.

"Deeds to Shamsi joon's properties."

"She probably had suspected Tirdad of some sort of mischief, and wanted to keep copies." Datam remarked casually.

"Yes. Well after he had turned the deed of the rented house to his name, she probably thought he would do the same with this one and the land at Varamin." Rose commented in English. He had to know and now was the time.

Perplexed, he swung his livid eyes to her and in English asked:

"What did you say?"

"A while ago, Kobra called to tell you what he had done, but you were not home. So she talked to me. She wanted you to join her in taking legal action against him. I told her you would not be interested in doing so."

"Why did you not tell me this at the time?" Datam protested in an angry tone.

"Would you have taken legal action against your brother?"

"No. But I had the right to know about my family affairs." Datam replied, his tone cutting.

"Had you known, what would you have done?" Rose asked calmly.

"Nothing."

"So, what would have been the point in me giving you news that would have upset and sickened you?"

"You treat me as though I already have a leg in my grave."

"Nonsense. We all die one day; nevertheless, I will not allow anything to aggravate your illness – I have that 'right'." She took his arm and squeezed it with affection. "You are my husband, and my life. Should anything happen to you, I will not be able to bear it. God has been kind to us, and I will not allow anyone to disturb what is left of our lives together. You must respect that Datam – if you love me as much as I love you."

Ashamed of his unreasonable outburst, he lowered his head and murmured: "I am sorry Rose. I did not intend to upset you."

"That is Ok. Now speak in Farsi. Homayon seems annoyed with us." She replied, her voice soft yet authentic. This was not the first time he was rebuking her for having protected him against the venoms of his siblings and she was getting annoyed with his forgiving nature that they all took for stupidity rather than humanity.

As Homayon opened the door a gust of stinking air rushed out. Repelled, they, each took a step back and stood astounded. The smell of death was too loathsome to bear. Rose took Datam's hand and said:

"Let's leave. We will search for a professional cleaner to come and clean the flat – I do not want you to enter it. It will be too upsetting for you."

Datam turned his back to the door, put his hand on his forehead to stop the throbbing pain that had invaded it.

Homayon closed and locked the door.

Opening her palm, Rose demanded: "Homayon joon, give me the keys please."

Homayon hiding his hand with the keys behind his back replied: "I do not have Kobra joon's permission. Could you please call her, and let me talk to her."

"Kobra doesn't have to give you permission to give me my mother's keys. I am the oldest son and her guardian."

"I am sorry but I cannot Agha Datam. Kobra joon specifically told me not to give 'you' the keys, because you might sell this flat and pocket the money."

"When did she tell you this Agha Homayon?" Rose asked.

"Only yesterday."

"Datam, get Kobra on the phone and let Agha Homayon talk to her. It seems he is in love with her." Rose said in a light, teasing tone.

Homayon rolled his eyes in delight and replied: "Oh yes, I am in love with her, and I think, she with me."

The two exchanged a long meaningful glance before Datam diverted his attention to the mobile he had pulled out of his jacket's pocket. He dialled Golnar's number. After a few rings he heard her soft 'hallo'.

"Salam Golnar joon, is Kobra there?" The urgency in his voice troubled Golnar.

"Is anything wrong Datam?"

"No. Is she there?"

"Yes, I will put her on." Golnar handed the phone to Kobra standing by her in the kitchen. "It is Datam and he sounds worried about something." Kobra grimaced, shrugged her shoulders and took the phone

"Salam Dadda."

"Salam. Your new boyfriend here wants to have a word with you."

Stupefied, Kobra exclaimed: "My boyfriend?" The receiver was in Homayon's grip now.

"Yes azizam, Homayon."

Hearing his voice suddenly frightened her. She felt cold sweat ooze out in the cleft of her breasts and a flow of adrenalin made her heart grip tight. She swallowed her saliva, took a deep breath, shook her head to get the ache out and asked: "What do you want Agha Homayon?"

"So now I am Agha Homayon?"

"We talk about that later. What do you want?"

Her impersonal tone surprised and agitated Homayon. He took a step away from the other two and whispered:

"Your brother wants the keys."

"Give it to him."

"Why did you yesterday tell me not to do so?" He asked in a loud voice so that Datam could hear.

"I never said such a thing – do not lie and never call me azizam again."

His simple mind now completely confused, he asked: "Why not, pussy cat?"

"Oh my God", Kobra heard herself exclaim. She dropped the receiver on its cradle and leaned against the kitchen cabinet trembling.

Homayon's jaw dropped when he heard the click of disengagement and his widened eyes began to roll in puzzlement. Rose sensed his anxiety and became concerned about his state of mind. He looked as though he was about to have a fit. Her mind began to race.

"What is it Kobra?" Golnar asked.

"Nothing – It is Rose being nasty to me again."

"I thought you were talking to Homayon."

"I was at first but then she took the phone from him."

"I am surprised. She is never nasty to anyone. Why is she always nasty to you?"

"She is jealous of me. That is why."

Jealous of her! Never! The woman has everything she needs in the world. Why would she be jealous of Kobra? Golnar reflected, picking up a glass, filling it with tap water. "Drink this; you seem to be on the verge of a breakdown over nothing." She said to Kobra.

Nothing! Kobra gasped as she took the glass.

Homayon, shaking his head in disbelief handed the keys to Datam saying, "Agha Datam, your sister is a liar."

"Homayon joon, I am sure there has been a misunderstanding. Don't worry about it at all."

Homayon locked his eyes into Datam's, stamped his foot down and replied: "No Agha there has been no misunderstanding at all. She told me not to give you the keys and that is the honest truth. You all think I am stupid and mix things up. Don't you?" Without waiting for an answer he turned and ran inside his home and banged the door shut and began hitting his head against the wall murmuring "Liar, now I am a liar as well as an imbecile?"

In the corridor the two stood still as though spellbound. "What did Kobra say to make him so upset?" Rose asked more of herself than Datam.

"I have not a clue." He whispered "it seems so strange for an intelligent girl like Kobra, to have an affair with a simple-minded fellow like Homayon. He probably is making it up."

"No. I don't think so."

"What do you mean Rose?" He asked fed up with the situation.

"I mean Kobra must have been using this boy to serve her."

"Serve her?"

"Yes. Serve her on a serious matter worth opening her legs for him."

"Do not be vulgar Rose."

"I am neither vulgar nor an idiot – just realistic."

"What do you exactly mean? Now my sister has become a whore in your view?"

She gave him a pitiful look and said: "Soon you will find out what I mean. Just trust me and let me do what I think is right." Rose replied, sure that the key to the riddle was hidden in the midst of the mess and the dirt in that rotten apartment and Homayon had something to do with it.

"I have always trusted you Rose "

"And you have never regretted it!" Rose snapped back, took his arm and pulled him towards the stairs.

Outside, they turned left and mindful of the steepness of the hill, descended the steps that leads to Avenue Africa and Golnar's home. They walked in silence – each plunged in thought, totally oblivious to the bumper to bumper traffic and the zigzagging motorists in a hurry.

At a zebra-crossing which meant nothing to the drivers, they clasped hands and cautiously negotiated their way across the road. They stopped at a florist, bought a basket of flowers and walked the short distance to her house. Datam pressed the intercom button.

"Who is it?" A female voice asked.

"Doctor Amiri."

The gate clicked open and they stepped inside. Datam closed the gate and saw Golnar rushing down the steps.

Greeting her with his Salam, he offered her the basket.

"You shouldn't have done this." She voiced her customary protest taking the basket with delight. She dipped her small head in the midst of the flowers, inhaled their pleasant aroma and exclaimed: "Oh, I simply adore tuberoses, and gladiolas, especially white ones. Thank you Datam joon."

"Nothing at all, you have been so kind to us all." Rose spoke approaching Golnar for a kiss. The greeting over, Golnar led the way into a large, ornately furnished formal living area at a corner of which sat Kobra staring at them with unwelcoming eyes..

Rose and Datam offered her a curt Salam before sitting by the coffee table on which was a large tray of cream pastries. Golnar put her basket in the middle of the dining table and joined her guests. Her maid arrived with a tea tray. The guests picked up a cup each with thanks. Golnar pointed to the pastry dish with her hand, "please help yourselves" before taking a seat. No one moved. "They are fresh. I bought them today for you." Golnar said looking at Rose. "They look delicious." Rose replied and put a piece on a plate and put it in front of Datam.

Then smiling said: "he is the only one who doesn't have to worry about his weight." Golnar threw a loving glance at him and agreed. She had not seen him since Mohammad's funeral and that was many years back. He seemed too aged for sixty and too pale to be healthy. She liked and respected him very much. They had been playmates in another world, centuries ago. Memories of the good old times had now become pleasant dreams. Unable to contain her constraint, in a voice hued by concern, she asked, "Datam joon have you been ill?"

"No. But I am devastated by what has happened to my mother and brother."

"You should be glad he died at home and not hanged in jail – and, before stripping us of Madar's inheritance." Kobra stated, crossing one leg over the other.

"Since when have you become so materialistic?" Datam asked his tone sour.

"Since unlike you, I have had to earn every rial I own." Kobra snapped, glaring at him with narrowed eyes.

"We have not come here to discuss anyone's destiny or wealth. We are here to plan for Shamsi joon." Rose remarked, directing her gaze at Golnar who, uncomfortable with Kobra's approach, was nervously cracking her knuckles.

Datam threw his sister a dismissive glance before addressing Golnar:

"Rose and I have decided to find a suitable Retirement Home for Madar, where she will be taken care of by professionals."

"This is a great idea. With none of you present in Iran, a Home is the best solution." Golnar responded relieved from the anxiety of a possible further responsibility. She was already looking after a sick mother and an addict brother.

Kobra sniffed, furrowed her brows, put her tea cup on its saucer, looked up at Golnar and said: "I do not agree. We must employ a qualified nurse to take care of her until Datam can get her a visa and take her to live with them at their palace in London. After all, he is rich enough to be able to look after his own mother for once!" The sarcasm in her voice bit them all. But in their wisdom they let its venom settle on her own ugly face in a twisted grin

Rose straightened up in her chair, elongated her neck and in a manner that barred further dispute replied: "We will not be able to do so Kobra. She never liked me; therefore I do not believe she will be happy living with us."

"Shahzadeh Khanum you remain as selfish as ever." Kobra ridiculed.

Golnar threw her a disapproving glance. Datam blushed and Rose just looked into her husband's eyes.

Kobra turned her wicked eyes to her brother. He met them without a flinch. The selfish girl was set to insult him by defying his proposal. That he wouldn't allow because it concerned the wellbeing of their mother. So he said in an assertive tone: "Madar will stay at a Home, here in Iran. Tomorrow you Kobra Khanum and I will start looking for the best around." Point made, he turned his back to her and asked Golnar: "Do you know of a professional cleaner who can clean Madar's apartment?"

"Yes, my maid's husband works for a firm that does professional cleaning. When would you like that to be done?"

"Tomorrow morning and I will be there myself." Rose responded, giving Kobra a side look.

"Shahzadeh, do you know how to deal with a cleaning team – you have never touched a broom before." Kobra commented with a mocking glow in her dark eyes.

Now looking at her full face Rose answered: "You are right my dear. I have not. But I do manage a team of domestics who work for me with remarkable efficiency."

At the end of his titters, Datam threw a livid glance at his sister. "Kindly behave like the lady that I am sure you are." He said with a tinge of pepper in his tone.

Her peace disturbed by the tension in her home, Golnar yelled for the maid to bring the phone. The sharp crescendo of her voice disturbed Rose's sense of propriety. She felt indignant for the dismal ambiance created by their disputes and decided to end it as quickly as possible.

Zahra, eavesdropping in the kitchen picked up the handset and carried it for her distressed mistress. "Here you are Khanum." Golnar looked into her understanding eyes, smiled and said, "Could you please call your husband and see if he can oblige Rose Khanum by cleaning my aunt's flat tomorrow?"

The maid turned to Rose,

"Khanum joon, you will be very happy with Agha Parvis's services. He is very efficient. Besides I will ask him to supervise your work himself – then you won't have to worry about a thing. You just tell him what you want him to do, leave and return to a sparkling home."

"Thank you Zahra Khanum." Both Datam and Rose spoke in unison.

Zahra dialled her husband's number and pushed the loud speaker's button so all could hear their conversation. After a few rings they heard a deep voice say:

"Allo?"

"Salam Agha Parvis."

"Salam Zahra. Are you well?"

"Yes I am well. Nothing is wrong. I called because Khanum's cousin wants you to clean his mother's apartment tomorrow."

"Tomorrow is rather difficult. I have already made an appointment with a regular client."

"No, you must cancel that appointment and oblige Khanum Amiri's request. They are here for a short while and the matter is urgent."

"Do they want me in the morning or the afternoon?"

Rose whispered: "first thing in the morning please."

Zahra repeated her sentence.

"Ok. I will be there at 9. Have you told them how much I charge?"

"I will pay him on hourly basis without any bargains." Rose whispered.

"Khanum Amiri will pay you on hourly basis and will not bargain with you, if you do a good job for her, which I am sure you will."

"All my clients are satisfied with my work. What is the address?"

"It is Shamsi Khanum's apartment. You have been there twice already."

"Yah. Would she be there?"

"No, the poor soul is in hospital."

"Ok I'll be there at 9 in the morning."

"Thank you Agha Parvis." Zahra said before clicking off the phone. She swept her victorious eyes over all and fixed them on Rose who opened her bag; extracted out a five thousand note and a set of keys. From the key ring she detached one and dropped the ring back into her bag. She rose, thanked the maid while handing her the money and the Key with a smile. "Zahra Khanum this key is for the front door of the building, in case Agha Parvis gets there before I do." Zahra took the key refusing the money. After Rose's insistence she accepted the generous gratuity with delight.

Golnar watching the scene appreciated Rose's decorum and then from below her long lashes stole a glance from Kobra's twitching face. The animosity shooting out of her piercing eyes disgusted her. She released a long woeful sigh and stood to see her guests to the door.

Datam followed his wife and together apologized to Golnar for the bitter afternoon and left the room without a glance at Kobra. Nor did Kobra rise in their respect. Instead she leaned back and stared at their silhouettes wishing them death.

Out, in the street, away from that suffocating atmosphere of hate and malevolence, the two breathed with ease. Datam locked his hand in the crook of Rose's arm and pulled her close to himself so that he could feel her warmth and in it find strength and safety. Now more than ever he needed security. Even his sister had turned against him. Why? What had he done to her? What? He knew not. Why did people shy away from loving, forgiving and forgetting? Why? He knew not. So he tightened his grip of her arm. At least here was one who had not lost the notion of love and kindness. "Oh God – how lucky I am to have her." He whispered.

Rose heard him and said: "I am lucky to have you too my love – a man without an ounce of malice inside him is indeed rare."

Datam turned to her and in a wistful tone asked:

"Why do you think Kobra has become so rude and defensive?"

"She always was unfriendly, but you never realized it. Nevertheless do not worry about her, she is a lost cause. Mother of a friend of mine is at a place called Farzanegan, in Shahrake Gharb. According to her, the personnel there take real good care of their inmates. But it is very expensive."

"That doesn't matter."

"I know. I will call her tonight to get the phone number and the exact address. You go there tomorrow while I go to the flat with the cleaners."

"I hope I get a good night's sleep tonight. I feel awful."

"When we get back, you go to the Gym of the hotel, do some light exercise, swim and take a sauna. That will relax you."

"Good idea and what will you do?"

"I will go to Tavazo confectionary store to buy the nuts and the dried fruit I want to take to London."

"Ok Madame boss – I shall do as you command."

"Good. I am glad you are wise enough to follow my orders without a fight."

"Arguments are good. They make the love-making afterwards more exciting."

"You men – always think of sex." She scolded him with a nudge.

It was another bright morning when the Hotel's doorman opened the taxi's door for Rose. She thanked and tipped him. Looking at what lay on his palm he smiled, turned and went to attend to the other waiting guests.

The drive, during the morning rush, was as slow as a snake's creep. However the taxi-driver was talkative and full of political gossip. Rose enjoyed talking with him but was very careful with her remarks. One never knew who was a genuine citizen or member of that dreadful Ministry. Half an hour later, the taxi dropped her in front of the building. And by the time she climbed up the steps and reached the apartment, the cleaning team had already installed their tools by its door and were waiting for her. Agha Parvis introduced himself and his team members to Rose. She politely greeted them, took the entrance key from Agha Parvis, and fitted it back on the ring she had already extracted from her coat pocket; swept her eyes on them all and said: "Please accept my apologies. When I open the door, you will be hit by an awful stink. I have been told the apartment is in an appalling state and needs a real good cleaning."

"Khanum, don't worry, we are accustomed to dirty and untidy places." Parvis replied with a grin. Rose turned to the door and unlocked it. The stench pushed them back. Startled, they exchanged meaningful glances and hesitated for a few seconds before following her inside. There they halted taking in the mess in sight with wide and distressed eyes. Rose's throat tightened and her eyes moistened. She ran to the windows and opened them wide. The men began to whisper their objections. Conscious of their murmuring, she sharpened her ears and heard their rightful complaints. She lingered by the window until she heard them bringing their stuff inside. She turned and saw Agha Parvis taking a bucket to the kitchen.

"Agha Parvis." She called. He stopped and looked at her. "I just want to tell you again that I am sorry about this awful state, but since our arrangement is on hourly payment, your team has no cause to worry about their remuneration. I promise they will be paid handsomely once all is done."

"Khanum joon, do not worry. We will do our best for you."

"Thank you. I need to go through each room first, and then your men can move into that room after me. Right now can you please start with the windows?"

"Shall do Khanum joon." he said turning to his two assistants who were busy choosing their equipment, "you heard what Khanum Amiri wants you to do?"

"Yes sir." They both replied without looking at him.

Rose did not know what she was looking for, but she was sure she would find something that would indicate foul play. She sensed it in the extraordinary mess around her. The detective in her began to speculate: Homayon must have done something for Kobra; something very special to merit her intimacy with him. Tirdad died of a fall but he also had bleeding dysentery or something alike – the signs are everywhere, the shit, blood and stench. He could have eaten something bad or been poisoned. Poison – that was it. Kobra was a chemist with access to all kinds of chemicals. She was also shrewd enough to plan well. That made sense – a lot of sense. But she was not in Iran when Tirdad died. No – but

Homayon was. She must have asked him to do something for her – that is it – that – is – it. She smiled as her search found a focus. She went to the bathroom and made a thorough examination of what was in the medicine cabinet and the bin. She found nothing there; then, the bedrooms, even inside the waste paper baskets – nothing. In the dining room she found an empty plate and a take away container that stank. On and around them were laid a lot of dead insects – 'why' she asked herself. 'Poison!' They must have eaten the poisoned left-over food. She went to the kitchen, drew out the cutlery drawer, picked up a spoon and returned to the dining table. She put the spoon by the black heap, pulled out a tissue from the box on the table and spread it on the table top. She picked and dug the spoon under the dead insects; shook the full spoon over the tissue, put the spoon down and very carefully folded the tissue over the collection. She neatly fitted the parcel into the pocket of her open bag, returned to the kitchen and threw the spoon into the kitchen's garbage bin. The bin was full to the brim. Suddenly a small narrow tube caught a ray of light and sparkled. She picked it up. It had a French label on it. She took it to her nose. A faint putrid odour, similar to the one exuding from the takeaway container offended her nostrils. Bingo – that was it. Her eyes glowing with a sense of achievement, she returned to the sitting room, dropped the tube into her bag and inhaled with ease. She smiled at the workers who had already cleaned the windows: "I have finished my inspection. The flat is all yours now." She glanced at her watch. It was already eleven thirty. She turned to Agha Parvis and asked: "How long do you think you be here?"

"Another two to three hours Khanum."

"I should be here at around three in the afternoon."

"If we finish before you arrive we will wait for you Khanum joon."

"Thank you, and please do not close the windows until I return." Rose said, heading for the door.

She did not take the steps. Instead she rang Turan's bell. Homayon opened the door.

"Salam Homayon joon, is Turan Khanum home?"

"No, Khanum."

"Good. I want to have a word with you."

"With me?"

"Yes, with you."

"Please come in." Surprised and a bit frightened Homayon stepped aside for her to enter.

Rose stepped in loosening the tie of her scarf.

"Please take a seat." Homayon pointed to the sofa.

Rose sat down, carefully placed her bag on the floor and crossed her legs.

"Shall I get you something to drink or eat?"

"No Agha." Tapping the sofa seat she looked up at him. "Just sit here and tell me the truth."

"The truth?"

"Yes – the truth – that is if you do not want to be an accomplice to murder."

"Murder?" colour drained from Homayon's face.

"Yes – murder!"

Unable to comprehend anything anymore, he settled on the sofa, looked at her with terrified eyes and began to crack his knuckles and tap the floor with the tip of his shoes.

Rose took out the container from her bag, put it on the coffee table, looked at him with taxing eyes and asked: "You know this container don't you?"

As his eyes fell on the tube his furrow disappeared, he inhaled a lung full of air and exhaled it with ease. "Yes, of course I do. It contained the powder to rehabilitate Tirdad from his alcoholism."

"Who gave it to you?"

"Kobra did. Though a liar, she is a kind person. She wanted to cure her brother from being an alcoholic. She had begged him to give up drinking but to no avail. He was such an obstinate man. Therefore she decided to take matters into her own hands. From Paris she brought this new medicine, "he pointed to the tub with his chin, "and asked me to shake it on the Nazri and give it to him."

"Was there a Nazri Homayon joon?"

"No, no." He smiled. "It was all a plan. I had to buy a takeaway, shake the powder over the food, and present it to him as a Nazri." He shook his head in regret, "had the poor soul not died of a fall, he probably would have been cured of his dreadful habit by now."

Rose's tight lips pouted and moving her head left and right she glared at him with piteous eyes. The glum in them was so morose that he panicked. "What is wrong Khanum? Have I done something wrong?"

"You have committed a murder." "Murder?" He exclaimed in fright. "Yes. That powder was a medicine to kill and not to cure. However since you have been honest with me, and I do believe in your innocence – I can vouch that you have just followed instructions from a murderer who has exploited your gullibility. Trust me." Sensing the awfulness of the man's state of mind, Rose took his cold hand and tapping it continued: "I will try to protect you Homayon. However, in case the situation gets out of my hands and the police knocks at your door – just tell everything as it happened – you are too innocent to lose your life for a serpent like Kobra."

"Lose my life?" Homayon stuttered.

"Yes – murderers are hanged."

"A murderer?" He howled in pain.

"Yes – a murderer; the powder in this tube was poison, and you fed it to Tirdad – you killed Tirdad unknowingly." The world began to whirl inside Homayon's head and his facial muscles contorted by the force of the avalanche inside him. He placed his palm over his burning forehead and stuttered:

"Th... at bitch... shee... told me shee was in love wi... th mee."

"All lies Homayon – she is mad – just mad. She is only in love with herself."

Utterly mystified, Homayon's eyes rolled round and round and then rested on Rose with hate. He tightened his eyebrows, moved his head so close to Rose that she could inhale his breath and snapped: "You... are lying." Pulling her head back and staring at him with tender eyes she asked:

"Dear, why should I lie to you?"

His mind was so agitated now that he couldn't answer her. He fell back and rested his head on the back of the sofa, his eyes staring at the ceiling on which loitered the image of Kobra turned into a huge venomous, hooded serpent like a cobra slithering towards him, hissing with anger at his failure and glaring at him with condemning black eyes from which emanated shafts of fire. As the snake's mouth opened to devour him he let out a scream, cupped his face with his quivering palms, bent low and burst into a loud heart rendering cry.

Rose inched closer to him, put her hand on his trembling back and said:

"Homayon, please trust me. I am not going to harm you. I will not utter a word to anyone about your involvement in this. But I want you to tell everything to your mother. She will be able to help you. She loves you very much – trust her. You only have her and she you."

No one had talked to him this way – with so much respect and compassion. Rose's sincerity and concern quelled his fears, touched his heart and ignited his dormant sense of self-respect. He removed his hands from his red face and raised his sad eyes to hers. She caught the quest for help in them. Her heart bled for him. She felt a desire to cuddle him. He seemed like a desperately sick child begging for a cure. Instead she took his hand and gently pressed it with love. A serene smile spread over his tormented face.

"Thank you Rose Khanum. Thank you for being a friend."

"I am your friend, but your best friend is your own mother Homayon joon – trust her."

Something snapped in Homayon's head and he fell silent. He closed his eyes and on the screen of his mind manoeuvred his mother's homely silhouette limp around the kitchen to prepare his favourite food and her concerned countenance when he felt ill and her joy when pampered with a kiss from him and her warning about Kobra the cobra. Like a gale lashing at the core of a tree, a rush of guilt whacked at his conscience and made him shiver. He opened his lethargic eyes. They fell on Rose's serene smile.

"You are right Khanum. She is the only person I have in this wide world and I have been a bad son. In my selfishness, I have never shown her any love and in my stupidity have fulfilled her wishes with reluctance. People think that I am an ass. But I am an ass with a heart – just like everyone else. I have just been unlucky to catch a disease that affected my brain. When I couldn't perform at school and dropped out, my family and friends began to treat me as though I was an imbecile. At first I tried to be like others but you see, I cannot think like them. That is why Kobra was able to use me – that bitch." He stopped and began hitting his legs with both hands.

Rose grabbed his hands and gently settled them on his thighs. Then she stretched across the sofa and hugged him.

Taken by this unusual show of affection, he rested his head on her shoulder and began to cry hard again. She held him tight and gently patted his back, as though calming a baby. When he stopped, she unfolded her arms, looked into his innocent eyes and smiled.

"Thank you a thousand times Rose Khanum." He dropped his head and whispered: "I hope that bitch burns in hell."

"She will. Do not worry about that." Rose murmured more to herself than him.

She picked up the tube, returned it to its place and rising said: "I have to leave you now. She may call. Act the loving person you have been – but do not obey her requests and whatever she says deliver them to your mother, word by word. Will you promise me that?"

"Yes, of course I will."

"Good and thank you Homayon. You have been a great help to me."

"May I kiss you Rose Khanum?"

"Of course you may." Homayon aimed for her hand. "No, No," She said offering him her cheek.

Rose, tightened the tie of her scarf, picked up her bag and waving at Homayon left for the hotel. She did not go to their room. From the phone in the lobby she called Asghari on his mobile. He answered.

"Salam Doctor joon."

"Salam Rose Khanum." He cried in such a merry tone as though he had won the lottery. Suddenly he remembered he had to sound grave and offer his commiseration to her.

"Rose Khanum, I have heard that doctor Tirdad is no longer with us. Please accept my condolences for his untimely departure."

"Thank you doctor. Who told you about his death?" Rose asked not surprised at all. The enigma had already unravelled itself.

"A friend of a friend." Asghari lied.

"Yes his demise was indeed untimely. But you know we all have a death day. Unfortunately his arrived too early."

"Yes Khanum joon. Yes."

"Doctor joon, you kindly told me I can call you when I need you."

"Yes Khanum joon and how is doctor Datam?"

"He is fine and hopes to see you soon."

"Enshallah and Rose Khanum what can I do for you?" He asked highly aroused.

"I have a tube the content of which I want you to test and, a heap of dead insects."

"Dead insects?"

"Yes dead insects which I think must have nibbled at the contents of the tube."

"You want me to examine content of a tube because of dead insects?"

"No. Because of a dead man."

"A dead man?" He asked astonished, then his mind put two and two together and a smile flowered on his face.

"I am at your disposal. Come when you wish. "

"We are staying at the Esteghlal Hotel. I will leave right now. Please do not go anywhere until I arrive."

"I will be here for you Khanum joon."

"Thank you doctor."

An hour later, when Datam was taking a sauna, Rose handed her finds to Asghari – without telling him anything else.

Trying to hide his thrill, he asked her to wait while he took the stuff to the lab. She smiled her gratitude and made herself comfortable on her metal chair in his stark office. Half an hour later he reappeared, followed by a janitor carrying a tea tray. "Well doctor?" She asked, her eyes flaming with curiosity.

"Let's have tea now."

It would be impolite to reject his request. So she veiled her impatience with a sweet smile. He occupied the visitor's chair next to her, took a tea glass from the janitor's tray and handed it to her.

"Sugar cubes, Khanum?"

"No thank you doctor."

They sipped their tea, engaged in small talk until, the door opened and his assistant asked permission to enter. With his finger Asghari gestured him in. Then he put his tea glass down and took the report and the tube from him.

"Thank you Zafar."

"Nothing at all doctor." The Assistant replied, turning to leave when he heard his boss command:

"Please leave the door open."

He did so while praising the doctor's cautiousness. A man and a young and beautiful woman, alone, behind closed doors was a career suicide.

Asghari put the tube upright on the table and then unfolded the report, read the contents and feigned a frown. "What is it?" asked Rose.

"Something very strange."

"What? Please tell me?" Rose asked fixing her knowing eyes on his face. He looked into them and within their glitter, detected the knowledge of the information he had been unable to reveal to the family. He dropped his head and began to contemplate as how to present his version.

"You performed an autopsy on Tirdad – didn't you?" Rose asked, her voice steady, her facial expression demanding the truth.

"Yes. And the left over residue in the tube here is the same poison that killed him. He was brought here with a police report of 'Accidental Death'. The signs of poison were written all over him. Because I knew him, I performed an autopsy and found this same substance in his intestines and stomach." He leaned close to Rose's ears and whispered: "He was murdered my lady."

"I know. But why was nothing of murder mentioned in your report?" Rose whispered back.

He couldn't answer her question without having to lie. So he ignored it. Instead he asked:

"How did you find out?" From the edge in his tone of voice, Rose realized she could dig no further. So she respected his abstention, leaned back and replied:

"Intuition."

"Do you know who did it?"

Rose lifted an eyebrow and said: "First, please tell me if there is anything special about this poison?"

"Yes. It is not something a layman can acquire from a pharmacy. It is very specialized and can be concocted only by a chemist with a purpose, in an elaborate, sophisticated lab. It is particularly effective on people with intestinal problems."

"Like spastic colitis!"

"Yes – like spastic colitis."

"But, with him being buried, who can prove murder?"

"Do you know who the murderer is?" Asghari asked, in an unusually impatient manner.

"Yes – his step-sister – a brilliant chemist who works for the French Government."

"Do you want to bring her to justice?"

"Oh yes – but how can I with him already buried?"

"You cannot legally, but do you believe that justice prevails?"

"It should, but does it always – particularly now?"

He inched close to her and whispered:

"Not always, but this time it might."

"Might it?"

"Yes – just leave it to me."

"Do not tell me you work for that dreadful organization?"

Slowly his index finger went to the tip of his nose and he whispered a "hush". Then, in a raised, voice asked:

"Do you believe God is just Sister?"

"Yes I did – until now."

"Do not doubt him my sister – do not doubt him."

"Enshallah, you are right doctor."

Asghari shook his head and turned his eyes skywards and fixed them on a small grill in the ceiling.

"Khanum, believe that in the Islamic Republic of Iran, no evil will escape punishment. That should give you peace of mind."

Rose saw the grill and suddenly realized Asghari was warning her that his room is electronically monitored. Unconsciously her hand clasped her mouth and she fixed her startled eyes on him. "Don't worry," he murmured with his head gesturing to the door. She picked up her bag, stood up and in a graciously subdued manner said: "Brother, thank you for guiding me to the right path. God bless you for your good deed. I pray for the day in which the sword of justice will fall upon our evil doer."

"Rest assured it will." He repeated with a shadow of a smile crossing his thick lips and his hand picking up the tube.

Hashem was still in his office when his direct line sounded.

He picked up the receiver.

"Salam Hashem."

"Why have you called me on this line?"

"You said you owed me one."

"Yes I did."

"What is punishment for murder?"

"Blood for blood."

"OK. Tirdad was murdered by his step-sister – blood for blood."

"What is your interest in this Asghari?"

"Justice – only justice."

"Tell me the truth."

"I know the family. I told you before that Tirdad's father, professor Amiri, was one of the most respected scientists of Iran and my professor of physics. I met his sons and his daughter-in-laws at his wake. They are decent people. Rose Amiri, the wife of Datam Amiri who is a very decent lady, suspecting foul play, did her own search of the flat and found a suspicious tube in the kitchen bin and some dead insects on the plate from which Tirdad had eaten. She brought her finds to me to pass through the lab, something your supposedly vigilant detective should have done. The poison in that tube was the same one that killed Tirdad. As I predicted, the substance was specially formulated to kill slowly and is most effective on people with spastic colitis. Amiri's step-sister is a chemist and works for the French Government. She has ample access to all sorts of chemicals found in elaborately sophisticated laboratories."

"She works for the French Government?"

"Yes."

"Then she must be a spy. We know how to take care of spies who sell their country to the non-believers. Rest assured friend that justice will prevail."

"Thank you Hashem."

Three days later Shamsi was confined to Farzanegan. Kobra left for Paris. Datam and Rose went to spend two weeks at Galandoak and Golnar was left to enjoy the privacy of her home in peace.

Summer turned into autumn. Trees began to strip naked. Annuals had already wilted and the fields harvested. Grass was no longer green and there was that particular melancholy in the air that precedes all ends. Above, the sky remained cloudless and the sun bright but powerless.

In France the clock was set back and darkness spread its wings at around five p.m. To save electricity and its cost, street lamps were lit sporadically, making pavements quite creepy for lonely passers-by. Kobra had to work late that evening and when she let herself into the building, it was well past nine. Her elderly neighbours were all locked behind their doors: either in bed or snoring in front of their television sets. The long day had not affected her bright and breezy spirit. Nothing could erode her happiness today except death. At last she had reached the apex of her career with a hefty increase in salary. Now she could move to a more prestigious residential area and buy a better car. Ascending the steps she was so entrenched in planning that she did not hear the faint footsteps that had followed her ever since she had left the metro station. Panting she arrived at her threshold and promised herself that she would go to gym and get fit. She took a deep breath, opened her bag, withdrew her key ring, unlocked the door and was about to step inside when two powerful hands pushed her in. Losing balance, she fell on the floor with a loud thud. As she moved to rise, a heavy weight fell on her back gluing her to the ground. It was the weight of a man stinking of stale tobacco and onion.

"Mix the content of the tube with water – hurry." She heard him order. She jerked to free herself. A karate stroke on her spine sent a cry of pain out of her mouth and tears out of her wide frightened eyes. She sprawled on the hard floor gasping for breath.

She heard the bang of her door, followed by footsteps going towards her kitchenette, water running and then footsteps approaching. The weight over her lifted. As she attempted to rise a kick landed on her spine. Then she felt the tip of a shoe push under her waist, lift her up and turn her over. As she landed on her back her eyes fell on a bearded ape sneering at her with an ugly grin. The intruder lifted a leg and put it over her stomach, pushing it down. She screamed. This time, as loud as she could, hoping a neighbour would hear and come to her rescue.

"Open her mouth Nasser." The man holding the wet tube ordered.

Nasser lifted his foot up and quickly squatted over her stomach with his legs caging her ribs. For an instant, thinking he wants to rape her she screamed and screamed. He squeezed her torso between his legs, rested his hard buttocks on her stomach, and pushed his large fingers between her lips to open her mouth. She clenched her teeth tight and with her hands tried to push the beast away. Angry he punched her on the face. As she opened her mouth to howl, he shoved his fingers inside and forced it open. She bit the tip of a finger. He screamed and protested: "Why couldn't we finish her off with an injection or cut of her throat – much easier than this shit?"

"Eye for an eye – remember!" Kobra heard being said. Unable to comprehend the meaning, she increased her struggle until overwhelmed by exhaustion. Then she slumped and surrendered. Nasser grabbed the tube from his accomplice, forced it into her mouth and let the white liquid pour inside. She tasted nothing – the liquid slid down her throat. Perhaps this was all a nightmare. She opened her eyes and saw two dark faces staring down at her with malignant eyes. She had never seen them before. What did they want from her? What? Suddenly a volcano erupted inside her. She let out a muffled cry, swinging her frightened eyes from one ugly face to another until they became black dots. Pain and pain shot through her. She was still conscious. A savage spasm pushed something out of her anus. She felt it. It was loose and warm. It was the pain gone out of her. She relaxed and a sigh escaped her half open lips. Then she inhaled an awful stench. She smiled. It was Tirdad's stench. No her father's. But they were both dead and gone. She jerked her head to avoid the stench. It wouldn't go away. Was it from her? No, no. It couldn't be. She had become immune to stench of foulness – there had been so much in her wretched life. So much!

Nasser disgusted by the smell kept looking at the woman's contorted face, waiting for her last breath. A master assassin he knew when death claimed its prey. This one wasn't going without a fight. Then he noticed her eyes – calm and fixed. He took her pulse. It did not throb. Smiling with satisfaction he stood up and said:

"Let's get on with it."

"No. Wait a little. We must be sure she is dead."

"She is."

"Just wait a bit longer."

"Ok Ghasem. But why did we have to kill her this way?"

"Because we were ordered to."

"What was her crime?"

"Spying for the French."

A few minutes later, Ghasem, withdrew a little mirror from his coat pocket, knelt by Kobra, put the mirror in front of her nose. It did not steam up.

"Already in hell." He assured rising up. He shoved the mirror back into his pocket.

"Shall we start?" Nasser asked.

"Yes. But don't take anything. We are not thieves."

"Ok."

Ten days later the stench drifting out of the dirty foreign neighbour's apartment made the old French lady complain to the concierge.

It was a calm, cool and sedate Friday afternoon. Jajeroud River was rushing down its stony path to reach the mouth of its dam. A lonely persimmon tree stood erect, it's sturdy branches bent under the weight of ripe, pink fruit. Other trees were naked and forlorn. A little yonder, Datam, Rose and doctor Asghari sat on a picnic blanket spread under Rose's weeping willow that had not as yet become entirely bare. They had enjoyed Gholam Reza's chicken Kebab, and were toying with their tea glasses when a breathless Gholam Reza, phone in hand arrived. He offered the phone to Datam. "It is Nazanin Khanum from Paris." Datam looked at his wife with questioning eyes. "Nazanin is Kobra's best friend darling." Rose remarked in a whisper in case the loud speaker was on. And it was.

"Oh, Yes." Datam murmured. He took the phone and politely greeted the girl.

"Salam Datam."

"Salam Nazanin Khanum."

A pause followed.

"Khanum are you there?" Datam enquired surprised at the silence.

"Yes I am still here and don't know how to break this awful news."

"Has anything happened to Kobra?"

"She is dead – murdered."

"What?" The scream in Datam's heart flew out in a moan.

Rose looked at Asghari with eyes that enquired if he knew anything.

The quick shake of his head told her it was news to him too.

"Apparently she died two weeks ago. I was told this by her neighbour when she saw me banging on her door."

"How did she die?" Datam asked his voice coming from the bottom of an abyss.

"Datam joon all I know is from what I was told."

"By whom?"

"By the detective on her case whose card the neighbour gave me and whom I called. He told me that she died of intestinal bleeding but since her apartment was ransacked and her body severely bruised the case is still open."

"Is she at a morgue?"

"No. In the absence of any relatives, the police arranged for a burial at a public cemetery outside Paris. You know she was my best friend – I miss her so much."

Datam heard her sob and squeezed his eyes to suppress the flow of his own tears. His heart bleeding for yet another loss he aimed to console the girl but all he could utter was a simple, "thank you for your concern."

"Sorry to have been the bearer of such bad news." She whined, refusing to let go of her lost link with a dear friend. She, like many other self-exiles, was left with her own shadow as a mate

Not knowing what to say anymore Datam blew out a: "Thank you my dear," and promptly disconnected so that she wouldn't go on. At that moment, he couldn't bear talking to anyone any more. Gholam Reza, staring at him with compassionate eyes took the phone from him and asked: "Agha would you like another cup of tea – it will calm you down?"

Datam still mystified, didn't hear him. He put his hand on his forehead and closed his burning eyes. He felt very ill. He opened his eyes and saw Rose staring at him with sympathy. She pulled out a Kleenex and handed it to him. He spread it over his face and began to cry. Rose inched closer and hugged him tight. His head on her shoulder she could hear the crazy throbbing of his heart, and feel the agony that was choking him. He was so agitated that he couldn't remain still. He gently moved out of her embrace. The breeze that was pleasant became freezing. He crossed his arms over his chest to bar the chill from biting him. It wasn't enough. He had to go inside. In a daze he rose and walked away, his back stooped, his steps slow and his mind shut to the world which he could comprehend no more. Instantaneously, he thought of death and craved for the peace it offered.

Rose and Asghari's gaze followed him into the villa. Then they turned that same gaze to each other with a smile.

"Khanum, I am so sorry for your loss." Gholam Reza said shaking his head in sorrow.

"Thank you my dear."

Still shaking his head he attempted to bend to collect the dirty dishes. A tremor of pain attacked his spine. He straightened up and grimaced.

"Gholam Reza, leave the dishes to us. We will bring them to the kitchen. Please go and brew Agha some camomile tea. He badly needs something to relax him, and make sure it is very hot and spiced with a touch of cardamom."

"I am so sorry Khanum joon."

"Now for what?" Rose asked with a reluctant smile.

"For leaving you with the dirty dishes."

"Don't be silly man. It is nothing at all. Go and prepare my husband's remedy."

"Shall do Khanum joon, and if I may suggest you should go to him right now. He is very upset."

"I will Gholam Reza, I will." Rose responded turning her eyes to Asghari, "marvellous individuals like him do not exist anymore."

Nodding his head in agreement Asghari said: "I will give him my private number and ask him to call me when in need of medical treatment. I can send him to the best clinics and hospitals where he won't be charged a rial."

"Are you aiming to buy a ticket to heaven for yourself?" Teased Rose

Smiling he nodded his 'yes'.

'Let's go inside and cheer my husband up.'

"Are you going to paint him Kobra's true colour?"

"No. He will neither like it nor believe me."

"He is a lucky man to have a wife like you, so wise and considerate."

"I am luckier than he is. You know, there are not many men who can tolerate a wife like me – bossy, demanding and ......"

"Absolutely adorable!"

"Are you intending to relinquish your ticket to heaven?"

"No. Can't you see – I am trying to secure it by also being totally honest?"

"You are too kind my friend. Now hurry, let's go. I don't want Datam to be left alone, he might break, so fragile is his health, so sensitive his soul and so pure and delicate his heart. That is why I love him so very much. " She threw a mischievous glance at Asghari and asked:

"Have you ever smelt the scent of love?"

"Yes. It is intoxicating."

"And so purifying." She whispered, inhaling a lung full of the cold, clean air. She looked skyward and whispered: "A heart filled with love will have no room for any other feeling, will it?"

Admiring her more than ever he teased: "My dear lady; now I know you are a philosopher as well as a detective."

Rose laughed and stood up.

"What about the dishes?"

"Behjat will attend to them."

On 20th September, an Emirate Airline flew Hashem, Nary and Ahmad out of Iran to Dubai and then Sydney. For the first time in their lives, experiencing the comfort and hospitality of First Class travel Nary and her son were beside themselves. And Hashem, holding a glass of Moet & Chandon, was even happier than them. He had become a privileged man with ample Australian dollars at Coutts in Hong Kong, a family who doted on him as though he was their God and, the liberty to enjoy his Champagne in peace.

Neither Hashem nor Nary had told anyone of their emigration – they just wanted to vanish from the sight and memory of those they knew and who knew them or of them.

Hashem, faithful to his vow, had resigned from the Ministry – his excuse: further education in Australia. No one could object to that – to have a PhD after one's name had become a coveted objective for the young bureaucrats running the country.

They lodged at Double Bay's Ritz Carlton Hotel where Hashem used to stay when in Sydney. Amongst the wealthy clienteles of the establishment, Nary in her Islamic coat and scarf looked odd. After a short rest during which Hashem shaved his face with the electrical shaver he had purchased in Dubai, they decided to go out, explore the neighbourhood and hunt for clothes that would match their new identity. They had left Iran with nothing but their essential documents and a few items they cherished most.

Hashem knew the area well and he intended to take his family to the Westfield Shopping centre at Bondi Junction. It was still too early for the shops to open. So they indulged in a hearty breakfast, strolled down to the nearby Double Bay beach and sat on a bench admiring the Ocean and its magnificent surrounding landscape. It was a brilliant day and the ocean was as clear as the blue sky. No one was around and to them it seemed as though they monopolised the world until the first Ferry arrived to unload and load its passengers.

"Nary joon, do you know that from here you can get this Ferry to the city?"

Mesmerised by the beauty that lay in her view and the security that engulfed her, instead of answering him, she put her arms around his neck and kissed him with all the love in her.

Ahmad sitting beside her looked away. He had not as yet warmed up to Hashem. The man had been very kind but there was something in his eyes that stung him and made him feel like an intruder. However, he was his stepfather and provider. He had no choice but to pretend to like him, be civil to him and for posterity's sake try to get to know him better. Perhaps it was the soreness in his heart that was making him prejudiced. The suddenness of their marriage had revealed their illicit liaison like the light of the day and made him ashamed of his mother's morality. He knew she was selfish and materialistic but not a whore. So, in a way he had to be grateful to Hashem for marrying her and returning her to respectability. Letting the ocean breeze sweep away the dirt of the past from his mind he looked at his watch and exclaimed: "It is past nine Hashem Agha. Shall we go?"

"You must be impatient for your new wardrobe son." Hashem commented trying to please the boy. He knew he had to please this fat boy otherwise he would find no peace with his wife. He took both Nary and Ahmad's hands and pulled them up. "The walk is a bit long but very pleasant." He pointed to the bridge that crossed the ocean with his hand, "the other side of this bridge is called North Shore. Here we are in the Eastern Suburb where most of the Sydney millionaires live. I am going to take you through Wallaroy road where several diplomats reside."

"Are you a millionaire Hashem Agha?" Ahmad asked looking up at his face. Without his stubble he looked quite handsome to him.

"God be thanked, yes son." Hashem replied with a genuine smile.

Surprised Ahmad fell silent, trying to figure out how the son of a baker on a salary could have become a millionaire.

As predicted by Hashem, their walk through Wallaroy road, up the steps to Roslindale Avenue and Edgecliff Road to the windy Bondi Junction was indeed agreeable, particularly passing under the purple wings of Jacaranda trees in full bloom and inhaling the aroma of Japanese Jasmines that had invaded most of the fences along their path. Here vegetation was very different from Iran, even the colour of the leaves was a different green. Indeed they had discovered a new world in which they were starting a new life. The thought itself was auspicious for them all.

Westfield was indeed a dream shopping centre chiefly for those who had never set foot in a shopping mall. Overwhelmed by the animated atmosphere and the grandeur of the venue they shopped and shopped until they could carry no more and walk no more. Hashem treated his family to a hearty rump steak the size of which amazed both Nary and Ahmad. They had never tasted such tender meat. It almost melted in their mouths. Unaccustomed to drinking red wine with their meal, half of the ordered bottle was wasted. When the bill was paid Nary took hold of the bottle to take home. Hashem took her hand and gently shook it off the bottle's neck. "Khanum, in this country, you have to act like a lady of substance."

"And what does that mean Agha?" She demanded unaccustomed to his firmness.

"It means you must act like a lady: gracious, generous and less materialistic."

"I am your slave, Master I shall abide by your wishes." She replied with a happy wink.

The next day, smart in their designer clothes (without being conscious of the brand names), the three explored the Real Estate Agencies located on each side of New South Head Road and within a week, Bobby Smith of Laing & Simmons found the relatives of the late Shah of Iran (the myth Hashem had created) a grand waterfront mansion, in the sought-after suburb of Darling Point, with a swimming pool and a tennis court, costing Hashem a mere $10,000,000. Such wealthy clients who had fled to Sydney in order to escape the brutal agents of the Islamic Regime's secret service, were worthy of a warm welcome in a country that gave second chances to its new residents. Bobby, successful, rich and well-established in Sydney society took it upon himself to introduce the couple to the cream of the cream of the Eastern Suburb. With the city's cosmopolitan society being small, pretentious and receptive, doors opened to the 'poor' Iranians who had sought the safety of their shores. The Aussies loved the myth Hashem had created. Soon, he made many friends who did not mind his Pidgin English or his crude table manners. Wealth speaks well in Australia. Two months into their stay, they moved to their new residence decorated and furnished by one of the best interior decorating houses of Sydney. Hashem, to provide his adored wife with as comfortable a life as possible, employed a live-in domestic whom Nary taught Persian cuisine. Ahmad was registered at Scott College, one of the two best private boys' schools of the Eastern Suburb. As the Iranian high school diploma was not acceptable for entrance to an Australian university, he had to study and pass his HSC (high school certificate) examinations. A private teacher taught the family members English and a tennis coach came every Friday morning. To add a touch of class to his accomplishments, Hashem employed a connoisseur to teach him all about wine. Once ready, they opened their house to their Australian friends and their dinner parties became feasts to remember and talked about. Nary, sharing her husband's appreciation for good wine, aimed to fill their large cellar with the best they could acquire. To this end they drove to Hunter Valley, the vineyards of Victoria and Southern Australia. During their absence, Ahmad studied harder and during weekends, weather permitting, he headed for the beach at Neilson's park. He loved sports, particularly swimming. All his fat had melted away. Lean and muscular he looked much taller. Girls were after him but in vain. All he wanted was to become a doctor and save lives.

Four years passed in the wink of an eye. Ahmad commenced studying medicine at the University of New South Wales. Nary, in command of good English, started to write a Persian cook book and Hashem took up surfing.

It was Easter Sunday and the trio were having breakfast on the veranda of their Surfer's Paradise waterfront luxury apartment. It was a bright day and the ocean was as blue as the sky itself. The air was cool, the waves alive and the wind just right for surfing. Hashem had already finished his coffee and muffins and was casually paging his Sydney Morning Herald, perusing the headlines. His mind was not really on the news. He was impatient for the rest to finish their breakfast so that he could pack his surf board in his Range Rover and head for the beach. He threw the paper down and fixed his eyes on the ocean. He saw the waves lash at the sands and retreat with the same fury, their movements inviting, their beauty mesmerising. Keen to ride them, he began to shake his right leg that was crossed over his left. Regular surfing and swimming had turned his figure into the muscular shape of a professional athlete. But his wife had put on a few kilos. She looked more voluptuous than ever, particularly now that happiness had erased her frown and given her eyes a soft glow. And Ahmad had turned into a sophisticated young man with a deep Australian accent. He too was very happy – happier than the other two – for he was not the prisoner of his past deeds. He had come into terms with the guilt of that one undelivered phone message, the memory of which had haunted him for years and had gradually faded away. Now he was comfortable with himself, Hashem and others. The study of science and philosophy had opened his mind to a new and logical perception of the world in which he existed. He believed man is gifted with the power of rationality and a free will. Thus he is responsible for the decisions he makes and the paths he chooses. Therefore, he will reap what he sows – and he intended to sow well.

Rising to clear the table, he faced his mother and asked: "What would you like to do today?"

"If you accompany me I would like to go for a walk on the beach."

Nary's request pricked Hashem's ears and brought a huge smile to his lips. Their company at the surfer's beach would enhance his joy of the exercise. He fixed his adoring eyes on her and suggested:

"Why don't you make a picnic basket and we will all go to my beach where I can surf and then have lunch with you?"

"That is a great idea. I shall make some chicken sandwiches and we already have some Russian salad left from last night. Would that be enough?" Nary asked, putting her hand on her husband's lap. She still enjoyed his warmth. He was the light of her life. He patted her hand and replied: "Don't forget some mangoes and put a bottle of pink Champagne and a couple of beer cans in the ice box."

"Shall do Captain." Nary smiled, saluted like a sailor and rose to go to her kitchen – where she spent most of her time, trying new recipes for her new book.

It was close to noon when, dressed in their beachwear, they fitted the ice box and the picnic basket in the back of the car, climbed in and headed for the surfer's beach. It was near and the beach packed with the holiday makers. They carried their stuff to a relatively secluded corner where Ahmad erected their sun-shade while Nary spread a couple of towels on the white sand. Hashem, already changed, handed his clothes to his wife, tucked his surf board under his arm and hastened to the ocean. At that moment he felt the happiest man in the world.

Nary neatly folded his shorts and T-shirt and put them in her large beach bag.

"Mother, are you going to swim, or do you want to laze under the umbrella?"

"I want to laze under the umbrella and enjoy watching you and your father have fun."

Ahmad laughed at her laziness; he stepped out of his shorts, kicked off his sandals and ran to the ocean.

Nary unwrapped her cotton sarong, she folded it carefully and placed it by the pole of the umbrella. She put on her straw hat, creamed her pale skin with sun blocker lotion, sat well within the shade, cuddled her knees, rested her chin on them and focused her eyes on her two sources of happiness. She saw Ahmad negotiate his direction, wisely avoiding the waves lapping across the coast line. She turned her head to the direction of the waves and saw Hashem surf with his arms wide spread as though flying in the air. The waves were just right and there were so many surfers that at times she couldn't spot him and feel proud of his skill. He had taken several courses and was very good at surfing. In fact he was the champion of his club.

After a while, hot, sticky and tired of her own company, Nary decided to go for a swim. She put her beer can down, removed her glasses and sun hat, rose and ambled towards the ocean. Her eyes on the waves she saw surfers riding the waves, but the sunlight was too glary for her to be able to discern one from the other. Nevertheless, one of them was her Hashem. And if she had her glasses on, she probably could spot him from his refined style and skill. He had become so very good. Not only at surfing but at everything he did. Now his English was perfect and he had become totally westernized which was a relief. No more talks about the fire of hell and the other bullshits in which she had never believed. She had changed too. But not like him. He was much cleverer than her and kinder. She was so lucky to have him. He had not only been a good husband but a perfect father to Ahmad. "God bless him." She heard herself pray as she walked and perused the waves. They had suddenly become angry. She didn't like the change. It was dangerous. She always worried about Hashem when the waves were too powerful. She halted to gauge the velocity of their movements. They were really not that bad. Then she saw something resembling an extraordinarily large white lizard's head protrude out of the water, seemingly take a breath and disappear within the folds of the waves. "What on earth was that?" She exclaimed loudly. No one heard her. The sound of helicopters was drowning all other noises. She looked around. There was a commotion towards and from the beach. Those in the water were hastening out. A speed boat appeared from a distance and then she heard someone scream:

"Great White – Great White!" She looked around and saw nothing white. A wave of presentiment disturbed her peace. She turned and ran towards the crowd.

"Great White – Great White!" She heard the scream again.

"For heaven's sake, what is a Great White?" She yelled into the air.

"A huge shark." A man replied.

Her eyes popping out of their sockets, she turned towards the voice and exclaimed, "a shark!"

"Yes. But it hardly ever comes so near. Don't worry mate. It just might be a false alarm."

"Enshallah." She murmured.

"What did you say mate?" The stranger asked;

"Nothing Sir. Nothing."

She joined the crowd. All eyes were on the ocean. From a distance she thought she saw Ahmad. She tightened her eye muscles and focused. Yes it was him. Her shoulders relaxed and she waited until he was within her reach and into her arms.

"Thank God you are here." She murmured kissing his ear and pressing him to herself. Embarrassed by her show of affection his eyes avoided onlookers who were glaring at them.

"Have you seen Hashem dear?" She whispered.

He pulled himself out of her arms, kissed her cheek, looked into her worried eyes and trying to comfort her said:

"Don't worry mother. He will be here soon. They say there has been a shark attack. But I don't believe them. Sharks never come this near the shore."

"I hope you are right dear." Murmured Nary in an uneasy tone.

Suddenly an amplifier burped, hissed loudly and a male voice blurted out:

"There has been a shark attack. Please stay away from the water."

The announcement went on and on.

Panic broke out. The beach lost the remnants of its peacefulness and the ocean turned into a monster.

"What does this mean?" Nary shrieked. "Mother, don't move from here." Ahmad cautioned before running to the life-guard he had earlier on spoken to. Reaching him he halted, pulled at his sleeve and blurted out: "My father has not returned yet?" The guard threw him a sympathetic glance, "Son wait, there are few who have not returned yet."

He ran back to his mother and together they joined the crowd that had now assembled around the Life-Guard's kiosk, their eyes fixed on the edge of the ocean.

As the surfers returned and joined their families the crowd disintegrated leaving behind the lifeguards and a mother and her son.

Time ticked away.

The wind subsided.

The waves subdued.

Hands clasped, they waited in hope.

The sun began its languid descent leaving behind a slowly melting sheet of gold glaze on the ripples of the ocean.

Unwilling to relinquish hope, Nary and Ahmad remained rooted to the ground praying in vain.

The cold breeze from the ocean bit deep into their skin. But they felt it not.

The lifeguard Ahmad had approached earlier, arrived on a motor cycle, detoured and halted with a skidding noise. He jumped off his motor, detached a surf-board, half chewed up by a shark and showing it to Ahmad asked:

"Was this your father's son?"

Ahmad took and reversed it. As his eyes fell on the small flag of Iran he had painted on it, his screams shattered the stillness of the dusk. Trembling hard, the board slipped out of his loose grip, somersaulted to the ground and sank in the sand.

"Mate I am so sorry." The Guard whispered, bent down, lifted the board and handed it back to Ahmad. Unconsciously he took it and pressed it to his heart as though it was Hashem.

Uncomprehending and totally oblivious to the reality of the event Nary stood still as though she was a tiny spec lost in the greater scheme of cosmic affairs. She didn't even feel the arm that hugged her shoulders.

"It is getting late now lady. Would you like me to ride you and your son to your car?"

His words fell on deaf ears. Their grief was too profound to break. They just stood there, hand in hand staring at the monster that had devoured the source of their happiness.

The man touched by their intense grief shook his head in sympathy, climbed up his motor, started its engine and speeding away disappeared in the cloud of sand he dragged behind.

The waves continued to lash at the shore, leaving behind a canopy of white fluff that eventually disintegrated within mounts of disturbed sands.

The air turned bitterly cold.

The Great White, better known as Dead White, retreated to his usual habitat in the deep waters.

The two bereaved, hand in hand, fingers intertwined, stood watching the waves, wondering at the temporariness of it all.

The sun sank deep.

The ocean disappeared in the darkness of the night. So did Ahmad and Nary's silhouettes. The only sound of life left was the roar of the ocean.

Years later, Ahmad a successful surgeon in Iran, taught Nary, his daughter named after his late mother, this poem:

O lovers

Love will lay a carpet of treasures under your feet.
Musicians
Love will fill your drums with gold.
Thirsty ones
Love will turn your scorched desert
into meadow of paradise.
Forsaken ones

Love will open the doors to the King's Palace.
Alchemists
Love's alchemy will reshape gallows into altars.
Sinners
Love will change your apathy to faith.
Kings of the world
In love's hands you will melt like a candle.
To the parched lips of those who are
willing to surrender
Love will bring the wine that changes darkness
into vision, cruelty into compassion
and dust into precious incense.

Jaleledin Rumi 13th Century.

www.ingramcontent.com/pod-product-compliance
Lightning Source LLC
Chambersburg PA
CBHW021952050726
47495CB00023B/2686